DIARY OF A MADMAN, THE GOVERNMENT INSPECTOR AND SELECTED STORIES

NIKOLAY VASILYEVICH GOGOL was born in 1809 in Poltava province, into a small gentry family of Ukrainian and Polish extraction. After finishing gymnasium in 1828, he went to St Petersburg and secured a minor post in an obscure government ministry. With the publication of his first collection of stories, *Evenings on a Farm Near Dikanka* (two volumes, 1831–2), he became famous, and began to meet important writers, notably Pushkin. During much of the 1830s, he experimented with different literary forms, including history, drama, essays and fiction. Two major collections of his stories, *Arabesques* and *Mirgorod*, were published in 1835; 'The Nose' and 'The Carriage' came out separately in 1836; and 'The Overcoat' was included in his collected works of 1842. His play *The Government Inspector* received its première in 1836, and Part I of his masterpiece, the novel *Dead Souls*, appeared in 1842 to nearly unanimous acclaim. After 1836, he lived mainly abroad, especially in Rome, insisting that he needed a distant perspective on Russia to write about it. Throughout the 1840s he was increasingly tormented by physical, psychological and religious problems, but produced several important works of non-fiction. He also worked steadily on Part II of *Dead Souls*, but burned much of it in 1845, and again in 1852, shortly before his death, possibly from self-starvation complicated by typhus and despair.

ROBERT A. MAGUIRE was the Boris Bakhmeteff Professor Emeritus of Russian Studies at Columbia University. He taught at Yale, Princeton and Harvard, and was a Visiting Fellow at St Antony's College, Oxford. His two main areas of specialization, on which he wrote widely, were the Soviet period and the early nineteenth century. Among his books are *Red Virgin Soil: Soviet Literature in the 1920s* (1968; 3rd edn, 2000), *Gogol from the Twentieth Century* (1974) and *Exploring Gogol* (1994). His translations include the works of several contemporary Polish poets, notably Wisława Szymborska and Tadeusz Różewicz, and Andrei Bely's Symbolist novel *Petersburg* (with John Malmstad, 1978). He received a Ford Foundation Grant, a Guggenheim Fellowship, and several awards for published work and service to his field of study. Robert A. Maguire died in 2005.

RONALD WILKS studied language and literature at Trinity College, Cambridge, after training as a Naval interpreter, and later Russian literature at London University, where he received his Ph.D. in 1972. Among his translations for Penguin Classics are *My Childhood, My Apprenticeship* and *My Universities* by Gorky, *Diary of a Madman* by Gogol, filmed for Irish Television, *The Golovlyov Family* by Saltykov-Shchedrin, *How Much Land Does a Man Need?, Master and Man and Other Stories* by Tolstoy, *Tales of Belkin and Other Prose Writings* by Pushkin, and *The Shooting Party* by Chekhov and several volumes of his stories. He has also translated *The Little Demon* by Sologub for Penguin.

NIKOLAY GOGOL

Diary of a Madman, The Government Inspector and Selected Stories

Translated with Notes by RONALD WILKS
With an Introduction by ROBERT A. MAGUIRE

PENGUIN BOOKS

FIC
GOGOL

PENGUIN CLASSICS

Published by the Penguin Group
Penguin Books Ltd, 80 Strand, London WC2R ORL, England
Penguin Group (USA) Inc., 375 Hudson Street, New York, New York 10014, USA
Penguin Group (Canada), 90 Eglinton Avenue East, Suite 700, Toronto, Ontario, Canada M4P 2Y3
(a division of Pearson Penguin Canada Inc.)
Penguin Ireland, 25 St Stephen's Green, Dublin 2, Ireland
(a division of Penguin Books Ltd)
Penguin Group (Australia), 250 Camberwell Road,
Camberwell, Victoria 3124, Australia (a division of Pearson Australia Group Pty Ltd)
Penguin Books India Pvt Ltd, 11 Community Centre,
Panchsheel Park, New Delhi – 110 017, India
Penguin Group (NZ), cnr Airborne and Rosedale Roads, Albany,
Auckland 1310, New Zealand (a division of Pearson New Zealand Ltd)
Penguin Books (South Africa) (Pty) Ltd, 24 Sturdee Avenue,
Rosebank, Johannesburg 2196, South Africa

Penguin Books Ltd, Registered Offices: 80 Strand, London WC2R ORL, England

www.penguin.com

Published in Penguin Classics 2005
7

Chronology and Introduction © Robert A. Maguire, 2004, 2005
Further Reading, Publishing History and Notes, and Table of Ranks © Ronald Wilks, 2005
'Nevsky Prospekt', 'The Carriage' and *The Government Inspector* translations © Ronald Wilks, 2005
All other translations © Ronald Wilks, 1972, revised 2005
All rights reserved

The moral right of the editors has been asserted

Set in 10.25/12.25 pt PostScript Adobe Sabon
Typeset by Rowland Phototypesetting Ltd, Bury St Edmunds, Suffolk
Printed in England by Clays Ltd, St Ives plc

ISBN-13: 978-0-14044-907-5

www.greenpenguin.co.uk

Penguin Books is committed to a sustainable future
for our business, our readers and our planet.
The book in your hands is made from paper
certified by the Forest Stewardship Council.

Contents

Chronology

1809 20 March: Born in Sorochintsy, Mirgorod district, Poltava province, Ukraine

1821 Enters Gymnasium at Nezhin (Ukraine)

1825 Death of father

1828 Graduates from Nezhin, leaves for St Petersburg

1829 Publication of 'Italy' (poem) and *Hans Küchelgarten*
(verse idyll)

Spends August–September in Lübeck, Germany. Secures
minor clerical job in civil service

1830 Publication of 'Bisavryuk' ('St John's Eve', story), and
one chapter of *The Hetman* (novel, never completed)

Auditions unsuccessfully for Imperial Theatres. Another
minor clerical job. Studies painting at Academy of Arts

1831 Publication of the article 'Woman' (the first under his
own name). Publication of *Evenings on a Farm Near
Dikanka*, Part I ('The Fair at Sorochintsy', 'St John's Eve',
'A May Night, or the Drowned Maiden', 'The Lost Letter')

Meets Aleksandr Pushkin for the first time. Becomes a history
teacher in a private girls' school

1832 Publication of *Evenings on a Farm Near Dikanka*, Part II
('Christmas Eve', 'A Terrible Vengeance', 'Ivan Fyodorovich
Shponka and His Aunt', 'A Bewitched Place')

1832–5 Intense writing activity, in fiction, plays, history,
essays, most never completed; includes sketches for a historical play *Alfred* (published 1889), and 'Sketches for a Drama
from Ukrainian History'

1834 Publication of 'How Ivan Ivanovich Quarrelled with Ivan
Nikiforovich' (story), and two articles on history

Appointed adjunct professor of history at St Petersburg University

1835 January: Publication of *Arabesques* (articles and three stories: 'Diary of a Madman', 'Nevsky Prospekt', 'The Portrait'). March: Publication of *Mirgorod* ('Old World Landowners', 'Taras Bulba', 'How Ivan Ivanovich Quarrelled with Ivan Nikiforovich', 'Viy')

Begins work on *Dead Souls*, Part I. December: Leaves teaching post.

1836 19 April: Première of *The Government Inspector* (play). Publication of stories 'The Nose', 'The Carriage'

6 June: Leaves for Western Europe, travels for the rest of the year

1837 29 January: Death of Pushkin. 26 March: Arrives in Rome

1838–41 Lives in Rome. Travels in Europe, makes two trips back to Russia. Works on *Dead Souls*

1842 Publication of collected works, which include a new story, 'The Overcoat'; two drastically revised earlier ones, 'The Portrait' and 'Taras Bulba'; and the plays *Marriage, The Gamblers* and *Leaving the Theatre After the Performance of a New Comedy*. 21 May: Publication of *Dead Souls*, Part I

In Russia. June: Returns to Europe

1843–6 In Europe, extensive travels. Begins work on *Dead Souls*, Part II.

1845–7 Writes *Meditations on the Divine Liturgy* (published 1857)

1846 Writes 'The Denouement of *The Government Inspector*' (published 1856) and 'Forewarning to Those Who Would Like to Play *The Government Inspector* Properly' (published 1889). Writes 'Foreword to the Second Edition [of *Dead Souls*]. To the Reader from the Author'

1847 January: Publication of *Selected Passages from Correspondence with Friends*.

In Europe. June–July: Works on apologia (published 1855 as 'An Author's Confession')

1848 Pilgrimage to the Holy Land. 11 April: Returns to Russia, never to leave

1849–51 Works on *Dead Souls*, Part II.

1852 11–12 February: Burns much of *Dead Souls*, Part II. 21 February: Dies in Moscow and buried there (25 February)

Introduction

New readers are advised that this Introduction makes details of the plot explicit.

Nikolay Vasilyevich Gogol made his major literary debut at the age of twenty-two with eight short stories collected in two modest-size volumes entitled *Evenings on a Farm Near Dikanka* (1831–2). By the time of his death in 1852 at the age of forty-two, he had published eleven more stories. It is these stories, the play *The Government Inspector* (1836) and the novel *Dead Souls* (1842, 1855) that made him one of the first Russian writers to achieve international celebrity.

His early years gave no evidence of exceptional talent of any kind. He was born in 1809 into a Polish-Ukrainian family of moderately prosperous landowners in rural Ukraine, and completed his formal education when he graduated in 1828 from the gymnasium in Nezhin, some one hundred miles northwest of his home. He set out at once for St Petersburg, the goal of many an ambitious young man. A year earlier he had confided to a friend that from early childhood he had 'burned with an unquenchable fervour to make my life necessary for the good of the state', and proposed a career in 'justice' as a clear possibility.[1] But after he established himself in the capital, prospects looked dimmer. He auditioned for the Imperial Theatres with hopes of becoming an actor, but met with crushing rejection; for a short time he taught at a girls' school; he secured a drastically underpaid position in an obscure branch of the civil service; he took some classes at the Academy of Arts. While still at school, he had turned out a few poems, but they made no impression on his fellow-students. His earliest effort at prose fiction, 'The Brothers Tverdislavich', also dates from his years at Nezhin. It prompted a schoolmate to remark: 'You'll never

make a fiction writer, that's obvious right now',[2] upon which
he tore up the manuscript and burned it. In 1830, he published
two poems: the brief and forgettable 'Italy', and a long and
laboured effort under the fashionably German rubric of *Hanz
Küchelgarten*, which garnered reviews so savage that he bought
up every copy he could find and burned them.

It seems remarkable that he would persist in a literary career
despite such rebuffs. But he was endowed with two characteristics which, when combined with a hitherto inconspicuous yet
spectacular talent, would soon elevate him into the front ranks
of promising writers, and, within ten years, make him a modern
master in the eyes of the public and most critics. They were
a conviction that he stood above the 'crowd', and a steely
ambition to create something out of himself. 'A cold sweat
broke out on my face,' he continued in the letter to his friend
in 1827, 'at the thought that perhaps it would be my lot to
perish in the dust without having distinguished my name with
a single beautiful deed. To be in the world and not distinguish
my existence – that would be dreadful for me.'[3] Writers, not
government officials, were the great celebrities of the time,
much like actors or rock musicians today, and Russian literature was in a state of throbbing, even frantic, development,
boasting of an ever-growing body of readers avid for new talent
that would not only prove entertaining, but would address
questions that the European Romantics in particular had taught
Russians to expect writers to engage. One of the most important
was national identity, or *narodnost'*. It had been in vogue since
the late eighteenth century, had taken on special urgency since
the defeat of Napoleon in the War of 1812, and had engaged the
energies of a pantheon of new writers, especially in novels,
short stories, ballads, folk tales and histories. Gogol, always
alert to opportunity, undoubtedly sensed it here. It presented
itself in the form of his homeland, the Ukraine.

Exotic climes and exotic people were very much in vogue
in the early nineteenth century. The Ukraine, although part
of Russia since 1654, had a language and culture distinctive
enough to make it 'exotic' in the eyes of Russian readers. As
early as 30 April 1829 – even before the disaster with *Hanz*

Küchelgarten – we find Gogol writing to his mother from St Petersburg, begging her to do him the 'greatest of favours': putting her 'fine, observant mind' and her knowledge of the 'customs and usages of our Little Russians' (as Ukrainians were officially designated at the time) to his service and providing him with detailed descriptions of folk customs and costume 'down to the last ribbon'. He does not tell her why this material is 'very, very necessary' to him, but we may safely assume that he was already intending to work on some Ukrainian subjects.[4] He could also have drawn material from the comedies that his father (dead since 1825) had written in Ukrainian, as well as from Ukrainian folklore and the work of writers who had been busy creating a Ukrainian literary renaissance. For the kind of national fame to which he aspired, however, it was essential to write in Russian, the official language of the Empire, and he did so throughout his career, while always retaining an interest in and affection for his Ukrainian heritage.

His earliest uses of these materials date from 1830, with the story 'Bisavryuk, or St John's Eve', fragments of a historical novel, *The Hetman*, which was never finished, and, the following year, two brief chapters of a horror story (also never completed) entitled 'The Terrifying Boar'.[5] But the crowning work of the early 1830s was the two volumes of *Evenings on a Farm Near Dikanka* (which included a heavily revised 'St John's Eve'). Its eight stories and two prefaces focused on ordinary people in rural settings, and partly on those most exotic of Ukrainian phenomena, the Cossacks, with colourful descriptions of folk customs, scary yet humorous intrusions of the supernatural, madness, magic spells, love intrigues and idyllic landscapes, sufficiently seasoned with quotidian detail and Ukrainian words to create the impression that they were intimations, if not evocations, of 'real' life. They enjoyed enormous popularity, and made Gogol an instant celebrity.

The short story had for some time been the most popular literary genre in Russian, as in European literature, and Gogol was always alert to literary fashions. As Russia's most influential critic, Vissarion Belinsky, wrote in 1834: 'In all literatures the short story now is the exclusive object of the attention and activity of all who write and read, our daily bread, our bedside book, which we read as we close our eyes at night and read as we open them in the morning.'⁶ The most famous early instance in Russia was Nikolay Karamzin's 'Poor Liza' (1792), with the well-used theme of the tragedy of two lovers who belong to very different social classes, and a style that was widely credited with canonizing a supple, rich Russian literary prose. Gogol proved highly skilful at adapting the techniques of the European story to subject matter, genres and styles that were unmistakably Ukrainian, and later Russian.

In the five years that followed the publication of *Evenings on a Farm Near Dikanka*, Gogol tried his hand at a number of different prose forms and genres, notably stories, plays and essays. Like many other writers of the time, he was fascinated by historical subjects and processes. To friends he confided his ambition to write a large-scale history of the Ukraine, as well as a history of the world. Part of his preparation consisted in securing a position at St Petersburg University as a teacher of history, which found him lamentably unprepared and was not renewed. He collected materials from folklore, and undertook a series of notebooks that would record unusual or odd usages of language, both Russian and Ukrainian. An overview of this period reveals a mind ranging in many different directions. The wonder is that he managed to bring anything to completion. But in 1834 he published the story 'How Ivan Ivanovich Quarrelled with Ivan Nikiforovich', and two articles on history. In January 1835 a substantial volume entitled *Arabesques* appeared, consisting mainly of thirteen essays on a variety of topics, such as Aleksandr Pushkin, the Ukraine, contemporary architecture, the Middle Ages, geography, the teaching of history, and sculpture, painting and music. It also made three new additions to Gogol's short stories: 'Diary of a Madman', 'Nevsky Prospekt', and 'The Portrait', the second of which has been freshly translated for the present collection. In March of the same year Gogol took readers back to the Ukraine with a collection of four long stories that appeared under the title *Mirgorod* (a district and town located in Poltava province): these were 'Old World Landowners', 'Taras Bulba', 'Viy' and the story about the two Ivans that had been separately published the year before. In 1836 his interest in drama culminated in *The Government Inspector*, which, unusually for Gogol, is set in provincial Russia, and received its première on 19 April in St Petersburg. That same month two new stories appeared in literary journals: 'The Nose', again set in St Petersburg, and 'The Carriage', which unfolds in the provinces. This busy period was followed by a hiatus, during which Gogol was working frantically to complete the novel *Dead Souls*, the first part of which was published in 1842. Finally, there came a fresh burst of published stories in 1842, with 'The Overcoat' and heavily revised versions of 'The Portrait' and 'Taras Bulba'. The final story was 'Rome' (1842), a tribute to the city in which he spent so much of his adult life, but a curiously flawed work which has never achieved much popularity even among devotees of Gogol.

Gogol lived until 1852 but never produced another short story. This final decade was given over to essays – many on personal, religious and moralistic themes – and to Part II of *Dead Souls*, which he twice burned and constantly rewrote in a vain effort to complete it. A substantial part of it remains, showing us a Gogol who was moving closer to what we have come to appreciate as the great 'psychological' novels by Russian writers of the next generation, but, it is widely agreed, a Gogol who had also moved out of his element. That element is best represented by Part I of *Dead Souls*, and by the cluster of nineteen splendid short stories that were produced over a period of some ten years and are well represented in the collection now before us.

It is hardly surprising that this impassioned literary activity, conducted over such a short span of time, strikes readers as all of a piece. Each of the stories is very different from the others; yet each draws on a pool of themes, situations, stylistic devices and ideas that run throughout his work, and are developed, modified, reconfigured and varied in ways so ingenious that we always feel that we are on new territory, while at the same time recognizing familiar landmarks. It is impossible to confuse a story by Gogol with a story by anyone else, despite the numerous imitators he has attracted during the century and a half since his death.

PLOTS AND IDYLLS

In most of his writings, whether short stories, plays or novels, Gogol employs essentially the same outwardly simple plot. A seemingly stable setting or situation – whether a household, a society or an individual – is suddenly and unexpectedly destabilized by the intrusion of an alien element. The result is confusion and fundamental change which usually cannot be undone. In *The Government Inspector* the life of a small provincial town is disrupted by the unexpected arrival of Khlestakov, a young man who is mistakenly identified as a government inspector. Even though he leaves towards the end of the play, the delicate systems of checks and balances that have enabled the town to operate cannot be restored. In a more psychological vein, 'How Ivan Ivanovich Quarrelled with Ivan Nikiforovich' opens with a picture of an ideal friendship between two men in a peaceable society. The intrusive agent is the rifle which incongruously appears in the yard belonging to one of them, stirs up envy and resentment in the other, and ends by ruining the friendship and permanently throwing the town out of kilter. 'The Overcoat' offers the most complex treatment. The first intrusion comes in the form of the cold winter wind of St Petersburg, which persuades Akaky that he needs a new coat; then the coat itself becomes an unmanageable intrusion which forever changes Akaky's life, considerably for the worse; finally, the ghostly figure at the end (presumably the deceased Akaky) intrudes on the life of the self-satisfied Important Person and changes it for the better, at least temporarily.

So strong is the note of pathos with which the decline of these self-contained entities is treated that we suspect we are really dealing with versions of the idyll. This literary form has been defined as a work in prose or poetry which 'describes a picturesque rural scene of gentle beauty and innocent tranquillity and narrates a story of some simple sort of happiness'.[7]

The most obvious exemplifications of this definition are the *Dikanka* stories. The tone is established by several great set pieces, like the summer night in Little Russia, in 'The Fair at Sorochintsy', the panorama of the mighty Dnieper River, in 'A Terrible Vengeance', and the moving scene in 'Ivan Fyodorovich Shponka and His Aunt' (included in this collection), where the emphasis is on the wonders of Nature and the human desire to share in them, even if only partially. Such passages evoke a universe of beauty and harmony, which also embraces the world that the human inhabitants have created in their dedication to fruitful and timeless pursuits like love, the kind of family in which everyone, young and old, has a part, and a celebration of natural processes and cycles like marriages, births, and deaths. Gogol subtitled *Hanz Küchelgarten* 'an idyll in pictures', and in several of his articles on history he posited a unity of this kind at various times in the past. But even in the *Dikanka* stories it has begun to unravel. In keeping with the strong fairy-tale coloration of this collection, the intruders are often supernatural beings, like witches, goblins or demons, sometimes malevolent, sometimes benevolent, even comic. At the end, a semblance of harmony is restored, as the intruding element is banished, placated or somehow incorporated into the life of the community. The one exception is the story 'Ivan Fyodorovich Shponka'. Here a curious reversal takes place: the hero, Shponka, though a fully-fledged member of the community, is himself the intruder, an utter misfit by virtue of not wishing to participate at all in his seemingly (albeit deceptively) idyllic society.

Another striking feature of the *Dikanka* stories is the way in which they are narrated. They are presented to the reader by one Rudy Panko, an old beekeeper, who has gathered them during long winter evenings in the village from various story-tellers, and is reproducing them exactly as he has heard them. We too are supposed to imagine that we are hearing them without the intervention of print. Michael Wood has pointed out that the 'birthplace' of the story form 'is not the solitary individual but the person who lives in a community and has experiences he/she can pass on'.[8] In other words, oral narrative promotes unity and in this sense is well suited to the idyll. This is a technique that Gogol followed throughout his storytelling career. Usually the oral narrator stands, intellectually and culturally, somewhere between the characters and the presumed author. The reader, then, finds himself at a double remove from the characters, and can never confidently identify himself with the 'real' author, or Gogol himself. This sense of remove is also part of the feeling that an idyll generates in the reader.

The *Dikanka* stories also provide some glimpses of psychological motivation, which are among the several features that tell us they are not 'pure' idylls. 'A Terrible Vengeance', for instance, follows the workings of a curse on the mind of an increasingly deranged Cossack wife. But nowhere in this cycle of stories are these elements stronger than in 'Ivan Fyodorovich Shponka'. This is a portrait of a young man who is beholden to an array of peculiar and powerful authority figures – the schoolmaster, a bullying neighbour and the aunt – who are frighteningly adept at manipulating him to their ends. He does have a semblance of an inner life – as virtually (though not all) of Gogol's main characters have – but it mostly finds expression in infantile sexual fantasies, which are ultimately frustrated or exposed. Only in solitude is he able to enjoy some measure of contentment; but as the story ends, he is about to be denied even that.

In its theme and its hints at characters who have a rather more fully developed psychological life, 'Ivan Fyodorovich Shponka' has always struck critics as being out of place in the *Dikanka* cycle. But it does point ahead to Gogol's second set of Ukrainian stories, published in 1835 under the title of *Mirgorod*. If these stories are longer and more complex than the *Dikanka* ones, that is partly because Gogol is now increasingly interested in psychological factors. In particular, he wants to explore a question that he has not addressed in any depth in the earlier collection (not even in 'Ivan Fyodorovich Shponka'): *why* does the idyll disintegrate and collapse?

The four stories in *Mirgorod* begin by looking like idylls, offering as they do prosperous estates, bountiful harvests, a smiling nature and a cohesive and fruitful family life. Before long, however, each of them betrays flaws that are ultimately fatal. In 'Old World Landowners', the first indication that something is wrong comes when we realize that the relationship of the old married couple is more like brother and sister than husband and wife, that boasting and teasing are the prevalent modes of discourse, and eventually become acidulous enough to unravel the relationship, bring about the death of the old woman, and with it, the estate. The undying friendship of the two Ivans provides a model for the town of Mirgorod, which was small enough to partake of many of the features of the countryside as well, and therefore to qualify at least as quasi-idyllic, but it is spoiled irreparably by jealousy and envy, and the much-vaunted 'closeness' of the two men becomes a prison of hatred and vindictiveness. In 'Taras Bulba' we are shown a close-knit Cossack community, which was always a positive phenomenon for Gogol, as he seems to have wanted to remind us by making this one of the two stories he completely rewrote towards the end of his active life as a creator of fiction. But it is gradually undone by a younger son who falls in love with a Polish girl, thereby betraying his birthright and his family (Poles being deadly enemies of the Cossacks). Finally, there is 'Viy', an untranslatable name for the monster who, in a throwback to the supernatural world of *Dikanka*, destroys the dreams and fantasies of an already weak-willed hero and of an entire Cossack family. In these more sophisticated stories, the invasive agents are often internal, and easily find fertile ground. The community or the individual carry within them the seeds of their own undoing, which merely await the appearance of a catalytic agent to begin to sprout. They may be flaws of character, infection by a hostile ideology or a return to the community after living outside it for too long. In *The Government Inspector*, all the townspeople are venal in one way or another – tainted with what the Mayor delicately refers to as 'little indiscretions' – but have found ways of living in harmony and creating what to all appearances is a flourishing community. But once the intruding agent, in the person of Khlestakov, is introduced, harmony turns disharmonious, compromise becomes chaos, and at length even life ceases, as Gogol strongly suggests in the mute scene that concludes the play.

THE IDYLL'S URBAN FORM

The three stories contained in *Arabesques* represent a sudden shift to St Petersburg as a setting. Two more were to follow: 'The Nose' and 'The Overcoat'. (This group is sometimes referred to as the 'Petersburg Stories', but that is an editorial convention, which was not observed by Gogol.) Gogol lived in the capital city between 1828, when he graduated from Nezhin, and 1836, when he went abroad and settled mainly in Rome for the better part of the following twelve years. But the fact that he knew the city well was not the only reason why it came to figure so prominently in some of his best stories.

St Petersburg had been founded by Peter the Great in 1703 as an outpost of the Russian Empire on the Baltic Sea to provide easy access to Europe. The famous equestrian statue of Peter, created by E. M. Falconet and dedicated in 1782 at the behest of Catherine the Great in the Senate Square, stood as an imposing symbol of the majesty of the city and of its determination to open itself to the West. In fact, Petersburg looked 'European' in many respects, with its rectilinear layout, its system of canals and its Italianate architecture. For at least a century it was regarded as a magnificent tribute to the ingenuity of the human mind, a proud emblem of Russia's 'modernity'. By the time Gogol got there, however, it had begun to stand for something else: foreignness, artificiality and impersonality. It was a place where many citizens, Gogol among them, simply did not feel at home. In a letter he wrote to his mother shortly after his arrival, he observed: 'In general, every city is characterized by its people, who imprint it with national traits, but Petersburg has no character: the foreigners who have settled here have made themselves at home and are not like foreigners at all, and the Russians for their part have turned foreign and have become neither one thing nor another. The silence of the city is extraordinary, there is no flash of spirit in the people, they're all office workers or officials . . . everything is crushed, everything is mired in idle, trivial pursuits.'[9] By then too a literary version of the city had grown up which emphasized all these negative traits.

The decisive work for Gogol, as for Russians generally, was Pushkin's *The Bronze Horseman* (1833). Throughout much of the eighteenth century, St Petersburg had been celebrated as a monument to the vision of Peter the Great and the ingenuity of the human mind in conquering a hostile nature and establishing an orderly, stable and magnificent city. This is the view that informs Part I of Pushkin's poem, with its catalogue of wonders, such as the 'now bustling banks' which 'Stand serried in well-ordered ranks / Of palaces and towers', the Neva River 'cased in granite clean', the 'stern and comely face' of the city, and even 'your winter's fierce embraces'. He concludes with the wish:

> Thrive, Peter's city, flaunt your beauty,
> Stand like unshaken Russia fast,
> Till floods and storms from chafing duty
> May turn to peace with you at last.

But an abrupt change of mood begins in the final stanza of Part I: 'There was a time – our memories keep / Its horrors ever fresh and near us.'[10] This 'time' is the great flood of November 1824, to whose horrendous consequences Pushkin devoted all of Part II, which makes up the bulk of the poem. Nature takes its revenge, in the form of a devastating flood, and the city itself turns dark, violent, despotic and even demonic. This is the version of Petersburg that became lodged in Russian literature and remains vital to this day. Gogol's stories extended and deepened it. A sampling of quotations from one of his stories would include: 'lonely and deserted [streets] . . . cheerless dark shapes of low-built huts . . . an endless square . . . a terrifying desert . . . a watchman's hut which seemed to be standing on the very edge of the world . . . a raging blizzard that whistled down the street . . . [a wind that] was blowing from all the corners of the earth and from every single side-street' ('The Overcoat'). It is a city where Piskarev, in his pursuit of the girl along Nevsky Prospekt, in the story of the same name, experiences one of those derangements of the senses that came to be associated with the literary city, perhaps most famously in the final paragraph of the story, where we are enjoined not to trust Nevsky Prospekt, where 'all is deception, all is a dream, all is not what it seems'.[11]

The city is deception because it is an imitation of an idyll, an artificial construct that was created to keep Nature out or to confine it in manageable ways. Although it contains thousands of inhabitants, there is no sense of community, as Gogol explained to his mother in the letter he wrote to her soon after his arrival. At best, it is an assemblage of disconnected bits, which can fool people into imagining that it is a whole.

In the rural idylls of earlier stories there is still some sense that humans are open to the universe, that society and Nature can communicate; but in St Petersburg Nature is regarded as an enemy, to be defended against (hence the powerful image of the flood in Pushkin's poem, and the cold wind in Gogol's 'The Overcoat'). The world outside Petersburg also came to include the spiritual world: nowhere in his stories is any serious mention made of God; human aspirations are therefore always framed in purely human terms. The city becomes a prison, from which there is no escape.

Cities and idylls are poles apart; yet Petersburg is the end result of the decaying idyll that Gogol has been tracing throughout his works, and, as such, it stands for him as the prime symbol of modern times. Gogol is by no means the first writer to view the city in this way, but he is one of the most powerful and effective, as the enduring impact and popularity of these 'Petersburg' stories attest.

What sort of characters inhabit this urban prison that Gogol has so ingeniously and persuasively fashioned? Most are what critics came to refer to as 'little men', often lower-grade civil servants, obscure army officers, students, medium- or even high-ranking government officials. They are typically beleaguered, imposed upon and bullied, and in these senses are versions of Ivan Fyodorovich Shponka, although frequently far more complex. Each is in the thrall of one obsession, which fully defines him (and it is always 'him': there are no women in this category of characters), prevents him from interacting with other people in any meaningful way and deprives him of any

connection with society as a whole except as something to be
feared or exploited. He is completely isolated (nearly all are
bachelors) and completely disconnected from any sense of a
higher spiritual power. Ultimately, what these obsessions
amount to is the pursuit of sex and rank, which Gogol seems
to see as the two most important human drives. Sex is of course
pervasive, but rank was one of the defining features of life in
St Petersburg, perhaps because the city was mainly given over
to the civil service, where everyone had a rank prescribed by
the government. Most people who inhabited this world, in
Gogol's fictional versions, had the illusion that the pursuit of
higher rank would lead to happiness. The most complex and
poignant exploration of this theme occurs in 'Diary of a Madman'. Poprishchin is already a titular counsellor (class nine: see
also Table of Ranks, p. xxxv), but aspires higher, so much
higher, in fact, that eventually he imagines himself to be King
of Spain, as he is confined to a madhouse and tormented by his
keepers. Worse, his new rank isolates him utterly from society,
as his final despairing outburst indicates: 'There's no place for
him in this world!'

What is it that stirs such ambitions? It is not money or
worldly goods, but rather power over others, and, above all,
the thirst for recognition and respect, which most of Gogol's
characters feel to be the ultimate validation of themselves as
human beings. They have never learned what any new recruit
into armies all over the world learns on his first day of service:
that respect is to be accorded to the rank of his superiors, not
to the persons who hold rank. To be a king or a general is to
run the risk of turning entirely into the rank itself and therefore
ceasing to exist as a person. This is Poprishchin's terrible discovery, and one definition of madness, as it had been in an
earlier unfinished play of Gogol's.[12] Rank functions, we might
say, the way Akaky Akakievich's overcoat does in 'The Overcoat': as a second self which, if lost or removed, makes the first
self unrecognized and therefore non-existent. The acquisition
of the coat sets Akaky on a level with his fellow-workers, who
not so long ago were mocking and even persecuting him. The
coat represents power not so much in the sense of encouraging

him to treat others despotically or even condescendingly, but more as conferring a sense of personal empowerment. We do not know, however, that, if faced with another humble copyist in his office, he would not proceed to act the way his fellow-copyists had acted towards him. Likewise, the ending of the story of the two Ivans is depressingly similar to the beginning. They are under intense social pressure to resume their old relationship but nothing helps, and they remain the closest of enemies, a situation that prompts the narrator's famous closing line: 'It's a dreary world, gentlemen!' Seen this way, the inability of Gogol's characters to escape their situations and to change is perhaps more the result of moral deficiency than of victimhood. This question was never answered in the stories or the plays. It would have to wait until *Dead Souls*, and even then until the unfinished Part II, where Gogol's narrator would show ways that people could live happily and productively in the here and now. In the stories, meanwhile, Gogol lets us understand that one reason that the consequences of ambition are usually so dire is that the characters in question have done nothing to merit higher rank, and that it is therefore difficult to sympathize with them too much.

So far little has been said about the female characters in Gogol's stories and plays. That is because they are usually one-dimensional and considerably less interesting than the men. The aunt in 'Ivan Fyodorovich Shponka' is a variant of one common type of woman in Gogol, the shrew, who in other *Dikanka* stories often appears as a witch. In 'How Ivan Ivanovich Quarrelled with Ivan Nikiforovich', this type is represented by Agafiya Fedoseyevna, who bites the governor's ear (a vampire, perhaps?) and is ultimately responsible for heating up the quarrel between the two men. In 'The Nose', she is Podtochina, whom Kovalyov suspects of having sexual designs on him. Another type of woman is readily apparent in *The Government Inspector*, in the personages of Anna Andreyevna and Marya Antonovna, the major's wife and daughter. They are both empty-headed females who are concerned only with the social niceties of provincial living, and with the possibility of catching the government inspector as a husband for the daughter (and perhaps a lover for the mother). The extreme variants of this type are the tease, the vamp and the prostitute. Idylls are built on stereotypes; and the continuing presence of such characters in Gogol's fiction is a sign that the impulses of the idyll remained strongly present to the end of his career as a writer of fiction. Pushkin had created a fully developed woman in Tatyana in his novel in verse, *Eugene Onegin* (1833), but otherwise it was not until the late 1850s and early 1860s that equal treatment was extended to them in prose fiction by writers like Goncharov, Turgenev and Dostoyevsky.

REALIA

Gogol's beginnings as a writer coincided with the development of a movement in the intellectual and cultural life of Europe and Russia that can be broadly termed 'realism'. It came in response to a growing desire to turn one's gaze outward, after the inner-directed preoccupations of Sentimentalism and Romanticism, and record the world as it actually was, preferably in as much detail as possible. Gogol was one of the first Russian writers who responded to this new imperative. If the *Dikanka* stories still depended largely on myth, folklore and the supernatural, then the later stories present a world that looks firmly rooted – at least, at first – in the daily details that can be observed by anyone. Gogol was passionately interested in the visual arts, which were also moving in the same direction; his works are filled with metaphors taken from painting, drawing, sculpture and architecture. One thing that strikes even a casual reader of his stories is the fine, detailed texture of his settings and the care he often lavishes on them, and on the physiognomies and gestures of his characters: the dusty provincial town in 'The Carriage', the opening description of Petersburg's main thoroughfare in 'Nevsky Prospekt', the birth and naming of Akaky Akakievich, the permutations of Kovalyov's nose – many of these could readily be transcribed to canvas by a painter. For all their vividness, however, these details are rarely static. Realism is life, and life is movement. Gogol's task, like that of a painter, is to create movement from an apparently static medium, without depending too much on the lazy assumption that the reader's eye will automatically accomplish that as it sweeps across the page.

His techniques of bringing detail to life are many and varied. The simplest is, of course, personification, as with Kovalyov's very ordinary nose, which, once it ceases to be a mere appendage, becomes a plausible individual in its own right. Another simple but effective trick is to view the object from several different angles, thereby enhancing its importance. Such is the case with the aunt's carriage in 'Ivan Fyodorovich Shponka', dating back perhaps to the time of Adam (mythological perspective), which is constantly besieged by dogs trying to 'lick the grease off the wheels' (object of desire) and tilting 'slightly to one side so it was much higher on the right than the left' (narrator's vantage point) and much to the aunt's liking, since 'it could accommodate five undersized ones and three the size of Auntie' (aunt's view). Realization or displacement of metaphor figures heavily, as in the famous naming scene in 'The Overcoat': 'His surname was Bashmachkin, which all too plainly was at some time derived from *bashmak* ['shoe'] ... Both his father and his grandfather, and even his brother-in-law and all other Bashmachkins, went around in boots [shoes] and had them soled only three times a year.' The attentive reader will find many other such techniques in operation, all of which function to pull ordinary objects out of an ordinary world, and present them in a new light.

The opening pages of 'The Two Ivans' are rife with such devices. There is first of all exaggeration, or hyperbole: 'You should see Ivan Ivanovich's marvellous short fur jacket! It's quite fantastic! ... I'll bet you anything you like *nobody* has lambskins to compare with his.' Hyperbole by definition calls attention to itself. Then comes a shift of vantage point, which confers a two-dimensionality, and, therefore, greater substance, on the jacket: 'Heavens – just take a look at them from the side ... simply gorge your eyes on them!' These devices seize our attention even if we find them unwarranted or absurd by what convention deems trivial; but Gogol is always intent on destroying preconceived notions and prejudged categories. In another instance, vantage point is enhanced by a subtlety of syntax: 'All that's at the front of the house, but you should take a look at his garden! What *doesn't* he have! Plums, cherries, every kind of vegetable, sunflowers, cucumbers, melons, chick-peas – even a threshing-floor and a forge.' Enumeration in itself confers a weight and importance on the objects in question; and the little word 'even' – one of Gogol's signature words throughout his work – heightens the reader's expectation that what follows will be even grander and more important. 'All that' already suggests abundance, and the sudden shift to the garden, which is presumably at the back of the house, creates the impression that even more will be found there: if what lies at the back is even *more* important, then what lies at the front must *already* be important.

Even though such details, which abound in each of the stories, are in constant movement, and require constant re-examination, they do not take the reader or the characters outside the boundaries of the narrative, but serve to redefine and strengthen those boundaries. They give the story a feeling of inevitability, for both characters and readers. Situation trumps character; and if *we* feel that we cannot escape the situations as Gogol creates them, then we cannot expect the characters to do so either. They have to deal with the world around them – a largely artificial world that has been created by others for them, especially in the Petersburg stories, and to which none of them is capable of adding anything of his own.

Two works from 1836 are set in provincial Russia, as *Dead Souls* (1842) would later be as well: 'The Carriage' and *The Government Inspector*. The first of these, which embodies many themes familiar from the earlier stories, such as the importance of rank, boasting, a childish attitude towards women and a desire to be what one is not, is a small masterpiece. The ending, where Chertokutsky is discovered hiding in the carriage by the unwanted visitors, has puzzled many readers, although it is really a more sophisticated version of the non-ending of 'Ivan Fyodorovich Shponka' or 'The Nose'. The major masterpiece from the same year is *The Government Inspector*. It was flanked by other plays: *The Order of Vladimir, Third Class* (1832–4) and *Marriage*, which, though written by 1835, did not reach final form until 1842, and was followed by *The Gamblers* (1842) and *Leaving the Theatre After the Performance of a New Comedy* (1842). *The Government Inspector* is a comedy of misunderstanding, but is brought off in unmistakably Gogolian ways that link it to the stories. It is set in an enclosed space (an isolated provincial town) that is suddenly invaded by an outside force (the putative government inspector) which throws everything into confusion and brings about such drastic changes that nothing can ever be put right again. As the mayor says, 'the whole world's gone topsy-turvy'. Khlestakov, who is mistaken for the inspector, is an empty and stupid young man, perhaps the most unaware of any of Gogol's characters, but, like most of them, driven by a single impulse, in this case the 'will to please', and not 'ulterior motives', as in Act IV, Scene II. It is one of the funniest plays in Russian literature, yet, like all of Gogol's work, has a sombre side. The theme of rank is now developed to the point where it is the townsfolk who confer it on someone unworthy – Khlestakov. The same would be true of Chichikov in *Dead Souls*, who presents himself to the inhabitants of the town and vicinity as merely a would-be landowner, but before long is endowed by them with a series of identities, one more absurd than the next: millionaire, Napoleon in disguise, forger of official banknotes, brigand, seducer of the governor's daughter, and so on. The point seems to be that people feel enlarged and ennobled by association with someone lofty, even if they suspect him to be a fraud. Here Gogol has moved a few steps closer to one of Dostoyevsky's seminal insights about human nature.

FICTION IN LIFE, LIFE IN FICTION

Pervasive themes in a writer's work often tempt readers to look for parallels in the writer's life. There are many in Gogol's: the fact that the Ukrainian stories are set less than fifty miles from his home, the impoverishment of his early years in Petersburg, his largely solitary life, unmarked by marriage or romance, his chronic feeling of being misunderstood and underappreciated, even his long nose – these by no means exhaust a possible list. Yet like many authors he took pains to distance himself from his fiction. At one point, for instance, he took exception to the fact that the 'object of talk and criticism has become not [my] book, but [its] author'.[13] He stated on many occasions that he could not write from direct observation, that he had to remove himself in order to see his subjects whole. His Ukrainian stories were written from the vantage point of St Petersburg. The Petersburg stories were written for the most part while he was residing there, but he felt like a foreigner in that city. The provincial Russia he described in *The Government Inspector* and 'The Carriage' was a place in which he had never lived for any period of time, and its most extensive treatment, in *Dead Souls*, was mostly written in Rome. And in his fiction he deploys an array of devices designed to set him at a distance from the texts. The most common one, from the early stories up to and including 'The Overcoat', is that of an oral narrator, who stands between the reader and the characters. The presumed author appears not to take direct responsibility for the story. This is what lends plausibility to the narrator's admission, in 'The Nose', that the story may seem far-fetched, but that it's 'beyond my comprehension' and 'I simply don't know *what* one can make of it', even though 'these things do happen'. The reader, then, stands at a double remove from the characters, and can never confidently identify any of them with the 'real' author, or Gogol himself.

Gogol's need for distance – geographical and psychological – became more imperative after 1836. That was the year, if we are to credit Gogol's own retrospective account of it, that marked the point where he ceased to be what he called mainly a 'comic writer' and decided to change his approach. As he put it in 'An Author's Confession': 'I perceived that in my [earlier] works I was laughing for nothing, in vain, without knowing why myself. If I was going to laugh, then it was certainly better to laugh loudly and at things that were truly worthy of general ridicule.'[14] The social and moral improvement of the audience now became pre-eminent. He identified *The Government Inspector* as the first work in which he put this new way of writing into practice. 'I ventured to bring everything bad in Russia that I was aware of at that time into one heap, all the injustices that are perpetrated in those places and those circumstances where it is justice that is required from a person most of all, and have a good laugh at them all at once.' It did not work out the way Gogol planned: some people criticized the play for a lack of originality, others regarded it as a slander on Russia and most seemed to have thought it was hilariously funny and little more. Gogol's reaction at the time is registered in a letter to a close friend: 'I am going abroad, there to shake off the anguish that my fellow-countrymen visit upon me daily ... A prophet has no honour in his own country.'[15] Thus began his twelve-year self-imposed exile in Rome. What changed, from then on, was his confidence that his audience would understand what he was trying to do. Like all performers, Gogol craved approval, and this for him meant approval by *all*. To his finely tuned ear, disapproval, though nearly always voiced by a minority, was almost tantamount to disapproval by *all*. After 1842 he never completed another piece of fiction, consigned much of Part II of *Dead Souls* to the flames, and fell into a depression from which he was rescued only by death in February 1852, just short of his forty-third birthday.

As the enormous popularity of biography demonstrates these days, we are keenly curious about the lives of eminent people. Gogol has defeated the most ingenious efforts to put together a plausible and compelling life for himself, precisely because he is so 'enigmatic', 'mysterious', 'enclosed', epithets that are commonly deployed when talk runs to him. But what really matters, after all, is the work he himself created. And judging by a selection such as the one that is presented here, Gogol will be part of the cultural heritage of English speakers for many decades to come.

NOTES

Abbreviation: *PSS* stands for *Polnoe sobranie sochinenii* (*Complete Works*) (14 vols (Moscow–Leningrad, AN SSSR, 1937–52)). All dates in this Introduction are given in so-called old style (OS), which refers to the Julian calendar. This calendar remained in force in Russia until 1918, when the Gregorian calendar (new style, or NS) was adopted, thereby matching Western practice. Generally, NS dates are twelve days later than OS. Translations from the stories included in this collection are by Ronald Wilks; all others are my own.

1. Letter to P. P. Kosyarovsky, 3 October 1827 (*PSS*, X, p. 11).
2. Quoted by V. V. Gippius, *Gogol* (1924), trans. and ed. Robert A. Maguire (Durham, NC: Duke University Press, 1989), p. 18.
3. Letter to P. P. Kosyarovsky, 3 October 1827 (*PSS*, X, p. 11).
4. Letter to M. I. Gogol, 30 April 1829 (*PSS*, X, p. 141).
5. 'Bisavryuk' was published in *Notes of the Fatherland* (*Otechestvennye zapiski*), February–March 1830. One section of *The Hetman* ('A Chapter from an Historical Novel') appeared in the literary almanac *Northern Flowers* (*Severnye tsvety*) for 1830; the remaining excerpts were published posthumously. Two very brief chapters of 'A Terrifying Boar' appeared in *The Literary Gazette* (*Literaturnaya gazeta*) on 1 January and 22 March 1831.
6. 'O russkoi povesti i povestyakh g. Gogolya ("Arabeski" i "Mirgorod")' (1835), in Belinsky, *PSS*, I (Moscow: AN SSSR, 1953), pp. 261–2.
7. J. E. C. (J. E. Congleton), 'Idyl [l]', *Encyclopedia of Poetry and Poetics*, ed. Alex Preminger (Princeton, NJ: Princeton University Press, 1965), p. 362.
8. Michael Wood, 'The Work of Solitude', *PEN America*, Issue 5 (Volume 3) (New York: PEN America, 2004), p. 23.
9. Letter to M. I. Gogol, 30 April 1829 (*PSS*, X, p. 139).
10. *The Bronze Horseman*, ed. and trans. Walter Arndt, in *Alexander Pushkin: Collected Narrative and Lyrical Poetry* (Ann Arbor, Mich.: Ardis, 1984), pp. 425–38.
11. None of Gogol's stories is set in Moscow, perhaps because this city, which is many centuries older than St Petersburg and was the original capital, was regarded as a community that had arisen 'naturally' and 'organically', and as such did not suit his purposes.
12. The play, *The Order of Vladimir, Third Degree* (1832–4), remains in only four fragments ('An Official's Morning', 'The

Lawsuit', 'The Servants' Quarters' and 'Fragment'). The hero, Barsukov, a high-ranking civil servant, is obsessed with the desire for a decoration. According to accounts by contemporaries, missing scenes depicted him standing in front of a mirror imagining that he is already wearing the decoration, after which he goes insane and believes that he himself has become the decoration. See the Commentaries, in *PSS*, V, pp. 478–9, and Gippius, *Gogol*, p. 78.

13. '<Avtorskaya ispoved'>' (1847) (*PSS*, VIII, p. 432). This work was published posthumously, in 1856, and the title was supplied by the editor, S. P. Shevyryov. In such cases, the Russian usage is to place it in angular brackets.

14. '<Avtorskaya ispoved'>', p. 440.

15. Letter to M. P. Pogodin, 10 May 1836 (*PSS*, XI, p. 41).

Further Reading

GENERAL

Chizhevsky, Dmitry, 'Gogol: Artist and Thinker', *Annals of the Ukrainian Academy of Arts and Sciences in the USA*, II, no. 2(4) (1952).

Debreczeny, Paul, 'Nikolay Gogol and His Contemporary Critics', *Transactions of the American Philosophical Society*, vol. 56, pt 3 (Philadelphia, 1966).

de Jonge, Alex, 'Gogol', in *Nineteenth-Century Russian Literature*, ed. J. L. I. Fennell (London, 1973).

Driessen, F. C., *Gogol as a Short-Story Writer* (The Hague, 1965).

Erlich, Victor, 'Gogol and Kafka: A Note on "Realism and Surrealism"', in *For Roman Jakobson* (The Hague, 1956).

—, *Gogol* (New Haven, Conn., and London, 1969).

Fanger, Donald, *The Creation of Nikolai Gogol* (Cambridge, Mass., 1979).

Fusso, Susanne, and Meyer, Priscilla (eds), *Essays on Gogol: Logos and the Russian Word* (Evanston, Ill., 1992).

Gippius, V. V., *Gogol*, ed. and trans Robert A. Maguire (Ann Arbor, 1981); 2nd edn (Durham, NC).

Karlinsky, Simon, *The Sexual Labyrinth of Nikolai Gogol* (Cambridge, Mass., and London, 1976).

Lavrin, J., *Gogol (1809–52). A Centenary Survey* (London, 1951).

Magarshack, David, *Gogol* (London, 1957).

Maguire, Robert A. (ed.), *Gogol from the Twentieth Century* (Princeton, NJ, 1974).

—, *Exploring Gogol* (Stanford, CT, 1994).

McLean, Hugh, 'Gogol and the Whirling Telescope', in *Russia: Essays in Literature*, ed. L. H. Legters (Seattle, Wash., 1972).

Nabokov, Vladimir, *Nikolai Gogol* (New York, 1961).

Passage, C., *The Russian Hoffmannists* (The Hague, 1963).

Peace, Richard, *The Enigma of Gogol* (Cambridge, 1981).

Proffer, Carl R. (ed.), *Letters of Nikolai Gogol* (Ann Arbor, Mich., 1967).

Rahv, Philip, 'Gogol as a Modern Instance', in *Russian Literature and Modern English Fiction*, ed. Donald Davie (Chicago and London, 1965).

Setchkarev, Vsevolod, *Gogol: His Life and Works* (New York, 1965).

Troyat, Henri, *Gogol: The Biography of a Divided Soul* (London, 1971).

Wilson, Edmund, 'Gogol: The Demon in the Overgrown Garden', *The Nation*, CLXXV (December, 1952).

Woodward, James B., *The Symbolic Art of Gogol: Essays on His Short Fiction* (Columbus, Ohio, 1981).

Yelistratova, Anna, *Nikolai Gogol and the Western European Novel*, trans Christopher English (Moscow, 1984).

Zeldin, Jesse, *Nikolai Gogol's Quest for Beauty* (Lawrence, Kan., 1978).

INDIVIDUAL STORIES AND PLAY

'Ivan Fyodorovich Shponka and His Aunt'

Rancour-Laferriere, Daniel, 'Shponka's Dream Interpreted', *Slavic and East European Journal*, 33 (1989).

'The Nose'

Bocharov, Sergey, 'Around "The Nose"', in Susanne Fusso and Priscilla Meyer (eds), *Essays on Gogol: Logos and the Russian Word* (Evanston, Ill., 1992)

Bowman, H. E., 'The Nose', *Slavonic and East European Review*, vol. 31, no. 76 (1952).

Shukman, Anna, 'Gogol's *The Nose* or the Devil in the Works', in Jane Grayson and Faith Wigzell (eds), *Nikolay Gogol: Text and Context* (London, 1989).

Yermakov, Ivan, 'The Nose', in Robert A. Maguire (ed.), *Gogol from the Twentieth Century* (Princeton, NJ, 1974).

'The Overcoat'

Bernheimer, Charles C., 'Cloaking the Self: The Literary Space of Gogol's "Overcoat", *PMLA*, 90 (1975).

Chizhevsky, Dmitry, 'About Gogol's "Overcoat"', in Robert A. Maguire (ed.), *Gogol from the Twentieth Century* (Princeton, NJ, 1974).

Eichenbaum, Boris, 'How Gogol's "Overcoat" is Made', in Robert A. Maguire (ed.), *Gogol from the Twentieth Century* (Princeton, NJ, 1974).

Rancour-Laferriere, Daniel, *Out of Gogol's 'Overcoat': A Psychological Study* (Ann Arbor, Mich., 1982)

Stilman, Leon, 'Gogol's Overcoat: Thematic Pattern and Origins', *American Slavic and East European Review*, XI, no. 1 (1952).

Trahan, Elizabeth (ed.), *Gogol's 'Overcoat': An Anthology of Critical Essays* (Ann Arbor, Mich., 1982).

'Diary of a Madman'

Gustafson, R. F., 'The Suffering Usurper: Gogol's Diary of a Madman', *Slavic and East European Journal*, vol. IX, 3 (1965).

Trott, Liz, 'Diary of a Madman': The Hidden Absurd', in Jane Grayson and Faith Wigzell (eds), *Nikolay Gogol: Text and Context* (London, 1989).

'The Carriage'

Garrard, John G., 'Some Thoughts on Gogol's "Kolyaska"', *PMLA*, 90, 1975.

The Government Inspector

Bertensson, S., 'The Première of "The Government Inspector"', *Russian Review*, VII, 1 (1947).

Bodin, P-A., 'The Silent Scene in Nikolaj Gogol's "The Government Inspector"', *Scando-Slavica*, 15 (1969).

Coleman, A. P., *Humour in the Russian Comedy from Catherine to Gogol* (New York, 1925).

Debreczeny, Paul, 'The Government Inspector', in 'Nikolay Gogol and His Contemporary Critics', *Transactions of the American Philosophical Society*, vol. 56, pt 3 (Philadelphia, 1966).

Ehre, Milton, 'Laughing Through the Apocalypse: The Comic Structure of Gogol's "Government Inspector"', *Russian Review*, 39 (1980).

Gippius, V. V., 'The Inspector General: Structure and Problems', in Robert A. Maguire (ed.), *Gogol from the Twentieth Century* (Princeton, NJ, 1974).

Ivanov, Vyacheslav, 'Gogol's *Inspector General* and the Comedy of Aristophanes', in Robert A. Maguire (ed.), *Gogol from the Twentieth Century* (Princeton, NJ, 1974).

Karlinsky, Simon, *Russian Drama from its Beginnings to the Age of Pushkin*, Berkeley, Calif. (1985).

LeBlanc, R. D., 'Satisfying Khlestakov's Appetite: The Semiotics of Eating in "The Inspector General"', *Slavic Review*, 47 (1988).

Slonim, Marc, *Russian Theatre: From the Empire to the Soviets* (Cleveland, Ohio, 1961).

Varneke, V. H., *History of the Russian Theatre (Seventeenth through Nineteenth Century)*, trans Boris Brasol, ed. Belle Martin (New York, 1951).

White, Duffield, 'Khlestakov as Representative of Petersburg in *The Inspector General*', in Susanne Fusso and Priscilla Meyer (eds), *Essays on Gogol* (Evanstown, Ill., 1992).

Wigzell, Faith, 'Gogol and Vaudeville', in Jane Grayson and Faith Wigzell (eds), *Nikolay Gogol: Text and Context* (London, 1989).

Table of Ranks

Since the different civil service ranks are mentioned frequently throughout this volume, notably in 'Nevsky Prospekt' and *The Government Inspector*, but also in the other St Petersburg stories, they are listed here for ease of reference. The Table of Ranks was introduced by Peter the Great in 1722 for the civil service. Each civil rank had its equivalent in the army and navy, the clergy and the imperial court. The system survived in slightly modified form until the 1917 Revolution.

The fourteen ranks are (beginning with the highest):

Class	Rank
1	Chancellor
2	Actual privy counsellor
3	Privy counsellor
4	Actual state counsellor
5	State counsellor
6	Collegiate counsellor
7	Court counsellor
8	Collegiate assessor
9	Titular counsellor
10	Collegiate secretary
11	Ship secretary
12	Government secretary
13	Provincial secretary
	Senate registrar
	Synod registrar
	Cabinet registrar
14	Collegiate registrar

Hereditary nobility was conferred on those holding minimum rank eight (collegiate assessor). Although civil ranks had their parallels in the army and navy, the armed services took precedence over the civil. Thus the highest civil servants were referred to as 'generals' (in *The Government Inspector* the mayor aspires to this rank as he imagines moving to St Petersburg). Kovalyov, the collegiate assessor in 'The Nose', always wishes to be known as 'major', because of the greater kudos.

DIARY OF A MADMAN AND
SELECTED STORIES

IVAN FYODOROVICH
SHPONKA AND HIS AUNT

Behind this story there is another one. We first heard it from
Stepan Ivanovich Kurochka who had just travelled up from
Gadyach.[1] Now, one thing you must know is that I have an
absolutely shocking memory. You can talk to me until you are
blue in the face, but everything goes in one ear and out the
other. It's like trying to fill a sieve with water. As I am only too
aware of this weakness of mine I asked our visitor to write the
story down for me specially in an exercise book. He was always
kind to me, God grant him good health, and he took the book
and wrote everything out. I put it on the small table, which I
think you know: it stands in the corner near the door. Oh
dear, I quite forgot, you have never even been here! My old
housekeeper, who has been with me for thirty years now, never
learned to read and write and there's no point in trying to
disguise the fact. Once I noticed she liked baking pies on paper.
Dear reader, she bakes absolutely wonderful pies, better than
you'll eat anywhere. So I had a look underneath them and what
do I see but some writing. It was as if I'd known deep down
already – I went up to the table and there was half of the
exercise book gone! She had torn the pages out for her pie
paper! What can you do? You can't quarrel at our time of life!

Last year I had to pass through Gadyach. So before I even
got near the place I tied a knot so I shouldn't forget to ask
Stepan Ivanovich about it. I'd assured myself that as soon as I
sneezed in the town, this would make me remember to call on
him. But it was all no use: I travelled through the town, sneezed,
blew my nose in my handkerchief, and still forgot to call. At
least, I didn't remember until I was about four or five miles

from the town gates. So there remained nothing else to do but print the story without an ending. However, if anyone really wants to know what happened in the end, all he has to do is go to Gadyach and ask Stepan Ivanovich. He will take great pleasure in telling you the story, although he'll insist on starting right from the beginning. He doesn't live very far from the stone church. You'll find a little lane there, and as soon as you turn into it, it's the second or third gate along. Better still, when you see a large pole with a quail on it and a fat woman wearing a green skirt coming out to meet you (there's no harm in my saying that Stepan leads the life of a bachelor) then you'll know it's his place. However, you could also try the market, where you can catch him every morning before nine choosing fish and green vegetables and having a chat with Father Antip or a Jewish tax-farmer.[2] You'll recognize him at once, for no one else has the same printed linen trousers or yellow cotton coat. And there's something else you can recognize him by: he always walks about waving his arms. The late-lamented local assessor Denis Petrovich always used to say when he spotted him coming some way off: 'Look! Look! Look at our windmill over there!'

IVAN FYODOROVICH SHPONKA

It is already four years since Ivan Fyodorovich Shponka retired and settled down on his farm at Vytrebenky.[3] When he was still a little boy he went to the local school at Gadyach and I must say he was exceedingly diligent and well-behaved. The Russian grammar teacher, Nikifor Timofeyevich Deyeprichastiye[4] used to say that if all his other boys applied themselves like Shponka there would be no need for that maplewood ruler of his. He was tired of caning idlers and mischief-makers, as he himself was the first to admit.

His exercise book was always immaculate, with a ruled margin and not a mark anywhere. He would always sit very quietly, his arms folded, his eyes riveted on his teacher. He never hung bits of paper on the back of the boy in front, never made carvings on the desks, and never played at shoving other boys off the benches just before the teacher came in. If anyone needed a knife for sharpening a pen, then he would go straight away to Ivan Fyodorovich, knowing he was bound to have one. Ivan Fyodorovich (at that time he was simply called Vanyusha) would take it out of its small leather sheath which he kept tied to the buttonhole of his greyish coat, and all he asked was that the sharp edge was not to be used for pens, insisting there was a blunt side for that. Before long his exemplary behaviour caught the attention of the Latin teacher, the sound of whose cough in the corridor was enough to terrify the whole class even before his woollen overcoat and pockmarked face made their appearance at the classroom door.

This frightening teacher, who always had two bundles of birch twigs lying on his chair, with half the boys kneeling in subjection around it, made Ivan Fyodorovich class monitor, although there were many far better qualified for the job.

Here we must not forget to mention one incident which was destined to have a lasting influence on the whole of his life. One of the boys under his command brought a buttered pancake wrapped in paper into the class, hoping this would induce his monitor to pass his work with a *scit*,[5] whereas in fact he had not prepared his lesson at all.

Now, although Ivan Fyodorovich was usually very correct in all he did, on this occasion he was very hungry and could not resist the temptation. He took the pancake, propped his book in front of him and began eating. He was so absorbed that he did not even notice the deathly silence that suddenly descended on the class. And it was only when he looked up in horror that he realized what was happening. By then that terrible hand stretching out of its woollen jacket had seized him by the ear and dragged him out into the middle of the room. 'Give me that pancake! Give it to me, you miserable wretch!' roared the terrible teacher, who snatched the pancake and flung it out of the window, with a strong warning to the boys running around the playground not to dare pick it up. After this he gave Ivan Fyodorovich a severe and very painful caning on the hands. According to his reasoning the hands alone were guilty, since they had taken the pancake and no other part of the body should therefore be punished. Anyway, from that time onwards his timidity – the first thing that struck you about him and which was quite bad enough already – grew even more pronounced. Perhaps this incident was the reason why he never showed any desire to enter government service, since experience had taught him it is not always possible to conceal one's crimes.

He was very nearly fifteen when he entered class two, where instead of the abridged catechism and four rules of arithmetic he grappled with more complex matters, such as the duties of man and fractions. But when he saw that the further one advances, the more pitfalls lie in the way, and when he heard that his father had taken leave of this world, he stayed on another two years and then, with his mother's consent, entered the P— Infantry Regiment. The latter was quite different from most normal infantry regiments, and, despite being stationed in little country villages most of the time, lived it up in such style that even most *cavalry* regiments could not compete with it. Most of the officers drank strong spirits made from frozen liquor[6] and even the Hussars could teach them nothing about pulling Jews around by their ringlets. A few of them even danced the mazurka, and the colonel never missed the opportunity of mentioning this when he was at social gatherings. Patting himself on the belly after each word, he used to say: 'Many of my officers dance the mazurka; a great many, my deah sir, oh, *ever* so many.'

To give the reader another example of the P— Regiment's high cultural level, we should add that two of the officers were so passionately fond of playing banker that they gambled away their uniforms, peak caps, greatcoats, sword knots, even their underclothes, something you would hardly ever come across even among *cavalry* regiments. Rubbing shoulders with such friends, however, did not make Ivan Fyodorovich any less shy. Since he never drank strong spirits, preferring a glass of vodka before dinner or supper, and since he did not dance the mazurka and did not play cards, quite naturally he was always left to his own devices. And so, when the others went gallivanting around on hired horses visiting small landowners, he stayed in his room doing the sort of thing you might expect of someone so meek and mild: sometimes he would polish his buttons; sometimes he would read a fortune-telling book, sometimes he would set up mousetraps in the corners of his room; sometimes he would just throw his uniform off and lie on his bed. But then, there was no one in the whole regiment so punctilious as Ivan Fyodorovich, and he drilled his platoon so well that the Company Commander always set him up as a shining example to the rest. Therefore, in a very short time, only eleven years after becoming an ensign, he was promoted second lieutenant.

During this period he learned from his aunt that his mother had passed away. This aunt (his mother's sister) he knew only because when he was a boy she used to bring by hand or send him (even as far as Gadyach) dried pears and very tasty honey cakes she made herself. She was on bad terms with his mother and so he had not seen her since his childhood. Now this aunt, being very kind-hearted, took over the management of his small estate, and duly informed him of this. Since Ivan Fyodorovich was quite sure his aunt was a very capable person, he carried on his military duties. Anyone else in his place would have gone around boasting about his important promotion. But pride was quite foreign to his nature, and after he became a second lieutenant he was just the same Ivan Fyodorovich as he had been when he was a mere ensign. When he had spent another four years in the army after this wonderful event in his life, and was getting ready to travel with the regiment from Mogilyov[7] to Russia proper, he received the following letter:

My dear nephew Ivan Fyodorovich,

I'm sending you some clothes: five pairs of cotton socks and four fine linen shirts. There's something I'd like to mention. As you've already reached quite an important rank, I think by now you should realize you're quite old enough to think of managing the estate, and there's no point in your staying on in the army. I'm getting on in years and I can't look after everything for you. And in fact there's a lot I'd like to tell you about *personally*. So do come home, Vanyusha.

Looking forward to the great pleasure of seeing you,
Your loving Auntie,
Vasilisa Tsupchevska.

P. S. The turnips in the kitchen garden are simply wonderful this year, more like potatoes than turnips.

Ivan Fyodorovich answered a week later:

Dear Auntie Vasilisa,

Many thanks for the clothes. In fact, my socks are so worn out my batman has darned them four times. As a result they've become very tight.

About my staying on in the army, I quite agree with what you say and the day before yesterday I resigned my commission. As soon as I get my papers I'll try and hire a cart.

I've had no luck at all with that seed-wheat and Siberian corn you asked me to get. There's none in the whole Mogilyov province. They feed the pigs here mainly on brewer's mash mixed with a little stale beer.

Your affectionate and ever-loving nephew,

Ivan Shponka.

Finally Ivan Fyodorovich was retired with the rank of full lieutenant. He found a Jew to take him from Mogilyov to Gadyach for forty roubles, and climbed into the covered cart just at that time of year when the trees were still sparsely clothed with young leaves, when the whole earth shone bright with fresh greenery and all the fields were fragrant with spring.

ON THE ROAD

Nothing very eventful happened during the journey, which took just over two weeks. Ivan Fyodorovich might have arrived sooner, but the orthodox old Jew had to celebrate the Sabbath by sticking his horse-cloth over his head and praying all day long. However, as I have mentioned before, Ivan Fyodorovich was not the kind of person to let himself get bored waiting.

While the Jew was at his devotions he unlocked his trunk, took out his linen, checked it over to see if it was properly laundered and folded, carefully picked the fluff off his new uniform, which was made without epaulettes, and then put everything back as neatly as he could. Generally speaking he was not very fond of reading; but if he chanced to look at a fortune-telling book it was because everything in it was familiar and he had already read it several times before, just as someone living in a town goes off to the club every day, not to hear anything new, but to meet those friends whom he is used to chatting to from time immemorial. In the same way a clerk in the civil service reads the address book[8] with great enjoyment several times a day, not from any *ulterior* motives, but because he simply loves reading a list of names in print. 'Ah, there's Ivan Gavrilovich So-and-so!' he says in a toneless voice. 'Ah, there's my name. Hm!' And then he reads it all over again, making exactly the same comments.

After two weeks' journey Ivan Fyodorovich reached a small village about eighty miles from Gadyach. This was on a Friday. The sun had set some time before he drove up to the inn with his Jew and his covered wagon. This inn was no different from any others you find in small villages. Usually no effort is spared to regale the traveller with hay and oats, just as if he were a post-horse. But if he wants a proper meal, like any *respectable* person, then he is obliged to conserve his appetite for another time.

Ivan Fyodorovich knew all about this and had equipped himself beforehand with two bundles of dough rings and a sausage. He asked for a glass of vodka, which *no* inn is short of, and sat down to supper at an oak table which was firmly riveted to the clay floor.

While he was eating his supper he suddenly heard a small carriage draw up. The gates creaked open, but it was some time before the carriage actually drove into the yard. He could hear a loud voice quarrelling with the old woman who owned the inn.

'All right, I'll stay the night, but if I'm bitten by a single bug then I'll smash your face in, you old bag! And I won't pay for the hay either!'

A minute later the door opened and there entered, or should I say there *squeezed* in, a fat man in a green jacket. His head was immovably fixed on a short neck, which was made to look even thicker by his double chin. Apparently he belonged to the class of people who have never let *little* things get them down and whose whole life has been plain sailing.

'Pleased to meet you, my dear fellow,' he said when he saw Ivan Fyodorovich.

Ivan Fyodorovich bowed and did not reply.

'And may I ask whom I have the honour of addressing?' the fat stranger asked.

This cross-examination made Ivan Fyodorovich involuntarily stand to attention, which he normally did when the colonel was speaking to him.

'Retired lieutenant Ivan Fyodorovich Shponka,' he answered.

'And may I ask where you're going?'

'To my estate, Vytrebenky.'

'Vytrebenky!' his formidable inquisitor exclaimed. 'Allow me, my dear sir!' he said, going up to him and waving his arms about as if someone were trying to hold him back, or as if he were struggling through a crowd. He came up to Ivan Fyodorovich and embraced him, kissing him first on the right cheek, then on the left, then again on the right. Ivan Fyodorovich did the same and found this kissing very enjoyable, as the stranger's large cheeks made soft cushions for his lips to plant themselves on.

'Please, my dear sir, allow me to introduce myself,' continued the fat man. 'I've an estate in the Gadyach district as well, and I'm your neighbour. I live at Khortishche, not more than four miles from Vytrebenky. My name's Grigory Grigoryevich Storchenko. We must, we really *must* get together, my dear sir. And I won't have anything to do with you if you don't come and visit me at Khortishche. But now I'm in rather a hurry ... What's that?' he asked a boy who came in wearing a Cossack-style short overcoat with patched elbows, a startled look on his face, and who began laying out bundles and boxes on the table.

'What's going on, eh?' Grigory Grigoryevich's voice grew more and more threatening. 'Did I tell you to put these here? Well, did I, you little devil? Didn't I tell you to warm the chicken up first, you rogue? Get out!' he shouted, stamping his foot. 'Wait a minute, you with the ugly mug. Where's the hamper with the bottles?'

'Ivan Fyodorovich,' he added, pouring some liqueur into a glass, 'do have some of my medicine!'

'No, really, I've had a drink already,' Ivan Fyodorovich said hesitantly.

'I won't hear of it, my dear chap,' the landowner said, raising his voice. 'I just won't hear of it! I'm not leaving this place until you join me . . .'

When he saw it was impossible to refuse, Ivan Fyodorovich drank a glass, which he did not find exactly unpleasant.

'Here's the chicken, my dear sir,' the fat Grigory Grigoryevich continued, carving it inside a wooden box. 'I must inform you that my cook Yavdokha sometimes has a drop too much and as a result everything gets overdone. Hey, step lively,' he said to the boy in the overcoat, who at that moment was carrying in a feather bed and some pillows. 'Lay my bed out in the middle of the room. And mind you put plenty of hay under the pillow. And pull some hemp from the women's distaff to stop my ears up with when I go to bed. I must tell you, my dear sir, that I've had the habit of stuffing up my ears even when I'm in bed, ever since that damned night when I was staying in some Russian inn[9] and a cockroach crawled into my left ear. Those blasted Russians, as I found out later, drink their cabbage soup with cockroaches in it. I can't describe what happened. There was such a tickling in my ear I felt like banging my head against a brick wall. A simple old woman helped me out in the end. And how do you think she did it? Just by whispering. What do you think about our doctors, my dear chap? All those devils do is make complete fools of us. Old peasant women know twenty times as much as all your doctors.'

'You're perfectly right,' said Ivan Fyodorovich. 'In fact, it sometimes happens . . .' At this point he stopped, as if he could not think of the right word. Here it won't hurt to mention that Ivan Fyodorovich was not really what you might call eloquent. Perhaps this was because of his shyness, or perhaps because he was always looking for better words.

'Give it a good shake now,' Grigory Grigoryevich said to his boy. 'The hay's so rotten here you'll get nasty twigs sticking out if you don't watch it. Allow me to wish you a very good night, my dear sir! We shan't see each other tomorrow, as I'm leaving before dawn. Your Jew will be praying all day, as it's a Saturday, so there's no point in your getting up early. Don't forget now, I won't have anything to do with you if you don't come and visit me at Khortishche.'

Here Grigory Grigoryevich's valet pulled his jacket and socks off for him and put a dressing-gown over him. Grigory Grigoryevich slumped on to his bed, which made it look as if one great feather mattress were lying on top of another.

'Aha, look alive there! Where have you gone, you devil? Straighten the blankets out. Move yourself, and put more hay under my head. You've watered the horses, haven't you? More hay. Under *this* side. Now straighten that blanket out properly, you little devil. That's it, some more. Ah!'

Grigory Grigoryevich sighed twice more and then filled the whole room with terrifying nasal whistles; now and again he snored so loud that the old woman dozing on the bench by the stove would wake up, peer round the room, and, relieved at finding nothing wrong, would drop off again.

When Ivan Fyodorovich woke up next day the fat landowner had already gone. This was the only event of note throughout the whole journey. Three days after this he was approaching his little farm. He felt his heart pounding when the windmill peeped out, waving its arms, and as the Jew drove his nags higher up the hill he could see rows of willows spreading beneath him. The pond glinted brightly and vividly through them, lending its freshness to everything. At one time he used to go swimming in that same pond, or wade up to his neck after crayfish with the other boys from the village. The cart reached the dyke and Ivan Fyodorovich at once caught sight of that same old-fashioned little house thatched with rush, those same apple and cherry trees he used to climb up when no one was around. The moment the cart entered the yard, dogs of every description came running from all directions: chestnut-coloured, black, grey, spotted. Some ran barking around the horses' hooves, others went round the back when they smelled the axle greased with fat. Another stood by the kitchen with its paw over a bone and howled for all it was worth. Another could be heard barking some way off as it ran backwards and forwards, wagging its tail as if to say: 'Look, everyone, what a fine young dog I am!' The village boys ran up in their dirty shirts to see what was going on. A sow taking a stroll around the yard with its sixteen piglets lifted up its snout with an inquiring look and gave a louder grunt than usual. Around the yard were scattered sheaves of wheat, millet and barley all drying in the sun. On the roof many different kinds of herbs such as chicory and hawkweed had been left to dry as well.

Ivan Fyodorovich was so engrossed with all this that he only came to his senses when the spotted dog bit the Jew on the thigh as he was climbing down from the cart. The household servants, comprising one cook, one old woman and two girls in woollen shifts all came running up. After shouting, 'Oh, our young master's back!', they announced that Auntie was planting Indian corn in the kitchen garden with the help of Palashka and Omelko the coachman, who performed the duties of kitchen gardener as well. But Auntie had spotted the covered cart when it was still some way off and now arrived on the scene. Ivan Fyodorovich was astonished when she almost lifted him right off his feet and could hardly believe this was the same Auntie who had written complaining she felt poorly and was getting too old to cope.

AUNTIE

At that time Aunt Vasilisa Kashporovna was about fifty. She had never married and used to say she valued a spinster's life more than anything else. Still, if my memory serves me right, no one had ever courted her. This was because she made everyone feel shy and no one could pluck up the courage to propose. Her suitors used to say, 'Vasilisa Kashporovna has a *very strong* character.' And they were right, since Vasilisa Kashporovna always wore the trousers. She could transform the drunken miller (who was not fit for anything) into a perfect treasure, just by pulling him by his curly tuft of hair every day with her own very manly hands. She looked like a giant and in fact had the proportions and strength of one. It seemed as if Nature had committed some unforgivable blunder in decreeing she should wear a dark-brown cloak with flounces on weekdays and a red cashmere shawl on Easter Sundays and her name-day, when a dragoon's moustache and high jackboots would have suited her much better. And the way she spent her time was a perfect reflection of what she wore: she went boating, wielding the oars even more skilfully than any fisherman; she went shooting wild game, and was for ever standing over the reapers at work; she could tell you exactly how many melons there were in the kitchen garden, and she made anybody who crossed her pastures in their wagon pay a toll of five copecks; she climbed trees and shook the plums down; she beat her lazy vassals with that awesome hand of hers – and that same terrible hand would offer a glass of vodka to those who earned it. Almost simultaneously she would tell everyone off, dye yarn, run into the kitchen, make kvass, preserves from honey, bustle around the whole day, and still manage to get everything done. As a result, Ivan Fyodorovich's little estate (according to the last census there were eighteen serfs) was flourishing in the true meaning of the word. What's more, Auntie was extremely fond of her nephew and carefully put away every copeck she could save for him.

After his arrival Ivan Fyodorovich's life was transformed and and took a completely new turn. It seemed as if Nature had created him specially to run that farm with its eighteen serfs. Even Auntie remarked that he would make a good farmer, but all the same did not let him have a say in *everything* to do with running the estate. Although Ivan Fyodorovich was not far short of forty she used to say: 'He's only a *young boy*, so how can you expect him to know everything?'

However, he was always to be found in the fields with the reapers and haymakers, something which brought inestimable pleasure to his gentle soul. The sweep of more than ten shining scythes in unison; the noise of grass falling in orderly rows; the reapers breaking into song now and then – gay songs for welcoming guests, sad ones for farewells; calm, fresh evenings – and what evenings! How free and pure the air is then! How everything springs to life! The steppe flames with red, then blue, simply burning with the colours of the flowers. Quails, bustards, gulls, grasshoppers, thousands of insects – all of them whistling, buzzing and chirping away, then suddenly breaking into one melodious chorus! Nothing is silent for one moment and the sun sets and hides below the horizon. Ah, how fresh and good it is! Here and there fires are lit in the fields, copper cauldrons are set up and the reapers with their big moustaches gather round them. Steam rises from the dumplings. Dark turns to grey . . . It is hard to say how Ivan Fyodorovich felt at these times. He would stand next to the reapers and forget to help himself to dumplings, a dish he was very fond of, standing motionless and following the flight of a gull disappearing into the heavens, or counting the sheaves of harvested wheat strung out over the fields like beads.

It was not long before Ivan Fyodorovich acquired the reputation of a first-class farmer. However, Auntie couldn't have been more pleased with her nephew and would never miss the opportunity of singing his praises. One day, towards the end of the harvesting, at the end of July to be exact, Vasilisa Kashporovna took Ivan Fyodorovich by the hand and with a mysterious look said she wanted to have a chat with him about something that had been on her mind for a long time.

'My dear Ivan Fyodorovich,' she began, 'you know very well there are eighteen serfs on the farm. However, that's only according to the last census, and by now there are probably twenty-four. But that's not what I want to talk to you about. You know that copse on the other side of our watermeadow and you must know there are some pastures beyond the copse. Not far short of sixty acres. And the grass is so lush, you can earn yourself more than a hundred roubles a year – especially if the cavalry happens to be stationed at Gadyach.'

'Why, of course I know, Auntie. The grass is very good there.'

'I know that without *you* telling me. But did you know that all that land is really yours? Why are you goggling like that? Listen, Ivan Fyodorovich! You remember Stefan Kuzmich? Are you listening? You were so small then, you couldn't even pronounce his name. I remember I came just before Advent and took you in my arms and you nearly ruined my dress. Luckily I managed to plump you on your nurse Matryona. You were so dirty then! But all that's neither here nor there. All the land on the other side of our farm, and the village of Khortishche too, belonged to Stefan Kuzmich. I must tell you – before you were born he used to ride over to see your mother. Of course, only when your father was out. But I'm not reproaching her for it, God rest her soul, even though she always treated me very unfairly. But that's another story. Anyway, Stefan Kuzmich, by deed of title, left you that estate I was talking to you about. But your late mother (strictly between ourselves) behaved very strangely at times. The Devil himself (God forgive me for using such a disgusting word) would have had a job understanding her. And where she put that title deed, God only knows. I think that old bachelor Grigory Grigoryevich Storchenko has it. That pot-bellied old devil managed to grab the whole estate, and I'd stake my life on it that he's got that deed hidden away somewhere.'

'May I ask, dear Auntie, if that's the same Storchenko I met at the inn?'

Here Ivan Fyodorovich told her about the meeting.

'Who knows?' she answered after a moment's reflection. 'Perhaps he's not a swindler after all. True, it's only six months since he came to live near us and you can't get to know anyone in such a short time. The old woman, his mother, is a very sensible woman and is a dab hand, so they say, at pickling cucumbers. And her maids make wonderful carpets. But if as you say he was very friendly, then go and see him. Perhaps the old rake's conscience will prick him and he'll give up what doesn't belong to him. You could have taken the small carriage, only those damned brats have pulled all the nails out of the back. You must tell Omelko to fasten the leather covering down much better in future.'

'Why do I need the carriage, Auntie? I'll take the old wagon, the one you use when you go shooting wildfowl.'

And with that the conversation ended.

THE DINNER

It was around dinner time when Ivan Fyodorovich entered the village of Khortishche and he felt certain misgivings as he approached the landowner's house. It was a long building, not thatched with reeds like other local landowners' houses, but with a wooden roof. The two barns in the yard had wooden roofs as well. The gates were made of oak. Ivan Fyodorovich felt like a dandy who arrives at a ball and sees that everyone is dressed more smartly than he is. Out of respect he left the old cart by one of the barns and walked the rest of the way to the front door.

'Ah, Ivan Fyodorovich,' fat Grigory Grigoryevich shouted as he crossed the yard, wearing a coat, but without any tie, waistcoat or braces. However, even these clothes were evidently too heavy and thick for someone of his size, for the sweat just poured off him. 'But didn't you say you'd come and visit me *as soon as* you'd seen your Auntie again?' After these words Ivan Fyodorovich's lips were welcomed by the familiar cheek cushions again.

'I've been very busy on the farm. I've only dropped in for a few minutes, because there's something I want . . .'

'Just for a few minutes? We can't allow that. Hey, step lively,' he shouted and the same boy in the Cossack-style overcoat came running from the kitchen. 'Tell Kasyan to shut the gates, and mind he does it properly! And unharness this gentleman's horses immediately. Please come in. It's so hot out here my shirt's soaked through.'

Ivan Fyodorovich went inside. He made up his mind not to waste any time, to try and overcome his shyness and get right down to business.

'My Auntie has the honour, so she said . . . to inform you that the late Stefan Kuzmich's deed of title . . .'

It is hard to imagine the disagreeable expression these words produced on Grigory Grigoryevich's broad, expansive face.

'Good God! I can't hear a thing!' he answered. 'I must tell you that a cockroach once crawled into my left ear. Those blasted Russians have started breeding the things in their huts. No pen could describe the torments I went through. It just went on tickling and tickling. An old woman got rid of it very simply . . .'

'What I wanted to say,' said Ivan Fyodorovich, taking the liberty of interrupting Grigory Grigoryevich, who was clearly trying to change the subject, 'what I wanted to say was that this deed of title is mentioned in the late Stefan Kuzmich's will and in connection with this . . .'

'I know what your aunt's been telling you. A complete lie, I tell you! My uncle made no such deed of title. However, some sort of deed *is* mentioned in the will, but where is it? No one's ever produced it. I'm telling you this, as I sincerely want to help you. I swear to God it's all a lie!'

Ivan Fyodorovich said nothing, and reflected that perhaps Auntie had really imagined everything.

'Ah, here comes Mother with my sisters,' said Grigory Grigoryevich. 'That means dinner's ready. Come on!' And with that he caught hold of Ivan Fyodorovich by the hand and pulled him into the next room, where there was a table laden with vodka and savouries. At this moment an old, shortish woman came in, a real coffee-pot in a nightcap, accompanied by two girls, one fair, the other dark. Ivan Fyodorovich, like the gentleman he was, first went up to kiss the old lady's hand, then kissed the hands of the two young ladies.

'Mother, I want to introduce a neighbour of ours, Ivan Fyodorovich Shponka!' said Grigory Grigoryevich.

The old lady stared at Ivan Fyodorovich, or at least, so it appeared. Anway, she was kindness itself. All she wanted to do, it seemed, was to ask Ivan Fyodorovich how much salt he used for pickling cucumbers during the winter.

'Did you have some vodka before you came?' she asked.

'Mother, you can't have had a proper nap,' said Grigory Grigoryevich. '*Who* asks a guest if he's had anything to drink *before* he arrives. You should offer him some, whether *we've* had any or not. Ivan Fyodorovich, some centaury-flavoured or Trokhimov vodka?[10] Which do you prefer? Ivan Ivanovich, why are you standing there?' Grigory Grigoryevich added, turning round. And Ivan Fyodorovich saw the gentleman of that name go up to the vodka in his long-tailed frock-coat with its enormous stand-up collar covering the whole of the back of his neck, which made his head look as though it were riding in a carriage.

Ivan Ivanovich went up to the vodka, wiped his hands, had a good look at his glass, poured some vodka out, lifted it up to the light, poured the whole glassful into his mouth, rinsed it round without swallowing it right away – and then gulped it down. After he had eaten some bread with some salted golden-brown mushrooms he went up to Ivan Fyodorovich.

'Do I have the pleasure of addressing Ivan Fyodorovich Shponka?'

'That's right, sir.'

'You've changed a lot since I saw you last. I remember when you were as tall as this,' continued Ivan Ivanovich, putting his hand about two feet from the floor. 'Your late father, God rest his soul, was a man of rare qualities. He grew such musk melons and watermelons as you'd never find anywhere these days. Just take this place, for instance,' he said, drawing Ivan Fyodorovich to one side. 'They serve you melons at table. What sort of melons are they supposed to be? Why, they're not even worth looking at! Believe me, my dear sir,' he added with a mysterious expression, opening his arms wide apart as if he were trying to embrace a thick tree, 'they were this size, I swear it!'

'Let's go in to dinner,' Grigory Grigoryevich said, and took Ivan Fyodorovich by the arm. Everyone went into the dining-room. Grigory Grigoryevich sat at his usual place at the end of the table. With his enormous napkin he looked like one of those heroes painted by barbers on their shop signs.

Ivan Fyodorovich sat blushing in his appointed place opposite the two girls. And Ivan Ivanovich did not let the chance slip of sitting next to him, terribly pleased that there was someone present to whom he could show off his knowledge.

'It's no good looking for the parson's nose, Ivan Fyodorovich,' the old lady said, turning to him. 'It's a hen turkey.' At this moment a rural waiter in a grey frock-coat with black patches all over it put a plate in front of him. 'Have some of the back.'

'Mother!' Grigory Grigoryevich said. 'No one asked *you* to interfere! You can rest assured our guest knows what he wants! Ivan Fyodorovich, have some wing or a piece of gizzard . . . There . . . Why have you taken so little? Have some leg.' Then he turned to the rural waiter and said: 'Why are you standing there gaping with that plate? Ask him to take some. Down on your knees, you old devil. Now ask our guest: "Ivan Fyodorovich, please take some leg".'

The waiter went down on his knees and bellowed: 'Do take some leg, Ivan Fyodorovich.'

'Hm, do you call that a turkey?' Ivan Ivanovich said to his neighbour in a contemptuous, low voice. 'If you want real turkeys, you should see mine! I swear any one of them has more fat on it than ten of these. Believe me, it makes you feel quite sick to see them running round the yard, they're so fat!'

'You're lying, Ivan Ivanovich,' said Grigory Grigoryevich, who had overheard this little speech.

Ivan Ivanovich pretended he had not heard and carried on talking to his neighbour: 'I'm telling you that last year, when I sent them to Gadyach, I was offered fifty copecks each. And I wouldn't take it.'

'And I say you're lying,' Grigory Grigoryevich said, in a louder voice this time, clearly enunciating each syllable. But Ivan Ivanovich pretended this remark was not directed at him at all and continued, in a far softer voice this time: 'No, I wouldn't take it. Not one squire in Gadyach . . .'

'Ivan Ivanovich, you're nothing but an idiot!' shouted Grigory Grigoryevich. 'Ivan Fyodorovich knows more about these things than you and won't believe a word you're saying.'

Ivan Ivanovich was very hurt by this remark. He did not say any more and started devouring the turkey – even though it was not as fat as those which make you feel sick just to look at them.

The clatter of knives, spoons and plates took the place of conversation for a while; but the loudest noise of all was made by Grigory Grigoryevich sucking the marrow out of a sheep's bone.

After a short silence Ivan Ivanovich stuck his head out of its 'carriage' and asked Ivan Fyodorovich: 'Have you read Korobey-

nikov's *Journey to the Holy Land*?[11] It's a book to delight heart
and soul! They don't publish books like that nowadays. I'm
only sorry I forgot to see what year it came out.'

When Ivan Fyodorovich heard the subject had changed to
books he diligently applied himself to the sauce.

'My dear sir, I find it quite amazing that a simple commoner
from the town should have visited all those places. More than
two thousand miles! More than two thousand miles, my dear
sir! Why, it's as if Our Lord Himself, by His divine grace,
enabled him to visit Palestine and Jerusalem.'

Ivan Fyodorovich, who had heard a lot about Jerusalem from
his orderly, remarked:

'You said he visited Jerusalem?'

'What did you say, Ivan Fyodorovich?' Grigory Grigoryevich
asked from the other end of the table.

'I had occasion to remark that the earth contains many far-off
places,' said Ivan Fyodorovich, deeply pleased with himself for
producing such a long and difficult sentence.

'Don't believe him, Ivan Fyodorovich,' said Grigory Grigoryevich, who evidently hadn't heard properly, 'he does nothing
but tell lies.'

Dinner was over. Grigory Grigoryevich went off to his room
for his usual little nap, while the guests followed the old lady
and the two girls into the drawing-room where that same table
at which they had been drinking vodka before dinner had
undergone a transformation and was now covered with dishes
containing various kinds of jam and plates of watermelons,
cherries and musk melons.

Grigory Grigoryevich was conspicuous by his absence. The
old lady became very talkative and, without being asked, re-
vealed a great many secrets about making fruit jelly flans and
drying pears. Even the girls opened their mouths. But the
blonde, who seemed six years younger than her sister and
who was actually about twenty-five, was not so talkative. Ivan
Ivanovich was livelier and said more than anyone else. Convinced that no one would try to contradict or muddle him, he
talked about growing cucumbers and sowing potatoes, about
how sensible everyone was in the old days – how *could* you

compare people at present? – and about how things were pro-
gressing and what wonderful inventions were being made. In
brief, he was one of those people who take the greatest pleasure
in sweetening their souls with conversation and will talk about
anything and everything under the sun. If the conversation
happened to be on a solemn or religious subject, then Ivan
Ivanovich would sigh after each word and slightly nod. If the
conversation turned to more domestic matters, he would stick
his head out of its 'carriage' and make such faces you could tell
from his expression alone how to make kvass[12] from pears,
how enormous were those melons of which he had been talking,
and how fat those geese running around his yard.

Finally, when it was already evening, Ivan Fyodorovich managed to bid them farewell, but only after great difficulty. Despite
his easy-going nature and pliancy, and although his hosts tried
their hardest to make him stay the night, he would not give in
and succeeded in making his escape.

AUNTIE'S NEW PLAN

'Well, did you get the deed out of the old devil?' This was
the question Ivan Fyodorovich's aunt greeted him with on his
return. She was so impatient that she had been waiting several
hours on the front steps and in the end could not resist running
outside the main gate.

'No, Auntie,' Ivan Fyodorovich said as he climbed down
from the cart. 'Grigory Grigoryevich has no deed of title.'

'And you believed him! He's lying, damn him! If I ever meet
him, I'll thrash him with my own hands. *I'll* strip that fat off
him! Anyway, we'd better have a talk with our solicitors to see
if we can take him to court over it. But we're not concerned
with that now. Did you have a good meal?'

'Yes, very good, Auntie.'

'Well, tell me what you had. I know the old girl's an excellent
cook.'

'There were cheese fritters with sour cream, Auntie. And
stuffed pigeons with sauce . . .'

'Did you have turkey and plums?' asked Auntie, who was an expert at preparing that very same dish.

'Yes, we had turkey as well. Grigory Grigoryevich's sisters are very pretty, especially the blonde!'

'Ah,' said Auntie and stared at Ivan Fyodorovich, who blushed and looked down at the ground. A new thought suddenly flashed through her mind. 'Well then,' she asked in a brisk, inquisitive voice, 'what were her eyebrows like?'

Here we should mention that Auntie always thought a woman's eyebrows were the most important part of her looks.

'Her eyebrows, Auntie, were just like the ones you said you had when you were young. And she's got little freckles all over her face.'

'Ah!' said Auntie, very pleased with this observation, although in fact he had not meant to pay her this compliment.

'What kind of dress was she wearing? Nowadays it's hard to find the high-quality material my cloak's made of, for example. But that's neither here nor there. What did you find to talk about?'

'Talk? Me, Auntie? Perhaps you're already getting ideas . . .'

'Well, what's so strange about that? It's all in the hands of the Good Lord. Perhaps you were destined from birth to live together as man and wife.'

'I don't know how you can say that, Auntie. It only goes to show you don't know me at *all*.'

'Oh, I've really touched a soft spot there!' said Auntie. 'A little boy,' she thought, 'he knows nothing! I *must* bring them together, and at least let them get to know each other.'

Here Auntie left Ivan Fyodorovich and went into the kitchen. But from now on all she could think of was seeing her nephew married as soon as possible and herself looking after some little grandchildren. All that filled her head now were the wedding preparations, and everyone noticed she was fussing around much more than usual, with the result that things took a turn for the worse, instead of improving. Often, when she was making a pie (normally she would never trust the cook with this), her thoughts would wander. She would imagine a little grandson was standing by her asking for a piece. Absent-mindedly she would hand him one of the best pieces, but one of the house dogs, seeing its chance, would seize the tasty morsel and wake her from her daydreams with its loud munching: for this it was invariably beaten with a poker. She even neglected her favourite pastimes and did not go shooting so often, especially after she even shot a crow instead of a partridge, something she had never done before.

Four days later everyone saw the old carriage finally come rumbling out of its shed into the yard. Omelko, the coachman (he was night-watchman and looked after the kitchen garden as well) had been hammering away from early morning, nailing on new leather, and constantly chasing off the dogs when they tried to lick the grease off the wheels. I must inform my readers that this was the very same carriage that Adam travelled in. Therefore, if you meet anyone trying to pass his carriage off as Adam's, then you can be sure that it must be a complete fake, an absolute forgery if ever there was one. God alone knows how it ever survived the Flood. One can only conclude that there was a special shed for it in Noah's ark. It's a great pity I haven't time to describe it in detail. Suffice it to say that Vasilisa Kashporovna was very satisfied with its architecture and was forever expressing her deep regret that carriages in the old style had gone out of fashion. Its actual structure – it tilted slightly to one side so it was much higher on the right than the left – was very much to her liking, since, as she said, an undersized person could get in on one side and a large one on the other. However, it could accommodate five undersized ones and three the size of Auntie.

Towards the afternoon Omelko, having fussed around the carriage, led three horses out of the stables – three horses not much younger than the carriage – and began harnessing them to the magnificent vehicle with a rope. Ivan Fyodorovich and his aunt – one from the left, the other from the right – climbed into the carriage and drove off. When the peasants they passed along the road saw such a sumptuous carriage (Auntie rarely used it) they respectfully stopped, doffed their caps and bowed very low. Two hours later the carriage came to a halt (I need hardly say where) at the front door of Storchenko's house. Grigory Grigory-evich was not in. The old lady and the two girls met the visitors in the dining-room. Auntie swept up to them quite magnificently, gracefully put one leg forward and said in a loud voice:

'Very glad to offer you my respects, my dear lady, and to offer my heartfelt gratitude for being so hospitable towards my nephew Ivan Fyodorovich who speaks highly of the welcome you gave him. What marvellous buckwheat you grow! I saw it when I drove up to the village. Do you mind telling me how many sheaves per acre you get from it?'

Thereupon everyone started kissing each other. When they were all settled in the drawing-room the old lady began:

'I can't tell you anything about the buckwheat, that's Grigory Grigoryevich's concern. I haven't had anything to do with that for a long time now, because I'm too old and incapable! I remember in the old days that our buckwheat used to grow right up to one's waist. God knows what it's like now, though they do say it's even better.' Here the old lady sighed. Anyone present would have detected in this sigh an echo of the eighteenth century.

'I hear your maids make wonderful carpets, my dear lady,' Vasilisa Kashporovna said, touching the old lady's most sensitive chord. At these words she seemed to liven up and started babbling away about dyeing yarn and preparing thread. From carpets the conversation quickly changed to pickling cucumbers and drying pears. In short, not an hour passed before both ladies were engaged in the friendliest conversation, as if they had known each other for ages. Vasilisa Kashporovna started telling her many things, in such a low voice that Ivan Fyodorovich could not make out one word.

'Well, would you like to have a look?' the old lady said, getting up.

Vasilisa Kashporovna and the girls stood up as well and they all went into the maids' room. However, Auntie signalled to Ivan Fyodorovich to stay where he was and whispered something to the old lady.

'Mashenka,' the old lady said, turning to the blonde sister. 'Stay and talk to our guest, so that he won't be bored.'

The blonde girl stayed behind and sat on the couch. Ivan Fyodorovich shifted about in his chair as though he was sitting

on a bed of thorns, blushing and looking down at the floor. But
the young lady was quite oblivious of this and sat quite coolly
on the couch, studiously inspecting the windows and walls or
watching the cat, which had taken fright and had run under a
chair.

Ivan Fyodorovich plucked up a little courage and tried to
start a conversation. But all the words seemed to have got lost
on the way. Not a single thought came into his head. The silence
lasted about a quarter of an hour. All this time the young lady
just sat there.

Finally Ivan Fyodorovich made a great effort and said in a
slightly trembling voice:

'There's a great many flies this summer, Miss.'

'An extraordinary number,' she answered. 'My little brother
made a swatter out of one of Mama's old shoes; but the place
is still full of them.'

The conversation came to an end once more. Ivan Fyodorovich just could not think of anything to say at all.

Finally the old lady, Auntie, and the dark-haired sister
returned. After chatting a little while longer Vasilisa Kashporovna took her leave, despite repeated invitations to stay the
night. The old lady and the sisters came out on to the front
steps with their guests to say goodbye, and for a long time
stood there curtsying to Auntie and her nephew, who kept on
looking back out of the departing carriage.

'Well, Ivan Fyodorovich, what did you talk about when you
were with the young lady?' Auntie asked as they drove along.

'She's a very unpretentious, well-bred young lady, Marya
Grigoryevna!'

'Listen, Ivan Fyodorovich, I want to have a serious talk with
you. Good God, you're thirty-eight now. You have a good
position. It's time to think about having children. You must get
yourself a wife . . .'

'*What*, Auntie!' Ivan Fyodorovich cried out in horror. 'A wife!
No, Auntie, please! You're making me blush! . . . I've never been
married before, I just wouldn't know what to *do* with a wife!'

'You'll find out,' she said, smiling, 'you'll find out.' Then she
said to herself: 'Whatever next? He's just like a little child, he

doesn't know a thing!' Then she continued aloud: 'Yes, Ivan Fyodorovich, you couldn't find a better wife than Marya Grigoryevna. And you're quite attracted to her, I know. I've had a good talk about it already with the old lady, and she'll be more than delighted to have you as her son-in-law. Of course, we still don't know what that old devil Grigory Grigoryevich will have to say. But let's not think about him. And if he doesn't give her a dowry, we can always take him to court . . .'

At this moment the carriage was approaching the yard and the ancient steeds livened up, sensing they were not far from their stalls.

'Listen, Omelko, don't take the horses to the watering-trough straight away – they're hot from the journey.' Auntie climbed down and continued: 'Ivan Fyodorovich, I advise you to consider this very carefully. Right this minute I'm needed in the kitchen. I forgot to tell Solokha about dinner and that lazy bitch won't have thought of doing anything herself.'

But Ivan Fyodorovich stood there thunderstruck. True, Marya Grigoryevna was quite pretty; but to get *married*! The idea seemed so strange, so far from his world, that he just could not think about it without a profound feeling of terror. Live with a *wife*! It was just inconceivable! He would never be alone in his room any more, because there would always be *two* of them, together, everywhere! The more engrossed he became in these thoughts, the more the sweat poured off his face.

He went to bed earlier than usual, but, however hard he tried, he just could not drop off. In the end long-awaited sleep, that universal comforter, descended on him. But what dreams he had! Never had he known such chaotic nightmares. First he dreamt that everything around him was making a terrific din and whirling round and he was running, running, without feeling the ground under his feet, until he was too exhausted to run any longer. Suddenly someone grabbed him by the ear. 'Ah, who's that?' 'It's me, your wife!' a voice shouted right into his ear. And he suddenly woke up. Then he had another dream, that he was already married, that everything in the house had become so weird, so peculiar, and that there was a *double* instead of a single bed in his room. His wife was sitting on a chair. He was completely at a loss what to do, whether to go up to her or speak to her, and then he noticed that she had the face of a goose. He happened to look the other way, and saw another wife, and she had a goose's face as well. He looked again and there was a third wife; he looked around – still another. He panicked and ran into the garden, but it was hot out there. He took off his hat – and there was a wife sitting in it.[13] Beads of sweat trickled down his face. He felt in his pocket for his handkerchief – and found a wife in it. He took some cotton wool out of his ear – there was a wife there too. Suddenly he started hopping on one foot, and Auntie looked at him and said with a serious expression: 'Yes, you may well hop about; because you're a married man now.' He went over to her, but Auntie had turned into a belfry and it seemed someone was hauling him up by a rope to the top. 'Who's pulling me up?' he asked in a pathetic voice. 'It's me, your wife, and I'm hauling you up because you're a bell.' 'No, I'm not a bell, I'm Ivan Fyodorovich!' he shouted. 'No, you're a bell,' said a certain colonel of the P— Infantry Regiment who happened to be passing at the time. Then he suddenly had another dream, that his wife was not a person at all, but some kind of woollen material. He had gone into a shop in Mogilyov. 'What kind of material could you like, sir?' asked the shopkeeper. 'Have some *wife*, it's the latest thing now! Lovely quality as well. Everyone's having coats made from it.' The shopkeeper made his measurements and cut the wife up. Ivan Fyodorovich took it under his arm and went off to a Jewish tailor, who said, 'No, that's *very poor* material. No one uses *that* kind of stuff for coats now . . .' Ivan Fyodorovich woke up terrified, in a frenzy, with cold sweat pouring off him.

As soon as he got up in the morning he immediately consulted his fortune-telling book, at the end of which some philan-thropically minded bookseller, out of rare kindness of heart and unprompted by any *mercenary* motives, had included an abridged *Interpretation of Dreams* as an appendix. But he could not find anything even remotely resembling such a wild dream.

Meanwhile Auntie had hatched a new plan which you will learn more about in the next chapter.

HOW IVAN IVANOVICH QUARRELLED WITH IVAN NIKIFOROVICH

I. Ivan Ivanovich and Ivan Nikiforovich

You should see Ivan Ivanovich's marvellous short fur jacket! It's quite fantastic! Good God – what lambskins! All dove-coloured and shot with frosty-white! I'll bet you anything you like *nobody* has lambskins to compare with his. Heavens – just take a look at them from the side, especially if Ivan Ivanovich happens to be talking to someone: simply gorge your eyes on them! I really can't describe them – velvet, silver, fire! Good heavens, by the name of St Nicholas the Miracle-Worker, why don't *I* have a coat like his? He had it made before Agafiya Fedoseyevna went to Kiev. Do you know Agafiya Fedoseyevna? She's the same woman who bit the Assessor's ear off.

Ivan Ivanovich is a very fine man! You should see his house in Mirgorod! It's completely surrounded by a veranda supported by oak pillars, with little benches all around. When the weather gets too hot Ivan Ivanovich throws off his fur jacket and some of his underclothes and relaxes in his shirtsleeves on the veranda, watching what's happening in the yard and the street. And those apple and pear trees growing right by his windows! Just open one window and the branches will poke right into the room. All that's at the front of the house, but you should take a look at his garden! What *doesn't* he have! Plums, cherries, every kind of vegetable, sunflowers, cucumbers, melons, chickpeas – even a threshing-floor and a forge.

Ivan Ivanovich is a very fine man! He loves melons; they're his favourite food. As soon as dinner is over he comes out on to the veranda in his shirtsleeves and immediately orders Gapka[1] to bring him his two melons. He slices them himself, collects the seeds in a special piece of paper and starts eating. Then he tells Gapka to bring him a bottle of ink and he makes the following entry: 'These melons were eaten by me on such-and-such a date.' If he happens to have company he adds: 'So-and-so joined me.'

The late judge in Mirgorod always used to admire Ivan Ivanovich's house and it is really quite pretty. I like the way it has numerous little rooms and lean-tos added to it on all sides, so that if you look at it from the distance all you can see are the roofs rising one above the other, making it look very much like a plateful of pancakes – better, tree fungi. The roofs are all thatched with reeds; a willow, oak and a couple of apple trees lean their spreading branches against them. Tiny windows with carved, whitewashed shutters peep out from among the trees and even stick out into the street.

He's a very fine man, Ivan Ivanovich! Even the commissioner from Poltava[2] knows him. Dorosh Tarasovich Pukhivochka always pops in to see him on his way back from Khorol.[3] And when Father Pyotr, who lives in Koliberda,[4] has five or six friends round, he always says that he knows no one who carries out his duties as a Christian so well and leads such a full life as Ivan Ivanovich.

God, how time flies! It's already more than ten years since his wife died. He never had any children. Gapka has some and they often run around the yard. Ivan Ivanovich is always giving them rolls, or slices of melon, or pears. Gapka keeps the keys to the storehouses and cellars, but Ivan Ivanovich keeps the key to the large chest in his bedroom and the middle storehouse himself, and he doesn't like letting anyone go in there. Gapka is a healthy girl, with fresh-looking thighs and cheeks, and she goes around in a coarse shift.

And Ivan Ivanovich is such a pious man! Every Sunday he puts on his fur jacket and goes to church. Once inside he bows in all directions and usually stands in the choir, singing a very good bass. And no sooner is the service over than Ivan Ivanovich goes rushing off to call on the poor of the parish. Perhaps he wouldn't have troubled himself with anything so boring if his own inborn goodness hadn't urged him on.

'Good morning, you poor thing,' he usually says when he has found the most badly crippled old woman, in her tattered, patched-up old dress. 'Where are you from, you poor woman?'

'From the farm, sir. I've had nothing to eat or drink for three days now, and my own children have driven me out of the house.'

'You poor thing! So, why did you come here?'

'To see if I could beg some bread from someone, sir.'

'Hm . . . so you want some *bread*?' Ivan Ivanovich will ask.

'I want some all right! I'm absolutely famished!'

'Hm . . . I suppose you want some meat as well?' Ivan Ivanovich will usually reply.

'I'd be grateful for anything you're kind enough to give me.'

'Hm . . . Isn't meat better than bread?'

'You can't be fussy when you're starving. Anything's welcome.'

With this the old woman would usually hold her hand out.

'God be with you,' Ivan Ivanovich will reply. 'Well, what are you standing there like that for? I'm not going to hit you!'

After putting the same question to one or two others he finally goes home or drops in at Ivan Nikiforovich's for a glass of vodka, or calls on the judge or the mayor.

Ivan Ivanovich loves receiving little gifts and presents. This pleases him immensely.

Ivan Nikiforovich is a fine man too. His yard adjoins Ivan Ivanovich's. They are friends the like of whom the world has never seen. Anton Prokofyevich Pupopuz,[5] who still goes around in a brown frock-coat with blue sleeves and who dines every Sunday at the judge's, often used to say that the devil himself tied Ivan Nikiforovich and Ivan Ivanovich together with a rope. Wherever one of them went the other was sure to follow.

Ivan Nikiforovich has never been married. Although some people say he has, that is a complete lie. I know Ivan Nikiforovich very well and and I'm in a position to say that he has never had the slightest intention of getting married. Where do all these rumours come from? For example, it has got round that he was born with a tail! But this idea is so ridiculous and indecent – and disgusting into the bargain – that I'm sure I needn't start trying to disprove it for my enlightened readers who doubtless know that only witches have tails (and even then very few), most of them tending to belong to the female sex rather than the male.

In spite of their great friendship these uncommon friends are really not very similar. The best way to find out about their respective characters is to compare them. Ivan Ivanovich has the gift of being able to make extremely agreeable conversation. God, how he can talk! The sensation can only be compared with the feeling you get when someone runs his hand through your hair or gently passes his finger across your heel. You listen and listen – and then your head droops. It's pleasant, extremely pleasant, like a snooze after a swim. Ivan Nikiforovich, on the other hand, tends to say very little, but if he should come out with one of his witticisms then watch out: his tongue is sharper than any razor. Ivan Ivanovich is on the thin side and tall. Ivan Nikiforovich is a little shorter, but he makes up for it in width. Ivan Ivanovich's head is like a radish with the tail pointing downwards, while Ivan Nikiforovich's is like a radish with the tail pointing up. It's only after dinner that Ivan Ivanovich stretches out on the veranda in his shirtsleeves. Later in the evening he puts on his fur jacket and goes off somewhere – either to the village stores, which he supplies with flour, or out into the fields to catch quail. But Ivan Nikiforovich lies in his porch all day – if it isn't too hot he turns his back to the sun – and there he stays. In the morning, if he should happen to think of it, he will wander around the yard, see to things in the house, and then come back for another lie-down. In bygone days he used to go round to see Ivan Ivanovich.

Ivan Ivanovich is a extraordinarily refined gentleman and you will never hear him utter a single indecent word in polite company – he is the first to take offence should he hear one. Ivan Nikiforovich sometimes forgets himself, which usually makes Ivan Ivanovich get up and say: 'Enough, enough Ivan Nikiforovich! You'd better lie in the sunshine than say such sacrilegious things!' Ivan Ivanovich is furious if a fly falls into his borsch: he loses his temper completely, throws the plate away and the innkeeper catches it. Ivan Nikiforovich is terribly fond of having a bath and when the water reaches his neck he has a table and a samovar put in the tub, for he loves drinking tea in the cool. Ivan Ivanovich shaves twice a week, Ivan Nikiforovich once. Ivan Ivanovich is extraordinarily inquisitive and God help you if you start telling him something and don't finish. If he's dissatisfied about something he lets you know right away. It's very hard to tell just from looking at Ivan Nikiforovich if he's angry or not – and if something has pleased him he certainly does not show it. Ivan Ivanovich is a rather timid person. Ivan Nikiforovich, on the other hand, has such wide folds in his trousers that if you inflated them there would be room enough for the whole farmyard, barn and outbuildings. Ivan Ivanovich has large, expressive, tobacco-coloured eyes and a mouth rather like the letter 'V'.[6] Ivan Nikiforovich has small yellowish eyes almost completely lost between bushy eyebrows and puffy cheeks, and a nose like a ripe plum. If Ivan Ivanovich offers you snuff, he will first lick the snuff-box lid, flip it open with his finger and hold it out, saying – if he happens to know you – 'I shall esteem it a favour, my dear sir, if you'll take some.' If he doesn't know you he'll say: 'Not having the honour of knowing your rank, name and patronymic, will you please do me the favour of taking some?' But Ivan Nikiforovich will plonk the snuff-box right in your hand and all he'll say is: 'Please take some.' Both Ivan Ivanovich and Ivan Nikiforovich cannot abide fleas and for this reason neither will let a Jewish trader go away without first buying some of his patent remedies in different jars for these insects – and not without giving him a good telling-off into the bargain for practising the Jewish faith.

But all in all, despite certain differences, both Ivan Ivanovich and Ivan Nikiforovich are fine people.

II. In which we learn what Ivan Ivanovich wanted, how the conversation arose between Ivan Ivanovich and Ivan Nikiforovich, and how it was concluded

One morning in July Ivan Ivanovich was lying on his veranda. It was a hot day and the dry air was rippling in waves. Ivan Ivanovich had already been to the other side of town to see the haymakers on the farm and to ask the peasant men and women he met what they were doing, where they were from and where they were going. He was terribly tired and had lain down for a rest. Lying there for a long time he surveyed his storehouses, his yard, his sheds and his chickens running around and he thought: 'Good Lord! All this belongs to me! I'm not short of *anything*. Poultry, buildings, granaries – everything I fancy. Genuine distilled vodka, pears and plums in the orchard, poppies, cabbages, peas in the kitchen garden . . . What else do I need!? I'd really like to know . . . !'

As he asked himself this profound question he began to reflect, but at the same time his eyes happened to wander over Ivan Nikiforovich's fence and settled on a curious scene. A skinny peasant woman was bringing out some clothes which had been packed away for some time, to air them on the line. Soon an old uniform with threadbare cuffs was stretching out its arms to embrace a woman's brocade jacket. Behind it spread out a gentleman's jacket with coats of arms on the buttons and a moth-eaten collar; and he could see some white twill trousers, stained all over, which had once been pulled up over his legs and which could fit his fingers now. Other clothes resembling the letter Π were soon hung out with them. Next came a dark-blue Cossack tunic that Ivan Nikiforovich had had made twenty years ago when he was preparing for the army and had let his whiskers grow. Then, one after the other, there were put out: a sword that resembled a church spire sticking up. Then the folds of something resembling a grassy-green tunic with brass buttons as big as copecks swung to and fro, with a waistcoat trimmed with gold lace and opening wide in front peeping

out from under one of its folds. This waistcoat was soon hidden
by an old petticoat which had belonged to his late grandmother,
with pockets big enough to hold a water melon. All these clothes
hanging together struck Ivan Ivanovich as very interesting, with
the sun's rays falling on a green or blue sleeve, a red cuff, some
gold brocade, or playing on the point of the sword and making
everything appear rather strange, like one of those puppet
shows performed by the strolling players who go from farm to
farm. Above all it recalled the scenes where the people crowd
close together and watch King Herod in his golden crown, or
Anton with his goat; when a violin screeches and a gypsy thrums
his lips to make them sound like a drum; when the sun sets and
the cool freshness of a southern night caresses more firmly the
shoulders and breasts of plump peasant women without them
even noticing it.

Soon the old woman crept out of the storeroom, puffing away
under the weight of an ancient saddle with ragged stirrups,
worn-out leather holsters and a saddle-cloth that had once been
red, with gold embroidery and brass discs.

'What a stupid woman!' thought Ivan Ivanovich. 'Next thing
she'll be bringing out Ivan Nikiforovich and airing *him!*' And
Ivan Ivanovich was not far wrong. Five minutes later Ivan
Nikiforovich's baggy nankeen trousers were hoisted into place
and took up nearly half the yard. Then she brought out a cap
and a rifle.

'What's she up to?' wondered Ivan Ivanovich. 'I never knew
Ivan Nikiforovich had a rifle. What does he want with that?
Whether he shoots with it or not what use can it be to him? But
it's a wonderful piece! I've wanted one like that for ages. I'd love
to get my hands on that rifle – I like having fun with rifles!'

'Hey there, woman!' shouted Ivan Ivanovich, beckoning with
his finger.

The old woman came up to the fence.

'What's that you've got there, grannie?'

'You've got eyes, haven't you? A rifle.'

'What kind?'

'How should I know? If it were mine I'd know what it's made
of, wouldn't I? But it's the Master's.'

Ivan Ivanovich got up and began examining the rifle all over, completely forgetting to tell the old woman off for hanging it out to air with the sword.

'I should think it's made of iron,' continued the old woman.

'Hm . . . Iron. Why's it made of iron?' Ivan Ivanovich said to himself. 'Has the Master had it long?'

'Maybe.'

'It's a very fine piece!' Ivan Ivanovich continued. 'I'll ask him if I can have it. What can *he* want it for? Perhaps he'll take something in part exchange. Well, is the Master home, grannie?'

'Yes.'

'What's he doing? Having a lie-down?'

'Yes.'

'Good, I'll go and see him.'

Ivan Ivanovich dressed, took the knotty stick he kept for dogs, since there were far more dogs in the streets than people, and set off.

Although Ivan Nikiforovich's yard adjoined Ivan Ivanovich's, so that you could get from one to the other by climbing over the wattle fence, Ivan Ivanovich took the long way round, by the street. This street led off into an alley which was so narrow that if two carts drawn by a single horse happened to meet they could not pass and had to stay put until they were hauled backwards by their rear wheels in opposite directions. Pedestrians made their way as best they could, creeping to one side like the flowers and burdock growing along both sides of the fence. Ivan Ivanovich's shed ran along one side of the alley and along the other were Ivan Nikiforovich's granary, front gates and dovecote.

Ivan Ivanovich went up to the gates and rattled the latch. This set off a loud barking inside, but when they recognized a familiar face the dogs – all a host of different colours – ran off wagging their tails. Ivan Ivanovich crossed the courtyard with its many-coloured Indian doves fed by Ivan Nikiforovich himself, melon rinds, greenery in places, in others broken wheels, barrel hoops – and a small boy lolling about in a dirty shirt – altogether the kind of scene dearly beloved by painters! The shadow cast by the clothes strung out along the line covered most of the yard and made it somewhat cooler. A peasant woman gave him a welcoming bow and stood there gaping, rooted to the spot. A small porch with its roof supported by two oak pillars adorned the front of the house: in the Ukraine this does not give much protection from the sun, which at this time of year is no laughing matter, soaking the traveller from head to foot in warm sweat. From this you will appreciate how much Ivan Ivanovich wanted the indispensable rifle when he actually decided to venture out in such heat, contrary to his usual habit of taking a stroll only in the evening.

The room Ivan Ivanovich entered was completely dark, as the shutters were closed. A ray of sunlight shining through a chink in them took on the colours of the rainbow and, as it struck the opposite wall, produced a colourful landscape of reflected thatched roofs, trees and the clothes hanging outside, with everything reversed. All of this filled the room with a wonderful half-light.

'Good day to you!' said Ivan Ivanovich.

'Ah, good day, Ivan Ivanovich,' came a voice from one corner. It was only then that Ivan Ivanovich noticed Ivan Nikiforovich lying on a rug spread out on the floor. 'Sorry you caught me in my birthday suit!' (Ivan Nikiforovich had nothing on – not even a nightshirt.)

'Don't worry. So, you've been having a rest today, Ivan Nikiforovich?'

'Yes. And how about you, Ivan Ivanovich?'

'I've been resting too.'

'But now you're up?'

'Up? For goodness sake, Ivan Nikiforovich! How can anyone sleep so late! I've just got back from the farm. You should see the beautiful barley fields along the road! Delightful! And the hay is so tall and soft and golden!'

'Gorpina!' Ivan Nikiforovich shouted. 'Bring Ivan Ivanovich some vodka and pastries with sour cream.'

'Lovely weather we're having today.'

'How can you say that! It can go to the devil! You just can't escape this heat.'

'You don't have to bring up the devil, Ivan Nikiforovich!

You'll remember my words when it's too late. You'll pay for these blasphemous words in the next world!'

'How have I offended you, Ivan Ivanovich? I haven't laid hands on your mother or father. I don't know how I've offended you.'

'Forget it, Ivan Nikiforovich. Forget it!'

'But I didn't insult you, I swear I didn't, Ivan Ivanovich!'

'Strange that quails don't rise to the whistle yet.'

'Think what you like, but in no way have I insulted you.'

'I really don't know why they don't come,' said Ivan Ivanovich, as if he had not heard. 'It's about time they came, but perhaps they're waiting until later.'

'You said the barley's good this year?'

'Marvellous barley, absolutely marvellous!'

Thereupon followed silence. Finally Ivan Ivanovich said:

'Tell me, Ivan Nikiforovich, why have you hung your clothes out like that?'

'Well, that damned woman went and let those beautiful clothes rot – almost new they were. So now I'm having them aired. The cloth's still good and they only need turning a bit to make them fit to wear.'

'One thing rather caught my fancy, Ivan Nikiforovich.'

'What was that?'

'Tell me, why do you need that rifle you've hung out to air with the clothes?' At this point Ivan Ivanovich offered him some snuff. 'Will you please help yourself, may I venture to suggest?' he said.

'No, you take a pinch of yours, I'll sniff mine!'

Ivan rummaged around in his pockets and produced a snuff-box. 'Don't tell me that stupid woman has put the rifle out to air. That Jew at Sorochintsy[7] makes very good snuff. I don't know what he puts in it to make it so fragrant. Like tansy, isn't it? Please do take some!'

'Now, please tell me, Ivan Nikiforovich. It's your *rifle* I'm interested in. What are you going to do with it? After all, you don't really need it.'

'Why don't I need it? Supposing I want to go shooting?'

'Good God, Ivan Nikiforovich – I'd like to see the day! At

the Second Coming, most likely. If I know you – and according
to what others say – you've never even shot a duck. The Good
Lord didn't make you the type to go shooting! Your bearing
and figure are far too *dignified*. How can you roam around the
marshes when a certain item of clothing, which is best left
unmentioned for propriety's sake, is hanging out to air? No,
you need *repose* and *relaxation*. (As I mentioned earlier, Ivan
Ivanovich had a very picturesque turn of phrase when he
wanted to be convincing. How he could talk! God, how he
could talk!) Yes, you should behave in a manner that becomes
you. Listen, give that rifle to me!'

'Don't be ridiculous! It's a valuable piece. You won't find a
rifle like that anywhere these days. I bought it from a Turk
when I was about to join the army. So, why should I suddenly
want to give it away? How could I? It's *necessary*.'

'For what is it necessary?'

'Do you really want to know? Supposing the house were to
be attacked by robbers? . . . I should say it's necessary! Good
heavens! Now my mind's at rest and I fear no one. And why?
Because I know I have a rifle in my storehouse!'

'It's a fine rifle! But the lock's broken, Ivan Nikiforovich.'

'What do you mean – *broken*? I could have it repaired. All it
needs is rubbing down with hemp oil to stop it going rusty.'

'From what you say, Ivan Nikiforovich, I conclude you're
not at all *amicably disposed* towards me. You don't want to do
anything for me as a token of our friendship.'

'How can you say, Ivan Ivanovich, that I'm not at all friendly
towards you? You ought to be ashamed of yourself! I let your
oxen graze on my pastures and not once have I asked for any
payment. You always ask if you can use my carts when you go
to Poltava. Oh yes! Have I ever refused you? Those brats of
yours are always climbing over my fence and playing with my
dogs and I've never complained. Let them play – as long as they
don't touch anything! Let them enjoy themselves!'

'If you don't want to give me the rifle then how about taking
something in exchange?'

'And what do you have in mind?' As he said this Ivan Nikiforovich leaned on one elbow and stared at Ivan Ivanovich.

'I'll give you my dark-brown sow for it, the one I've kept fattened up in the sty. A splendid sow! You'll see, she'll present you with a litter next year.'

'How *can* you say that, Ivan Ivanovich? What do I need a sow for? To eat at the devil's own funeral dinner?'

'You're at it again! You just can't do without the devil, can you! It's a mortal sin to swear, Ivan Nikiforovich – a mortal sin!'

'And what a liberty on your part, Ivan Ivanovich, offering the devil knows what for my rifle. A pig!'

'And why is my pig "the devil knows what"?'

'Why? You should be able to judge for yourself. Everyone knows about rifles – but what the hell is a pig after all! If it weren't you speaking I could easily take that as an insult!'

'And have you seen anything wrong with the sow?'

'Who do you take me for? Don't I know a good sow when I see one?'

'Now sit down! I shan't mention it any more. You can keep your rifle – let it stand in a corner of the storehouse and rot. I shan't mention it again.'

Thereupon silence followed.

'They say,' Ivan Ivanovich began, 'that three kings have declared war on the Tsar.'

'Yes, Petr Fyodorovich was telling me. What kind of war is it?' What's the reason?'

'I really can't say for sure, Ivan Nikiforovich. I assume the three kings want to convert us to the Turkish faith.'

'The stupid fools! Fancy wanting to do that!' pronounced Ivan Nikiforovich, raising his head.

'So you see, now the Tsar's declared war on *them*. "No," he told them, "you adopt the *Christian* faith!"'

'I wouldn't worry about it. We'll beat them easily enough, Ivan Ivanovich!'

'Of course we will. So, you don't feel like swapping your rifle, Ivan Nikiforovich?'

'I can't understand it, Ivan Ivanovich: you're a man who's known for his learning, yet you talk like a child. I'd really be a fool . . .'

'Sit down, sit down! To hell with the rifle! Let it rot! I shan't so much as mention it again.'

Just then some savouries were brought in.

Ivan Ivanovich poured himself a glass of vodka and ate a pie filled with sour cream.

'Listen, Ivan Nikiforovich. Besides the pig I'll give you two sacks of oats – you haven't sown any yet and you'll have to buy some sooner or later this year.'

'Good God, Ivan Ivanovich, it's like talking to a brick wall!' (That's nothing – Ivan Nikiforovich can produce even stronger phrases.) 'Whoever heard of swapping a rifle for two sacks of oats? Now – what about that fur jacket of yours!'

'But you're forgetting there's a sow thrown in as well.'

'What!? Two sacks of oats and a sow for a *rifle*?'

'Well, that's fair enough, isn't it?'

'For my *rifle*?'

'That's what I said.'

'Two sacks of oats for a rifle?'

'Not empty sacks, of course, but full of oats. And you've forgotten the sow.'

'Go and kiss your sow. If you don't want to – then go to hell!'

'Oh – get away from me! You'll see – in the next world they'll stick red-hot needles in your tongue for such sacrilegious words! A man needs to wash his face and hands after talking to you and fumigate himself!'

'If you don't mind, Ivan Ivanovich! A rifle's a noble object, a most interesting item of amusement. What's more, it looks very decorative in a room.'

'And you, Ivan Nikiforovich, are behaving like a child with a new toy, what with that rifle of yours,' Ivan Ivanovich said, the annoyance creeping into his voice: he was getting really angry now.

'And you, Ivan Ivanovich, are a perfect *goose*.'*

If Ivan Nikiforovich had not used this word they would not have had their quarrel and then – as ever – parted good

---

* That is, a gander [Gogol's note].

friends. But now exactly the opposite happened. Ivan Ivanovich immediately flared up.

'What was that you said, Ivan Nikiforovich?' he asked, raising his voice.

'I said you look like a goose, Ivan Ivanovich.'

'How dare you, sir, be so oblivious of the honour and respect due to my rank and station? How dare you insult me with such a defamatory word?'

'What's defamatory about it? And why are you waving your arms about, Ivan Ivanovich?'

'I repeat, what's happened to your sense of decency, that you can go so far as to call me a goose?'

'I'd like to spit in your face, Ivan Ivanovich! What on earth are you cackling about?'

Ivan Ivanovich could not control himself any more: his lips trembled, his mouth changed from its normal 'V' shape and began to look like an 'O'. He started blinking in a terrifying way.

This was something exceedingly rare for Ivan Ivanovich. He had to be really incensed to look like this.

'For your information,' said Ivan Ivanovich, 'I don't want to have anything more to do with you.'

'What a shame! Don't worry, I won't lose any sleep over it!' Ivan Nikiforovich replied.

He was lying, lying. God, how he was lying! He was really very upset.

'I shall never set foot in your house again.'

'Aha!' exclaimed Ivan Nikiforovich as he rose to his feet. He was so furious he just could not think what to do. Contrary to his normal practice he stood up and shouted: 'Hey there woman! Boy!' At this the same skinny woman appeared together with a small boy wrapped in a long, wide coat. 'Take hold of Ivan Ivanovich and show him the front door!'

'What! You'd do this to a *gentleman*?' shouted Ivan Ivanovich, his feeling of dignity mingled with indignation. 'Just you dare! Come on then! I'll thrash the living daylights out of you and your stupid master. The crows won't even find the bones!' (Ivan Ivanovich used extremely strong language when aroused.)

All together they made a striking picture:[8] Ivan Nikiforovich standing in the middle of the room in his full natural beauty, unadorned; the peasant woman with her mouth wide open and the most stupid, terrified look on her face; and Ivan Ivanovich, his arm raised high like a Roman senator's. It was a truly great moment, a magnificent spectacle! And there was only one person to see it – the boy in the immense coat who stood there fairly calmly, picking his nose.

At length Ivan Ivanovich reached for his hat.

'A fine way to behave, Ivan Nikiforovich, absolutely wonderful! I'll see you don't forget it in a hurry.'

'Get out! And keep out of my way, or I'll bash your ugly mug in.'

'And that's for you, Ivan Nikiforovich,' replied Ivan Ivanovich, making an obscene gesture with two fingers and slamming the door so hard it rattled on its hinges and banged open again.

Ivan Nikiforovich appeared in the doorway and was about to add something more, but Ivan Ivanovich did not stop to look round and flew out of the yard.

III. *What happened after the quarrel between Ivan Ivanovich and Ivan Nikiforovich*

And that is how two respectable gentlemen, the pride and glory of Mirgorod, came to quarrel. And because of what? A stupid trifle – a goose! They refused to see each other again, and broke off all relations – yet these two friends were formerly known to be absolutely inseparable. Every day Ivan Ivanovich and Ivan Nikiforovich had been in the habit of sending a servant over to inquire about the other's health and they often used to chat to each other from their verandas, saying such pleasant things it warmed your heart to listen to them. On Sundays they used to set out for church arm-in-arm, Ivan Ivanovich in his light woollen jacket and Ivan Nikiforovich in his yellowish-brown velveteen Cossack coat.

If Ivan Ivanovich, who had very keen eyesight, happened to spot a puddle or some refuse in the middle of the street (quite a common sight in Mirgorod) before his friend did, then he always used to say: 'Careful now, don't step there, it's dirty.' For his part Ivan Nikiforovich displayed the same touching signs of friendship and, wherever he happened to be standing, always offered Ivan Ivanovich his snuff-box with the words: 'Do take some – please!' And how well they ran their households. And these two friends . . . When I heard about the quarrel I was simply thunderstruck. Ivan Ivanovich had quarrelled with Ivan Nikiforovich! Such a worthy pair! Is there nothing lasting in this world?

When Ivan Ivanovich arrived home he remained extremely agitated for some time. Usually he first went to the stables to see whether the mare was eating her hay (Ivan Ivanovich had a grey mare with a white patch on her forehead and she was a very fine horse). Then he would read some books printed by Lyubya, Garya and Popov[9] (Ivan couldn't remember their titles as one of the kitchen maids had long ago torn off the top half of the title page when she was playing with one of her children); or he would have a rest on the veranda.

But now he did not busy himself with a single one of the things he usually did. Instead, he gave Gapka a telling-off for lazing around, whereas in fact she was busy carrying barley into the kitchen. He flung his stick at a cock that had come up to the porch for its customary offering; and when the filthy little boy in the torn shirt ran up to him shouting: 'Uncle, uncle, give me some gingerbread', he threatened him so violently and stamped so hard that the terrified child ran off God knows where.

In the end he thought better of it and busied himself as usual in the house again. He dined very late and it was almost dark when he stretched out on the veranda. A good plate of borsch with pigeon, cooked by Gapka, had completely banished the morning's events from his mind. Once again he took pleasure in surveying his possessions. Finally he looked at the neighbouring yard and said to himself: 'I haven't been to Ivan Nikiforovich's today. I think I'll pay him a visit', whereupon he took his stick and went out into the street. He had hardly passed through the gates, though, when he remembered the quarrel. He spat and went back. Almost identical movements took place at Ivan Nikiforovich's. Ivan Ivanovich saw a peasant woman put her foot on the wattle fence, evidently intending to climb across into his yard, when he suddenly heard Ivan Nikiforovich shout: 'Come back, come back. Don't go in there!' Ivan Ivanovich found all this rather tiresome. It was highly probable, however, that the two worthy gentlemen could easily have patched things up the very next day had not something that happened in Ivan Nikiforovich's house destroyed all hope of reconciliation and poured oil on the hostile fires which were ready to die out.

That very same evening Agafiya Fedoseyevna came to see Ivan Nikiforovich. Agafiya Fedoseyevna was neither a relative, nor his sister-in-law, nor even his godmother. There was no reason at all, it seemed, why she should visit him, and Ivan Nikiforovich was not exactly pleased when she did. All the same, she was in the habit of coming to stay with him for weeks on end, sometimes even longer, keeping the keys in her possession and taking charge of the whole house. All this Ivan Nikiforovich found very unpleasant but, surprisingly enough, he obeyed her like a child, and although he sometimes tried to argue with her she always got her way.

I must confess that I have no idea how women can grab us by the nose as deftly as they take hold of a teapot handle. Either their hands are adapted for this, or else that is all our noses are fit for. And although Ivan Nikiforovich's nose looked rather like a plum, she would catch hold of it and lead him around like a dog. When she was around he couldn't help altering his normal routine: he would not lie in the sun so long, and when he did he would never lie in the nude, but would always wear a shirt and his broad velveteen trousers, although Agafiya Fedoseyevna never requested him to. On the contrary, she did not like ceremony and when Ivan Nikiforovich felt feverish, she would wash him from head to foot with turpentine and vinegar, with her own hands. Agafiya Fedoseyevna wore a cap and a coffee-coloured cloak with yellowish flowers, and she had three warts on her nose. She had a figure like a small tub and it was just about as difficult to make out where her waist was as trying to see one's own nose without a mirror. Her little feet were shaped like cushions. She loved scandalmongering, ate boiled beetroot in the mornings, swore like a trooper – and whichever one of these varied activities she happened to be engaged in her expression never altered for one second. This is a gift that normally only *women* are blessed with.

The moment she arrived everything was turned inside out.

'You mustn't apologize to him, Ivan Nikiforovich, or try and make it up – he wants to ruin you, he's that kind of man! You don't really know him at all.' The wretched woman babbled on and on, until in the end Ivan Nikiforovich didn't want to know any more about Ivan Ivanovich.

Sweeping changes took place: if a neighbour's dog strayed into the yard it was beaten with the first thing that came to hand; children who climbed over the fence came back howling, their shirts lifted up to show where they had been thrashed. Even the old peasant woman, when Ivan Ivanovich wanted to ask her something or other, gave such an obscene reply that Ivan Ivanovich, being an extremely sensitive person, spat on the ground and muttered: 'What a filthy woman! Worse than her master!'

Finally, to add insult to injury, his hateful neighbour had a goose shed built just where he used to climb over the fence, apparently with the specific intention of making the insult even worse. This shed that Ivan Ivanovich found perfectly hideous was built with devilish speed – in a single day.

All this filled Ivan Ivanovich with malice and a longing for vengeance. However, he did not show any signs of annoyance, despite the fact that the shed actually encroached on his land. But his heart began to beat so fast that he found it very difficult to keep up this outward show of calm. This was how he spent the rest of the day.

Night came. Oh, if only I were a painter I could portray to wonderful effect all the enchantment of night! I would paint the whole of Mirgorod as it slept; the countless motionless stars looking down upon it; the almost visible distance; the lovelorn sexton rushing past and climbing over the fence with the boldness of knights of old; the white walls of the houses caught by moonlight becoming even whiter, and the overhanging trees turning even darker and casting even deeper shadows; the flowers and silent grass smelling more fragrant; and the crickets, those restless cavaliers of the night, singing their friendly chirruping songs in unison in every corner.

I would paint the black-browed village maiden tossing about on her lonely bed in one of the tiny low-roofed clay cottages, her bosom heaving as she dreamt of some hussar's moustache and spurs. I would paint the black shadows of bats flitting along the white road and settling on chimney pots blanched in the moonlight. But to paint Ivan Ivanovich as he went out that night, saw in hand, is beyond my powers. His face registered a hundred different expressions. Quietly, quietly, he crept up and crawled under the goose shed. Ivan Nikiforovich's dogs had not yet heard about the quarrel so they treated him as an old friend and let him go up to the shed which was supported by four oak posts. He crawled over to the nearest one and started sawing. The noise produced by the saw made him constantly look round, but the thought of the insult restored his courage. The first post was sawn through; he started on another. His eyes seemed to be on fire and he was blinded with terror. Suddenly Ivan Ivanovich cried out loud and went numb all over: he thought he had seen a ghost. But he quickly recovered when he realized it was a goose sticking its neck out at him. He spat with annoyance and carried on with his work. The second post was sawn through. The shed tottered. His heart started beating so hard when he attacked the third that he had to stop several times. When he had sawn more than halfway through, the shaky building suddenly leaned right over. Ivan Ivanovich barely had time to jump back when the whole shed crashed to the ground. Scared out of his wits, he grabbed the saw and ran home, threw himself on the bed and did not even dare to look out of his window to see the results of his terrible deed. He imagined Ivan Nikiforovich's entire household had assembled – the old woman, Ivan Nikiforovich himself, the boy in the enormous coat: all armed with staves and led by Agafiya Fedoseyevna, they were coming to smash his house up.

The whole of the following day Ivan Ivanovich was feverish. He had continual visions of his neighbour avenging himself by burning down his house – at the very least. So he ordered Gapka to keep a constant lookout everywhere in case someone had hidden some dry straw away somewhere.

Finally he decided to dash straight off to the Mirgorod District Court and file a complaint before Ivan Nikiforovich could take any action. The gist of this complaint will be found in the next chapter.

IV. *What took place in the Mirgorod District Court*

Mirgorod is a wonderful town! There are so many different buildings there! Some with straw roofs, others thatched with reeds, some even with wooden roofs. There are streets to right and left, and a fine wattle fence everywhere. Hop vines twine along the fence, pots hang on it. Behind, sunflowers poke their sun-shaped heads out, poppies blush, fat pumpkins gleam. Such richness! The wattle fence is always decorated with objects that render it even more picturesque: women's petticoats and check woollen underclothes or broad velveteen trousers. Theft or swindling are unknown in Mirgorod, therefore everyone can hang up what he likes. If you walk along to the square you certainly *must* stop for a while and admire the view: in the middle is a pond – an amazing pond! It's unique, the finest you ever set eyes on! It takes up nearly the whole of the square. Houses and cottages, easily mistaken for haystacks from the distance, stand all around and wonder at its beauty.

But I am inclined to agree with those who say there's no finer building than the courthouse. I'm not concerned whether it's made of oak or birch, but, my dear sirs, it has eight windows! Eight windows all in a row and they look right on to the square and that watery expanse I have just described and which the mayor calls a lake! It is the only building painted the colour of granite. All the other houses in Mirgorod are simply whitewashed. The whole roof is made of wood that might even have been painted red if the clerks had not flavoured the primer with onion (during a fast, of course) and drunk it, with the result that the roof never got painted. A porch juts out into the square and often one can see chickens running about in it, since grains of barley (or anything else they can eat) are almost always being spilt all over it – not on purpose, but solely through the carelessness of the petitioners. It is divided into two sections: one is the courtroom, the other is where the cells are. The courtroom section comprises two spotless whitewashed rooms – one of them for clients and the other housing a table covered all over with ink spots. On this table stands a Mirror of Justice.[10] There are four oak chairs with high backs and along the wall stand some iron-bound chests containing bundles of documents relating to local libel cases. At this time a pair of wax-polished boots stood on one of them.

The court had been sitting since morning. The judge, who was a rather stout man, but slightly thinner than Ivan Nikiforovich, with a kindly face, a greasy housecoat, holding a pipe and a cup of tea, was having a chat with the clerk of the court. The judge's lips were situated right under his nose, so his nose could easily sniff along the upper lip to its heart's content. In fact, this lip was as good as a snuff-box, since the snuff that was destined for his nose almost invariably settled along it. As I was saying, the judge was chatting with the clerk of the court. A bare-footed girl stood by them with a tray and tea cups.

At the end of the table a secretary was reading out some verdict or other, in such a monotonous and doleful voice that it would have sent any defendant straight off to sleep just listening to it. The judge himself, no doubt, would have succumbed before anyone else had he not become involved in a very interesting conversation.

'I made a special point of finding out,' he was saying as he sipped his tea, which was already cold, 'how they manage to sing so well. I had a splendid thrush about two years ago. And what do you think? It suddenly went haywire and began to sing God knows what. As time went on it got worse and worse: it began burring its letters and wheezing: its voice became very hoarse and I was ready to throw it out! And do you know what the reason was? Why, really nothing at all. There was a small swelling under its throat – smaller than a pea. All you had to do was prick it with a needle. That's what Zakhar Prokofyevich taught me and if you want to know any more I'll tell you exactly what happened. I went to see him . . .'

'Shall I read out another verdict, Demyan Demyanovich?' interrupted the secretary, who had stopped reading several minutes before.

'Finished already? Well I never – that was quick! And I didn't hear a word. Where is it? Give it to me and I'll sign it. Do you have anything else?'

'There's the case of the Cossack Bokitko and the stolen cow.'

'Good! Read it out. As I was saying, I went to see him . . . I can even remember every single thing we had to eat. With the vodka he served dried sturgeon – wonderful! Not the kind you get here' (at this point the judge licked his lips and smiled, whereupon his nose took a sniff from its perpetual snuff-box) 'from the Mirgorod grocer. I didn't have any herring – as you know, they give me heartburn. But I tried some caviar. It was *excellent* – no mistake about it! Then I drank some peach vodka distilled with real centaury. Then there was saffron vodka – as you know, I don't drink it, though they say it's very good for whetting the appetite and finishing a meal with afterwards . . . Ah! Talk of the devil,' the judge suddenly cried out when he saw Ivan Ivanovich enter.

'Good day, gentlemen! I hope you are well!' Ivan Ivanovich said, bowing all round with his unique brand of geniality. Heavens, he really was a great charmer! Nowhere have I seen such refinement! He had a very exalted opinion of himself and expected everyone to show him the respect he thought he deserved. The judge himself handed Ivan Ivanovich a chair and his nose inhaled all the snuff resting on his upper lip, which was invariably a sign of great pleasure.

'What can we give you, Ivan Ivanovich?' he asked. 'A cup of tea perhaps?'

'No, thank you very much,' answered Ivan Ivanovich as he bowed and took his seat.

'Please! Just one little cup,' the judge said.

'Really, not at the moment. But I appreciate your hospitality,' answered Ivan Ivanovich as he stood up, bowed and sat down again.

'Just *one* cup,' repeated the judge.

'No, please don't worry, Demyan Demyanovich.' Ivan Ivanovich got up and bowed again.

'A teeny weeny cup, then?'

'All right, just one cup!' said Ivan Ivanovich, reaching towards the tray.

Good God, there's no end to some people's refinement! It is impossible to describe the very pleasant impression that good manners can make.

'Would you care for another cup?'

'No, thank you very much,' replied Ivan Ivanovich as he put his cup upside down on the tray and bowing.

'*Please* have some more, Ivan Ivanovich!'

'I just can't. I'm really most grateful to you.' With these words Ivan Ivanovich bowed and sat down again.

'Ivan Ivanovich! I insist you have another cup, for friendship's sake!'

'No, but I do appreciate your hospitality.' Once again he got up and bowed – and then sat down.

'Just a small cup, just *one* more!'

Ivan Ivanovich reached out and took a cup from the tray. Lord, what man will do to bolster his own dignity!

'Demyan Demyanovich,' said Ivan Ivanovich, draining his cup to the last drop. 'I've come on urgent business. I want to issue a writ.'

Ivan Ivanovich put his cup down and took from his pocket a sheet of paper that bore an official stamp and had writing all over it. 'It's against my enemy, my *mortal* enemy.'

'And who may that be?'

'Ivan Nikiforovich Dovgochkun.'[11]

At these words the judge nearly fell off his chair.

'What did you say?' he said clasping his hands. 'Did you say *you* are taking him to court?'

'You can see for yourself – it's me.'

'Well, by all that's holy! *You*, Ivan Ivanovich, are now Ivan Nikiforovich's *enemy*? Can it be *you* saying this? Repeat what you just said. Are you sure there's no one standing behind you and speaking instead?'

'And what's so strange about it? I just can't bring myself to look at him. He's guilty of a deadly insult and he's blackened my name.'

'By the Holy Trinity! How can I expect my mother to believe what I say now? Every day, after I've been quarrelling with my sister, the old woman says: "You two are at each other the whole time, just like two dogs fighting. If only you could follow Ivan Ivanovich's and Ivan Nikiforovich's example. They're what you call real friends. That's true friendship for you. Such worthy gentlemen!" But tell me exactly what on earth has happened?'

'It's a delicate matter, Demyan Demyanovich, and I can't tell you in just a few words. You'd better have the writ read out. Here, take it from this side – it's more proper.'

'Read it out, Taras Tikhonovich,' said the judge, turning to his secretary.

Taras Tikhonovich took the document and began to read, after he had blown his nose as only secretaries in provincial courthouses know how to – with two fingers.

From a gentleman and landowner of the Mirgorod District, Ivan Perepenko, son of Ivan, a plaint as hereinafter detailed:

1) Ivan Dovgochkhun, son of Nikifor, landowner, known to the whole world for his impious acts, which inspire universal repugnancy and violate the law in every way, did, on 7 July 1810, inflict a deadly insult, with direct bearing on my personal dignity and defamatory towards my rank and name. The aforementioned gentleman, besides being of loathsome appearance, is very quarrelsome by nature and nearly everything he says is blasphemous or insulting.

Here the secretary stopped to blow his nose again. The judge folded his arms admiringly and muttered to himself: 'What a lively pen! Good Lord, how that man can write!'

Ivan Ivanovich asked the secretary to carry on, and Taras Tikhonovich continued:

The said gentleman, Ivan Dovgochkhun, son of Nikifor, when I approached him with friendly intentions, did call me publicly by a most insulting and defamatory epithet, namely, a *goose*, whereas it is known to all and sundry in the whole Mirgorod district that I was never christened after that disgusting animal, and I have no intention of being christened after it in the future. Evidence of my noble origin can be found in the baptismal register in the Church of the Three Bishops, in which is inscribed my date of birth and where my baptism is likewise recorded. Anyone with any pretension to learning will be aware that a goose is a bird, and not a human being; this fact must be familiar even to someone who has never attended a seminary. But the aforesaid malicious gentleman, being aware of all these facts, insulted me by using the aforementioned word with the sole intention of bringing the most terrible slander on my name and rank.

(2) This same indecent and gross gentleman did attempt to damage my property, inherited by me from my father, Ivan Pererepenko, clergyman and son of Onisiyev, of blessed memory, in that, in flagrant violation of the law he erected a goose shed directly in front of my porch, with the sole intent of rubbing in the insult; for this aforementioned shed up to that time had stood in a very convenient position and was quite strong into the bargain. But the vile motive of the aforementioned gentleman consisted in this alone: viz.: to make me a direct witness of indecent actions, for it is known to everyone that no man goes into a shed – and least of all a goose shed – for reasons that can be mentioned in polite society. In carrying out this illegal act, the two front posts encroached on my land, handed down to me by my father when he was still alive, Ivan Pererepenko, son of Onisiyev, of blessed memory, starting from the granary and extending in a straight line to the place where the women wash their pots.

(3) The gentleman described above, whose name inspires nothing but disgust, cherishes in his soul a desire to set fire to me in my own home. Indubitable evidence of this intention is substantiated by the following: firstly, the above-mentioned malicious gentleman has acquired the habit of leaving his house quite often, which never was the case formerly, on account of his laziness and revolting corpulence; secondly, in the servants' quarters, adjoining the fence, which encloses the land inherited from my father of blessed memory, Ivan Pererepenko, son of Onisiyev, a light can be seen burning for an

extraordinarily long time every day, which is irrefutable evidence, since hithertofore, as a result of his hateful niggardliness, not only the tallow candle, but even the oil lamp has always been extinguished during the day. And therefore I request that the same gentleman, Ivan Dovgochkhun, son of Ivan, guilty of arson, of insulting my name and family, of rapacious arrogation of my property and, worst of all, of appending the vulgar and offensive name of *goose* to my surname, be called to account by the court for full recompense, costs, and damages, that the criminal be clapped in irons and locked up in the town prison, and that judgement may be brought to bear on this my plaint without delay. Written and compiled by Ivan Pererepenko, son of Ivan, gentleman and landowner of Mirgorod.

When the plaint had been read out the judge went over to Ivan Ivanovich, grabbed one of his buttons and spoke to him as follows:

'What *are* you thinking of, Ivan Ivanovich? Fear the Lord! Throw this plaint away, get rid of it! Send it to the devil! Shake hands with Ivan Nikiforovich, make it up with him, then go and buy some Santurinsky or Nikopolsky liqueur,[12] or just make a little punch and invite me over! We'll have a drink and forget the whole thing!'

'No, Demyan Demyanovich. It's not as easy as that!' Ivan Ivanovich proclaimed with that certain tone of authority that so became him. 'This is not something that can be settled by any amicable agreement. Goodbye! And goodbye to you, gentlemen,' he said with the same authority in his voice, turning to the rest. 'I trust the appropriate action will be taken.' And he walked out, leaving everyone in the courthouse utterly stunned.

The judge sat down without a word. His secretary took a pinch of snuff and the other clerks upset some broken pieces of bottle that served as inkwells. Even the judge, in a fit of absent-mindedness, smeared a puddle of ink all over the table with his finger.

'So, what do you think of that, Dorofey Trofimovich?' said the judge, turning to the clerk of the court after a short silence.

'I'd rather not say,' replied the clerk.

'The things that happen nowadays,' the judge added. He had

barely time to finish his sentence when the front door creaked
and the front portion of Ivan Nikiforovich made its appearance
in the courtroom, leaving the rear portion outside in the vestibule. Ivan Nikiforovich's arrival in the courtroom was so
unexpected that the judge gave a loud shriek. The secretary
stopped reading. One of the clerks, clad in something made of
frieze resembling a dress-coat, stuck his pen between his lips;
another swallowed a fly. Even a soldier invalided out of the
army, who acted as messenger and warder as well and who up
to this time had been standing by the door scratching himself
through his dirty shirt with stripes on the arms – even *he* gaped
and trod on someone's foot.

'Fancy seeing you here! To what do we owe this honour?
How are you, Ivan Nikiforovich?'

But Ivan Nikiforovich was more dead than alive, as he had
got stuck in the door and could not move forwards or backwards. In vain the judge called out into the vestibule for someone to shove Ivan Nikiforovich forwards into the courtroom.
Only an old woman was there, with a petition, and despite all
the efforts she made with her bony hands, could not budge him.
Then a thick-lipped clerk with broad shoulders, a fat nose, eyes
that could not focus straight from drink and with a jacket that
was coming away at the elbows, approached the front portion
of Ivan Nikiforovich, crossed his hands for him as though he
were a child and winked at the old soldier, who used his knee
as a lever against Ivan Nikiforovich's belly: in spite of his pitiful
groans he was squeezed back out into the vestibule. Then the
bolts were drawn back and the other half of the door was
opened. This combined effort made the clerk and soldier produce such powerful exhalations, that as a result the whole
courtroom was filled with a smell so strong, it seemed to be
momentarily transformed into a tavern.

'I hope I haven't hurt you, Ivan Nikiforovich. I'll ask my
mother to send you a hot infusion to rub your back and stomach
down with. That'll take the pain away!'

But Ivan Nikiforovich slumped down on a chair and all he
was able to articulate was a continual stream of 'ohs'. Finally
he said in a faint voice, barely audible from exhaustion: 'Would

you like some?' Taking his snuff-box out of his pocket he added, 'Help yourself, please!'

'Delighted to see you,' the judge replied. 'But I still can't imagine what prompted you to take all the trouble to come here and honour us with such an agreeable and unexpected visit.'

'I've a plaint,' Ivan Nikiforovich faintly burbled.

'A plaint!? What sort of plaint?'

'A summons . . .' At this point he completely ran out of breath and there was a long pause. 'Yes, a summons against that scoundrel . . . Ivan Ivanovich Pererepenko.'

'Good God! And you were such friends! How can you want to take proceedings against such a kind-hearted man?'

'He's the devil in disguise!' snapped Ivan Nikiforovich.

The judge crossed himself.

'Here's the plaint if you care to read it.'

'I suppose you'd better read it out then, Taras Tikhonovich,' the judge said, turning angrily to the secretary. At this point his nose happened to take a sniff at his upper lip, something that it normally did only when it was feeling very pleased. To see his nose do just what it liked made the judge angrier still. He pulled out his handkerchief and wiped all the snuff from his upper lip to punish his nose for its impudence.

After he had completed his normal nose-blowing procedure before reading out documents, the secretary began as follows:

Ivan Dovgochkhun, son of Nikifor, a gentleman residing in the Mirgorod district, presents his plaint in connection with the following:

(1) Through hateful malice and obvious ill-will, Ivan Perepenko, son of Ivan, who calls himself a gentleman, has been inflicting on me every conceivable kind of harm, perpetrating damage and other pernicious acts which fill me with terror. Yesterday evening, just like a robber and a common thief, armed with axes, saws, chisels and various locksmith's tools, he climbed into my courtyard and then into my own goose shed, which is situated in the said courtyard. With his own hands, and in the most offensive manner, he chopped it down. On my part I gave no cause whatsoever for such illegal and outrageous behaviour.

(2) This same gentleman Pererepenko has been making attempts on my life, and on the 7th ultimo, concealing his real purpose, in the most insidiously friendly way, called on me and begged me to let him have my rifle, which was in my room, and with characteristic stinginess, offered in exchange several worthless things: his brown sow and two sacks of oats. Anticipating his criminal intentions, I tried in every way to put him off. But that same swindler and rogue, Ivan Pererepenko, son of Ivan, swore at me like a peasant and ever since has nurtured undying hatred towards me. Moreover, the said raging madman and confirmed criminal Ivan Pererepenko, son of Ivan, is of very low birth: everyone knows that his sister was a prostitute and followed a regiment of chasseurs which was stationed in Mirgorod five years ago. And she entered her husband in the register as a serf. His father and mother were also lawless people and incredible drunkards. The above-mentioned robber Pererepenko, in his bestial and venal behaviour, surpasses all his family and under the guise of piety does the most scandalous things. He does not fast, for on the eve of St Philip's Day this same heretic bought a sheep and the following day ordered his mistress to kill it, trying to justify himself by alleging that he needed tallow fat straight away for the lamps and candles. In the light of the foregoing I request that this landed gentleman, a declared robber, church thief, scoundrel, already found guilty of larceny and burglary, be clapped in irons and locked up in the town jail or government prison, and, under police escort, stripped of his rank and gentleman's status, before being given a thorough flogging and banished to forced labour in Siberia. And that he be ordered to pay costs and damages, and that judgement be carried out forthwith.

To this plaint Ivan Dovgochkhun, son of Nikifor, gentleman of the Mirgorod district, appends his signature below.

As soon as the secretary had finished, Ivan Nikiforovich grabbed his hat and made for the door.

'Where are you off to, Ivan Nikiforovich?' the judge shouted. 'Please wait a minute! Stay for some tea. Oryshko, what are you standing there for, winking at the clerks? You stupid girl! Now, go and bring us some tea!'

But Ivan Nikiforovich, who was frightened at being so far from home territory, and to have endured such a dangerous quarantine, had already managed to squeeze through the door, saying as he left: 'Don't worry, it's been a pleasure . . .' and with that he slammed the door after him, leaving everyone completely stunned.

There was nothing to be done. Both plaints were filed and, just when events looked as if they might turn out interestingly enough, a totally unexpected incident lent them even more piquancy. Just when the judge left the court with his clerk and secretary, and the other clerks were stuffing chickens, eggs, crusts, pies, rolls and other oddments left behind by plaintiffs into a sack – at that very moment in rushed the brown sow and, to the amazement of the whole assembly, ignoring the pies and crusts, made straight for Ivan Nikiforovich's plaint, which was lying at the end of the table with some pages hanging down. Seizing the documents, the brown porker ran off so quickly that not one of the clerks could catch it, despite hurling inkwells and rulers after it.

This extraordinary event led to the most terrible confusion as no copy of the plaint had been made. The judge, his secretary and his clerk had a long debate about this unprecedented incident. Finally they decided to report it to the mayor, since the matter was really the concern of the police. Letter no. 389 was dispatched that very same day, producing a rather curious sequel, as the reader will discover in the next chapter.

V. In which is described the conference between two important personages of Mirgorod

As soon as Ivan Ivanovich had seen to things in the house and had gone out on to his veranda for his customary rest, to his indescribable amazement he saw something red at the gate. This was the red cuff of the mayor's uniform, which, like the collar, was kept highly polished and resembled varnished leather along its edges. Ivan Ivanovich thought to himself: 'I'm rather pleased Pyotr Fyodorovich has come to talk it over,' but he was amazed to see that the mayor was walking extremely quickly and waving his arms, which was very unusual for him.

He had eight buttons on his uniform – the ninth had been torn off during a procession at the consecration of some church two years before and the village police had not recovered it, although the mayor always used to ask if the button had been found when he read the daily reports handed in by the police officers. The manner in which these eight buttons were sewn on was reminiscent of the way peasant women sow beans: one on the right, one on the left. His left leg had been shot through during the last campaign and this made him limp and stick his leg out so far to one side that it well-nigh cancelled out all the efforts of the other. The faster the mayor sent his infantry into the attack, the less progress he made. Consequently, while he was struggling towards the veranda, Ivan Ivanovich had plenty of time to hazard a guess as to why the mayor was waving his arms so vigorously. The more he thought about it, the more importance he attached to this visit, especially as the mayor was carrying a new sword.

'Good morning, Pyotr Fyodorovich,' cried Ivan Ivanovich who, as we have already mentioned, was extremely inquisitive. He could barely suppress his impatience as the mayor stormed the flight of steps up to the veranda, not looking up once and grumbling at his leg which he could not swing up each step at one go.

'Good day to my good friend and benefactor, Ivan Ivanovich,' answered the mayor.

'Please do be seated. I can see you're exhausted, what with that crippled leg of yours . . .'

'My leg!' cried the mayor, giving him the kind of look a giant might give a pygmy, or a pedant a dancing-master. Then he stretched his leg out and stamped on the floor. This boldness cost him dearly, for his whole body lurched forwards and his nose struck the railings. However, this wise guardian of law and order tried to make out nothing had happened by immediately regaining his balance and feeling in his pocket, as if he wanted his snuff-box. 'I can tell you, my dear friend and benefactor Ivan Ivanovich, that never in all my born days have I ever taken part in such a campaign. I mean that in all seriousness. Take the one of 1807 . . . Ah, I could tell you how I once climbed over a fence to see a pretty little German girl.' At this the mayor winked and produced a diabolically roguish smile.

'Where have you been today?' asked Ivan Ivanovich, wishing to cut the mayor short and discover the reason for his visit as soon as possible. He was dying to ask what it was that the mayor intended to tell him, but his fine awareness of the ways of the world made him realize that such an approach would be totally indiscreet. And so Ivan Ivanovich had to hold himself in check and wait for the explanation. All this time his heart pounded away with unusual force.

'Let me tell you where I've been,' the mayor answered. 'But first I must inform you that it's very nice weather we're having today . . .'

Ivan Ivanovich nearly died when he heard these last words. The mayor continued, 'I've come here today to see you on a very important matter.' Here his face and bearing took on that same anxious look as when he was storming the steps.

Ivan Ivanovich breathed again, trembled feverishly, and came to the point, as was his habit, without further delay: 'Important matter? Why is it important?'

'Allow me to explain: may I inform you first of all, my dear friend and benefactor, Ivan Ivanovich, that you . . . from my point of view . . . I . . . let me explain, I've nothing to do with it, but that's what the law of the country demands. You have violated the rules of law and order . . . !'

'What are you saying, Pyotr Fyodorovich? I don't understand at all.'

'Please, Ivan Ivanovich! What do you mean, you don't understand! An animal owned by you has stolen a very important document and all you can say is you don't understand!'

'What animal?'

'If I may say so, your own brown sow!'

'But how am *I* to blame? Why did the court usher leave the door open?'

'But the animal is your property, therefore you are guilty.'

'Thanks very much for putting me on the same level as a pig!'

'But I didn't say that, Ivan Ivanovich! As God is my witness! Just examine your own conscience: you must know, without a shadow of doubt, that according to the laws of the country unclean animals are prohibited from roaming around the town – and especially the main streets. You must agree that it's illegal.'

'God knows what you're talking about! So, it's a great tragedy that a pig ran loose!'

'Please let me inform you, Ivan Ivanovich, *please*! It's completely against the law. So, what are we going to do? The authorities say the law must be obeyed. I'm not denying that at times even chickens and geese run out into the street – even on to the main square. Just think of it! But only last year I issued an order for pigs and goats to be banned from public squares. And I had that order read out at a public assembly.'

'No, Pyotr Fyodorovich! All I can see is that you're doing your level best to insult me in every possible way.'

'You can't really say, my dear friend and benefactor, that I'm trying to insult you. Cast your memory back a little: last year I never said one word to you when you had a roof built a full two feet higher than regulations allow. On the contrary – I pretended not to notice at all. My dearest friend, please believe that even at this stage, so to speak . . . but I have my duty to do and I'm required to keep a close watch on public hygiene. Just imagine if suddenly, in one of the main streets . . .'

'To hell with your main streets! All the old women go there to dump any old rubbish they please.'

'Allow me to inform you, Ivan Ivanovich, that *you* are insulting me now! True, it does happen sometimes, but as a rule they dump their rubbish by fences, sheds or storehouses. But for a pregnant sow to sneak into the main street or on to the square is so . . .'

'Is so . . . *what*, Pyotr Fydorovich? Surely a sow is one of God's creatures.'

'Agreed! The whole world knows you are a man of learning, deeply versed in science, among other subjects. I never studied science myself. I only learned to write longhand in the thirtieth year of my life. As you know, I came up through the ranks.'

'Hm . . .' Ivan Ivanovich muttered.

'Yes,' continued the mayor. 'In 1801 I was serving in the

42 Chasseur Regiment, as a lieutenant in the Fourth Company. This Company was commanded by a Captain Yeremeyev.' At this the mayor plunged his fingers into the snuff-box which Ivan Ivanovich held up, stirring the snuff.

'Hm . . .' replied Ivan Ivanovich.

'But it's my duty to observe the laws of the state,' continued the mayor. 'Did you know, Ivan Ivanovich, that it's a criminal offence to steal an official document from a courtroom?'

'I'm well aware of that and I can tell you a thing or two in that respect. It only concerns people – for example, if *you* stole a document. But a pig is an animal, one of God's creatures.'

'That may be, but the law says: "guilty of theft . . ." I beg you to listen carefully: guilty! No species is mentioned, or sex or rank, therefore an animal can be ajudged guilty. You can say what you like, but before sentence is passed the animal must be committed to the charge of the police, just like someone who commits a breach of the peace.'

'No, Pyotr Fyodorovich!' coolly retorted Ivan Ivanovich. 'You can't do that!'

'Think what you like, but I must carry out what the law demands.'

'Are you trying to scare me? Why don't you send that one-armed soldier of yours after it? In that case I'll tell one of my women to chase him off with a poker. Then he'll get his other arm broken.'

'I don't dare argue with you. Since you don't feel inclined to give the sow up to the police, then do what you like with it: kill it for Christmas and make some gammon, or eat it as it is. All I ask – in case you decide to make sausages – is to send me a couple – you know, those Gapka makes so well, with pig's blood and fat. My Agrafena Trofimovna is very fond of them.'

'I'll send you a couple if you like.'

'I'd be very grateful, my dear friend and benefactor. And now allow me to say just one more thing: I have been instructed by the judge, as well as all our friends, to try and bring about a reconciliation between yourself and Ivan Nikiforovich.'

'What – with that boor? Make it up with that lout? I'd like to see the day!'

Ivan Ivanovich was in a very determined mood.

'As you wish,' replied the mayor, regaling both nostrils with snuff. 'I daren't offer any more advice, but just allow me to inform you, that since you're now at loggerheads, if you can only make it up . . .'

But Ivan Ivanovich began to talk about catching quails, which he usually did when he wanted to change the subject.

And so the mayor had no option but to go home, having achieved nothing.

VI. *From which the reader can easily discover all it contains*

In spite of all the judge's efforts to hush the matter up, by the next day all Mirgorod knew that Ivan Ivanovich's sow had made off with Ivan Nikiforovich's plaint: in a moment of absent-mindedness the mayor forgot himself and was the first to let the cat out of the bag.

When Ivan Nikiforovich was told about it, all he did was reply: 'Was it the *brown* sow by any chance?'

But Agafiya Fedoseyevna, who was there at the time, started nagging Ivan Nikiforovich again. 'What's the matter with you? Everyone will laugh and think you're a complete idiot if you don't do something. And you won't be fit to call yourself a gentleman any more. You'll be lower than the woman who sells those sweetmeats you're so fond of!'

And the terrible nagger managed to persuade him to take action. Somewhere she found a swarthy middle-aged man with spots all over his face, who wore a dark-blue frock-coat patched at the elbows – a regular government pen-pusher! He blacked his boots with tar, wore three pens behind his ear, and instead of an inkwell had a glass phial tied to his buttonhole by a piece of bootlace. He could eat as many as nine pies at one sitting, keeping a tenth in his pocket, and he was a master at filling one sheet of chancery notepaper with so much libel that no one could read it through at one go without alternately coughing and sneezing in between. This pitiful semblance of a man rummaged around in the files, scribbled away for all he was worth, and finally concocted the following statement:[13]

To the District Judge of Mirgorod from the gentleman Ivan Dovgoch-khun, son of Nikifor:

Pursuant to my aforesaid plaint presented to me, Ivan Dovgochkun, son of Nikifor, conjointly with that of the aforesaid Ivan Pererepenko, son of Ivan, concerning which the Mirgorod District Judge has demonstrated his own illegal connivance. And that the said taking the law into his own hands on the sow being furtively concealed and becoming known through third disinterested parties. Inasmuch as the aforesaid criminal admission and illegal connivance being maliciously contrived must forthwith be judged in a court of law; inasmuch as the aforesaid pig is a stupid animal and thus all the more capable of documentary embezzlement. From which it is obviously evident that this oft-mentioned pig was incited by our opponent, to wit, Ivan Pererepenko, son of Ivan, calling himself gentleman, and already convicted of robbery, attempted murder, and sacrilege. But the aforesaid Mirgorod Court, with its characteristic partiality gave its authority clandestinely. For without such authority the aforesaid pig could never have gained entry to the courthouse to carry off the documents. Inasmuch as the Mirgorod Court is well supplied with staff, we need only adduce as evidence one invalided soldier who is always to be found in the vestibule and who, despite having only one eye and a rather crippled arm, has abilities proportionate to the task of chasing off the said pig and clubbing it with a large cudgel. From which is patently evident the illegal connivance of the aforesaid Mirgorod Court and the indisputable mutual distribution of the profits accruing therefrom as a result of Jew-like double dealing. The same aforesaid abovementioned robber has thus incriminated himself in larceny. Therefore I, Ivan, a gentleman son of Nikifor, Dovgochkhun, bring proper and fitting notification to the ears of the Court that: if the aforementioned plaint concerning the abovementioned brown sow (or the gentleman Pererepenko in league with it) is not investigated and decided in my favour and advantage, then, I, Ivan, gentleman, son of Nikifor, Dovgochkhun, will take the plaint to the High Court about the illegal connivance according to the fit and proper formal transference of the matter. Signed, Ivan, gentleman, son of Nikifor, Dovgochkhun, of the Mirgorod District Court.

This plaint had the desired effect. Like all good people, the judge was the timid sort. He consulted his secretary, but the secretary produced a throaty 'Hm' and displayed that indifferent and diabolically equivocal expression assumed only by Satan himself when he sees his victim rushing to throw himself at his feet. Only one course of action remained open to him: to reconcile the two friends. But how was he to set about this, when all efforts up to then had been futile? However, he decided to have one more try. But Ivan Ivanovich told him straight out that he would not hear of it and, what was more, became very angry, while Ivan Nikiforovich answered by turning his back on him and not saying a word.

Subsequently the case proceeded with that abnormal rapidity our courts normally pride themselves on. Documents were dated, entered, numbered, sewn together, recorded – all in one day and the case was filed away in a cupboard where it just lay and lay and lay – one, two, three years. During that time many girls found themselves husbands; a new street was laid out in Mirgorod; one of the judge's double teeth fell out, together with two eye-teeth; more children than ever ran around Ivan Ivanovich's yard – God alone knows where they came from. To insult Ivan Ivanovich, Ivan Nikiforovich built a new goose shed, slightly further back than the other one, and completely blocked himself off from him, so that these worthy gentlemen hardly ever set eyes on each other. And the papers continued to lie in the cupboard, which became mottled with ink-spots. Meanwhile an event of the greatest importance for Mirgorod took place: the mayor gave a reception. Where can I find brush and palette to portray the varied gathering at that magnificent banquet? Take your watch, open it up and see what's going on inside. You won't deny that it's dreadful nonsense! Now try and imagine about the same number of wheels – if not more – all standing in the mayor's courtyard. What carriages and wagons were there! One was wide behind and narrow in the front, another narrow behind and wide in the front, a third a carriage and wagon combined, and a fourth neither carriage nor wagon. One looked like a huge haystack or a fat merchant's wife, another resembled a dishevelled Jew or a skeleton not quite freed from the skin. Another, if you viewed it from the side, looked just like a long-stemmed pipe, while yet another looked like nothing on earth, suggesting some strange, shapeless, absolutely fantastic object.

In the middle of all this chaos of wheels and coach boxes one could glimpse what appeared to be a carriage with a window with a heavy transom, just like in a house. The drivers, in grey Cossack overcoats, short Ukrainian coats, sheepskin hats and caps of varying sizes, all holding their pipes, led the unharnessed horses through the courtyard. What a reception the mayor gave! If you will allow me, I will just run through the guests.

There were: Taras Tarasovich, Yevpl Akinfovich, Yevtikhy Yevtikhiyevich, Ivan Ivanovich (another one), Savva Gavrilovich, our own Ivan Ivanovich, Yelevfery Yelevferiyevich, Makar Nazaryevich, Foma Grigoryevich . . . that's enough for now. I've no strength left, my hand's tired from all this writing. And so many ladies! Dark- and fair-complexioned, short and tall, some of them fat, like Ivan Nikiforovich, and others so thin you could easily picture them hiding in the scabbard of the mayor's sword. And the hats and dresses! Red, yellow, coffee-coloured, green, blue, new, turned, recut; and the shawls, ribbons and handbags! Farewell, my poor eyes! You will never see properly again after such a sight. And the long table they laid out!

What a noise they made with all their chatter – a mill, with all its stones, wheels, pinions and cogs would be silent in comparison. I can't tell you exactly what they talked about, but the conversation must have been about a whole host of pleasant and useful subjects, such as the weather, dogs, wheat, nightcaps, colts. Finally, Ivan Ivanovich – not ours, but another Ivan Ivanovich with one eye – said:

'Strange, but my right eye' (this Ivan Ivanovich always talked sarcastically about himself) 'does not see Ivan Nikiforovich Dovgochkhun.'

'He didn't want to come,' the mayor replied.

'Why not?'

'Good God, it's already two years since they had their quarrel – I mean Ivan Ivanovich and Ivan Nikiforovich. If one of them knows where the other is, you couldn't drag him here for all the tea in China.'

'What are you talking about?' The one-eyed Ivan Ivanovich looked up and folded his arms. 'If people with good eyes can't get on together, then how am I supposed to live on good terms with everyone, seeing I've only one eye?'

This produced a loud guffaw. Everyone loved the one-eyed Ivan Ivanovich for his witticisms which suited the modern taste extremely well.

A tall, thin man in a felt coat, with a plaster on his nose, who until then had been sitting in the corner with a face that remained absolutely motionless, even when a fly flew up his nose – this same gentleman left his seat and moved closer to the crowd surrounding the one-eyed Ivan Ivanovich.

'Listen,' the one-eyed Ivan Ivanovich said when he saw a fair crowd had gathered around him. 'Listen! Instead of your staring at my bad eye, why don't we all try to get our two friends to make it up! Ivan Ivanovich is having a chat with the women and girls right now – let's send for Ivan Nikiforovich on the quiet and then bring them together.'

Ivan Ivanovich's proposal met with universal approval and they decided to send someone round to Ivan Nikiforovich's to try and persuade him to come to the mayor's house without fail. But the important question – whom to entrust with this difficult mission – foxed everyone.

For a long time they argued as to who was best versed in the methods of diplomacy. Finally they decided unanimously to entrust Anton Prokofyevich Golopuz with the job.

But first we must acquaint the reader with this remarkable personage. In every sense of the word, Anton Prokofyevich was a highly virtuous man: if one of Mirgorod's worthy citizens happened to give him a scarf or some item of underwear he would even thank him. He would also thank someone for giving him a gentle flick on the nose. If someone were to ask him: 'Why are you wearing a brown frock-coat with blue sleeves?' he would usually reply: 'But *you* don't have one like that! You wait, when it begins to wear out, it will be the same colour all over!' And it was just as he said: the sun began to turn the blue cloth of the sleeves brown, so that it now matched the rest of the frock-coat perfectly. But the strange thing was, Anton Prokofyevich had the habit of wearing woollens in the summer and nankeen in the winter. Anton Prokofyevich does not have a house of his own now. He did have one once, on the outskirts, but he sold it, and with the proceeds bought a team of three bay horses and a small carriage, in which he rode around visiting local landowners. But as he had a lot of trouble with the horses and at the same time needed money for oats, Anton Prokofyevich exchanged them for a violin and a housemaid, plus a twenty-five-rouble note. Then he sold the violin and exchanged the girl for a gold and morocco tobacco pouch. And now he has a pouch like no one else. Because of this little luxury he cannot go riding around the villages any more, but has to stay in town and spend the night at different houses, especially where the owners take delight in flipping him on the nose. Anton Prokofyevich is quite a gourmet and plays a good hand at cards.

He has always been in his element taking orders and he immediately set off with his hat and cane. However, as he walked along he began to wonder how he could best persuade Ivan Nikiforovich to come to the reception. But the rather intractable character of that otherwise very worthy gentleman rendered his task almost impossible.

And how on earth could he induce him to come, when it was an effort for him just to get out of bed? But supposing he did get up – how could *anyone* expect him to come to a place where he knew without any shadow of doubt he would find his mortal enemy?

The more Anton Prokofyevich thought about it, the more obstacles he found. It was a stifling day, the sun beat down, and the sweat just poured off him. Although he did get rapped on the nose from time to time, Anton Prokovyevich was quite a cunning man in many respects. He was not so clever when it came to bargaining, however. He knew when to pretend to be stupid and could sometimes cope very well in circumstances from which a clever person would seldom be able to extricate himself.

While his inventive mind was devising some way of persuading Ivan Nikiforovich to come (he had already set out boldly on his mission), he was rather disconcerted by something he was not in the least expecting. At this stage there would be no harm in mentioning that, among other things, Anton Prokofyevich had such a peculiar pair of trousers that when he wore them dogs always bit him in the calves. Unfortunately he was wearing this pair of trousers that day and he had not progressed very far in his deep reflections before his ears were deafened by a terrifying barking all around him. Anton Prokofyevich yelled so loud – no one could yell as loud as him – that not only a peasant woman he knew and the possessor of that vast coat, but all the brats from Ivan Ivanovich's yard as well, came running out to meet him. Although the dogs managed to sink their teeth into one leg only, this had a shattering effect on his ardour and he approached the front steps very gingerly.

VII. And the Last

'Ah! Good morning! Why are you tormenting the dogs?' said Ivan Nikiforovich when he saw Anton Prokofyevich – everyone treated everything as a joke whenever they spoke to Anton Prokofyevich.

'I wish they'd all drop dead! Who's tormenting them?' replied Anton Prokofyevich.

'You're lying!'

'I swear to God I'm not! Pyotr Fyodorovich wants to you have dinner with him.'

'Hm . . .'

'I swear to God it's true! I really cannot put into words how badly he wants to see you. "Why," he said, "does Ivan Nikiforovich avoid me like the plague? He never drops in for a chat or a little rest."'

Here Ivan Nikiforovich started stroking his chin.

' "If," he said, "Ivan Nikiforovich doesn't come now, I shan't know what to make of it and I'll begin to think he has evil designs on me. Do me a favour, Anton Prokofyevich, persuade

Ivan Nikiforovich to come!" Well, Ivan Nikiforovich! What are we waiting for? Let's go! There's a wonderful crowd there now.'

Ivan Nikiforovich began scrutinizing a cock which stood on the porch crowing for all it was worth.

The zealous messenger continued: 'If you could only see the sturgeon and fresh caviar Pyotr Fyodorovich's been sent!'

At this point Ivan Nikiforovich turned his head and began to listen attentively, which encouraged the messenger.

'Let's not waste any more time! Foma Grigoryevich is there as well!' Then, seeing Ivan Nikiforovich was still lying in the same position, he added: 'Well, what do you say? Shall we go or not?'

'I don't want to.'

This '*I don't want to*' startled Anton Prokofyevich. He had already begun to think that he had won that worthy man over by his persuasive arguments. But all he had achieved was a decisive: 'I don't want to.'

'But why not?' he asked, speaking in a tone of annoyance, which was extremely rare for him, even when people put burning paper on his head – a trick that the judge and the mayor were very fond of playing on him.

Ivan Nikiforovich took a pinch of snuff.

'Please yourself, Ivan Nikiforovich, but I don't see what's holding you back.'

'What do I want to go for?' he muttered at length. 'That cut-throat will be there.' (He was in the habit of calling Ivan Ivanovich by that name.)

Heavens, and it wasn't so very long ago that . . .

'I swear to God he won't be there! May I be struck down if he is!' answered Anton Prokofyevich, who was prepared to swear ten oaths within a single hour. 'Let's go, Ivan Niki-forovich!'

'I can see you're lying, Anton Prokofyevich – he *is* there!'

'By all that's holy, I swear he's not. May I never move one limb again if he's there! And just think about it – why should I tell you lies? I'd rather my legs and arms withered and fell off. May I be struck dead before your very eyes! May my father and mother – and myself as well – never reach heaven! You still don't believe me?'

With these assurances Ivan Nikiforovich's mind was set completely at rest and he ordered his valet (the boy in the enormous coat) to fetch his baggy trousers and nankeen Cossack coat.

I imagine it would be superfluous to describe how Ivan Nikiforovich put on his trousers, or how his servant tied his cravat and finally pulled on his Cossack coat, which burst under the left sleeve. Suffice it to say that he remained cool and collected throughout the whole operation and ignored Anton Prokofyevich's offer of swapping something for his Turkish tobacco pouch.

Meanwhile the whole assembly impatiently awaited the critical moment when Ivan Nikiforovich would turn up and the reconcilation would finally take place between those two worthy gentlemen – something everyone was hoping for. Many of them felt almost certain that Ivan Nikiforovich would not come. The mayor even wanted to bet the one-eyed Ivan Ivanovich that he would not turn up, but withdrew when this Ivan Ivanovich offered to stake his own bad eye against the mayor's crippled leg, a suggestion that infuriated the mayor, but made everyone else chuckle. No one had sat down to eat yet, although it was long past one – by which time everyone in Mirgorod has usually eaten, even on special occasions like this.

As soon as Anton Prokofyevich appeared at the door he was surrounded. All inquiries met with a categorical 'He's not coming'. He had hardly said this and a hail of reproaches, abuse and perhaps nose flicks were already about to descend on him for failing in his mission, when suddenly the door opened and in came Ivan Nikiforovich. If Satan himself or a ghost had appeared he would not have created such a sensation among the whole assembly as Ivan Nikiforovich's unexpected arrival. But Anton Prokofyevich nearly split his sides laughing and was tickled pink at having made everyone look so silly.

Whatever, no one could really bring himself to believe that he had dressed himself up to look like a gentleman in such a short time. Ivan Ivanovich was not present at that precise moment, having gone outside. When they had recovered from their amazement, everyone inquired about Ivan Nikiforovich's health and said how pleased they were to see that he had put on weight. Ivan Nikiforovich kissed them all and said: 'I'm very grateful to you.'

Meanwhile the smell of borsch drifted across the room and agreeably titillated the nostrils of the hungry guests. They all piled into the dining-room. Quiet ladies and talkative, fat ladies and thin – all surged forward together and the long table was suddenly resplendent with every conceivable colour. I shall not attempt to describe all the dishes on that table. I will remain silent about the dumplings and sour cream, and the giblets served with the borsch, and the turkey with plums and raisins, or the dish that closely resembled a pair of old boots soaked in kvass, and the sauce, the swansong of the old-fashioned chef – a sauce that was served enveloped in brandy flames, which the ladies found very amusing as well as frightening. I shall not describe these dishes because I much prefer eating them to expatiating about them. Ivan Ivanovich was delighted with the fish dressed with horseradish. He paid this particular attention through the following useful and nourishing exercise, picking the finest bones out, laying them on his plate – and then he happened to glance across the table. God in heaven! He could not believe his eyes! Ivan Nikiforovich was sitting opposite him!

At that very moment Ivan Nikiforovich happened to look up . . . No, I can't go on! . . . Bring me a different pen to describe the scene, mine has gone sluggish, dead; its nib is too fragile. Their faces registered mutual amazement and seemed to turn to stone. Each saw a long-familiar face opposite him, a face he could quite easily have approached, like some unexpected friend, without even thinking about it, offering his snuff-box with the words: 'Please take some' or 'I shall esteem it a favour'. But now those faces looked terrifying, omens of some impending disaster. The sweat just poured off Ivan Ivanovich and Ivan Nikiforovich.

All of those present, every single person who was seated at the table, looked on numbly and did not take their eyes off the former friends for one second.

The ladies, who up to this point had been engaged in a very

interesting conversation on the preparation of capons, suddenly cut short their discussion. Everything went quiet. Only a great painter could have done the scene justice.

Finally Ivan Ivanovich pulled out his handkerchief and started blowing his nose, while Ivan Nikiforovich looked around until his eyes came to rest on the open door. The mayor noticed this movement and ordered the door to be shut more firmly. Then the friends started eating without giving each other so much as a glance.

As soon as dinner was over, the two erstwhile friends leapt from their seats and started looking for their hats with the intention of making their escape.

Then the mayor winked and Ivan Ivanovich – not our Ivan Ivanovich but the one with the bad eye – stationed himself behind Ivan Nikiforovich, while the mayor took up a similar position behind Ivan Ivanovich and both tried to push them back towards each other, not intending to release them until they shook hands. The one-eyed Ivan Ivanovich – although by a slightly circuitous route – was quite successful in pushing Ivan Nikiforovich towards the spot where Ivan Ivanovich was standing. But the mayor steered too much to one side, as he was quite unable to control his wayward 'infantry', which on this occasion disobeyed all orders and – as if from spite – kicked out completely in the opposite direction, possibly under the influence of the startling variety of drinks that had been served at dinner, making Ivan Ivanovich fall over a lady in a red dress who, out of curiosity, had forced her way into the middle of the room. This did not augur at all well.

However, to put matters right, the judge took the mayor's place and after sweeping all the snuff from his upper lip with his nose pushed Ivan Ivanovich in the opposite direction.

This is how they usually try to patch things up in Mirgorod and it is rather like playing a ball game. As soon as the judge had given Ivan Ivanovich a shove, the one-eyed Ivan Ivanovich strained every muscle and pushed Ivan Nikiforovich, from whom the sweat was pouring like rainwater from a roof. Although both friends put up a very stiff resistance, they were, however, finally pushed together, since both parties received strong reinforcement from the other guests. Then they were closely hemmed in and not released until they had agreed to shake hands.

'Come now, Ivan Nikiforovich and Ivan Ivanovich! Look in your hearts and tell us what the quarrel's about. You must admit it's about nothing at all. Don't you feel ashamed before everyone – and before God?'

'I don't know,' Ivan Nikiforovich said, breathless from exhaustion (one could see that he was very close to being reconciled). 'I really don't know what I did to annoy Ivan Ivanovich. Why did he chop my goose shed down and try to ruin me?'

'I'm not guilty of any malicious intent,' Ivan Ivanovich said without looking at Ivan Nikiforovich. 'I swear before God and before all you good people that I never harmed my enemy. Why did he have to drag my name in the mud and slander my rank and reputation?'

'But what harm have I done you, Ivan Ivanovich?' said Ivan Nikiforovich.

Just one minute more and that long-standing enmity would have been extinguished. Ivan Nikiforovich was already feeling about for his snuff-box, to offer it with his customary 'Please do take some, please do'.

'If it isn't harm, then what is it,' answered Ivan Ivanovich, looking down, 'when you, my dear sir, insulted my name and rank with such an indecent word that I really can't repeat it in polite society?'

'Let me tell you, as one friend to another, Ivan Ivanovich!' (at this point Ivan Nikiforovich touched one of Ivan Ivanovich's buttons, a sure sign that he was quite ready to make it up), 'God only knows why you took such offence, as all I did was call you a *goose* . . .'

Ivan Nikiforovich saw immediately that he had committed a terrible blunder in saying this word, but it was too late: he had said it! Everything went to the devil . . .

Ivan Ivanovich had once before lost his temper when this word was pronounced without anybody else there to hear it and had flown into such a rage (God spare us from such a spectacle again!) that our dear readers can judge for themselves the effect when the fateful word was now uttered before a large social gathering, with many ladies present, and in whose company Ivan Ivanovich was always so careful about his language. Had Ivan Nikiforovich said *bird* instead of *goose*, the matter could still have been put right. But all was lost now!

He glanced at Ivan Nikiforovich – and what a glance! If that look had had any physical power behind it, it would have literally pulverized Ivan Nikiforovich. The guests recognized that look and rushed to separate them. And that same gentleman, a model of humility, who would not let a beggar woman go past without asking if she needed anything, tore out in the most terrible rage. So violent are the storms aroused by human passions!

For a whole month nothing was heard of Ivan Ivanovich. He shut himself up in his house. The ancestral chest was opened – and what were taken out? Why, the old silver roubles that had belonged to his grandfather! And these silver roubles passed into the inkstained hands of legal scribes. The case went to the High Court. And only when Ivan Ivanovich received the glad tidings that the case would be decided the following day – only then did he take a look at the outside world and decide to leave the house. But, alas, from that day onwards, the court announced each day that the case was going to be decided tomorrow – and so it went on for ten years!

Five years ago I happened to be passing through Mirgorod. I had picked a bad time. It was autumn and the weather was miserable – damp and misty with mud everywhere. A kind of unnatural green substance, produced by continual, tiresome rain, covered the fields and meadows with a thin network, which suited them as much as frolics an old man or a rose an old crone. At that time I was very sensitive to the weather – when it was miserable, so was I. In spite of this, my heart started beating violently when I approached Mirgorod. The memories that place holds for me! It was twelve years since I had last visited the town, where two men who were quite inseparable had lived together in friendship which was truly touching to see. How many important people had died since then! Judge Demyan Demyanovich had passed away and the one-eyed Ivan Ivanovich had breathed his last. I went into the main street. Everywhere there were poles with bundles of straw tied to the tops. Some large-scale alterations were in progress. A few huts had been pulled down. The remains of wattle fences and hedges stuck out depressingly.

It was a high holiday. I ordered the covered wagon to stop at the church and entered very quietly, so that no one would notice.

But I need not have worried. The church was almost deserted – there was hardly anyone there. Evidently the mud had frightened away even the most pious. The candles looked strangely unpleasant in that gloomy, rather sickly light. The dark porch had a melancholy look, and the oblong windows with their circular panes were streaming with tears of rain. I went into the porch and approached a venerable-looking old man with grey hair: 'Can you tell me if Ivan Nikiforovich is still alive?'

At that moment the lamp in front of the icon flared up and the light shone straight into the old man's face. You can imagine how astonished I was to see those familiar features again. Yes, it was Ivan Nikiforovich himself. But how he had changed!

'Are you keeping well, Ivan Nikiforovich? Goodness, how you've aged!'

'Yes, I have indeed. I've just got back from Poltava.'

'What's that! You went to Poltava on a day like this?'

'What else can I do? There's a lawsuit pending . . .'

At this I could not help sighing. Ivan Nikiforovich noticed and said: 'Don't worry. I've had news from a reliable source that the case will be decided in my favour.'

I shrugged my shoulders and went off to see what I could find out about Ivan Ivanovich.

'Ivan Ivanovich is here,' someone said. 'Over there, in the choir.'

Then I saw a gaunt figure. Was that really Ivan Ivanovich? His face was covered with wrinkles and his hair had turned completely white. But he was still wearing the same short fur coat. After we had greeted each other, Ivan Ivanovich turned to me with that cheerful smile which suited his funnel-shaped face so well and said: 'Have you heard the good news?'

'What news?' I asked.

'My case will be decided tomorrow – without fail. The High Court said it's absolutely certain.'

I heaved an even deeper sigh, hurriedly made my farewell, as I had some very important business to attend to and climbed into my covered wagon. Some skinny horses, known as the post-haste type in Mirgorod, made an unpleasant squelching as they trod in the grey mass of mud. The rain poured down on a Jew who was sitting on the horse-box with a mat over him.

The dampness soaked right through me. The wretched turnpike and its sentry-box, with an old soldier sitting there mending his grey armour slowly passed by. Those fields again, with black ploughed patches in places, showing green in others, the drenched crows and jackdaws, monotonous rain and a tearful sky without one ray of sunlight ... It's a dreary world, gentlemen!

NEVSKY PROSPEKT

There is nowhere finer than Nevsky Prospekt[1] – at least, not in St Petersburg. It is its very life blood. What brilliance does it lack, this crowning beauty of our capital! I know that not one of her pale-faced government clerks would exchange Nevsky Prospekt for all the blessings of this world. Not only the young fellow of twenty-five, sporting a handsome moustache and a splendidly cut frock-coat, but also the elderly gentleman with white hairs sprouting on his chin and a pate as smooth as a silver dish, is enraptured by Nevsky Prospekt. And as for the ladies! Well, the ladies are even more taken with Nevsky Prospekt. And who would not find it agreeable? The moment you step on to Nevsky Prospekt you are carried away by its gaiety. Even though you may have some urgent, vital work to do, as soon as you step on to Nevsky Prospekt you forget all about any kind of business. It is the one place where people do not appear because they are compelled to, without being driven by necessity or those mercantile interests engulfing all of St Petersburg. And the person you meet on Nevsky Prospekt seems less of an egotist than on Morskaya, Gorokhovaya, Liteynaya, Meshchanskaya and other streets,[2] where greed, avarice and self-interest distinguish all who walk there or fly past in carriages or droshkies.

Nevsky Prospekt is St Petersburg's principal artery. Here one who resides in the Petersburg or Vyborg[3] districts, who has not visited his friend at Peski[4] or the Moscow Gate for years, can be sure to encounter him. No directory at an information bureau provides such reliable information as Nevsky Prospekt. Mighty Nevsky Prospekt! – sole place of entertainment for the poor

man in St Petersburg. How cleanly its pavements are swept and
– my God! – how many feet have left their traces there. Both
the muddy, clumsy boot of the discharged soldier under whose
very weight the granite appears to crack, and the miniature
shoes, as light as a puff of smoke, of the young lady who, like
a sunflower to the sun, turns her head towards the glittering
shop windows, the rattling sabre of the ambitious ensign that
leaves a sharp scratch – everyone displays his own particular
strength or weakness. What a bewildering phantasmagoria
within one day! How many transformations between dawn and
dusk!

Let us begin with early morning, when all St Petersburg smells
of hot, freshly baked loaves and is filled with old women in
tattered clothes and cloaks making their forays on churches and
compassionate passers-by. Then Nevsky Prospekt is well-nigh
deserted: stout shopkeepers and their assistants are still slum-
bering in their holland nightshirts or lathering their noble
cheeks or drinking coffee. Beggars gather at the door of a pastry
shop where a sleepy Ganymede,[5] who the previous day had
been darting about like a fly, bearing cups of chocolate, emerges
broom in hand, tieless, and throws them stale pies and leftovers.
Working folk trudge down the streets, occasionally crossed by
peasants hurrying to work in boots so caked with lime that
even the Yekaterinsky Canal,[6] famed for its cleanliness, could
not wash it off. At this hour of the day it is normally unseemly
for ladies to be out walking, since Russian folk like to express
themselves in strong language that they would never hear even
in the theatre.[7] Sometimes a drowsy civil servant will plod past,
briefcase under arm, if the route to his office lies along Nevsky
Prospekt. One can say without hesitation that at this time of
day – that is, up to twelve o'clock, Nevsky Prospekt is no one's
final destination, merely the means of reaching it. Gradually
it becomes filled with people weighed down with their own
preoccupations, problems and vexations and who do not give
it a moment's thought. Peasants speak of ten copecks or cop-
pers, old men and women wave their arms about, or talk to
themselves – occasionally with wild gesticulations – but no one
listens to them or laughs at them, with the possible exception

of street urchins in their coarse cotton smocks, racing down
Nevsky Prospekt like lightning with empty vodka bottles or
newly repaired boots in their hands. At this time you can wear
what you like – even if you put on a cap instead of a felt hat,
even if your collar sticks out too far above your cravat, no one
will take the slightest notice.

At twelve o'clock tutors of all nationalities with their charges
in cambric collars descend upon Nevsky Prospekt. English
Joneses and French Coqs walk arm-in-arm with the nurslings
entrusted to their parental care and, with appropriate gravity,
explain to them that shop signs are there to inform people what
lies within. Governesses, pale misses and rosy-cheeked Slav
maidens walk in stately fashion behind their lissom, fidgety
young charges, instructing them not to drop their shoulders
and to keep their backs straight. In short, at this hour Nevsky
Prospekt becomes a pedagogical Nevsky Prospekt. But as two
o'clock approaches, the tutors, pedagogues and children become fewer, until they are finally supplanted by doting papas
walking arm-in-arm with their colourfully attired, weak-nerved
spouses. Gradually they are joined by all who have completed
their fairly important domestic duties – namely, discussing the
weather with their doctor, for instance, and the tiny pimple
that has sprung up on their nose, inquiring about the health of
their horses and their children (who both, incidentally, show
remarkable promise) and who have perused a theatre poster or
an important announcement in the newspapers about depar-
tures and arrivals, finally drinking their cup of coffee or tea.
And then they are joined by those whom fate has blessed with
the enviable title of official on special commissions and by those
who serve in the Foreign Collegium[8] and are distinguished by
the nobility of their occupations and habits. My God! What
splendid positions and services there are! How they elevate and
delight the soul! But alas! I am not in government service and
therefore am denied the pleasure of seeing myself addressed in
refined fashion by heads of departments. Everything you meet
with on Nevsky Prospekt is remarkable for its decorum: gentlemen in long frock-coats, hands in pockets, ladies in pink, white
or pale-blue satin redingotes and modish bonnets. Here you

will encounter unique sidewhiskers, allowed with consummate skill to extend below the cravat; velvety, satiny side-whiskers as black as sable or coal – but alas! – belonging only to officials at the Foreign Collegium. Providence has denied black side-whiskers to civil servants in other departments and they are compelled, to their extreme displeasure, to sport ginger ones instead. Here you will find wondrous moustaches that no pen or brush could portray, moustaches to which the best part of a life has been devoted, the objects of prolonged vigils by day and night, moustaches sprinkled with the most ravishing perfumes and fragrances, anointed with the most precious and rarest kinds of pomade, twisted at night in the finest vellum curl-papers, moustaches towards which their owners display the most touching devotion and which are the envy of every passer-by. The thousands of varieties of hats, dresses, kerchiefs – so wispy and brightly coloured – sometimes held in affection by their owners for two whole days on end, are enough to dazzle anyone walking down Nevsky Prospekt. An entire sea of butterflies seems to have suddenly risen from their flower stalks and is hovering in a shimmering cloud above the black beetles of the male sex. Here you will encounter waists beyond your wildest dreams – slender and narrow, no thicker than the neck of a bottle, at the sight of which you step respectfully to one side for fear of inadvertently nudging them with an impolite elbow. Your heart is overcome with timidity and apprehension, lest by a careless breath you might snap this exquisite creation of nature in two. And the ladies' sleeves you will see on Nevsky Prospekt! Ah – sheer delight! They are rather like two hot-air balloons and it seems the lady might suddenly soar into the air should the gentleman with her fail to hold her down; in fact, it is just as easy and pleasant lifting a lady into the air as raising a glassful of champagne to the lips. Nowhere do people bow so nobly and naturally as on Nevsky Prospekt. Here you will see a unique smile that is the very pinnacle of art, that will sometimes make you melt with pleasure, sometimes make you bow your head and feel lower than grass, or hold it high, making you feel loftier than the Admiralty spire.[9] Here you will hear people discussing a concert or the weather with extraordinary refinement and sense of their own importance. Here you will encounter a thousand incredible characters and events. Good heavens! What strange types you will meet on Nevsky Prospekt! Many are those who will not fail to look at your boots on meeting and when you have passed will look around to inspect your coat-tails. To this day I cannot understand why this should be. At first I thought they were bootmakers – but no, far from it. For the most part they are clerks in various departments; many of them can draft a memorandum from one department to the other with consummate skill. Or they are simple people who stroll along or read the paper in pastry shops: in other words, they are normally highly respectable citizens.

At this blessed hour, between two and three o'clock in the afternoon, when everything on Nevsky Prospekt reaches its climax, the finest products of man's genius are most grandly displayed. Someone will sport a dandyish frock-coat with the best beaver collar, another – a handsome Greek nose, a third – superb whiskers, a fourth – a pair of pretty eyes and a wonderful hat, a fifth – a signet ring with seal, ostentatiously worn on the little finger, a sixth – a dainty foot in an enchanting shoe, a seventh – a stunning tie, an eighth – simply astounding moustaches. But on the stroke of three the exhibition is over, the crowd begins to thin out. At three o'clock there is a fresh transformation: spring has suddenly come to Nevsky Prospekt! It is bustling with civil servants in green uniforms. Hungry titular, court and other counsellors[10] try to quicken their pace. Young collegiate registrars, provincial and collegiate secretaries, hasten to make the most of their time and they stroll down Nevsky Prospekt with a dignified air, as if to prove that they had not spent the last six hours cooped up in an office. But the elderly collegiate secretaries, titular and court counsellors walk briskly, with heads bowed: they are disinclined to scrutinize passers-by; as yet they have not torn themselves away from their daily cares, their muddled heads are simply bursting with a whole archive of completed and uncompleted files. For a long time, instead of seeing shop signs, all they see is piles of documents or the plump face of the departmental director.

From four o'clock Nevsky Prospekt is deserted and you are

unlikely to encounter a single government clerk. The odd seamstress might dash out of a shop across Nevsky, box in hand; or
the hapless booty of some philanthropic bailiff with nothing in
the world but his coarse frieze overcoat; or an eccentric visitor
for whom all hours are the same; or a tall, thin Englishwoman
with reticule and a little book in her hands; or the occasional
thick-bearded Russian workman in his high-waisted denim
frock-coat, reduced to scraping a living, his back, legs and head
– in fact everything about him in motion – slinking meekly
along the pavement; or the occasional humble artisan – but you
will meet no one else at this time on Nevsky Prospekt.

The moment dusk descends on the houses and streets, when
the night-watchman with a mat on his back climbs his ladder
to light the lamps, while engravings that dare not show themselves by day peep out from the lower shop windows – it is
then that Nevsky Prospekt springs to life and all is astir. Now
comes that mysterious time when the street lamps cast an allur-
ing, magical light over everything. You will meet many young
men, mostly bachelors, in warm frock-coats and overcoats. At
this time everything suggests a purpose – better, something
resembling a purpose and extremely difficult to explain. Everyone's footsteps quicken and generally become very uneven.
Long shadows flit along walls and pavement, almost touching
the Police Bridge with their heads. Young collegiate registrars,
provincial and collegiate secretaries, stroll about for hours on
end. But elderly collegiate registrars, titular and court counsellors stay at home for the most part, either because they are
married or because their live-in German cooks prepare very
tasty dinners for them. Here you will meet those venerable old
gentlemen who at two o'clock walked along Nevsky Prospekt
with such dignity and amazing elegance. You will see them
tearing along just like young collegiate registrars to peep under
the bonnet of some lady espied from afar, a lady whose fleshy
lips and rouge-plastered cheeks appeal to so many – but above
all to those shop assistants, craftsmen and merchants who
always wear German coats and who promenade in large
crowds, usually arm-in-arm.

'Stop!' cried Lieutenant Pirogov on such an evening, tugging at a young man who was walking beside him in tail-coat and cloak. 'Did you see her?'

'Oh yes – wonderful! The image of Perugino's Bianca!'[11]

'But which one do you mean?'

'Why, the one with the dark hair. And what eyes! God, what eyes! Her whole demeanour, her figure, the cast of her face – miraculous!'

'I'm talking about the blonde who followed her! Well, why don't you go after the brunette, since she attracts you so much?'

'Oh, how can you talk like that?' the young man in tails exclaimed, turning red. 'As if she were one of those women who walk Nevsky at night! She must be a very distinguished lady,' he continued with a sigh. 'Her cloak alone must be worth eighty roubles!'

'You ass!' Pirogov shouted, pushing him in the direction of her bright, billowing cape. 'Hurry up, you silly fool or you'll lose her. I'm going after the blonde!'

The two friends parted.

'We know your type,' Pirogov thought with a smug, self-satisfied smile, convinced that no beauty could resist him.

The young man in tails and cloak, stepping nervously and timidly, went off in the direction of the colourful, billowing cape, at one moment brightly shining as it approached a street lamp, and the next momentarily veiled in darkness as it moved away. His heart pounded and he unconsciously quickened his pace. He dared not think for one moment that he had any claim on the attention of the beauty who was flying into the distance – even less that he should entertain for one moment those lewd thoughts that Lieutenant Pirogov had hinted at: his sole wish was to see the house, to discover the abode of that ravishing creature who seemed to have flown straight from heaven on to Nevsky Prospekt and would surely fly off God knows where. He dashed along so fast that he constantly kept knocking respectable looking, grey-whiskered gentlemen off the pavement.

This young man belonged to the class which constitutes a rather strange phenomenon among us and has as much connection with our regular Petersburger as someone we dream of has with reality. This exceptional class is extremely rare in a city where everyone is either civil servant, merchant or German craftsman. Our young man was an *artist*. Is that not strange? A St Petersburg artist! An artist in the land of snow, of Finns, where all is wet, smooth, flat, pale, grey and misty! These artists are utterly different from their Italian counterparts, as proud and fiery as Italy herself and her sky. On the contrary: they are generally kind, self-effacing, carefree people quietly devoted to their art, who drink tea with a couple of friends in their tiny rooms, modestly discussing their favourite topics and totally indifferent to anything unrelated to them. They are always inviting some old beggarwoman to their rooms, making her sit six hours on end in order to transfer her pathetic, blank features on to canvas. They sketch in perspective their rooms, filled with all kinds of artist's clutter: plaster-of-Paris arms and legs that accumulated time and dust have turned coffee coloured, broken easels, overturned palettes, a friend playing the guitar, walls smeared with paint, an open window through which can be glimpsed the pale Neva and poor fishermen in their red smocks. Usually almost all of them use greyish, muddy paint – the indelible imprint of the North. But for all that they labour over their productions with genuine enjoyment. Often they are endowed with real talent and if only the fresh winds of Italy were to blow on them they would surely blossom as freely, luxuriantly and brightly as a potted plant at last taken outdoors into the fresh air. On the whole they are timid people – a star and thick epaulettes will so thoroughly confuse them that they cannot help lowering their prices. At times they like to cut a dash, but in their case this is invariably overdone and stands out rather like a badly matching patch. Occasionally you will find them wearing an excellent tail-coat with a soiled cape, or an expensive velvet waistcoat and frock-coat covered in paint: it is exactly the same with their unfinished landscapes, where you will sometimes see an inverted nymph which the artist, for want of another place, has sketched over the muddied background of an earlier composition that he once painted with great enjoyment. These artists will never look you straight in the eye and, if they do, then their expression will be vague and indefinite. They do not transfix you with the hawk-like stare of some observer, or with the falcon-like glance of a cavalry officer. This is because they will be simultaneously taking note of your features and those of some plaster-of-Paris Hercules standing in their room. Or because they are visualizing a painting that they dream of producing one day. This often leads them to reply incoherently, sometimes quite irrelevantly, and the muddle in their heads only increases their shyness.

To such a class belonged our young man, the artist Piskarev, so shy and withdrawn, but harbouring sparks of feeling in his heart that were ready to burst into flame – given the chance. With secret tremors he hurried after the lady who had made such a powerful impression on him and he himself appeared to be amazed at his own audacity. The unknown creature who had been the cynosure of his eyes, thoughts and feelings, suddenly turned her head and glanced at him. God! What divine features! That most enchanting of brows, of dazzling whiteness, was framed by hair as lovely as agate. Those wonderful tresses fell in curls, straying from under her hat and brushing those cheeks flushed with a delicate fresh hue by the evening chill. Her lips were sealed by a whole flock of the most enchanting reveries. All that remained of childhood memories, bringing sweet daydreams and quiet inspiration by the gleaming lamplight – all seemed to blend and intermingle, and be reflected on those harmonious lips.

She glanced at Piskarev – and at this glance his heart missed a beat: it was stern and betrayed indignation at his audacious pursuit. But even anger was enchanting on that lovely face. Overcome with shame and timidity, he stopped and lowered his eyes. But how could he lose that divine creature without even discovering that holy of holies where she dwelt? Such were the thoughts that crowded into our young dreamer's head, and he decided to pursue her. But to keep out of sight he stayed a good distance away, casually glancing around and inspecting the shop signs and at the time not missing one step taken by the young lady. Passers-by were fewer, the street grew quieter. The beauty looked back and he fancied a faint smile gleamed on her lips. He trembled all over and could not believe his eyes. No: it was the street lamp's deceptive light that had brought a semblance of a smile to her lips; no, it was his own daydreams that were mocking him. He gasped for breath, he trembled all over, his feelings were on fire and everything became enveloped in mist. The pavement seemed to be rushing away beneath his feet, carriages with their galloping horses seemed to stand stock-still, the bridge stretched and broke its arch, houses turned upside down and a sentry's halberd, the gilt letters of a shop sign with its painted scissors, appeared to gleam on his very eyelash. This was what one turn of that pretty head had produced. Hearing nothing, seeing nothing, conscious of nothing, he swiftly followed the light traces of those beautiful feet, endeavouring to moderate his steps which moved in unison with his heartbeats. Now he was seized by doubt as to whether her glance really offered encouragement – and then he would stand still for a moment. But the beating of his heart, the irresistible power and violence of his feelings, spurred him on. He did not even notice the four-storey house that suddenly loomed in front of him or those four rows of brightly illuminated windows that looked at him all at once, or the iron railings at the entrance that rudely brought him to a sudden halt. He saw the beautiful stranger fly up the staircase, turn round, put one finger to her lips and beckon to him to follow. His knees trembled, his every feeling and thought was ablaze. A thrill of almost unbearable joy pierced his breast like a knife. No – it was no dream! Good God! So much happiness in one instant! A lifetime of bliss in two minutes! But had he not dreamt all this? Could that creature, for one divine glance from whom he would willingly have sacrificed his life, to approach whose abode he considered the very height of felicity – could she really have been so gracious, so attentive towards him a moment ago? He flew up the stairs. No earthly thoughts entered his mind, nor did any earthly passion inflame him. No: at that moment he was as pure and chaste as an innocent youth who still nurtures a vague, spiritual yearning for love. And all that would have aroused base thoughts in a depraved man only made his all the more chaste. The trust shown him by that frail, lovely creature imposed the strict code of chivalry upon him, made it his duty slavishly to carry out her every command. All he desired was that those commands should be as difficult and demanding as possible, so that he should strive all the more to surmount every obstacle. He did not doubt that some mysterious, momentous event had compelled the unknown woman to place her trust in him and that she would ask for significant service from him – and already he felt that he possessed sufficient strength and determination for anything.

The staircase spiralled upwards and with it spiralled his fleeting fantasies. 'Mind how you go!' a voice rang out like a harp, filling his whole being with a renewed flush of excitement. On the gloomy landing, high up on the fourth floor, the beautiful stranger knocked on a door: it opened and they entered together. They were greeted by a woman of fairly attractive appearance, with a candle, but she stared at Piskarev so strangely, so brazenly, that he looked down. Three female figures in different corners met his eyes. One was laying out cards, another was sitting at a piano, giving some pathetic rendition of an old polonaise with two fingers. The third was sitting before a mirror, combing her long hair, and she evidently had no intention of abandoning her toilette at the arrival of a stranger. The sort of disagreeable untidiness, usually only to be found in a carefree bachelor's room, was everywhere in evidence. The furniture (of quite good quality) was covered in dust. A spider had stretched its web over the moulded cornice. Through the open door of another room glinted a spurred boot and the red piping of a uniform. A man's loud voice and a woman's laughter rang out, without any inhibition.

Good Lord! Where had he come to? At first he could not believe his eyes and started scrutinizing more closely the objects that filled the room. But the bare walls and curtainless windows betrayed the complete absence of a caring housewife's hand. The worn faces of those pathetic creatures, one of whom had settled right in front of his nose and was surveying him coolly, as if he were a stain on another woman's dress, convinced him that he had arrived at one of those loathsome dens which wretched depravity, spawned by tawdry education and the terrible overcrowding of the city, had made its abode. It was a den of iniquity, where man sacrilegiously tramples and mocks all that is pure and holy, all that enhances life, where woman, the beauty of this world, the crown of creation, is transformed into some strange, equivocal being, where she loses all purity of soul, all that is womanly and where she adopts the loathsome habits of the male and has ceased to be the delicate, beautiful creature that differs from us so much. Piskarev measured her from head to foot with astonished eyes, as if trying to convince himself that this really was the same person who had so bewitched him and lured him away from Nevsky Prospekt. But she stood there before him, as lovely as before; her hair was just as beautiful, her eyes still looked heavenly. She was fresh – just seventeen. He could see that only recently had she sunk into depravity. He dared not touch her cheeks, which were as fresh and as faintly flushed as ever: she was beautiful.

He stood motionless before her and was ready to let himself be carried away again by that same simplicity of heart. But the beautiful girl was bored with this lengthy silence and smiled knowingly, looking him straight in the eye: that smile was filled with a kind of shameless provocativeness, as strange and as ill-suited to her face as a pious expression to a bribetaker or an accounts ledger to a poet. He shuddered. She parted her lovely lips and began to speak, but everything she said was so stupid, so vulgar. It was as if her intelligence had deserted her along with her virtue! He wanted to hear no more. Our artist was really ridiculous and as naïve as a child. Instead of taking advantage of such encouragement, instead of rejoicing at such an opportunity as anyone in his place would have done, he tore headlong from the room and out into the street like a startled gazelle.

His head bowed and his arms drooping at his side, he sat in his room like some beggar who has found a priceless pearl and immediately let it fall into the sea. 'Such beauty, such heavenly features – and *where*!? In that dreadful place!' He could say no more.

In fact, nothing arouses pity so much as the sight of beauty tainted by the putrid breath of corruption. Ugliness can go hand in hand with depravity, but never beauty, tender beauty . . . in our minds beauty is invariably linked with chastity and purity. The beautiful girl who had so bewitched our poor Piskarev was a wondrous, rare creature and her presence in those despicable surroundings was all the more astonishing. Her every feature was so cleanly moulded, her beautiful face expressed such nobility that one would never think that debauchery now held her in its terrible clutches. She would have been a pearl beyond price, the whole universe, the paradise, the radiant quiet star of some obscure family circle and with one movement of her beautiful lips would have issued sweet commands. She would have been a goddess in a crowded ballroom, gliding over bright parquet, in the brilliant light of candles, silently adored by crowds of admirers prostrate at her feet. But alas! By the terrible will of some infernal spirit intent on destroying the whole harmony of life, she had been cast into the abyss, to the sound of mocking laughter.

Racked with heart-rending pity, he sat before the candle that had burnt low in its socket. Midnight had long passed and the belfry clock struck half past twelve, but he sat there motionless, neither asleep nor fully awake. Drowsiness, taking advantage of his stillness, began to overcome him; the room was beginning to disappear – only the light of the candle still shone through the dreams that were taking possession of him – when suddenly a knock at the door made him start and come to his senses. The door opened and in came a footman in magnificent livery. Never had a richly liveried footman peered into his lonely room, especially at that time of night! He was completely baffled and stared at the footman with impatient curiosity.

'The lady,' announced the footman with a polite bow, 'whom you were pleased to visit a few hours ago, has instructed me to invite you and sent her carriage for you.'[12]

Piskarev was speechless with astonishment. 'A carriage! A liveried footman! No, this must be some mistake . . .' he thought.

'Listen, my good man,' he said timidly, 'it seems you've come to the wrong address. Your mistress must have sent you for someone else, not me.'

'Oh no, sir, I'm not mistaken. Wasn't it you, sir, who accompanied my mistress to a house on Liteynaya, to a room on the fourth floor?'

'Yes, it was.'

'Well, if you don't mind hurrying, sir, the mistress is very eager to see you and asks you to come direct to her house.'

Piskarev flew down the stairs. Sure enough, a carriage was waiting in the courtyard. He climbed in, the doors slammed, the cobblestones in the road clattered under the wheels and hooves, and the illuminated vista of shops with their bright signs flashed past the carriage windows. Piskarev sat deep in thought the whole way, unable to make sense of this adventure. Her own house, a carriage, a footman in rich livery – he could make none of this tally with the fourth-floor room, the dusty windows and untuned piano.

The carriage stopped in front of a brightly lit entrance and Piskarev was immediately struck by the procession of carriages, the coachmen's conversation, the brilliantly illuminated windows and the sounds of music. The richly liveried footman helped him out of the carriage and respectfully escorted him into a hall with marble pillars, a porter in gold braid, cloaks and fur coats scattered here and there and a brilliant lamp. A staircase, seemingly suspended in midair, with gleaming banisters and smelling strongly of perfume, led upwards. He was already mounting it and had reached the first hall, when the swelling crowd of people made him recoil in terror at the first step he took. The extraordinary variety of people threw him into complete confusion. It seemed as if a demon had crumbled the whole world into thousands of little pieces and mixed them all together, quite at random. The gleaming shoulders of the ladies, the black tail-coats, the chandeliers, lamps, the shimmery gauze, the ethereal ribbons and the stout double bass visible through the railings of the magnificent gallery – all this dazzled him beyond measure. At one glance he could see great numbers of venerable old and middle-aged men with stars on their dress-coats, ladies gliding so lightly, proudly and gracefully over the parquet floor or sitting in rows. He could hear so many French and English words; and those young men in their black tail-coats displayed such nobility of bearing, conversed or remained silent with such dignity, incapable of uttering one word too many, related jokes so majestically, smiled so politely, sported such wonderful whiskers, moved their elegant hands so skilfully as they adjusted their cravats, while the ladies were so ethereal, so completely immersed in their own self-satisfaction and so conscious of their charms, lowering their eyes so enchantingly that ... but Piskarev's subdued look as he nervously leaned against a column showed that he was completely bewildered.

At that moment a crowd formed a circle around some dancers. Off they flew across the floor, draped in the diaphanous creations of Paris, in dresses fashioned from the air itself. Nonchalantly they glided over the floor with their glittering slippers and seemed more airy and weightless than if they had been treading on air. But one of them was lovelier, more sumptuously and brilliantly dressed than the others. An indescribable, most subtle refinement of taste distinguished her whole attire and yet it seemed she had taken no pains over her appearance, as if it had come into being of its own accord. She looked – and did not look – at the surrounding crowd, her long eyelashes were lowered indifferently, and the brilliant whiteness of her face was still more dazzling as she bowed her head and a faint shadow fell across her enchanting brow.

Piskarev made a great effort to force his way through the crowd, so that he could get a better look. But to his annoyance an enormous head of dark curly hair continually screened her from him. And he was so hemmed in that he dared not try to step forward or backward, afraid he might jostle some privy counsellor. But at last he managed to get to the front – and then he took a look at his clothes, wanting everything to be just right. But heavens above! What was this! The frock-coat (the one he usually wore) was covered all over with paint. In his haste he had forgotten to change into something respectable. He blushed furiously, let his head drop and wanted the ground to swallow him up. But there was absolutely nowhere to hide. Kammerjunkers[13] in their brilliant tunics formed a solid wall behind him. By now he wanted to be as far as possible from the beauty with the lovely brow and eyelashes. In fear and trembling he raised his eyes to see if she were looking at him: heavens! There she was, facing him ... But what was this? 'It's *her*!' he cried almost at the top of his voice. In fact it really was her, the very woman whom he had met on Nevsky Prospekt and whom he had escorted home.

Meanwhile, she raised her eyelashes and gazed at everyone with her radiant eyes. 'Oh, oh, how lovely!' was all he could say, catching his breath. She surveyed the whole circle that was eager for her attention, but soon she looked away with an air of bored indifference – and her eyes met Piskarev's. 'Oh, what heaven! What paradise! Give me strength, Lord, to bear this. Life cannot contain it – it will destroy and bear my soul away.' She beckoned, but not with her hand, or with an inclination of the head – no! This sign was expressed so subtly and imperceptibly in her ravishing eyes that it was visible to no one. But *he* could see it – and he alone understood it. The dance continued for a long time and the weary music would seem to be dying away – and then it would burst into life again, shrill and thunderous. At last it was over. She sat down, her bosom heaving beneath the shimmering gauze of her veil; her hand (heavens, what a wondrous hand!) dropped on to her knees, crushing her filmy dress, which seemed to be breathing music and its delicate lilac hue accentuated the dazzling whiteness of that beautiful hand! If only to touch it – and nothing more ... He had no other desires – they were all too audacious. He stood beneath her chair, not daring to speak or breathe.

'Were you bored?' she asked. 'I was bored too. I can see that you hate me,' she added, lowering her long eyelashes.

'Hate you? *Me?*' Piskarev stammered, completely at a loss – and he would surely have poured out a stream of the most incoherent words, but at that moment a gentleman-in-waiting with a wonderfully curled tuft of hair on his head came up and made some pleasant and witty remarks. Rather appealingly he displayed a row of fine teeth and with every jest drove a sharp nail into Piskarev's heart. At last another guest – fortunately – came up to him with a question.

'It's unbearable!' she exclaimed, raising her heavenly eyes to him. 'I shall go and sit at the other end of the room. Be there!'

She glided through the crowd and disappeared. Like one possessed he forced his way through – and he was there like lightning.

So it was her, sitting like a queen, the best of all, the most beautiful, seeking him with her eyes.

'Oh, you are here!' she softly said. 'I shall be frank with you. No doubt the circumstances of our meeting struck you as very odd. Surely you cannot think that I could belong to that contemptible class of beings among whom you met me? My behaviour may seem strange to you, but I shall tell you a secret – will you promise,' she asked, fixing her eyes on him, 'never to reveal it?'

'Oh, I will, I will, I will!'

But just then a fairly elderly gentleman came up, spoke to her in some language Piskarev did not understand and offered his hand. She gave Piskarev an imploring look, motioning to him to stay where he was and await her return. But he was so impatient that he felt unable to obey orders – even from her lips. No longer could he see the lilac dress. Extremely agitated, he went from room to room and mercilessly pushed everyone he met out of his way. But everywhere sat distinguished looking personages playing whist and plunged in deathly silence. In one corner a few elderly gentlemen were debating the superiority of military over civilian service. In another, some men in superb tail-coats were indulging in light repartee about the voluminous *oeuvre* of some hard-working poet. Piskarev felt one of the elderly, venerable-looking gentlemen grab one of his coat buttons and submit a most just observation for his judgement, but he rudely thrust him aside, without even noticing that he was wearing a fairly important order around his neck. He ran into another room – she was not there. He ran into another – she was not there. He ran into a third – she was not there either. 'Where can she be? Give her to me! I cannot live without seeing her again . . . I must hear what she was meaning to tell me.' But all his searching was in vain. Anxious and exhausted he huddled in one corner and surveyed the crowd. But to his straining eyes everything appeared blurred. Finally he began to distinguish the walls of his room. He looked up: before him was a candlestick, the flame flickering at the very bottom of the socket: the whole candle had burnt down and the melted tallow had spilt on to his table.

So he had been sleeping! God, what a marvellous dream! But why had he woken up? Why could that dream not have lasted one more minute – surely she would have reappeared? Unwelcome daybreak was peering through his windows with its unpleasant, dull light. His room was in terrible, grey, murky chaos. Oh, how repulsive reality was! What was it compared to dreams? Quickly he undressed and climbed into bed, wrapping himself in his blanket, eager to recapture, if only for a moment, that fugitive vision. And in fact sleep was not slow in coming, but presented him with the exact opposite of what he wanted to see. First Lieutenant Pirogov smoking his pipe, then the Academy porter, then an actual state counsellor, then the head of a Finnish girl whose portrait he had once painted – and similar nonsense.

He lay in bed until noon, yearning to dream. But she did not appear. If only for one moment her lovely features would reappear, if only he could hear her footsteps, if only he could see her naked arm, as bright as virgin snow! Having dismissed and forgotten everything he sat with a shattered, hopeless expression, thinking only of that dream: he was not interested in anything else. His eyes gazed vacantly, lifelessly at the window, through which he could see a grubby water-carrier pouring out water that froze in the air, and the goat-like voice of a rag-and-bone man bleated: 'Any old clothes!' The sounds of pedestrian reality rang strangely in his ears. Thus he sat until evening and then he eagerly flung himself into bed. He struggled for hours with sleeplessness, but finally succumbed. Again a dream so vile and vulgar. 'God have mercy! Let me see her – if only for one minute!' Again he waited for evening, again he fell asleep, again he dreamt of some government clerk who was a clerk and a bassoon at the same time. Oh, it was unbearable! But at last she appeared! Her head, her tresses . . . she was gazing at him. But for such a fleeting moment! And again that mist, again a ridiculous dream.

In the end he lived only for dreams and from that time his whole life took a strange turn: he could be said to sleep while waking and was awake only when sleeping. If someone had seen him sitting silently at his empty table or walking down the street he would surely have taken him for a lunatic or a man ruined by drink. His expression was completely vacant, his innate absentmindedness grew worse and drove all feeling, all movement from his face. Only at nightfall did he come to life.

Such a state undermined his strength and the most agonizing part was when sleep began to abandon him altogether. In order to save the only precious thing that remained he used every possible means of restoring it. He had heard that there was a way of ensuring sleep – one had to take opium. But where was he to get opium? Then he remembered a Persian who kept a shawl shop and who, whenever he met Piskarev, almost invariably asked him to paint a pretty girl for him. Assuming that he was bound to have opium he decided to call on him. The Persian received him sitting cross-legged on a divan.

'What do you want opium for?' he asked.

Piskarev told him about his insomnia.

'All right, I'll give you some, but you must paint me a beautiful woman. She must be very beautiful, with black eyebrows and eyes as large as olives! And paint me lying beside her, smoking my pipe! Do you hear? She must be a real beauty!'

Piskarev promised to do everything. The Persian went out and returned with a small jar filled with a dark liquid and carefully poured some of it into another jar, which he handed to Piskarev with instructions to take no more than seven drops in water. Piskarev eagerly seized that precious jar which he would not have exchanged for a pile of gold and he tore off home.

Once there he poured a few drops into a glass of water, gulped it down and fell into bed.

Good God! What joy! It was her – her again, but now in a different world. Oh, how charming she looked as she sat at the window of a bright country cottage. Her dress was simplicity itself – the simplicity that invests a poet's thought . . . heavens, how simple and how well it suited her! A short kerchief was casually thrown around her graceful neck. Everything about her was modest, everything displayed mysterious, inexplicable taste. How charming her graceful walk! How musical the sound of her footsteps and the rustle of her simple dress! How pretty her arm, encircled by a hair bracelet. With a tear in her eye she told him:

'Do not despise me. I am not what you take me for. Just look at me, look closer and tell me: could I be capable of what you imagine?'

'Oh, no, no! Let him who dares think that then let him . . .' But then he woke up, deeply moved, distraught, with tears in his eyes. 'Better you had not existed, that you had never lived in this world, but had been the creation of some inspired artist! I would never have left the canvas, I would have gazed upon you for eternity and kissed you, I would have lived and breathed you – as in the most wonderful dream – and then I would have been happy. I would have wanted for nothing else, I would have summoned you as my guardian angel, sleeping or in my waking hours. I would have waited for you if ever I had to portray the divine and holy. But as things are . . . how terrible life is! What use is it that she lives? Can a madman's life be pleasing for his relatives and friends who once loved him? God, what is our life? Only perpetual discord between dream and reality!'

Almost the same thoughts occupied him incessantly. He thought of nothing, hardly ate, and with the impatience and eagerness of a lover waited for nightfall and those longed-for dreams. This constant concentration on one and the same object finally took such a hold on his whole existence and imagination that the desired image appeared almost every day, always the very opposite of reality, since his thoughts were as pure as a child's. Through these dreams the object itself became somehow purer and was completely transformed.

The draughts of opium inflamed his mind even more and if ever there was a man who loved impetuously, ruinously, tempestuously, to the utmost degree of insanity, then he was that unfortunate.

Of all his dreams one brought him more joy than any other: he imagined himself in his studio, in such high spirits, sitting so cheerfully, palette in hand. And *she* was there. She was already his wife, sitting at his side, leaning her lovely elbow on the back of his chair and looking at his work. Her languorous, weary eyes expressed overwhelming bliss. Everything in his room spoke of paradise. It was so bright, so neat. Heavens! She lay her enchanting head on his breast. He had never had such a wonderful dream. Afterwards he rose feeling somehow fresher and less absent-minded than before. Strange thoughts arose in his head. 'Perhaps,' he thought, 'she has been drawn into vice against her will, by some dreadful circumstances. Perhaps her heart is inclined towards remorse, perhaps she herself longs to escape from her appalling condition? And how could I be so indifferent and allow her to perish, when I only need to hold out a hand to save her from drowning?'

His thoughts wandered even further. 'No one knows me,' he told himself. 'Besides, why should anyone be concerned about me? And I have nothing to do with anyone either. If she shows genuine remorse and changes her life I will marry her. I *must* marry her. That way I would be acting far better than many who marry their housekeepers – and even the most despicable creatures. But my course of action will be disinterested and might even be noble. I shall return to the world its finest embellishment.'

After drawing up this light-headed plan, he felt his cheeks flush. He went over to the mirror and was alarmed when he saw those hollow cheeks and how pale his face was. He started to dress and groom himself with the utmost care. He washed, smoothed his hair, put on a new tail-coat and a smart waistcoat, threw his cloak over his shoulders and went out into the street. He breathed fresh air and felt totally invigorated, like a convalescent who has gone out for the first time after a long illness. His heart pounded as he drew near the street where he had not set foot since that fateful encounter. He spent a long time looking for the house and his memory seemed to have played him false. Twice he walked up and down the street, unsure in front of which house to stop. Finally one of them looked the likely one. He dashed up the stairs and knocked at the door. It opened – and who should come out to greet him? His ideal, his mysterious image, the original of those visions in his dreams – she, in whom he had lived so terribly and painfully – and so sweetly. Yes, she was standing before him! He shuddered and

could barely keep to his feet for weakness, simply overwhelmed
by a surge of joy. She looked as beautiful as ever, although her
eyes seemed sleepy, although a pallor had crept over her face
that was no longer so fresh – but she was still lovely.

'Ah!' she cried, seeing Piskarev and rubbing her eyes (it was
already two o'clock in the afternoon). 'Why did you run away
from us that day?'

Weak with exhaustion he sat on a chair and looked at her.
'I've only just woken up. This morning they brought me home
at seven – I was dead drunk,' she added, smiling.

Oh, better you were dumb, quite unable to say a thing, than
utter such words! She had suddenly shown him her whole life,
as if in a panorama. Despite all, he summoned up courage and
decided to try and see if his exhortations would have any effect
on her. He pulled himself together and in a trembling but
passionate voice began by explaining her appalling position to
her. She listened to him with an attentive look and with the same
feeling of wonderment we display at the sight of something
unexpected and strange. Faintly smiling, she looked at her
friend who was sitting in one corner and stopped cleaning
her comb to give her full attention to this new preacher.

'Yes, it's true I'm poor,' Piskarev finally said after a lengthy
and instructive homily, 'but we shall work. We shall vie with one
another to improve our lives. Nothing is more agreeable than to
be one's own master. I shall sit at my painting while you will
sit at my side, inspiring me in my work, busy with embroidering
or some other handicraft. And we shall want for nothing!'

'You don't say!' she interrupted in a rather contemptuous
voice. 'I'm no laundrymaid or seamstress that I should have to
work!'

God! In these words her whole vile, despicable life was
summed up – a life of emptiness and idleness, those loyal com-
panions of depravity.

'Will you marry *me*!' her friend chimed in with a brazen air
– until then she had been silently sitting in one corner. 'When
I'm your wife I'll sit like this!'

Then her pathetic face assumed a stupid grin, which greatly
amused the beauty.

Oh, this was too much! That was more than he could stand. He rushed out of the room, seeing nothing, feeling nothing, hearing nothing. His mind clouded over. The whole day was spent stupidly, aimlessly – and he did not hear or feel a thing. No one would have known that he had spent the night away somewhere. Only next day blind instinct led him back to his room, looking dreadful, pale-faced, his hair dishevelled and with signs of insanity on his face. He locked himself in his room and admitted no one; he asked for nothing. Four days passed and his door never opened. Finally, after a week had gone by and the room was still locked, people rushed to the door and called him, but there was no reply. Finally they broke down the door and found his lifeless body with the throat cut. A bloodstained razor lay on the floor. From his convulsively parted hands and his terrifyingly distorted expression one could infer that his hand had faltered and that he had suffered for a long time before his sinful soul left his body.

Thus perished a victim of insane passion – poor Piskarev, as gentle, meek and mild and as ingenuous as a child, bearing the sparks of talent that might with time have blossomed into the full flower of genius. No one shed tears over him, no one was to be seen beside his lifeless body apart from the usual district police chief and the indifferent face of the town doctor. Without even any religious rites his coffin was swiftly taken to Okhta.[14] Only one old soldier followed it and wept – and only then because he had drunk a bottle of vodka too many. Even Lieutenant Pirogov did not come to see the body of the poor devil to whom – when he was alive – he had given his exalted patronage: he had no time to think about such things and, besides, he was too involved in some extraordinary adventure. But let us return to him.

I have no liking for corpses and it is always disagreeable when a long funeral procession crosses my path, when some old soldier, dressed like a Capucin friar, takes snuff with his left hand because he has a torch in his right. I always feel most annoyed when I see an ornate catafalque with a coffin draped in velvet. But my annoyance is tinged with sorrow when I see a carrier hauling the uncovered pine coffin of some poor wretch, with only some old beggarwoman (who has met the procession at a crossroads) plodding after it for want of something better to do.

If I remember correctly, we left Lieutenant Pirogov at the moment when he parted company with poor Piskarev and went in hot pursuit of the blonde. The blonde was a rather attractive but frivolous little creature. She would stop before every shop and gaze at the sashes, scarves, earrings, gloves and other trifles in the windows, constantly wriggling and gawking in all directions. 'You, my sweetie, shall be mine!' Pirogov said with confidence as he continued his pursuit, turning up his overcoat collar in case he met one of his friends. But it would not come amiss to acquaint the reader with our Lieutenant Pirogov's character.

Before we go on to describe Lieutenant Pirogov, however, it would be a good idea to say a few words about the kind of society to which Pirogov belonged. There are officers who make up a kind of middle class in St Petersburg. You will always come across one of them at a soirée or dinner given by a state counsellor who has finally risen to that rank after forty years' hard work. The pale-faced daughter, as colourless as St Petersburg, many of whom are past their prime, the customary tea table, piano, domestic balls – all this tends to be inseparable from bright epaulettes gleaming in the light of a lamp between a virtuous blonde and the black tail-coat of her brother or some family friend. It is exceedingly difficult to rouse and amuse these cold-blooded maidens: to achieve that requires much skill – better, the absence of any skill. One has to say things that are neither too clever nor too funny, intermingled with those trivialities so beloved by women. And here one must give the gentlemen in question their due. They have a special knack for making these colourless beauties laugh and listen. Often their greatest reward is to hear exclamations (smothered by laughter) such as: 'Ooh, please stop! You'll make me die laughing!' Only rarely – perhaps never – are they to be seen in the highest circles. From these they have generally been ousted by so-called aristocrats. Nonetheless, they are considered cultured, highly educated men. They love discussing literature; they praise

Bulgarin,[15] Pushkin and Grech[16] and speak disdainfully and sarcastically about A. A. Orlov.[17] They never miss a public lecture, whether on book-keeping or even forestry. You will always find one of their number at the theatre, whatever the play – unless it's one of those *Filatkas*,[18] which are deeply offensive to their fastidious taste. They are permanently in the theatre and are the greatest source of revenue for theatrical directors. They are particularly fond of fine verses in a play and like to call loudly for the actors. Many of them, who by teaching in government institutions or by preparing candidates for them, finally come to be proud owners of a carriage and pair. Then their circle widens. In the end they manage to marry a merchant's daughter who can play the piano, with a hundred thousand (or around that figure) in ready cash and a whole swarm of bearded kinsfolk. But they cannot achieve this honour until they have reached at least colonel's rank. This is because – despite giving off a slight whiff of cabbage – our bearded merchants are most reluctant to see their daughters married to anyone except a general, or at least a *colonel*.

Such are the chief characteristics of this class of young men. But Lieutenant Pirogov possessed an abundance of talents that were his own particular preserve. He could declaim verses from *Dmitry Donskoy*[19] and *Woe from Wit*[20] superbly, and he had a special gift for blowing smoke rings from his pipe – so skilfully that he was able to string ten of them together in a chain at a time. He could tell the anecdote about a cannon being one thing and a unicorn another[21] most agreeably. But it is rather difficult to enumerate *all* the talents and fine qualities that fate had lavished on Pirogov. He loved to discuss actresses and ballet dancers, but never as crudely as young ensigns usually discourse on the subject. He was delighted with his army rank, to which he had been recently promoted and, although he would occasionally utter as he reclined on his couch: 'Oh, oh! All is vanity! What of it if I'm a lieutenant?', deep down he was secretly flattered by this newly acquired status. He often tried to hint at it in a roundabout way in conversation and on one occasion, when he bumped into some copy clerk in the street who struck him as impolite, immediately made him stop and gave him to understand, in few but cutting words, that a *lieuten-ant* was standing before him and not a common or garden officer. And then he tried to express his views even more elo-quently when two exceedingly attractive young ladies happened by pass by. Generally speaking, Pirogov displayed a passion for all that was refined and consequently he encouraged the artist Piskarev. However, this was possibly because he dearly wanted him to paint a portrait of his own manly countenance. But enough about Pirogov's virtues. Man is such a wonderful crea-ture that you can never enumerate all his finer qualities in one attempt and, the more you examine him, the more fresh features come to light.

And so Pirogov did not abandon his pursuit of the unknown pretty blonde and occasionally plied her with questions, to which she replied with rather brusque and vague sounds. They passed through the dark Kazan Gates to Meshchanskaya Street – a street of tobacconists and cheap bric-a-brac shops, German artisans and Finnish nymphs. The blonde ran even faster and flew through the gates of a rather dingy looking house. Pirogov followed her. Then she ran up a dark narrow staircase and passed through a doorway, through which Pirogov also boldly made his way. He found himself in a large room with black walls and grimy ceiling. On the table lay a pile of iron screws, sundry locksmith's tools, shining coffee pots and candlesticks. The floor was littered with brass and iron filings. Pirogov could see at once that it was a workman's lodgings. The unknown blonde flew away through a side door. For a moment Pirogov hesitated but, following the Russian rule, decided to press on. He entered a room that was quite unlike the first, very neat and tidy, showing that a German lived there. Then he was struck by an extremely weird spectacle. Before him sat Schiller – not the Schiller who wrote *William Tell* and a *History of the Thirty Years War*, but the *famous* Schiller, master tinsmith of Meshchanskaya Street. Beside Schiller stood Hoffmann – not the writer Hoffmann, but a rather competent bootmaker from Ofitserskaya Street and a great pal of Schiller's. Schiller was drunk and sitting on a chair stamping and excitedly gabbling away. None of this would have surprised Pirogov, but what did surprise him were the extraordinarily peculiar positions of the two figures. Schiller was sitting with his rather fleshy nose sticking up, his head held high, while Hoffmann was gripping the nose between two fingers and holding the blade of his cobbler's knife close to the surface. Both individuals were speaking German and, since all the German Lieutenant Pirogov knew was 'Gut Morgen', he could not make head or tail of what was going on. However, what Schiller was saying is as follows:

'I don't vant it, I don't need ein nose!' he said, waving his arms. 'Mein nose cost me three pounds of snuff a month. And I buy it from lousy Russian shop, because Germans don't stock Russian snuff. So I pay lousy Russian shop forty copecks a pound. That comes to one rouble twenty copecks. Twelve times one rouble twenty makes fourteen roubles forty. Do you hear, mein dear Hoffmann? Fourteen roubles forty just on mein nose! And on holidays I take a pinch of rappee,[22] as I don't want to use filthy Russian snuff on holidays. Over the year I used two pounds of snuff at two roubles a pound. Now, six plus fourteen comes to twenty roubles – on snuff alone! That's daylight robbery! I'm asking you, mein dear friend Hoffmann – aren't I right?' Hoffmann, who was drunk as well, replied affirmatively. 'Twenty roubles forty copecks! I'm a Swabian[23] German, loyal subject of a German king. I don't want any nose! Cut mein nose off – here!!'

But for Pirogov's sudden appearance Hoffmann would without a shadow of doubt have sliced off Schiller's nose – and quite without rhyme or reason – because he had just positioned his knife as if he was about to cut out a boot sole.

Schiller was furious that a complete stranger, someone uninvited, should have so inopportunely interrupted proceedings. Despite the fact that he was befuddled by beer and wine, Schiller felt that it was rather unbecoming to be seen in such a posture and having such things done to him, in the presence of an outsider.

Pirogov performed a slight bow and asked with his customary affability: 'Oh! Please do forgive me!'

'Clear off!' drawled Schiller in reply.

At this Pirogov was completely taken aback. This treatment was something quite new for him. The smile that had been faintly glimmering on his face vanished at once. With a feeling of wounded dignity he announced: 'I find this all very strange, my dear sir . . . obviously the fact that I'm an *officer* has escaped you.'

'So, vot's an officer! I'm a Swabian German. Me meinself' (here Schiller banged his fist on the table) 'vill be officer. Eighteen months junker, two years lieutenant and tomorrow I shall be officer immediately. But I don't want to serve. This is what I'd do to officer – phooo!' And Schiller opened his hand and snorted into it.

Lieutenant Pirogov saw that all he could do now was make himself scarce. However, the kind of treatment he had received was most unbecoming for one of *his* rank and highly disagreeable. Several times he stopped on the stairs as if trying to pluck up courage and think how to make Schiller pay for his impertinence. Finally, he concluded that Schiller might be excused, since his head was so befuddled with beer. Besides, he visualized the pretty little blonde and so he decided to consign these considerations to oblivion.

Early next morning Lieutenant Pirogov appeared at the tinsmith's workshop. He was met in the hall by the pretty blonde, who asked him in a severe voice which suited her little face very well: 'What do you want?'

'Ah, good morning, my sweetie! Don't you recognize me? You little minx, you! What absolutely ravishing eyes!' And as he spoke Lieutenant Pirogov wanted to raise her chin very charmingly with one finger. But the blonde produced a frightened cry and asked with the same severity: 'What do you want?'

'To see *you* – that's all I desire!' replied Lieutenant Pirogov, smiling agreeably as he went nearer. But when he noticed that the timorous blonde was about to slip through the door he added: 'I want to order some spurs, sweetie. Can you have them made for me? But I need no spurs to love you – I need a curb, rather! What pretty little hands!'

Lieutenant Pirogov was always particularly courteous when making such declarations.

'I'll go and fetch my husband right away,' the German cried

out and left. A few moments later Pirogov saw sleepy-eyed Schiller enter – he had not recovered from yesterday's hangover. With one glance at the officer he remembered, as if in a vague dream, the events of the previous day. He could not remember *everything*, exactly as it had happened, but he felt that he had blurted out something very silly, so he greeted the officer with a very sombre look.

'I can't take less than fifteen roubles for a pair of spurs,' he said, wanting to get rid of Pirogov – as an honest German he was deeply ashamed of having to look at anyone who had seen him in such an unseemly condition. Schiller loved drinking without anyone else for company – apart from two or three of his close pals – on which occasions he kept the door locked, even to his workmen.

'Why are they so expensive?' Pirogov asked amiably.

'German workmanship!' Schiller nonchalantly replied, stroking his chin. 'A Russian would ask two roubles for them.'

'Well, to show you that I like you and want to get to know you better, I'll pay fifteen.'

Schiller reflected for a moment; being an honest German he felt rather ashamed. As he hoped to put him off ordering, he announced that the quickest he could make them was a fortnight. Pirogov made no objection and readily agreed.

The German pondered once again and then began wondering how best to do the job, to make the spurs really worth fifteen roubles. Just then the pretty blonde came into the workshop and started rummaging around on the table that was cluttered with coffee pots. The lieutenant took advantage of Schiller's musings, went over to her and squeezed her arm that was bare to the shoulder. This did not please Schiller one bit.

'Mein Frau!' he shouted.

'Was vollen Sie doch?' replied the blonde.

'Genzi into kitchen!'

The blonde retreated.

'So, in a fortnight?' asked Pirogov.

'Yes, a fortnight,' Schiller replied, still reflecting. 'I've a lot of work on at the moment.'

'Well, goodbye then, I'll look in again.'

'Goodbye,' replied Schiller, shutting the door after him.

Lieutenant Pirogov was firmly resolved not to abandon his pursuit, even though the German girl had so obviously rebuffed him. He failed to understand how anyone could resist him, especially as his personal charms and distinguished rank entitled him to full recognition. But it must be mentioned that, for all her attractiveness, Schiller's wife was extremely stupid. Stupidity, however, can be particularly appealing in a pretty wife. At least, I know of many husbands who are delighted by their wives' stupidity and see evidence in it of childlike innocence. Beauty can work perfect miracles. Instead of inspiring revulsion, all spiritual defects in a beautiful woman become unusually attractive: even vice can be attractive in them. But should beauty fade, then a woman needs to be twenty times cleverer than her husband to inspire, if not love, at least respect. For all her stupidity Schiller's wife always fulfilled her wifely duties faithfully and so it was rather hard for Pirogov to succeed in his daring enterprise. But there is always enjoyment in overcoming obstacles and with every day that passed the blonde attracted him more. He took to making fairly frequent inquiries about the spurs, so that in the end Schiller grew sick and tired of it and made every effort to finish the spurs as soon as he could. Finally they were ready.

'Ah, what excellent workmanship!' exclaimed Lieutenant Pirogov when he saw them. 'Heavens – they're so well made! Even our general doesn't have spurs like these.'

A feeling of self-satisfaction flooded through Schiller's heart. His eyes became quite cheerful and he felt completely reconciled to Pirogov. 'That Russian officer is a clever chap,' he thought to himself.

'So, I suppose you can make a sheath for a dagger, for example, or other things?'

'Well, of course I can!' Schiller replied, smiling.

'So, make me a sheath for a dagger – I'll go and fetch it – I've a very fine Turkish one, but I'd like a different sheath.'

This struck Schiller like a bombshell. He suddenly knitted his brows. 'Well, how d'ye like that!' he thought, inwardly cursing for bringing the work on himself. However, to refuse it now

he considered dishonourable. Besides, the Russian officer had
praised his workmanship. With a slight shake of the head he
consented. But the kiss that Pirogov audaciously planted on the
lips of the pretty blonde as he left utterly bewildered him.

I do not consider it out of place to make the reader a little
better acquainted with Schiller. Schiller was a typical German,
in the fullest sense of the word. From the age of twenty, that
happy time when a Russian is leading a devil-may-care existence, Schiller had already planned his whole life and never once
deviated from it, whatever the circumstances. He made it a rule
to get up at seven, to dine at two, to be ever-punctual and to get
drunk every Sunday. He set himself the target of accumulating
capital of 50,000 roubles within ten years and this was as fixed
and immutable as fate itself, for a civil servant would sooner
forget to look in at the porter's lodge of his superior than a
German to alter his routine. Under no circumstances would he
increase his spending and if the price of potatoes was higher
than usual he would not pay a copeck more and was perfectly
content with buying less. Although this sometimes left him
feeling rather hungry, he grew used to it. His punctiliousness
was so thorough that he resolved never to kiss his wife more
than twice in twenty-four hours and to ensure he did not exceed
this total never added more than one teaspoonful of pepper to
his soup. However, on Sundays this rule was not so strictly
observed, since Schiller would then drink two bottles of beer
and one of caraway vodka which he nonetheless always cursed.
He did not drink at all like an Englishman who locks his door
immediately after dinner and gets drunk in solitude. On the
contrary: as a true German he always drank in inspired fashion,
either with Hoffmann the cobbler or with Kuntz the carpenter,
also German and a great drunkard. Such was the character of
our worthy Schiller, who was now in a very ticklish position:
although he was phlegmatic and a German, Pirogov's behaviour
aroused in him something akin to jealousy. He racked his brains
and just could not think how to get rid of that Russian officer.
Meanwhile Pirogov was smoking his pipe in the company of
his fellow officers – Providence has decreed that wherever an
officer is to be found, so is a pipe, and he alluded with great

pomp and ceremony and with a pleasant smile to his little intrigue with the pretty German with whom, so he maintained, he was already on the most intimate terms and that he still entertained hopes of winning her over.

One day as he was strolling down Meshchanskaya Street, looking at the house adorned with Schiller's sign advertising coffee pots and samovars, to his unbounded delight he spotted the blonde with her head thrust out of the window, watching passers-by. He stopped, blew a kiss and said: 'Gut Morgen!'

The blonde leaned towards him as if he were an old friend.

'Tell me, is your husband home?'

'Yes,' replied the blonde.

'And when is he out?'

'Usually on Sundays,' the stupid little blonde replied.

'That sounds promising!' thought Pirogov. 'I mustn't let the chance slip.'

The following Sunday he appeared before the blonde like a bolt from the blue. Schiller was in fact out. The pretty wife took fright, but on this occasion Pirogov proceeded rather cautiously, treating her with the utmost respect and when exchanging bows displayed the full beauty of his supple figure in its tightly fitting tunic. He made pleasant and polite jokes, but the stupid German replied to everything in monosyllables. Finally, having tried every kind of attack from all sides and realized nothing would amuse her, he invited her to dance. The German agreed in a flash, since all German women love to dance. Pirogov pinned all his hopes on this approach: firstly, because it would give her pleasure and secondly because he would be able to impress her with his graceful bearing and agility, thirdly because while dancing he could get much closer, put his arm round the pretty German and thus set the ball rolling. In brief, he envisaged complete success. He began with a variety of gavotte, knowing that one has to take things gradually with German women. The pretty German stepped out into the middle of the room and raised her shapely foot. This pose so enchanted Pirogov that he rushed to kiss her. The German girl started screaming and this only enhanced her charms in Pirogov's eyes. He was showering her with kisses when suddenly the door opened and in came Schiller and Hoffmann, together with Kuntz the carpenter. All these worthy craftsmen were as drunk as lords.

But I leave it to the reader to judge for himself Schiller's anger and indignation.

'You oaf!' he shouted, utterly incensed. 'How dare you kiss my wife? You're a scoundrel and no Russian officer! To hell with it, mein friend Hoffmann, I'm a German and no Russian pig!'

Hoffmann replied in the affirmative.

'Oh no, I don't want any horns! Grab him by the scruff of the neck, mein dear friend, Hoffmann, I won't put up with this!' he continued, wildly gesticulating, his face turning as red as the cloth of his waistcoat. 'Eight years I've been living in St Petersburg, I have mother in Swabia and uncle in Nurnberg. I'm a German and not a cuckolded chunk of meat! Off with his clothes, Hoffmann mein friend. Hold him by the arm and leg, comrade Kuntz!'

And the Germans grabbed Pirogov by his arms and legs.

In vain he struggled to fight them off. These three craftsmen were among the sturdiest Germans in all St Petersburg and treated him so roughly and rudely that I must confess I cannot find the words to portray this melancholy event.

I am convinced that next day Pirogov was running a high fever, that he was trembling like a leaf as he waited for the police to arrive any minute, that he would have given heaven knows what for all yesterday's events to have been nothing but a dream. But what has been cannot be changed. Nothing bears comparison with Pirogov's anger and indignation. The mere thought of such a terrible insult drove him into a frenzy. He considered Siberia and a flogging the very least punishment Schiller deserved.[24] He flew home to dress and then proceeded straight to the general's, to describe in the most lurid colours those German craftsmen's outrageous behaviour. At the same time he wanted to lodge a written complaint with the General Staff: should the punishment designated by it be inadequate[25] in his opinion he would go straight to the Council of State – if not to the Tsar himself.

But all this ended rather peculiarly. On the way he dropped into a pastry shop, ate two puff pastries, read something in the *Northern Bee*[26] and emerged with his wrath somewhat diminished. And the fairly pleasant cool evening encouraged him to take a little stroll along Nevsky Prospekt. By nine o'clock he had completely calmed down and realized that he should not disturb the general on a Sunday. Besides, the general was sure to have been called away somewhere and so off he went to a soirée given by a director of the Control Commission,[27] where he found a highly congenial gathering of civil servants and officers from his regiment. There he spent a most enjoyable evening and so distinguished himself in the mazurka that not only the ladies but even the cavaliers were in raptures.

'How wonderfully this world of ours is arranged!' I thought as I walked the day before yesterday along Nevsky Prospekt and recalled those two events. 'How strangely, how inscrutably fate plays with us! Do we ever get what we really desire? Do we ever achieve what our powers have ostensibly equipped us for? No: everything works by contraries. Fate has allotted the most beautiful horses to one person and he nonchalantly drives them without even noticing their beauty, whereas another, whose heart burns with passion for horses, has to lump it on foot and his only solace is to click his tongue when a trotter is led past. Someone may have an excellent cook, but unfortunately his mouth is so small it cannot accommodate more than two little morsels of food. Another has a mouth the size of the arch of the Staff Headquarters.[28] But alas! – he has to be content with a German supper of potatoes. What strange tricks fate plays on us!

But strangest of all are the events that take place on Nevsky Prospekt. Oh, do not trust this Nevsky Prospekt! I always wrap myself tighter in my cloak when I walk along it and try to ignore every object I see on my way. All is deception, all is a dream, all is not what it seems. So you think that gentleman strolling along in his superbly tailored frock-coat is exceedingly wealthy? Not a bit of it. His frock-coat is his entire fortune. You imagine that those two stout gentlemen who have stopped in front of a church that is being built[29] are commenting on its architecture? Far from it: they are discussing how strangely two crows are sitting opposite each other. You think that the enthusiastic character waving his arms about is telling of how his wife threw a ball out of the window at some officer who was a complete stranger to him? Not a bit of it . . . he's discussing Lafayette.[30] You think that these ladies . . . but ladies are least of all to be trusted. Try not to look into shop windows so often: the trifles on display are charming, but they smack of great piles of banknotes. But God forbid you peep under women's hats! However invitingly the cape of some beauty in the distance flutters, not for anything would I follow her to satisfy my curiosity . . . Keep away, for God's sake, keep away as far as you can from street lamps. Hurry past them, as fast as you can! You will be lucky if you escape without your foppish frock-coat having stinking oil spilt on it. But, apart from the lamp, everything here breathes deception. This Nevsky Prospekt lies at all hours, but most of all when the thick pall of night descends upon it and throws into relief the white and pale-yellow walls of the houses, when the whole city turns into noise and glitter, when myriad carriages pour from the bridges, when postilions shout, leap up and down on their horses and when the devil himself lights the street lamps, only to show everything in an unreal guise.

THE NOSE

I

An extraordinarily strange event took place in St Petersburg on 25 March. Ivan Yakovlevich, a barber who lived on Voznesensky Prospekt (his surname has been lost and all that his shop sign shows is a gentleman with a lathered cheek and the inscription 'We also let blood'), woke up rather early one morning and smelt hot bread. Raising himself slightly on his bed he saw his wife, who was a quite respectable lady and a great coffee-drinker, taking some freshly baked rolls out of the oven.

'I don't want any coffee today, Praskovya Osipovna,' said Ivan Yakovlevich, 'I'll make do with a hot roll and onion instead.' (Here I must explain that Ivan Yakovlevich would really have liked to have had some coffee as well, but knew it was quite out of the question to expect both coffee *and* rolls, since Praskovya Osipovna did not take very kindly to these whims of his.) 'Let the old fool have his bread, I don't mind,' she thought. 'That means extra coffee for me!' And she threw a roll on to the table.

Ivan pulled his frock-coat over his nightshirt for decency's sake, sat down at the table, poured out some salt, peeled two onions, took a knife and with a determined expression on his face started cutting one of the rolls.

When he had sliced the roll in two, he peered into the middle and was amazed to see something white there. Ivan carefully picked at it with his knife, and felt it with his finger. 'Quite thick,' he said to himself. 'What on earth can it be?'

He poked two fingers in and pulled out – a nose!

Ivan Yakovlevich let his arms drop to his sides and began rubbing his eyes and feeling around in the roll again. Yes, it was a nose all right, no mistake about that. And, what's more, it seemed a very familiar nose. His face filled with horror. But this horror was nothing compared with his wife's indignation.

'You beast, whose nose is *that* you've cut off?' she cried furiously. 'You scoundrel! You drunkard! I'll report it to the police myself, I will. You thief! Come to think of it, I've heard three customers say that when they come in for a shave you start tweaking their noses about so much it's a wonder they stay on at all!'

But Ivan felt more dead than alive. He knew that the nose belonged to none other than Collegiate Assessor[1] Kovalyov, whom he shaved on Wednesdays and Sundays.

'Wait a minute, Praskovya! I'll wrap it up in a piece of cloth and put it over there in the corner. Let's leave it there for a bit, then I'll try and get rid of it.'

'I don't want to know! Do you think I'm going to let a sawn-off nose lie around in *my* room . . . you fathead! All you can do is strop that blasted razor of yours and let everything else go to pot. Layabout! Night-bird! And you expect me to cover up for you with the police! You filthy pig! Blockhead! Get that nose out of here, out! Do what you like with it, but I don't want that thing hanging around here a minute longer!'

Ivan Yakovlevich was absolutely stunned. He thought and thought, but just didn't know what to make of it.

'I'm damned if I know what's happened!' he said at last, scratching the back of his ear. 'I can't say for certain if I came home drunk or not last night. All I know is, it's crazy. After all, bread is something you bake, but a nose is quite different. Can't make head or tail of it! . . .'

Ivan Yakovlevich lapsed into silence. The thought that the police might search the place, find the nose and afterwards bring a charge against him, very nearly sent him out of his mind. Already he could see that scarlet collar beautifully embroidered with silver, that sword . . . and he began shaking all over. Finally he put on his undergarments and boots, pulled on all that nonsense and with Praskovya Osipovna's vigorous invective ringing in his ears, wrapped the nose up in a piece of cloth and went out into the street.

All he wanted was to stuff it away somewhere, either hiding it between two curb-stones by someone's front door or else 'accidentally' dropping it and slinking off down a side-street. But as luck would have it, he kept bumping into friends, who would insist on asking: 'Where are *you* off to?' or 'It's a bit early for shaving customers, isn't it?' with the result that he didn't have a chance to get rid of it. Once he *did* manage to drop it, but a policeman pointed with his halberd and said: 'Pick that up! Can't you see you dropped something!' And Ivan Yakovlevich had to pick it up and hide it in his pocket. Despair gripped him, especially as the streets were getting more and more crowded now as the shops and stalls began to open.

He decided to make his way to St Isaac's Bridge and see if he could throw the nose into the River Neva without anyone seeing him. But here I am rather at fault for not having told you before something about Ivan Yakovlevich, who in many ways was a man worthy of respect.

Ivan Yakovlevich, like any honest Russian working man, was a terrible drunkard. And although he spent all day shaving other people's beards, his own was perpetually unshaven. His frock-coat (Ivan Yakovlevich never wore a dress-coat) could best be described as piebald: that is to say, it was black, but with brownish-yellow and grey spots all over it. His collar was very shiny, and three loosely hanging threads showed that some buttons had once been there. Ivan Yakovlevich was a great cynic, and whenever Kovalyov the collegiate assessor said 'Your hands always stink!' while he was being shaved, Ivan Yakovlevich would say: 'But why *should* they stink?' The collegiate assessor used to reply: 'Don't ask me, my dear chap. All I know is, they *stink*.' Ivan Yakovlevich would answer by taking a pinch of snuff and then, by way of retaliation, lather all over Kovalyov's cheeks, under his nose, behind the ears and beneath his beard – in short, wherever he felt like covering him with soap.

By now this respectable citizen of ours had already reached St Isaac's Bridge. First of all he had a good look round. Then he leant over the rails, trying to pretend he was looking under the bridge to see if there were many fish there, and furtively threw the packet into the water. He felt as if a couple of hundredweight had been lifted all at once from his shoulders and he even managed to produce a smile.

Instead of going off to shave civil servants' chins, he headed for a shop bearing the sign 'Hot Meals and Tea' for a glass of punch. Suddenly he saw a policeman at one end of the bridge, looking very impressive with broad whiskers, a three-cornered hat and a sword. He went cold all over as the policeman beckoned to him and said: 'Come here, my friend!'

Recognizing the uniform, Ivan Yakovlevich took his cap off before he had taken half a dozen steps, tripped up to him and greeted him with: 'Good morning, Your Honour!'

'No, no, my dear chap, none of your "Honour". Just tell me what you were up to on the bridge?'

'Honest, officer, I was on my way to shave a customer and stopped to see how fast the current was.'

'You're lying. You really can't expect me to believe that! You'd better come clean at once!'

'I'll give Your Honour a free shave twice, even three times a week, honest I will,' answered Ivan Yakovlevich.

'No, no, my friend, that won't do. Three barbers look after me already, and it's an *honour* for them to shave me. Will you please tell me what you were up to?'

Ivan Yakovlevich turned pale . . . But at this point everything became so completely enveloped in mist it is really impossible to say what happened afterwards.

2

Collegiate Assessor Kovalyov woke up rather early and made a 'brring' noise with his lips. He always did this when he woke up, though, if you asked him why, he could not give any good reason. Kovalyov stretched himself and asked for the small mirror that stood on the table to be brought over to him. He wanted to have a look at a pimple that had made its appearance on his nose the previous evening, but to his extreme astonishment found that instead of a nose there was nothing but an absolutely flat surface! In a terrible panic Kovalyov asked for some water and rubbed his eyes with a towel. No mistake about it: his nose had gone. He began pinching himself to make sure he was not sleeping, but to all intents and purposes he was wide awake. Collegiate Assessor Kovalyov sprang out of bed and shook himself: still no nose! He asked for his clothes and off he dashed straight to the Head of Police.

In the meantime, however, a few words should be said about Kovalyov, so that the reader may see what kind of collegiate assessor this man was. You really cannot compare those collegiate assessors who acquire office through academic qualifications with the variety appointed in the Caucasus.[2] The two species are quite distinct. Collegiate assessors with diplomas from learned bodies . . . But Russia is such an amazing country, that if you pass any remark about *one* collegiate assessor, every assessor from Riga to Kamchatka will take it personally. And the same goes for all people holding titles and government ranks. Kovalyov belonged to the Caucasian variety.

He had been a collegiate assessor for only two years and therefore could not forget it for a single minute. To make himself sound more important and to give more weight and nobility to his status he never called himself collegiate assessor, but 'Major'.[3] If he met a woman in the street selling shirt fronts he would say: 'Listen dear, come and see me at home. My flat's in Sadovaya Street. All you have to do is ask if Major Kovalyov lives there and anyone will show you the way.' If he happened to meet a pretty girl he would whisper some secret instructions and then say: 'Just ask for Major Kovalyov, my dear.' Therefore, throughout this story, we will call this collegiate assessor 'Major'.

Major Kovalyov was in the habit of taking a daily stroll along Nevsky Prospekt.[4] His shirt collar was always immaculately clean and well-starched. His whiskers were the kind you usually find among provincial surveyors, architects and regimental surgeons, as well as those who have some sort of connection with the police, with anyone in fact who has full rosy cheeks and plays a good hand at whist. These were the kind of whiskers that usually reach from the middle of the face right across to the nostrils. Major Kovalyov always carried plenty of seals with him – seals bearing coats of arms or engraved with the words: 'Wednesday, Thursday, Monday', and so on. Major Kovalyov had come to St Petersburg with the express purpose of finding a position in keeping with his rank. If he was successful, he would get a vice-governorship, but failing that, a job as an administrative clerk in some important government department would have to do. Major Kovalyov was not averse to marriage, as long as his bride happened to be worth 200,000 roubles. And now the reader can judge for himself this major's state of mind when, instead of a fairly presentable and reasonably sized nose, all he saw was an absolutely preposterous smooth flat space. As if this were not bad enough, there was not a cab in sight, and he had to walk home, keeping himself huddled up in his cloak and with a handkerchief over his face to make people think he was bleeding. 'But perhaps I dreamt it! How could I be so stupid as to go and lose my nose?' With these thoughts he dropped into a coffee-house to take a look at himself in a mirror. Fortunately the shop was empty, except for some waiters sweeping up and tidying the chairs. A few of them, rather bleary-eyed, were carrying trays laden with hot pies. Yesterday's newspapers, covered in coffee stains, lay scattered on the tables and chairs. 'Well, thank God there's no one about,' he said. 'Now I can have a look.' He approached the mirror rather gingerly and peered into it. 'Damn it! What kind of trick is this?' he cried, spitting on the floor. 'If only there were *something* to take its place, but there's nothing!'

He bit his lips in annoyance, left the coffee-house and decided not to smile or look at anyone, which was not like him at all. Suddenly he stood rooted to the spot near the front door of some house and witnessed a most incredible spectacle. A carriage drew up at the entrance porch. The doors flew open and out jumped a uniformed, stooping gentleman who dashed up the steps. The feeling of horror and amazement that gripped Kovalyov when he recognized his own nose defies description! After this extraordinary sight everything went topsy-turvy. He could hardly keep to his feet, but decided at all costs to wait until the nose returned to the carriage, although he was shaking all over and felt quite feverish.

About two minutes later a nose really did come out. It was wearing a gold-braided uniform with a high stand-up collar and chamois trousers, and had a sword at its side. From the plumes on its hat one could tell that it held the exalted rank of state counsellor.[5] And it was abundantly clear that the nose was going to visit someone. It looked right, then left, shouted to the coachman 'Let's go!', climbed in and drove off.

Poor Kovalyov nearly went out of his mind. He did not know what to make of it. How, in fact, could a nose, which only yesterday was in the middle of his face, and which could not possibly walk around or drive in a carriage, suddenly turn up in a uniform! He ran after the carriage which fortunately did not travel very far and came to a halt outside Kazan Cathedral.[6] Kovalyov rushed into the cathedral square, elbowed his way through a crowd of beggarwomen who always used to make him laugh because of the way they covered their faces, leaving only slits for the eyes, and made his way in. Only a few people were at prayer, all of them standing by the entrance. Kovalyov felt so distraught that he was in no condition for praying, and his eyes searched every nook and cranny for the nose in uniform. At length he spotted it standing by one of the walls to the side. The nose's face was completely hidden by the high collar and it was praying with an expression of profound piety.

'What's the best way of approaching it?' thought Kovalyov. 'Judging by its uniform, its hat, and its whole appearance, it must be a state counsellor. But I'm damned if I know how to go about it!'

He tried to attract its attention by coughing, but the nose did not interrupt its devotions for one second and continued to perform low bows.

'My dear sir,' Kovalyov said, summoning up his courage, 'my dear sir . . .'

'What do you want?' replied the nose, turning round.

'I don't know how best to put it, sir, but it strikes me as very peculiar . . . Don't you know where you belong? And where do I find you? In church, of all places! I'm sure you'll agree that . . .'

'Please forgive me, but would you mind telling me what you're talking about? . . . Explain yourself.'

'How can I make myself clear?' Kovalyov wondered. Nerving himself once more he said: 'Of course, I am, as it happens, a major. You will agree that it's not done for someone in my position to walk around minus a nose. It's all right for some old woman selling peeled oranges on the Voskresensky Bridge[7] to sit there without one. But as I'm hoping to be promoted soon . . . Besides, as I'm acquainted with several highly placed ladies: Madame Chekhtaryev, for example, a state counsellor's wife and others . . . you can judge for yourself . . . I really don't know what to say, my dear sir . . . (He shrugged his shoulders as he said this.) 'If one considers this from the point of view of duty and honour . . . then you yourself will understand.'

'I don't understand a thing,' the nose replied. 'Please make yourself clear.'

'My dear sir,' continued Kovalyov in a smug voice, 'I really don't know what you mean by that. It's plain enough for anyone to see . . . Unless you want . . . Don't you realize you are *my own nose*!'

The nose looked at the major and frowned a little.

'My dear fellow, you are mistaken. I am a person in my own right. Furthermore, I don't see that we can have anything in common. Judging from your uniform buttons, I should say you're from another government department.'

With these words the nose turned away and continued its prayers.

Kovalyov was so confused he did not know what to do or think. At that moment he heard the pleasant rustle of a woman's dress, and an elderly lady, bedecked with lace, came by, accompanied by a slim girl wearing a white dress, which showed her shapely figure to very good advantage, and a pale yellow hat as light as pastry. A tall footman, with enormous whiskers and what seemed to be a dozen collars, stationed himself behind them and opened his snuff-box. Kovalyov went closer, pulled the linen collar of his shirt front up high, straightened the seals hanging on his gold watch chain and, smiling all over his face, turned his attention to the slim girl, who bent over to pray like a spring flower and kept lifting her little white hand with its almost transparent fingers to her forehead.

The smile on Kovalyov's face grew even more expansive when he saw, beneath her hat, a little rounded chin of dazzling white, and cheeks flushed with the colour of the first rose of spring.

But suddenly he jumped backwards as though he had been burnt: he remembered that instead of a nose he had absolutely nothing, and tears streamed from his eyes. He swung round to tell the nose in uniform straight out that it was only masquerading as a state counsellor, that it was an impostor and a scoundrel, and really nothing else than his own private property, *his* nose . . . But the nose had already gone: it had managed to slip off unseen, probably to pay somebody a visit.

This reduced Kovalyov to utter despair. He went out, and stood for a minute or so under the colonnade, carefully looking around him in the hope of spotting the nose. He remembered quite distinctly that it was wearing a plumed hat and a gold-embroidered uniform. But he had not noticed what its greatcoat was like, or the colour of its carriage, or its horses, or even if there was a liveried footman at the back. What's more, there were so many carriages careering to and fro, so fast, that it was practically impossible to recognize any of them, and even if he could, there was no way of making them stop.

It was a beautiful sunny day. Nevsky Prospekt was packed. From the Police Headquarters right down to the Anichkov Bridge[8] a whole floral cascade of ladies flowed along the pavements. Not far off he could see that court counsellor whom he referred to as lieutenant-colonel,[9] especially if there happened to be other people around. And over there was Yarygin, a head clerk in the Senate, and a very close friend of his who always lost at whist when he played in a party of eight. Another major, a collegiate assessor, of the Caucasian variety, waved to him to come over and have a chat.

'Blast and damn!' said Kovalyov, hailing a droshky. 'Driver, take me straight to the Chief of Police.'

He climbed into the droshky and shouted: 'Drive like the devil!'

'Is the Police Commissioner in?' he said as soon as he entered the hall.

'No, he's not, sir,' said the porter. 'He left only a few minutes ago.'

'This really *is* my day.'

'Yes,' added the porter, 'you've only just missed him. A minute ago you'd have caught him.'

Kovalyov, his handkerchief still pressed to his face, climbed into the droshky again and cried out in a despairing voice: 'Let's go!'

'Where?' asked the driver.

'Straight on!'

'Straight on? But it's a dead end here – you can only go right or left.'

This last question made Kovalyov stop and think. In his position the best thing to do was to go first to the City Security Office, not because it was directly connected with the police, but because things got done there much quicker than in any other government department. There was no sense in going for satisfaction direct to the head of the department where the nose claimed to work since anyone could see from the answers he had got before that the nose considered nothing holy and was just as capable now of lying as it had done before, claiming never to have set eyes on him.

So just as Kovalyov was about to tell the driver to go straight to the Security Office, it again struck him that the scoundrel and impostor who had behaved so shamelessly at their first encounter could quite easily take advantage of the delay and slip out of the city, in which event all his efforts to find it would be futile and might even drag on for another month, God forbid. Finally inspiration came from above. He decided to go straight to the newspaper offices and publish an advertisement, giving such a detailed description of the nose that anyone who happened to meet it would at once turn it over to Kovalyov, or at least tell him where he could find it. Deciding this was the best course of action, he ordered the driver to go straight to the newspaper offices and throughout the whole journey never once stopped pummelling the driver in the back with his fist and shouting: 'Faster, damn you, faster!'

'But sir . . .' the driver retorted as he shook his head and flicked his reins at his horse, which had a coat as long as a spaniel's. Finally the droshky came to a halt and the breathless Kovalyov tore into a small waiting-room where a grey-haired bespectacled clerk in an old frock-coat was sitting at a table with his pen between his teeth, counting out copper coins.

'Who sees to advertisements here?' Kovalyov shouted. 'Ah, good morning.'

'Good morning,' replied the grey-haired clerk, raising his eyes for one second, then looking down again at the little piles of money spread out on the table.

'I want to publish an advertisement.'

'Just one moment, if you don't mind,' the clerk answered, as he wrote down a figure with one hand and moved two beads on his abacus with the other.

A footman who, judging by his gold-braided livery and generally very smart appearance, obviously worked in some noble house, was standing by the table holding a piece of paper and, considering it the right thing to display a certain degree of bonhomie, started rattling away:

'Believe me, sir, that nasty little dog just isn't worth eighty copecks. I mean, I wouldn't even give eight for it. But the Countess adores it, just dotes on it she does, and she'll give anyone who finds it a reward of a hundred roubles! If we're going to be honest with one another, I'll tell you quite openly, there's no accounting for taste. I can understand a fancier paying anything up to five hundred, even a thousand for a deerhound or a poodle, as long as it's a good dog.'

The worthy clerk listened to him solemnly while he carried on totting up the words in the advertisement. The room was crowded with old women, salesmen and house-porters, all holding advertisements. In one of these a coachman of 'sober disposition' was seeking employment; in another a carriage, hardly used, and brought from Paris in 1814, was up for sale; in another a nineteen-year-old servant girl, with laundry experience, and

prepared to do *other* work, was looking for a job. Other advertisements offered a droshky for sale – in good condition apart
from one missing spring; a 'young' and spirited dapple-grey
colt seventeen years old; radish and turnip seeds only just
arrived from London; a country house, with every modern
convenience, including stabling for two horses and enough land
for planting an excellent birch or fir forest. And one invited
prospective buyers of old boot soles to attend certain auction
rooms between the hours of eight and three daily. The room
into which all these people were crammed was small and
extremely stuffy. But Collegiate Assessor Kovalyov could not
smell anything as he had covered his face with a handkerchief
– and he could not have smelt anything anyway, as his nose
had disappeared God knows where.

'My dear sir, if I may request your . . . it's really most urgent,'
he said, beginning to lose patience.

'Just a minute, if you *don't* mind! Two roubles forty-three
copecks. Nearly ready. One rouble sixty-four copecks,' the
grey-haired clerk muttered as he shoved pieces of paper at the
old ladies and servants standing around. Finally he turned to
Kovalyov and said: 'What do you want?'

'I want . . .' Kovalyov began. 'Something very fishy's been
going on, whether it's some nasty practical joke or a plain case
of fraud I can't say as yet. All I want you to do is to offer a
substantial reward for the first person to find the black-
guard . . .'

'May I inquire as to your name, sir?'

'Why do you need that? I can't tell you. Too many people
know me – Mrs Chekhtaryev, for example, who's married to a
state counsellor, Mrs Palageya Podtochin, a staff officer's wife
. . . they'd find out who it was at once, God forbid! Just put
"Collegiate Assessor", or even better, "Gentleman holding the
rank of major".'

'And the missing person was a household serf of yours?'

'Household serf? The crime wouldn't be half as serious! It's
my *nose* that's disappeared God knows where.'

'Hm, strange name. And did this Mr Nose steal much?'

'*My* nose, I'm trying to say. You don't understand! It's my own nose that's disappeared. It's a diabolical practical joke someone's played on me.'

'How did it disappear? I don't follow.'

'I can't tell you how. But please understand, my nose is driving at this very moment all over town, calling itself a state counsellor. That's why I'm asking you to print this advertisement announcing the first person who catches it should return the nose to its rightful owner as soon as possible. Imagine what it's like being without such a conspicuous part of your anatomy! If it were just a small toe, then I could put my shoe on and no one would be any the wiser. On Thursdays I go to Mrs Chekhtaryev's (she's married to a state counsellor) and Mrs Podtochin, who has a staff officer for a husband – and a very pretty little daughter as well. Also, they're all very close friends of mine, so just imagine what it would be like . . . In *my* state I can't possibly visit any of them.'

The clerk's tightly pressed lips showed he was deep in thought. 'I can't print an advertisement like that in our paper,' he said after a long silence.

'What? Why not?'

'I'll tell you. A paper can get a bad name. If everyone started announcing his nose had run away, I don't know how it would all end. And enough false reports and rumours get past editorial already . . .'

'But why does it strike you as so absurd? *I* certainly don't think so.'

'That's what *you* think. But only last week there was a similar case. A clerk came here with an advertisement, just like you. It cost him two roubles seventy-three copecks, and all he wanted to advertise was a runaway black poodle. And what do you think he was up to really? In the end we had a libel case on our hands: the poodle was meant as a satire on a government cashier – I can't remember what ministry he came from.'

'But I want to publish an advertisement about my nose, not a poodle, and that's as near myself as dammit!'

'No, I can't accept that kind of advertisement.'

'But I've lost my *nose*!'

'Then you'd better see a doctor about it. I've heard there's a

certain kind of specialist who can fix you up with any kind of
nose you like. Anyway, you seem the cheery sort, and I can see
you like to have your little joke.'

'By all that's holy, I swear I'm telling you the truth. If you
really want me to, I'll *show* you what I mean.'

'I shouldn't bother if I were you,' the clerk continued, taking
a pinch of snuff. 'However, if it's *really* no trouble,' he added,
leaning forward out of curiosity, 'then I shouldn't mind having
a quick look.'

The collegiate assessor removed his handkerchief.

'Well, how very peculiar! It's quite flat, just like a freshly
cooked pancake. Incredibly flat.'

'So much for your objections! Now you've seen it with your
own eyes and you can't possibly refuse. I will be particularly
grateful for this little favour, and I'm delighted that this incident
has afforded me the pleasure of making your acquaintance.'

The major, evidently, had decided that a little toadying might
do the trick.

'Of course, it's no problem *printing* the advertisement,' the
clerk said. 'But I can't see what you can stand to gain by it. If
you like, why not give it to someone with a flair for journalism,
then he can write it up as a very rare freak of nature and have
it published as an article in the *Northern Bee*[10] (here he took
another pinch of snuff) so that young people might benefit from
it (here he wiped his nose). Or else, as something of interest to
the general public.'

The collegiate assessor's hopes were completely dashed. He
looked down at the bottom of the page at the theatre guide.
The name of a rather pretty actress almost brought a smile to
his face, and he reached down to his pocket to see if he had a
five-rouble note, since in his opinion staff officers should sit
only in the stalls. But then he remembered his nose, and knew
he could not possibly think of going to the theatre.

Apparently even the clerk was touched by Kovalyov's terrible
predicament and thought it would not hurt to cheer him up
with a few words of sympathy.

'I deeply regret that such a strange thing has happened to
you. Would you care for a pinch of snuff? It's very good for

headaches – and puts fresh heart into you. It's even good for piles.'

With these words he offered Kovalyov his snuff-box, deftly flipping back the lid which bore a portrait of some lady in a hat.

This unintentionally thoughtless action made Kovalyov lose patience altogether.

'I don't understand how you can joke at a time like this,' he said angrily. 'Are you so blind you can't see that I've nothing to smell with? To hell with your snuff! I can't bear to look at it, and anyway you might at least offer me some real French rappee,[11] not that filthy Berezinsky[12] brand.'

After this declaration he strode furiously out of the newspaper office and went off to the local Inspector of Police (a fanatical lover of sugar whose hall and dining room were crammed full of sugar cubes presented by merchants who wanted to keep well in with him). At that moment the cook was removing the Inspector's regulation jackboots. His sword and all his military trappings were hanging peacefully in the corner and his three-year-old son was already fingering his awesome tricorn. And he himself, after a warrior's life of martial exploits, was now preparing to savour the pleasures of peace. Kovalyov arrived just when he was having a good stretch, grunting, and saying, 'Now for a nice two hours' nap.' Our collegiate assessor had clearly chosen a very bad time for his visit.

The Inspector was a great patron of the arts and industry, but most of all he loved government banknotes. 'There's nothing finer than banknotes,' he used to say. 'They don't need feeding, take up very little room and slip nicely into the pocket. And they don't break if you drop them.'

The Inspector gave Kovalyov a rather cold welcome and said that after dinner wasn't at all the time to start investigations, that Nature herself had decreed a rest after meals (from this our collegiate assessor concluded the Inspector was well versed in the wisdom of antiquity), that *respectable* men do not get their noses ripped off, and that there were no end of majors knocking around who were not too fussy about their underwear and who were in the habit of visiting the most disreputable places.

These few home truths stung Kovalyov to the quick. Here I must point out that Kovalyov was an extremely sensitive man. He did not so much mind people making personal remarks about him, but it was a different matter when aspersions were cast on his rank or social standing.

As far as he was concerned they could say what they liked about subalterns on the stage, but staff officers should be exempt from attack.

The reception given him by the Inspector startled him so much that he shook his head, threw out his arms and said in a dignified voice, 'To be frank, after these remarks of yours, which I find very offensive, I have nothing more to say . . .' and walked out. He arrived home hardly able to feel his feet beneath him. It was already getting dark. After his fruitless inquiries his flat seemed extremely dismal and depressing. As he entered the hall he saw his footman Ivan lying on a soiled leather couch spitting at the ceiling, managing to hit the same spot with a fair degree of success. The nonchalance of the man infuriated him and Kovalyov hit him across the forehead with his hat and said: 'You fat pig! Haven't you anything better to do!'

Ivan promptly jumped up and rushed to take off Kovalyov's coat. Tired and depressed, the major went to his room, threw himself into an armchair and after a few sighs said:

'My God, my God! What have I done to deserve this? If I'd lost an arm or a leg it wouldn't be so bad. Even without any *ears* things wouldn't be very pleasant, but it wouldn't be the end of the world. A man without a nose, though, is God knows what, neither fish nor fowl. Just something to be thrown out of the window. If my nose had been lopped off during the war, or in a duel, at least I might have had some say in the matter. But to lose it for no reason at all and with nothing to show for it, not even a copeck! No, it's absolutely impossible . . . It can't have gone just like that! Never! Must have been a dream, or perhaps I drank some of that vodka I use for rubbing down my beard after shaving instead of water: that idiot Ivan couldn't have put it away and I must have picked it up by mistake.'

To convince himself that he was not in fact drunk the major pinched himself so hard that he cried out in pain, which really did convince him he was awake and in full possession of his senses. He stealthily crept over to the mirror and screwed up his eyes in the hope that his nose would reappear in its proper place, but at once he jumped back, exclaiming:

'That ridiculous blank space again!'

It was absolutely incomprehensible. If a button, or a silver spoon, or his watch, or something of that sort had been missing, that would have been understandable. But for his *nose* to disappear from his own flat ... Major Kovalyov weighed up all the evidence and decided that the most likely explanation of all was that Mrs Podtochin, the staff officer's wife, who wanted to marry off her daughter to him, was to blame, and no one else. In fact he liked chasing after her, but never came to proposing. And when the staff officer's wife told him straight out that she was offering him her daughter's hand, he politely withdrew, excusing himself on the grounds that he was still a young man, and that he wanted to devote another five years to the service, by which time he would be just forty-two. So, to get her revenge, the staff officer's wife must have decided to ruin him and for that purpose had hired some old witches – it was quite inconceivable that his nose had been cut off – no one had visited him in his flat, his barber Ivan Yakovlevich had shaved him only last Wednesday, and the rest of that day and the whole of Thursday his nose had been intact. All this he remembered quite clearly. Moreover, he would have been in pain and the wound could not have healed as flat as a pancake in such a short time. He began planning what to do: either he would sue the staff officer's wife for damages, or he would go and see her personally and accuse her point blank.

But he was distracted from these thoughts by the sight of some chinks of light in the door, which meant Ivan had lit a candle in the hall. Soon afterwards Ivan appeared in person, holding the candle in front of him, so that it brightened up the whole room. Kovalyov's first reaction was to seize his handkerchief and cover up the bare place where only yesterday his nose had been, to stop that stupid man gaping at his master's weird appearance. No sooner had Ivan gone back to his cubby-hole than a strange voice was heard in the hall:

'Does Collegiate Assessor Kovalyov live here?'

'Please come in. The major's home,' said Kovalyov, springing to his feet and opening the door.

A smart-looking police officer, with plump cheeks and whiskers that were neither too light nor too dark – the same police officer who had stood on St Isaac's Bridge at the beginning of our story – made his entrance.

'Are you the gentleman who has lost his nose?'

'Yes, that's me.'

'It's been found.'

'What did you say?' cried Major Kovalyov. He could hardly speak for joy. He looked wide-eyed at the police officer, the candle-light flickering on his fat cheeks and thick lips.

'How did you find it?'

'Very strange. We intercepted it just as it was boarding the stagecoach bound for Riga. Its passport was made out in the name of some civil servant. Strangely enough, I mistook it for a gentleman at first. Fortunately I had my spectacles with me so I could see it was really a nose. I'm very short-sighted, and if you happen to stand just in front of me, I can only make out your face, but not your nose, or beard, or anything else in fact. My mother-in-law (that's to say, on my *wife's* side) suffers from the same complaint.'

Kovalyov was beside himself.

'Where is it? I'll go right away to claim it.'

'Don't excite yourself, sir. I knew how much you wanted it back, so I've brought it with me. Very strange, but the main culprit in this little affair seems to be that swindler of a barber from Voznesensky Street: he's down at the station now. I've had my eyes on him a long time now on suspicion of drunkenness and larceny, and only the day before yesterday he was found stealing a dozen buttons from a shop. You'll find your nose just as it was when you lost it.'

And the police officer dipped into his pocket and pulled out the nose wrapped up in a piece of paper.

'That's it!' cried Kovalyov, 'no mistake! You *must* stay and have a cup of tea with me.'

'That would give me great pleasure, but I just couldn't. From here I have to go direct to the House of Correction ... The price of food has rocketed ... My mother-in-law (on my *wife's* side) is living with me, and all the children as well; the eldest boy seems very promising, very bright, but we haven't the money to send him to school ...'

Kovalyov guessed what he was after and took a note from the table and pressed it into the officer's hands. The police officer bowed very low and went out into the street, and almost simultaneously Kovalyov could hear him telling some stupid peasant who had driven his cart up on the pavement what he thought of him.

When the police officer had gone, our collegiate assessor felt rather bemused and only after a few minutes did he come to his senses at all, so intense and unexpected was the joy he felt. He carefully took the nose in his cupped hands and once more subjected it to close scrutiny.

'Yes, that's it, that's it!' Major Kovalyov said, 'and there's the pimple that came up yesterday on the left-hand side.' The major almost laughed with joy.

But nothing is lasting in this world. Even joy begins to fade after only one minute. Two minutes later, and it is weaker still, until finally it is swallowed up in our everyday, prosaic state of mind, just as a ripple made by a pebble gradually merges with the smooth surface of the water. After some thought Kovalyov concluded that all was not right: yes – the nose had been found but there still remained the problem of putting it back in place.

'What if it doesn't stick?'

And this question which he now asked himself made the major turn pale.

With a feeling of inexpressible horror he rushed to the table, and pulled the mirror nearer, as he was afraid that he might stick the nose on crooked. His hands trembled. With great care and caution he pushed it into place. But oh! the nose just would not stick. He warmed it a little by pressing it to his mouth and breathing on it, and then pressed it again to the smooth space between his cheeks. But try as he might the nose would not stay on.

'Come on now – stay on, you fool!' he said. But the nose

seemed to be made of wood and fell on to the table with a strange cork-like sound. The major's face quivered convulsively. 'Perhaps I can graft it,' he said apprehensively. But no matter how many times he tried to put it back, all his efforts were futile.

He called Ivan and told him to fetch the doctor, who happened to live in the same block, in the best flat, on the first floor.

This doctor was a handsome man with fine whiskers as black as pitch, and a fresh-looking, healthy wife. Every morning he used to eat apples and was terribly meticulous about keeping his mouth clean, spending at least three quarters of an hour rinsing it out every day and using five different varieties of toothbrush to polish his teeth. He came right away. When he had asked the major if he had had this trouble for very long the doctor lifted Major Kovalyov's head by the chin and prodded him with his thumb in the spot once occupied by his nose – so sharply that the major hit the wall very hard with the back of his head. The doctor told him not to worry and made him stand a little way from the wall and lean his head first to the right. Pinching the place where his nose had been the doctor said 'Hm!' Then he ordered him to move his head to the left and produced another 'Hm!' Finally he prodded him again, making Kovalyov's head twitch like a horse having its teeth inspected.

After this examination the doctor shook his head and said: 'It's no good. It's best to stay as you are, otherwise you'll only make it worse. Of course, it's possible to have it stuck on, and I could do this for you quite easily. But I assure you it would look terrible.'

'That's *marvellous*, that is! How can I carry on without a nose?' said Kovalyov. 'Things can't get any worse! The devil knows what's going on! How can I go around looking like a freak? I mix with nice people. I'm expected at two soirées today. I know nearly all the best people – Mrs Chekhtaryev, a state counsellor's wife, Mrs Podtochin, a staff officer's wife . . . after the way *she's* behaved I won't have any more to do with *her*, except when I get the police on her trail.' Kovalyov went on pleading: 'Please do me this one favour – isn't there *any* way?

Even if you only get it to hold on, it wouldn't be so bad, and if there were any risk of it falling off, I could keep it there with my hand. I don't dance, which is a help, because any violent movement might make it drop off. And you may rest assured I wouldn't be slow in showing my appreciation – as far as my pocket will allow of course . . .'

The doctor then said in a voice which could not be called loud, or even soft, but persuasive and arresting: 'I never practise my art from purely mercenary motives. That is contrary to my code of conduct and all professional ethics. True, I make a charge for private visits, but only so as not to offend patients by refusing to take their money. Of course, I could put your nose back if I wanted to. But I give you my word of honour, if you know what's good for you, it would be far worse if I tried. Let nature take its course. Wash the area as much as you can with cold water and believe me you'll feel just as good as when you had a nose. Now, as far as the nose is concerned, put it in a jar of alcohol; better still, soak it in two tablespoonsful of sour vodka and warmed-up vinegar, and you'll get good money for it. I'll take it myself if you don't want it.'

'No! I wouldn't sell it for anything,' Kovalyov cried desperately. 'I'd rather lose it again.'

'Then I'm sorry,' replied the doctor, bowing himself out. 'I wanted to help you . . . at least I've tried hard enough.'

With these words the doctor made a very dignified exit. Kovalyov did not even look at his face, and felt so dazed that all he could make out were the doctor's snowy-white cuffs sticking out from the sleeves of his black dress-coat.

The very next day he decided – before going to the police – to write to the staff officer's wife to ask her to put back in its proper place what belonged to him, without further ado. The letter read as follows:

Dear Mrs Alexandra Grigoryevna,

I cannot understand this strange behaviour on your part. You can be sure, though, that it won't get you anywhere and you certainly won't force me to marry your daughter. Moreover, you can rest assured that, regarding my nose, I am familiar with the whole history of this affair from the very beginning, and I also know that you, and no one else, are the prime instigator. Its sudden detachment from its rightful place, its subsequent flight, its masquerading as a civil servant and then its re-appearance in its natural state, are nothing else than the result of black magic carried out by yourself or by those practising the same very honourable art. I consider it my duty to warn you that if the above-mentioned nose is not back in its proper place by today, then I shall be compelled to ask for the law's protection.

 I remain, dear Madam,

Your very faithful servant,

Platon Kovalyov.

Dear Mr Kovalyov!

 I was simply staggered by your letter. To be honest, I never expected anything of this kind from you, particularly those remarks which are quite uncalled-for. I would have you know I have never received that civil servant mentioned by you in my house, whether disguised or not. True, Philip Ivanovich Potanchikov used to call. Although he wanted to ask for my daughter's hand, and despite the fact that he was a very sober, respectable and learned gentleman, I never gave him any cause for hope. And then you go on to mention your nose. If by this you mean to say I wanted to make you look foolish,[13] that is, to put you off with a formal refusal, then all I can say is that I am very surprised that you can talk like this, as you know well enough my feelings on the matter are quite different. And if you care to make an official proposal to my daughter, I will gladly give my consent, for this has always been my dearest wish, and in this hope I am always at your disposal.

Yours sincerely,

Alexandra Podtochin.

'No,' said Kovalyov when he had read the letter. 'She's not to blame. Impossible! A guilty person could never write a letter like that.' The collegiate assessor knew what he was talking about in this case as he had been sent to the Caucasus several times to carry out legal inquiries. 'How on earth did this happen then? It's impossible to make head or tail of it!' he said, letting his arms drop to his side.

Meanwhile rumours about the strange occurrence had spread throughout the capital, not, need we say, without a few embellishments. At the time everyone seemed very preoccupied with the supernatural: only a short time before, some experiments in magnetism had been all the rage. Besides, the story of the dancing chairs in Konyushenny Street[14] was still fresh in people's minds, so no one was particularly surprised to hear about Collegiate Assessor Kovalyov's nose taking a regular stroll along Nevsky Prospekt at exactly three o'clock every afternoon. Every day crowds of inquisitive people flocked there. Someone said they had seen the nose in Junker's Store and this produced such a crush outside that the police had to be called.

One fairly respectable-looking, bewhiskered entrepreneur, who sold stale cakes outside the theatre, knocked together some handsome, solid-looking wooden benches, and hired them out at eighty copecks a time for the curious to stand on.

One retired colonel left home especially early one morning and after a great struggle managed to barge his way through to the front. But to his great annoyance, instead of a nose in the shop window, all he could see was an ordinary woollen jersey and a lithograph showing a girl adjusting her stocking while a dandy with a small beard and cutaway waistcoat peered out at her from behind a tree – a picture which had hung there in that identical spot for more than ten years. He left feeling very cross and was heard to say: 'Misleading the public with such ridiculous and far-fetched stories shouldn't be allowed.'

Afterwards it was rumoured that Major Kovalyov's nose was no longer to be seen strolling along Nevsky Prospekt but was in the habit of walking in Tavrichesky Park[15] and that it had been doing this for some time. When Khozrev-Mirza[16] lived there, he was astonished at this freak of nature. Some of the students from the College of Surgeons went to have a look. One well-known, very respectable lady wrote specially to the head park-keeper, asking him to show her children this very rare phenomenon and, if possible, give them an instructive and edifying commentary at the same time.

These events came as a blessing to those socialites (indispensable for any successful party) who loved amusing the ladies and whose stock of stories was completely exhausted at the time.

A few respectable and high-minded citizens were very upset. One indignant gentleman said that he was at a loss to understand how such absurd cock-and-bull stories could gain currency in the present enlightened century, and that the complete indifference shown by the authorities was past comprehension. Clearly this gentleman was the type who likes to make the government responsible for everything, even their daily quarrels with their wives. And afterwards . . . but here again the whole incident becomes enveloped in mist and what happened later remains a complete mystery.

3

This world is full of the most outrageous nonsense. Sometimes things happen which you would hardly think possible: that very same nose, which had paraded itself as a state counsellor and created such an uproar in the city, suddenly turned up, as if nothing had happened, in its rightful place, that is, between Major Kovalyov's two cheeks. This was on 7 April. He woke up and happened to glance at the mirror – there was his nose! He grabbed it with his hand to make sure – but there was no doubt this time. 'Aha!' cried Kovalyov, and if Ivan hadn't come in at that very moment, he would have joyfully danced a trepak round the room in his bare feet.

He ordered some soap and water to be brought right away, and as he washed himself looked into the mirror again: the nose was there. He had another look as he dried himself – yes, the nose was still there!

'Look, Ivan, I think I've got a pimple on my nose.'

Kovalyov thought: 'God, supposing he replies: "Not only is there no pimple, but no nose either!"' But Ivan answered: 'Your nose is quite all right, sir, I can't see any pimple.'

'Thank God for that,' the major said to himself and clicked his fingers.

At this moment Ivan Yakovlevich the barber poked his head round the corner, but timidly this time, like a cat which had just been beaten for stealing fat.

. 'Before you start, are your hands clean?' Kovalyov shouted from the other side of the room.

'Perfectly clean.'

'You're lying.'

'On my life, sir, they're clean!'

'Well, they'd better be!'

Kovalyov sat down. Ivan Yakovlevich covered him with a towel and in a twinkling, with the help of his shaving brush, had transformed his whole beard and part of his cheeks into the kind of cream served up at merchants' birthday parties.

'Well, I'll be damned,' Ivan Yakovlevich muttered to himself, staring at the nose. He bent Kovalyov's head to one side and looked at him from a different angle. 'That's *it* all right! You'd never credit it . . .' he continued and contemplated the nose for a long time. Finally, ever so gently, with a delicacy that the reader can best imagine, he lifted two fingers to hold the nose by its tip. This was how Ivan Yakovlevich normally shaved his customers.

'Come on now, and mind what you're doing!' shouted Kovalyov. Ivan Yakovlevich let his arms fall to his side and stood there more frightened and embarrassed than he had ever been in his life. At last he started tickling Kovalyov carefully under the chin with his razor. And although with only his olfactory organ to hold on to without any other means of support made shaving very awkward, by planting his rough, wrinkled thumb on his cheek and lower gum (in this way gaining some sort of leverage) he finally succeeded in overcoming all obstacles.

When everything was ready, Kovalyov rushed to get dressed and took a cab straight to the café. He had hardly got inside before he shouted, 'Waiter, a cup of chocolate,' and went straight up to the mirror. Yes, his nose was there! Gaily he turned round, screwed up his eyes and looked superciliously at two soldiers, one of whom had a nose no bigger than a *waistcoat* button. Then he went off to the ministerial department where he was petitioning for a vice-governorship. (Failing this he was going to try for an administrative post.) As he crossed the entrance hall he had another look in the mirror: his nose was still there!

Then he went to see another collegiate assessor (or major), a great wag whose sly digs Kovalyov used to counter by saying: 'I'm used to your quips by now, you old niggler!'

On the way he thought: 'If the major doesn't split his sides when he sees me, that's a sure sign everything is in its proper place.' But the collegiate assessor did not pass any remarks. 'That's all right then, dammit!' thought Kovalyov. In the street he met Mrs Podtochin, the staff officer's wife, who was with her daughter, and they replied to his bow with delighted exclamations: clearly, he had suffered no lasting injury. He had a long chat with them, made a point of taking out his snuff-box, and stood there for ages ostentatiously stuffing both nostrils as he murmured to himself: 'That'll teach you, you old hens! And I'm not going to marry your daughter, simply *par amour*, as they say! If you *don't* mind!'

And from that time onwards Major Kovalyov was able to stroll along Nevsky Prospekt, visit the theatre, in fact go everywhere as though absolutely nothing had happened. And, as though absolutely nothing *had* happened, his nose stayed in the middle of his face and showed no signs of absenting itself. After that he was in perpetual high spirits, always smiling, chasing all the pretty girls, and on one occasion even stopping at a small shop in the Gostiny Dvor[17] to buy ribbon for some medal, no one knows why, as he did not belong to any order of knighthood.

And all this took place in the northern capital of our vast empire! Only now, after much reflection, can we see that there is a great deal that is very far-fetched in this story. Apart from the fact that it's *highly* unlikely for a nose to disappear in such a fantastic way and then reappear in various parts of the town dressed as a state counsellor, it is hard to believe that Kovalyov was so ignorant as to think newspapers would accept advertisements about noses. I'm not saying I consider such an advertisement too expensive and a waste of money: that's nonsense, and what's more, I don't think I'm a mercenary person. But it's all very nasty, not quite the thing at all, and it makes me feel very awkward! And, come to think of it, how *did* the nose manage to turn up in a loaf of bread, and how *did* Ivan Yakovlevich . . . ? No, I don't understand it, not one bit! But the strangest, most incredible thing of all is that authors should write about such things. That, I confess, is beyond my comprehension. It's just . . . no, no, I don't understand it at all! Firstly, it's no use to the country whatsoever; secondly – but even then it's no use either . . . I simply don't know *what* one can make of it . . . However, when all is said and done, one can concede this point or the other and perhaps you can even find . . . well then you won't find much that *isn't* on the absurd side *somewhere*, will you?

And yet, if you stop to think for a moment, there's a grain of truth in it. Whatever you may say, these things do happen in this world – rarely, I admit, but they do happen.

THE OVERCOAT

In one of our government departments ... but perhaps I had better not say exactly *which* one. For no one's more touchy than people in government departments, regiments, chancelleries or, in short, *any* kind of official body. Nowadays every private citizen thinks the whole of society is insulted when he himself is. They say that not so long ago a complaint was lodged by a district police inspector (I cannot remember which town he came from) and in this he made it quite plain that the state and all its laws were going to rack and ruin, and that his own holy name had been taken in vain without any shadow of doubt. To substantiate his claim he appended as supplementary evidence an absolutely enormous tome, containing a highly romantic composition, in which nearly every ten pages a police commissioner made an appearance, sometimes even in an inebriated state. And so, to avoid any *further* unpleasantness, we had better call the department in question *a certain department*.

In a certain department, then, there worked *a certain civil servant*. On no account could he be said to have a memorable appearance; he was shortish, rather pockmarked, with reddish hair, and also had weak eyesight, or so it seemed. He had a small bald patch in front and both cheeks were wrinkled. His complexion was the sort you might call haemorrhoidal ... but there's nothing anyone can do about that: the Petersburg climate is to blame.

As for his rank in the civil service[1] (this must be determined before we go any further) he belonged to the species known as eternal titular counsellor, for far too long now, as we all know, mocked and jeered by certain writers with the very commendable habit of attacking those who are in no position to retaliate. His surname was Bashmachkin, which all too plainly was at some time derived from *bashmak*.[2]

But exactly when and what time of day and how the name originated is a complete mystery. Both his father and his grandfather, and even his brother-in-law and all the other Bashmachkins, went around in boots and had them soled only three times a year. His name was Akaky Akakievich. This may appear an odd name to our reader and somewhat far-fetched, but we can assure him that no one went out of his way to find it, and that the way things turned out he just could not have been called *anything* else. This is how it all happened: Akaky Akakievich was born on the night of 22 March, if my memory serves me right. His late mother, the wife of a civil servant and a very fine woman, made all the necessary arrangements for the christening. At the time she was still lying in her bed, facing the door, and on her right stood the godfather, Ivan Ivanovich Yeroshkin, a most excellent gentleman who was a chief clerk in the Senate, and the godmother, Arina Semyonovna Belobrushkova, the wife of a district police inspector and a woman of the rarest virtue. The mother was offered a choice of three names: Mokkia, Sossia or Khozdazat, after the martyr. 'Oh no,' his mother thought, 'such awful names they're going in for these days!' To try and please her they turned over a few pages in the calendar[3] and again three peculiar names popped up: Triphily, Dula and Varakhasy. 'It's sheer punishment sent from above!' the woman muttered. 'What names! For the life of me, I've never seen anything like them. Varadat or Varukh wouldn't be so bad but as for Triphily and Varakhasy!' They turned over yet another page and found Pavsikakhy and Vakhtisy. 'Well, it's plain enough that this is fate. So we'd better call him after his father. He was an Akaky, so let's call his son Akaky as well.' And that was how he became Akaky Akakievich. The child was christened and during the ceremony he burst into tears and made such a face it was plain that he knew there and then that he was fated to be a titular counsellor. So, that's how it all came about. The reason for all this narrative is to enable our reader to judge for himself that the whole train of events was absolutely

predetermined and that for Akaky to have any other name was
quite impossible.

Exactly *when* he entered the department, and who was
responsible for the appointment, no one can say for sure. No
matter how many directors and principals came and went, he
was always to be seen in precisely the same place, sitting in
exactly the same position, doing exactly the same work – just
routine copying, pure and simple. Subsequently everyone came
to believe that he had come into this world already equipped
for his job, complete with uniform and bald patch. No one
showed him the least respect in the office. The porters not only
remained seated when he went by, but they did not so much as
give him a look – as though a common housefly had just flown
across the waiting-room. His superiors treated him icily and
despotically. Some assistant to the head clerk would shove some
papers right under his nose, without even so much as a 'Please
copy this out', or 'Here's an interesting little job', or some
pleasant remark you might expect to hear in refined establish-
ments. He would take whatever was put in front of him without
looking up to see who had put it there or questioning whether
he had any right to do so, his eyes fixed only on his work. He
would simply take the documents and immediately start copying them out. The junior clerks laughed and told jokes at his
expense – as far as office wit would stretch – telling stories they
had made up themselves, even while they were standing right
next to him, about his seventy-year-old landlady, for example,
who used to beat him, or so they said. They would ask when
the wedding was going to be and shower his head with little
bits of paper, calling them snow.

But Akaky Akakievich did not make the slightest protest, just
as though there were nobody there at all. His work was not
even affected and he never copied out one wrong letter in
the face of all this annoyance. Only if the jokes became too
unbearable – when somebody jogged his elbow, for example,
and stopped him from working – would he say: 'Leave me
alone, why do you have to torment me?' There was something
strange in these words and the way he said them. His voice had
a peculiar sound which made you feel sorry for him, so much

so that one clerk who was new to the department, and who was about to follow the example of the others and have a good laugh at him, suddenly stopped dead in his tracks, as though transfixed, and from that time onwards everything seemed to have changed for him and now appeared in a different light. Some kind of supernatural power alienated him from his colleagues whom, on first acquaintance, he had taken to be respectable, civilized men. And for a long time afterwards, even during his gayest moments, he would see that stooping figure with a bald patch in front, muttering pathetically: 'Leave me alone, why do you have to torment me?' And in these piercing words he could hear the sound of others: 'I am your brother.' The poor young man would bury his face in his hands and many times later in life shuddered at the thought of how brutal men could be and how the most refined manners and breeding often concealed the most savage coarseness, even, dear God, in someone universally recognized for his honesty and uprightness . . .

One would be hard put to find a man anywhere who so lived for his work. To say he worked with zeal would be an understatement: no, he worked *with love*. In that copying of his he glimpsed a whole varied and pleasant world of his own. One could see the enjoyment on his face. Some letters were his favourites, and whenever he came to write them out he would be beside himself with excitement, softly laughing to himself and winking, willing his pen on with his lips, so you could tell what letter his pen was carefully tracing, so it seemed, just by looking at him. Had his rewards been at all commensurate with his enthusiasm, he might perhaps have been promoted to state counsellor,[4] much to his own surprise. But as the wags in the office put it, all he got for his labour was a badge in his buttonhole and piles in his posterior. However, you could not say he was *completely* ignored. One of the directors, a kindly gentleman, who wished to reward him for his long service, once ordered him to be given something rather more important than ordinary copying – the preparation of a report for another department from a completed file. All this entailed was altering the title page and changing a few verbs from the first to the third person. This caused him so much trouble that he broke out in a sweat, kept mopping his brow, and finally said: 'No, you'd better let me stick to plain copying.' After that they left him to go on copying for ever and ever. Apart from this copying nothing else existed as far as he was concerned. He gave no thought at all to his clothes: his uniform was not what you might call green, but a mealy white tinged with red.

His collar was very short and narrow, so that his neck, which could not exactly be called long, appeared to stick out for miles, like those plaster kittens with wagging heads foreign street-pedlars carry around by the dozen. Something was always sure to be sticking to his uniform – a wisp of hay or piece of thread. What is more, he had the strange knack of passing underneath windows when walking down the street just as some rubbish was being emptied and this explained why he was perpetually carrying around scraps of melon rind and similar refuse on his hat. Not once in his life did he notice what was going on in the street he passed down every day, unlike his young colleagues in the Service, who are famous for their hawk-like eyes – eyes so sharp that they can even see whose trouser-strap has come undone on the other side of the pavement, something which never fails to bring a sly grin to their faces. But even if Akaky Akakievich did happen to notice something, all he ever saw were rows of letters in his own neat, regular handwriting.

Only if a horse's muzzle appeared from out of nowhere, propped itself on his shoulder and fanned his cheek with a gust from its nostrils – only then did he realize he was not in the middle of a sentence but in the middle of the street.[5] As soon as he got home he would sit down at the table, quickly swallow his cabbage soup, and eat some beef and onions, tasting absolutely nothing and gulping everything down, together with whatever the Good Lord happened to provide at the time, flies included. When he saw that his stomach was beginning to swell he would get up from the table, fetch his inkwell and start copying out documents he had brought home with him. If he had no work from the office, he would copy out something else, just for his own personal pleasure – especially if the document in question happened to be remarkable not for its stylistic beauty, but because it was addressed to some newly appointed or important person.

Even at that time of day when the light has completely faded from the grey St Petersburg sky and the whole clerical brotherhood has eaten its fill, according to salary and palate; when everyone has rested from departmental pen-pushing and running around; when his own and everyone else's absolutely indispensable labours have been forgotten – as well as all those other things that restless man sets himself to do of his own free will – sometimes even more than is really necessary; when the civil servant dashes off to enjoy his remaining hours of freedom as much as he can (one showing a more daring spirit by careering off to the theatre; another sauntering down the street to spend his time looking at cheap little hats in the shop windows; another going off to a party to waste his time flattering a pretty girl, the shining light of some small circle of civil servants; while another – and this happens more often than not – goes off to visit a friend from the office living on the third or second floor, in two small rooms with hall and kitchen, and with some pretensions to fashion in the form of a lamp or some little trifle which has cost a great many sacrifices, refusals to invitations to dinner or country outings); in short, at that time of day when all the civil servants have dispersed to their friends' little flats for a game of whist, sipping tea from glasses and nibbling little biscuits, drawing on their long pipes, and giving an account while dealing out the cards of the latest scandal which had wafted down from high society – a Russian can *never* resist stories; or when there is nothing new to talk about, retelling the age-old anecdote about the Commandant who was told that the tail of the horse in Falconet's statue[6] of Peter the Great had been cut off; briefly, even when everyone was doing his best to amuse himself, Akaky Akakievich did not abandon himself to any such pleasures.

No one could remember ever having seen him at a party. After he had copied to his heart's content he would go to bed, smiling in anticipation of the next day and what God would send him to copy. So passed the uneventful life of a man who, on a salary of four hundred roubles, was perfectly happy with his lot; and this life might have continued to pass peacefully until ripe old age had it not been for the various calamities that lie in wait not only for titular counsellors, but even privy, state, court and all types of counsellor, even those who give advice to no one, nor take it from anyone.

St Petersburg harbours one terrible enemy of all those earning four hundred roubles a year – or thereabouts. This enemy is nothing else than our northern frost, although some people say it is very good for the health. Between eight and nine in the morning, just when the streets are crowded with civil servants on their way to the office, it starts dealing out indiscriminately such sharp nips to noses of every description that the poor clerks just do not know where to put them.

At this time of day, when the foreheads of even important officials ache from the frost and tears well up in their eyes, the humbler titular counsellors are sometimes quite defenceless. Their only salvation lies in running the length of five or six streets in their thin, wretched little overcoats and then having a really good stamp in the lobby until their faculties and capacity for office work have thawed out. For some time now Akaky Akakievich had been feeling that his back and shoulders had become subject to really vicious onslaughts no matter how fast he tried to sprint the official distance between home and office. At length he began to wonder if his overcoat might not be at fault here.

After giving it a thorough examination at home he found that in two or three places – to be exact, on the back and round the shoulders – it now resembled coarse cheesecloth: the material had worn so thin that it was almost transparent and the lining had fallen to pieces.

At this point it should be mentioned that Akaky Akakievich's coat was a standing joke in the office. It had been deprived of the status of overcoat and was called a dressing-gown instead. And there was really something very strange in the way it was made. As the years went by the collar had shrunk more and more, as the cloth from it had been used to patch up other parts. This repair work showed no sign of a tailor's hand, and made the coat look baggy and most unsightly. When he realized what was wrong, Akaky Akakievich decided he would have to take the overcoat to Petrovich, a tailor living somewhere on the third floor up some backstairs and who, in spite of being blind in one eye and having pockmarks all over his face, carried on quite a nice little business repairing civil servants' and other gentlemen's trousers and frock-coats, whenever – it goes without saying – he was sober and was not hatching some plot in that head of his.

Of course, there is not much point in wasting our time describing this tailor, but since it has become the accepted thing to give full details about every single character in a story, there is nothing for it but to take a look at this man Petrovich.

At first he was simply called Grigory and had been a serf belonging to some gentleman or other. People started calling him Petrovich after he had gained his freedom, from which time he began to drink rather heavily on every church holiday – at first only on the most important feast-days, but later on every single holiday marked by a cross in the calendar.[7] In this respect he was faithful to ancestral tradition, and when he had rows about this with his wife he called her a worldly woman and a German.

As we have now brought his wife up we might as well say a couple of words about her. Unfortunately, little is known of her except that she was Petrovich's wife and she wore a bonnet instead of a shawl. Apparently she had nothing to boast about as far as looks were concerned. At least only *guardsmen* were ever known to peep even under her bonnet as they tweaked their moustaches and made a curious noise in their throats.

As he made his way up the stairs to Petrovich's (these stairs, to describe them accurately, were running with water and slops, and were anointed with that strong smell of spirit which makes the eyes smart and is a perpetual feature of all backstairs in Petersburg), Akaky Akakievich was already beginning to wonder how much Petrovich would charge and had made up his mind not to pay more than two roubles. The door had been left open as his wife had been frying some kind of fish and had made so much smoke in the kitchen that not even the cockroaches were visible.

Mrs Petrovich herself failed to notice Akaky Akakievich as he walked through the kitchen and finally entered a room where Petrovich was squatting on a broad, bare wooden table, his feet crossed under him like a Turkish Pasha. As is customary with tailors, he was working in bare feet. The first thing that struck Akaky was his familiar big toe with its deformed nail, thick and hard as tortoiseshell. A skein of silk and some thread hung round his neck and some old rags lay across his lap. For the past two or three minutes he had been trying to thread a needle without any success, which made him curse the poor light and even the thread itself. He grumbled under his breath: 'Why don't you go through, you swine! You'll be the death of me, you devil!'

Akaky Akakievich was not very pleased at finding Petrovich in such a temper: his real intention had been to place an order with Petrovich after he had been on the bottle, or, as his wife put it, 'after he'd bin swigging that corn brandy again, the old one-eyed devil!'

In this state Petrovich would normally be very amenable, invariably agreeing to any price quite willingly and even concluding the deal by bowing and saying thank you. It is true that afterwards his tearful wife would come in with the same sad story that that husband of hers was drunk again and had not charged enough. But even so, for another copeck or two the deal was usually settled. But at this moment Petrovich was (or so it seemed) quite sober, and as a result was gruff, intractable and in the right mood for charging the devil's own price. Realizing this, Akaky Akakievich was all for making himself scarce, as the saying goes, but by then it was too late. Petrovich had already screwed up his one eye and was squinting steadily at him. Akaky Akakievich found himself saying:

'Good morning, Petrovich!'

'Good morning to you, sir,' said Petrovich, staring at Akaky's hand to see what kind of booty he'd brought.

'I . . . er . . . came about that . . . Petrovich.'

The reader should know that Akaky Akakievich spoke mainly in prepositions, adverbs and resorted to parts of speech which had no meaning whatsoever. If the subject was particu-

larly complicated he would even leave whole sentences unfinished, so that very often he would begin with: 'That is really
exactly what . . .' and then forget to say anything more, convinced that he had said what he wanted to.

'What on earth's that?' Petrovich said, inspecting with his
solitary eye every part of Akaky's uniform, beginning with the
collar and sleeves, then the back, tails and buttonholes. All of
this was very familiar territory, as it was his own work, but
every tailor usually carries out this sort of inspection when he
has a customer.

'I've er . . . come . . . Petrovich, that overcoat you know, the
cloth . . . you see, it's quite strong in other places, only a little
dusty. This makes it look old, but in fact it's quite new. Just a
bit . . . you know . . . on the back and a little worn on one
shoulder, and a bit . . . you know, on the other, that's all. Only
a small job . . .'

Petrovich took the 'dressing-gown', spread it out on the table,
took a long look at it, shook his head, reached out to the
window sill for his round snuff-box bearing the portrait of
some general – exactly which one is hard to say, as someone
had poked his finger through the place where his face should
have been and it was pasted over with a square piece of paper.

Petrovich took a pinch of snuff, held the coat up to the light,
gave it another thorough scrutiny and shook his head again.
Then he placed it with the lining upwards, shook his head once
more, removed the snuff-box lid with the pasted-over general,
filled his nose with snuff, replaced the lid, put the box away
somewhere, and finally said: 'No, I can't mend that. It's in a
terrible state!'

With these words Akaky Akakievich's heart sank.

'And why not, Petrovich?' he asked almost in the imploring
voice of a child. 'It's only a bit worn on the shoulders. After
all, you could patch it up with a few scraps of cloth.'

'I've got plenty of patches, plenty,' said Petrovich, 'But there's
nothing to sew them on to. The coat's absolutely rotten. It'll
fall to pieces if you so much as touch it with a needle.'

'Well, if it falls to bits you can patch it up again.'

'But it's too far gone. There's nothing for the patches to hold on to – it's all worn terribly thin. You can hardly call it cloth any more. One gust of wind and the whole lot will blow away.'

'But patch it up just a *little*. It can't, hm, be, well . . .'

'I'm afraid it can't be done, sir,' replied Petrovich firmly. 'It's too far gone. You'd be better off if you cut it up for the winter and made some leggings with it, because socks aren't any good in the really cold weather. The Germans invented them as they thought they could make money out of them.' (Petrovich liked to have a dig at Germans.) 'As for the coat, you'll have to have a *new* one, sir.'

The word 'new' made Akaky's eyes cloud over and everything in the room began to swim round. All he could see clearly was the pasted-over face of the general on Petrovich's snuff-box.

'What do you mean, a *new* one?' he said as though in a dream. 'I've got no money for that.'

'Yes, you'll have to have a new one,' Petrovich said in a cruelly detached voice.

'Well, um, if I had a *new* one, how would, I mean to say, er . . . ?'

'You mean, how much?'

'Yes.'

'You can reckon on three fifty-rouble notes or more,' said Petrovich pressing his lips together dramatically. He had a great liking for strong dramatic effects, and loved producing some remark intended to shock and then watching the expression on the other person's face out of the corner of his eye.

'A hundred and fifty roubles for an overcoat!' poor Akaky shrieked for what was perhaps the first time in his life – he was well known for his low voice.

'Yes, sir,' said Petrovich. 'And even then it wouldn't be much to write home about. If you want a collar made from marten fur and a silk-lined hood then it could set you back as much as two hundred.'

'Petrovich, please,' said Akaky imploringly, not hearing, or at least trying not to hear, Petrovich's 'dramatic' pronouncement, 'just do what you can with it, so I can wear it a little longer.'

'I'm afraid it's no good. It would be sheer waste of time and money,' Petrovich added, and with these words Akaky left, feeling absolutely crushed.

After he had gone Petrovich stayed squatting where he was for some time without continuing his work, his lips pressed together significantly. He felt pleased he had not cheapened himself or the rest of the sartorial profession.

Out in the street Akaky felt as if he were in a dream. 'What a to-do now,' he said to himself. 'I never thought it would turn out like this, for the life of me . . .' And then, after a brief silence, he added: 'Well now then! So this is how it's turned out and I would never have guessed it would end . . .' Whereupon followed a long silence, after which he murmured: 'So that's it! Really, to tell the truth, it's so unexpected that I never would have . . . such a to-do!' When he had said this, instead of going home, he walked straight off in the opposite direction, quite oblivious of what he was doing. On the way a chimney-sweep brushed up against him and made his shoulder black all over. And then a whole hatful of lime fell on him from the top of a house that was being built. To this he was blind as well; and only when he happened to bump into a policeman who had propped his halberd up and was sprinkling some snuff he had taken from a small horn on to his wart-covered fist did he come to his senses at all, and only then because the policeman said:

'Isn't the pavement wide enough without you having to crawl right up my nose?'

This brought Akaky to his senses and he went off in the direction of home.

Not until he was there did he begin to collect his thoughts and properly assess the situation. He started talking to himself, not in incoherent phrases, but quite rationally and openly, as though he were discussing what had happened with a sensible friend in whom one could confide when it came to matters of the greatest intimacy.

'No, I can see it's impossible to talk to Petrovich now. He's a bit . . . and it looks as if his wife's been knocking him around. I'd better wait until Sunday morning: after he's slept off Saturday night he'll start his squinting again and will be dying for a drink to see him through his hangover. But his wife won't give him any money, so I'll turn up with a copeck or two. That will soften him up, you know, and my overcoat . . .'

Akaky Akakievich felt greatly comforted by this fine piece of reasoning, and waiting for the next Sunday and after seeing from a distance that Petrovich's wife had left the house, he went straight off to see him. Just as he had expected, after Saturday night, Petrovich's eye really was squinting for all it was worth, and there he was, his head drooping towards the floor, and looking very sleepy. All the same, as soon as he realized why Akaky had come, he became wide awake, just as though the devil had given him a sharp kick.

'It's impossible, you'll have to have a new one.' At this point Akaky Akakievich shoved a ten-copeck piece into his hand.

'Much obliged, sir. I'll have a quick pick-me-up on you,' said Petrovich. 'And I shouldn't worry about that overcoat of yours if I were you. It's no good at all. I'll make you a *marvellous* new one, so let's leave it at that.'

Akaky Akakievich tried to say something about having it repaired, but Petrovich pretended not to hear and said:

'Don't worry, I'll make you a brand-new one, you can depend on me to make a good job of it. And I might even get some silver clasps for the collar, like they're all wearing now.'

Now Akaky Akakievich realized he would *have* to buy a new overcoat and his heart sank. Where in fact was the money coming from? Of course he could just about count on that holiday bonus. But this had been put aside for something else a long time ago. He needed new trousers, and then there was that long-standing debt to be settled with the shoemaker for putting some new tops on his old boots. And there were three shirts he had to order from the seamstress, as well as two items of underwear which cannot decently be mentioned in print. To cut a long story short, all his money was bespoken and he would not have enough even if the Director were so generous as to raise his bonus to forty-five or even fifty roubles. What was left was pure chicken-feed; in terms of *overcoat* finance, the merest drop in the ocean. Also, he knew very well that at times Petrovich would suddenly take it into his head to charge the devil's own price, so that even his wife could not help shouting at him:

'Have you gone out of your mind, you old fool! One day he'll work for next to nothing, and now the devil's making him charge more than he's worth himself!'

He knew very well, however, that Petrovich would do the job for eighty roubles; but the question still remained, where was he to get these eighty roubles from? He could just about scrape half of it together, perhaps a little more. But what about the balance? Before we go into this, the reader should know where the *first* half was coming from.

For every rouble he spent, Akaky Akakievich would put half a copeck away in a small box, which had a little slot in the lid for dropping money through, and which was kept locked. Every six months he would tot up his savings and change them into silver. He had been doing this for a long time, and over several years had amassed more than forty roubles. So, he had half the money, but what about the rest?

Akaky Akakievich thought and thought, and at last decided he would have to cut down on his day-to-day spending, for a year at least: he would have to stop drinking tea in the evenings; go without candles; and, if he had copying to do, go to his landlady's room and work by the light of her candle. He would have to step as carefully and lightly as possible over the cobbles in the street – almost on tiptoe – so as not to wear his shoe soles out before their time; avoid taking his personal linen to the laundress as much as possible; and, to make his underclothes last longer, take them off when he got home and only wear his thick cotton dressing-gown – itself an ancient garment and one which time had treated kindly. Frankly, Akaky Akakievich found these privations quite a burden to begin with, but after a while he got used to them. He even trained himself to go without any food at all in the evenings, for his nourishment was *spiritual*, his thoughts always full of that overcoat which one day was to be his. From that time onwards his whole life seemed to have become richer, as though he had married and another human being was by his side. It was as if he was not alone at all but had some pleasant companion who had agreed to tread life's path together with him; and this companion was none other than the overcoat with its thick cotton-wool padding and strong lining, made to last a lifetime. He livened up and, like a man who has set himself a goal, became more determined.

His indecision and uncertainty – in short, the vague and hesitant side of his personality – just disappeared of its own accord. At times a fire shone in his eyes, and even such daring and audacious thoughts as: 'Now, what about having a *marten* collar?' flashed through his mind.

All these reflections very nearly turned his mind. Once he was not far from actually making a *copying mistake*, so that he almost cried out 'Ugh!' and crossed himself. At least once a month he went to Petrovich's to see how the overcoat was getting on and to inquire where was the best place to buy cloth, what colour they should choose, and what price they should pay. Although slightly worried, he always returned home contented, thinking of the day when all the material would be bought and the overcoat finished. Things progressed quicker than he had ever hoped. The Director allowed Akaky Akakievich not forty or forty-five, but a whole *sixty* roubles bonus, which was beyond his wildest expectations. Whether that was because the Director had some premonition that he needed a new overcoat, or whether it was just pure chance, Akaky Akakievich found himself with an extra twenty roubles. And as a result everything was speeded up. After another two or three months of mild starvation Akaky Akakievich had saved up the eighty roubles. His heart, which usually had a very steady beat, started pounding away. The very next day off he went shopping with Petrovich. They bought some *very* fine material, and no wonder, since they had done nothing but discuss it for the past six months and scarcely a month had gone by without their calling in at all the shops to compare prices. What was more, even Petrovich said you could not buy better cloth anywhere. For the lining they simply chose calico, but calico so strong and of such high quality that, according to Petrovich, it was finer than silk and even had a smarter and glossier look.

They did not buy marten for the collar, because it was really too expensive, but instead they settled on cat fur, the finest cat they could find in the shops and which could easily be mistaken for marten from a distance. In all, Petrovich took two weeks to finish the overcoat as there was so much quilting to be done. Otherwise it would have been ready much sooner. Petrovich charged twelve roubles – anything less was out of the question. He had used silk thread everywhere, with fine double seams, and had gone over them with his teeth afterwards to make different patterns.

It was . . . precisely *which* day it is difficult to say, but without any doubt it was the most triumphant day in Akaky Akakievich's whole life when Petrovich at last delivered the overcoat. He brought it early in the morning, even before Akaky Akakievich had left for the office. The overcoat could not have arrived at a better time, since fairly severe frosts had already set in and were likely to get even worse. Petrovich delivered the overcoat in person – just as a good tailor should. Akaky Akakievich had never seen him looking so solemn before. He seemed to know full well that his was no mean achievement, and that he had suddenly shown by his own work the gulf separating tailors who only relined or patched up overcoats from those who make new ones, right from the beginning. He took the overcoat out of the large kerchief he had wrapped it in[8] and which he had only just got back from the laundry. Then he folded the kerchief and put it in his pocket ready for use. Then he took the overcoat very proudly in both hands and threw it very deftly round Akaky Akakievich's shoulders. He gave it a sharp tug, smoothed it downwards on the back, and draped it round Akaky Akakievich, leaving some buttons in the front undone. Akaky Akakievich, who was no longer a young man, wanted to try it with his arms in the sleeves. Petrovich helped him, and even this way it was the right size. In short, the overcoat was a perfect fit, without any shadow of doubt. Petrovich did not forget to mention it was only *because* he happened to live in a small backstreet and *because* his workshop had no sign outside, and *because* he had known Akaky Akakievich such a long time, that he had charged him such a low price. If he had gone anywhere along Nevsky Prospekt they would have rushed him seventy-five roubles for the labour alone. Akaky Akakievich did not feel like taking Petrovich up on this and in fact was rather intimidated by the large sums Petrovich was so fond of

mentioning just to try and impress his clients. He settled up
with him, thanked him and went straight off to the office in his
new overcoat. Petrovich followed him out into the street, stood
there for a long time taking a look at the overcoat from some
way off, and then deliberately made a small detour up a side-
street so that he could have a good view of the overcoat from
the other side, i.e. coming straight towards him.

Meanwhile Akaky Akakievich continued on his way to the
office in the most festive mood. Not one second passed without
his being conscious of the new overcoat on his shoulders, and
several times he even smiled from inward pleasure. And really
the overcoat's advantages were two-fold: firstly, it was warm;
secondly, it made him feel good. He did not notice where he
was going at all and suddenly found himself at the office. In the
lobby he took the overcoat off, carefully examined it all over,
and then handed it to the porter for special safe-keeping.

No one knew how the news suddenly got round that Akaky
Akakievich had a new overcoat and that his 'dressing-gown'
was now no more. The moment he arrived everyone rushed
out into the lobby to look at his new acquisition. They so
overwhelmed him with congratulations and good wishes that he
smiled at first and then he even began to feel quite embarrassed.
When they all crowded round him saying they should have a
drink on the new overcoat, and insisting that the *very least* he
could do was to hold a party for all of them, Akaky Akakievich
lost his head completely, not knowing what to do or what to
answer or how to escape. Blushing all over, he tried for some
considerable time, rather naïvely, to convince them it was not
a new overcoat at all but really his old one. In the end one of
the civil servants, who was nothing less than an assistant head
clerk, and who was clearly anxious to show he was not at all
snooty and could hobnob even with his inferiors, said: 'All right
then, *I'll* throw a party instead. You're all invited over to my
place this evening. It so happens it's my name-day.'

Naturally the others immediately offered the assistant head
clerk their congratulations and eagerly accepted the invitation.
When Akaky Akakievich tried to talk himself out of it, everyone
said it was impolite, in fact quite shameful, and a refusal was

out of the question. Later, however, he felt pleased when he remembered that the party would give him the opportunity of going out in his new overcoat that very same evening.

The whole day was like a triumphant holiday for Akaky Akakievich. He went home in the most jubilant mood, took off his coat, hung it up very carefully and stood there for some time admiring the cloth and lining. Then, to compare the two, he brought out his old 'dressing-gown', which by now had completely disintegrated. As he examined it he could not help laughing: what a *fantastic* difference! All through dinner the thought of his old overcoat and its shocking state made him smile. He ate his meal with great relish and afterwards did not do any copying but indulged in the luxury of lying on his bed until it grew dark. Then, without any further delay, he put his clothes on, threw his overcoat over his shoulders and went out into the street. Unfortunately the author cannot say exactly where the civil servant who was giving the party lived: his memory is beginning to let him down badly and everything in Petersburg, every house, every street, has become so blurred and mixed up in his mind that he finds it extremely difficult to say where *anything* is at all. All the same, we do at least know for certain that the civil servant lived in the *best part* of the city, which amounts to saying that he lived miles and miles away from Akaky Akakievich. At first Akaky Akakievich had to pass through some badly lit, deserted streets, but the nearer he got to the civil servant's flat the more lively and crowded they became, and the brighter the lamps shone. More and more people dashed by and he began to meet beautifully dressed ladies, and men with beaver collars. Here there were not so many cheap cabmen[9] with their wooden basketwork sleighs studded with gilt nails. Instead, there were dashing coachmen with elegant cabs, wearing crimson velvet caps, their sleighs lacquered and covered with bearskins. Carriages with draped boxes simply flew down the streets with their wheels screeching over the snow.

Akaky Akakievich surveyed this scene as though he had never witnessed anything like it in his life. For some years now he had not ventured out at all in the evenings.

Filled with curiosity, he stopped by a brightly lit shop window to look at a painting of a pretty girl who was taking off her shoe and showing her entire foot, which was really quite pretty, while behind her a gentleman with side-whiskers and a fine goatee was poking his head round the door of an adjoining room. Akaky Akakievich shook his head and smiled, then went on his way. Why did he smile? Perhaps because this was something he had never set eyes on before, but for which, nonetheless, each one of us has some instinctive feeling. Or perhaps, like many other civil servants he thought: 'Oh, those Frenchmen! Of course, if they happen to fancy something, then really, I mean to say, to be exact, something . . .' Perhaps he was not thinking this at all, for it is impossible to probe deep into a man's soul and discover all his thoughts. Finally he arrived at the assistant head clerk's flat. This assistant head clerk lived in the grand style: a lamp shone on the staircase, and the flat was on the first floor.

As he entered the hall Akaky Akakievich saw row upon row of galoshes. Among them, in the middle of the room, stood a samovar, hissing as it sent out clouds of steam. The walls were covered with overcoats and cloaks; some of them even had beaver collars or velvet lapels. From the other side of the wall he could hear the buzzing of voices, which suddenly became loud and clear when the door opened and there emerged a footman carrying a tray laden with empty glasses, a jug of cream and a basketful of biscuits. There was no doubt at all that the clerks had been there a long time and had already drunk their first cup of tea.

When Akaky Akakievich had hung up his overcoat himself he went in and was struck all at once by the sight of candles, civil servants, pipes and card tables. His ears were filled with the blurred sound of little snatches of conversation coming from all over the room and the noise of chairs being shifted backwards and forwards. He stood very awkwardly in the middle of the room, looking around and trying to think what to do. But they had already spotted him and greeted him with loud shouts, everyone immediately crowding into the hall to have another look at the overcoat. Although he was somewhat overwhelmed by this reception, since he was a rather simple-minded and ingenuous person, he could not help feeling glad at the praises showered on his overcoat. And then, it goes without saying, they abandoned him, overcoat included, and turned their attention to the customary whist tables. All the noise and conversation and crowds of people – this was a completely new world for Akaky Akakievich. He simply did not know what to do, where to put his hands or feet or any other part of himself. Finally he took a seat near the card-players, looking at the cards, and examining first one player's face, then another's. In no time at all he started yawning and began to feel bored, especially as it was long after his usual bedtime.

He tried to take leave of his host, but everyone insisted on his staying to toast the new overcoat with a glassful of champagne. About an hour later supper was served. This consisted of mixed salad, cold veal, meat pasties, pastries and champagne. They made Akaky Akakievich drink two glasses, after which everything seemed a lot merrier, although he still could not forget that it was already midnight and that he should have left ages ago.

So that his host should not stop him as he left, he crept silently from the room, found his overcoat in the hall (much to his regret it was lying on the floor), shook it to remove every trace of fluff, put it over his shoulders and went down the stairs into the street.

Outside it was still lit up. A few small shops, which house-serfs and different kinds of people use as clubs at all hours of the day, were open. Those which were closed had broad beams of light coming from chinks right the way down their doors, showing that there were still people talking inside, most probably maids and menservants who had not finished exchanging the latest gossip, leaving their masters completely in the dark as to where they had got to. Akaky Akakievich walked along in high spirits, and once, heavens know why, very nearly gave chase to some lady who flashed by like lightning, every part of her body showing an extraordinary mobility. However, he stopped in his tracks and continued at his previous leisurely

pace, amazed at himself for breaking into that inexplicable trot.
Soon there stretched before him those same empty streets which
looked forbidding enough even in the daytime, let alone at
night. Now they looked even more lonely and deserted. The
street lamps thinned out more and more – the local council was
stingy with its oil in this part of the city. Next he began to pass
by wooden houses and fences. Not a soul anywhere, nothing but
the snow gleaming in the streets and the cheerless dark shapes
of low-built huts which, with their shutters closed, seemed to
be asleep. He was now quite near the spot where the street was
interrupted by an endless square with the houses barely visible
on the other side: a terrifying desert. In the distance, God knows
where, a light glimmered in a watchman's hut which seemed to
be standing on the very edge of the world. At this point Akaky
Akakievich's high spirits drooped considerably. As he walked
out on to the square, he could not suppress the feeling of dread
that welled up inside him, as though he sensed that something
evil was going to happen. He looked back, then to both sides:
it was as though he was surrounded by a whole ocean. 'No, it's
best not to look,' he thought, and continued on his way with
his eyes shut. When at last he opened them to see how much
further he had to go he suddenly saw two men with moustaches
right in front of him, although it was too dark to make them out
exactly. His eyes misted over and his heart started pounding.

'Aha, that's *my* overcoat all right,' one of them said in a
thunderous voice, grabbing him by the collar. Akaky Akakievich was about to shout for help, but the other man stuck a fist
the size of a clerk's head right in his face and said: 'Just one
squeak out of you!' All Akaky Akakievich knew was that they
pulled his coat off and shoved a knee into him, making him fall
backwards in the snow, after which he knew nothing more. A
few minutes later he came to and managed to stand up, but by
then there was no one to be seen. All he knew was that he was
freezing and that his overcoat had gone, and he started shouting. But his voice would not carry across the vast square. Not
once did he stop shouting as he ran desperately across the
square towards a sentry box where a policeman stood propped
up on his halberd looking rather intrigued as to who the devil

was shouting and running towards him. When he had reached the policeman Akaky Akakievich (in between breathless gasps) shouted accusingly that he had been asleep, that he was neglecting his duty and could not even see when a man was being robbed under his very nose. The policeman replied that he had seen nothing, except for two men who had stopped him in the middle of the square and whom he had taken for his friends; and that instead of letting off steam he would be better advised to go the very next day to see the police inspector, who would get his overcoat back for him. Akaky Akakievich ran off home in the most shocking state: his hair – there was still some growing around the temples and the back of his head – was terribly dishevelled. His chest, his trousers, and his sides were covered with snow. When his old landlady heard a terrifying knocking at the door she leaped out of bed and rushed downstairs with only one shoe on, clutching her nightdress to her bosom out of modesty. But when she opened the door and saw the state Akaky Akakievich was in, she shrank backwards. After he had told her what had happened she clasped her hands in despair and told him to go straight to the District Police Superintendent, as the local officer was sure to try and put one over on him, make all kinds of promises and lead him right up the garden path. The best thing was to go direct to the Superintendent himself, whom she actually happened to know, as Anna, the Finnish girl who used to cook for her, was now a nanny at the Superintendent's house. She often saw him go past the houses and every Sunday he went to church, smiled at everyone as he prayed and to all intents and purposes was a thoroughly nice man. Akaky Akakievich listened to this advice and crept sadly up to his room. What sort of night he spent can best be judged by those who are able to put themselves in someone else's place. Early next morning he went to the Superintendent's house but was told that he was asleep. He returned at ten o'clock, but was informed that he was still asleep. He came back at eleven, and was told that he had gone out. When he turned up once again round about lunchtime, the clerks in the entrance hall would not let him through on any account, unless he told them first what his business was, why he had come, and what had happened. So in the end Akaky Akakievich, for the first time in his life, stood up for himself and told them in no uncertain terms that he wanted to see the Superintendent *in person*, that they dare not turn him away since he had come from a government department on official business, and that they would know all about it if he made a complaint. The clerks did not have the nerve to argue and one of them went to fetch the Superintendent who reacted extremely strangely to the robbery. Instead of sticking to the main point of the story, he started cross-examining Akaky Akakievich with such questions as: 'What was he doing out so late?' or 'Had he been visiting a house of ill-repute?', which left Akaky feeling very embarrassed, and he went away completely in the dark as to whether they were going to take any action or not. The whole of that day he stayed away from the office – for the first time in his life.

The next morning he arrived looking very pale and wearing his old 'dressing-gown', which was in an even more pathetic state.

The story of the stolen overcoat touched many of the clerks, although a few of them could not refrain from laughing at Akaky Akakievich even then. There and then they decided to make a collection, but all they raised was a miserable little sum since, apart from any *extra* expense, they had nearly exhausted all their funds subscribing to a new portrait of the Director as well as to some book or other recommended by one of the heads of department – who happened to be a friend of the author. So they collected next to nothing.

One of them, who was deeply moved, decided he could at least help Akaky Akakievich with some good advice. He told him not to go to the local police officer, since although that gentleman might well recover his overcoat somehow or other in the hope of receiving a commendation from his superiors, Akaky did not stand a chance of getting it out of the police station without the necessary legal proof that the overcoat was really his. The best plan was to apply to a certain *Important Person*, and this same Important Person, by writing to and contacting the proper people, would get things moving much faster. There was nothing else for it, so Akaky Akakievich decided to go and see this Important Person.

What exactly this Important Person did and what position he held remains a mystery to this day. All we need say is that this Important Person had become important only a short while before, and that until then he had been an *unimportant* person. However, even now his position was not considered very important if compared with others which were still more important. But you will always come across a certain class of people who consider something unimportant which for other people is in fact important. However, he tried all manners and means of buttressing his importance. For example, he was responsible for introducing the rule that all low-ranking civil servants should be waiting to meet him on the stairs when he arrived at the office; that no one, on any account, could walk straight into his office; and that everything must be dealt with in the *strictest* order of priority: the collegiate registrar was to report to the provincial secretary who in turn was to report to the titular counsellor (or whoever it was he *had* to report to) so that in this way the matter reached him according to the prescribed procedure. In this Holy Russia of ours everything is infected by a mania for imitation, and everyone apes and mimics his superior. I have even heard say that when a certain titular counsellor was appointed head of some minor government department he immediately partitioned off a section of his office into a special room for himself, an 'audience chamber' as he called it, and stationed two ushers in uniforms with red collars and gold braid outside to open the doors for visitors – even though you would have a job getting an ordinary writing desk into this so-called chamber.

This Important Person's methods and routine were very imposing and impressive, but nonetheless simple. The whole basis of his system was strict discipline. 'Strictness, strictness . . . and strictness' he used to say, usually looking very solemnly into the face of the person he was addressing when he had repeated this word for the third time. However, there was really no good reason for this strict discipline, since the ten civil servants or so who made up the whole administrative machinery of his department were all duly terrified of him anyway. If they saw him coming from some way off they would stop what they were doing and stand to attention while the Director went through the office. His normal everyday conversation with his subordinates simply *reeked* of discipline and consisted almost entirely of three phrases: 'How dare you? Do you know who you're talking to? Do you realize who's standing before you?'

However, he was quite a good man at heart, pleasant to his colleagues and helpful. But his promotion to general's rank had completely turned his head; he became all mixed up, somehow went off the rails, and just could not cope any more. If he happened to be with someone of equal rank, then he was quite a normal person, very decent in fact and even far from stupid in many respects.

But put him with people only one rank lower, and he was really at sea. He would not say a single word, and one felt sorry to see him in such a predicament, all the more so as even *he* felt that he could have been spending the time far more enjoyably.

Sometimes one could read this craving for interesting company and conversation in his eyes, but he was always inhibited by the thought: would this be going too far for someone in his position, would this be showing too much familiarity and therefore rather damaging to his status? For these reasons he would remain perpetually silent, producing a few monosyllables from time to time, and as a result acquired the reputation of being a crashing bore. This was the Important Person our Akaky Akakievich went to consult, and he appeared at the worst possible moment – most inopportune as far as *he* was concerned – but most opportune for the Important Person. The Important Person was in his office having a very animated talk with an old childhood friend who had just arrived in Petersburg and whom he had not seen for a few years.

At this moment the arrival of a certain Bashmachkin was announced. 'Who's he?' he asked abruptly and was told, 'Some clerk or other.' 'Ah, let him wait, I can't see him just now,' the Important Person replied. Here we should say that the Important Person told a complete lie: he had plenty of time, he had long since said all he wanted to his friend, and for some considerable time their conversation had been punctuated by very long silences broken only by their slapping each other on the thigh and saying:

'Quite so, Ivan Abramovich!' and 'Well yes, Stepan Varlamovich!'

Even so, he still ordered the clerk to wait, just to show his old friend (who had left the Service a fair time before and was now nicely settled in his country house) how long he could keep clerks standing about in his waiting-room. When they really had said all that was to be said, or rather, had sat there in the very comfortable easy chairs to their heart's content without saying a single word to each other, puffing away at their cigars, the Important Person suddenly remembered and told his secretary, who was standing by the door with a pile of papers in his hands: 'Ah yes now, I think there's some clerk or other waiting out there. Tell him to come in.' One look at the timid Akaky Akakievich in his ancient uniform and he suddenly turned towards him and said: 'What do *you* want?' in that brusque and commanding voice he had been practising especially, when he was alone in his room, in front of a mirror, a whole week before his present appointment and promotion to general's rank.

Long before this Akaky Akakievich had been experiencing that feeling of awe which it was proper and necessary for him to experience, and now, somewhat taken aback, he tried to explain, as far as his tongue would allow him and with an even greater admixture than ever before of 'wells' and 'that is to says', that his overcoat was a new one, that he had been robbed in the most barbarous manner, that he had come to ask the Important Person's help, so that through his influence, or by doing this or that, by writing to the Chief of Police or someone else (whoever it might be), the Important Person might get his overcoat back for him.

Heaven knows why, but the general found this approach rather too familiar.

'What do you mean by this, my dear sir?' he snapped again. 'Are you unaware of the correct procedure? Where do you think you are? Don't you know how things are conducted here?

It's high time you knew that first of all your application must be handed in at the main office, then taken to the chief clerk, then to the departmental director, then to my secretary, who *then* submits it to me for consideration . . .'

'But Your Excellency,' said Akaky Akakievich, trying to summon up the small handful of courage he possessed, and feeling at the same time that the sweat was pouring off him, 'I took the liberty of disturbing Your Excellency because, well, secretaries, you know, are a rather unreliable lot . . .'

'What, what, what?' cried the Important Person. 'Where did you learn such impudence? Where did you get those ideas from? What rebellious attitude towards their heads of department and superiors has infected young men these days?'

Evidently the Important Person did not notice that Akaky Akakievich was well past fifty. Of course, one might call him a young man, relatively speaking; that is, if you compared him with someone of seventy.

'Do you realize who you're talking to? Do you know who is standing before you? Do you understand, I ask you, do you understand? I'm asking you a question!'

At this point he stamped his foot and raised his voice to such a pitch that Akaky Akakievich was not the only one to be scared out of his wits. Akaky Akakievich almost fainted. He reeled forward, his body shook all over and he could hardly stand on his feet. If the porters had not rushed to his assistance he would have fallen flat on the floor. He was carried out almost lifeless. The Important Person, very satisfied that the effect he had produced exceeded even *his* wildest expectations, and absolutely delighted that a few words from him could deprive a man of his senses, peeped at his friend out of the corner of one eye to see what impression he had made. He was not exactly displeased to see that his friend was quite bewildered and was even beginning to show unmistakable signs of fear himself.

Akaky Akakievich remembered nothing about going down the stairs and out into the street. His hands and feet had gone dead. Never in his life had he received such a savage dressing-down from a general – and what is more, a general from another department.

He continually stumbled off the pavement as he struggled on with his mouth wide open in the face of a raging blizzard that whistled down the street. As it normally does in St Petersburg the wind was blowing from all four corners of the earth and from every single side-street. In a twinkling his throat was inflamed and when he finally dragged himself home he was unable to say one word. He put himself to bed and broke out all over in swellings. That is what a 'proper and necessary' dressing-down can sometimes do for you!

The next day he had a high fever. Thanks to the generous assistance of the Petersburg climate the illness made much speedier progress than one might have expected, and when the doctor arrived and felt his pulse, all he could prescribe was a poultice – and only then for the simple reason that he did not wish his patient to be deprived of the salutary benefits of medical aid. However, he *did* advance the diagnosis that Akaky Akakievich would not last another day and a half, no doubt about that, and then: *kaput*. After which he turned to the landlady and said:

'Now, don't waste any time and order a pine coffin right away, as he won't be able to afford oak.'

Whether Akaky Akakievich heard these fateful words – and if he did hear them, whether they shocked him into some feeling of regret for his wretched life – no one has the slightest idea, since he was feverish and delirious the whole time. Strange visions, each weirder than the last, paraded endlessly before him: in one he could see Petrovich the tailor and he was begging him to make an overcoat with special traps to catch the thieves that seemed to be swarming under his bed. Every other minute he called out to his landlady to drag one out which had actually crawled under the blankets.

In another he was asking why his old 'dressing-gown' was hanging up there when he had a *new* overcoat. Then he imagined himself standing next to the general and, after being duly and properly reprimanded, saying: 'I'm sorry, Your Excellency.' In the end he started cursing and swearing and let forth such a torrent of terrible obscenities that his good landlady crossed herself, as she had never heard the like from him in all her born days, especially as the curses always seemed to follow right after those 'Your Excellencies'. Later on he began to talk complete gibberish, until it was impossible to understand anything, except that this jumble of words and thoughts always centred on one and the same overcoat. Finally poor Akaky Akakievich gave up the ghost. Neither his room nor what he had in the way of belongings was sealed off,[10] in the first place, because he had no family, and in the second place, because his worldly possessions did not amount to very much at all: a bundle of goose quills, one quire of white government paper, three pairs of socks, two or three buttons that had come off his trousers, and the 'dressing-gown' with which the reader is already familiar. Whom all this went to, God only knows, and the author of this story confesses that he is not even interested. Akaky Akakievich was carted away and buried. And St Petersburg carried on without its Akaky Akakievich just as though he had never even existed.

So vanished and disappeared for ever a human being whom no one ever thought of protecting, who was dear to no one, in whom no one was the least interested, not even the naturalist who cannot resist sticking a pin in a common fly and examining it under the microscope; a being who endured the mockery of his colleagues without protesting, who went to his grave without achieving anything in his life, but to whom, nonetheless (just before the end of his life) a shining visitor in the form of an overcoat suddenly appeared, brightening his wretched life for one fleeting moment; a being upon whose head disaster had cruelly fallen, just as it falls upon the kings and great ones of this earth . . .

A few days after his death a messenger was sent from the Department with instructions for him to report to the office *immediately*: it was the Director's own orders. But the messenger was obliged to return on his own and announced that Akaky would not be coming any more. When asked why not he replied: ' 'Cos 'e's dead, bin buried three days ago.' This was how the office got to know about Akaky Akakievich's death, and on the very next day his place was taken by a new clerk, a much taller man whose handwriting was not nearly so upright and indeed had a pronounced slope.

But who would have imagined that this was not the last of Akaky Akakievich, and that he was destined to create quite a stir several days after his death, as though he were trying to make up for a life spent being ignored by everybody? But this is what happened and it provides our miserable story with a totally unexpected, fantastic ending. Rumours suddenly started going round St Petersburg that a ghost in the form of a government clerk had been seen near the Kalinkin Bridge,[11] and even further afield, and that this ghost appeared to be searching for a stolen overcoat. To this end it was to be seen ripping all kinds of overcoats from everyone's shoulders, with no regard for rank or title: overcoats made from cat fur, beaver, quilted overcoats, raccoon, fox, bear – in short, overcoats made from every conceivable fur or skin that man has ever used to protect his own hide. One of the clerks from the department saw the ghost with his own eyes and immediately recognized it as Akaky Akakievich. He was so terrified that he ran off as fast as his legs would carry him, with the result he did not manage to have a very good look: all he could make out was someone pointing a menacing finger at him from the distance. Complaints continually poured in from all quarters, not only from titular counsellors, but even such high-ranking officials as privy counsellors, whose backs and shoulders were being subjected to quite nasty colds through this nocturnal ripping off of their overcoats. The police were instructed to run the ghost in, come what may, dead or alive, and to punish it most severely, as an example to others – and in this they very nearly succeeded. To be precise, a policeman, part of whose beat lay along Kirushkin Alley, was on the point of grabbing the ghost by the collar at the very scene of the crime, just as he was about to tear a woollen overcoat from the shoulders of a retired musician who, in his day, used to tootle on the flute. As he seized the ghost by the collar the policeman shouted to two of his friends to come and keep hold of it, just for a minute, while he felt in his boot for his birch-bark snuff-box to revive his nose (which had been slightly frost-bitten six times in his life). But the snuff must have been one of those blends even a ghost could not stand, for the policeman had barely managed to cover his right nostril with a finger and sniff half a handful up the other when the ghost sneezed so violently that they were completely blinded by the spray, all three of them. While they were wiping their eyes the ghost disappeared into thin air, so suddenly that the policemen could not even say for certain if they had ever laid hands on it in the first place. From then on the local police were so scared of ghosts that they were frightened of arresting even the living and would shout instead: 'Hey you, clear off!' from a safe distance. The clerk's ghost began to appear even far beyond the Kalinkin Bridge, causing no little alarm and apprehension among fainter-hearted citizens. However, we seem to have completely neglected the Important Person, who, in fact, could almost be said to be the *real* reason for the fantastic turn this otherwise authentic story has taken. First of all, to give him his due, we should mention that soon after the departure of our poor shattered Akaky Akakievich the Important Person felt some twinges of regret. Compassion was not something new to him, and, although consciousness of his rank very often stifled them, his heart was not untouched by many generous impulses. As soon as his friend had left the office his thoughts turned to poor Akaky Akakievich.

Almost every day after that he had visions of the pale Akaky Akakievich, for whom an official wigging had been altogether too much. These thoughts began to worry him to such an extent that a week later he decided to send someone round from the office to the flat to ask how he was and if he could be of any help. When the messenger reported that Akaky Akakievich had died suddenly of a fever he was quite stunned. His conscience began troubling him, and all that day he felt off-colour.

Thinking that some light entertainment might help him forget that unpleasant experience he went off to a party given by one of his friends which was attended by quite a respectable crowd. He was particularly pleased to see that everyone there held roughly the same rank as himself, so there was no chance of any embarrassing situations. All this had an amazingly uplifting effect on his state of mind. He unwound completely, chatted very pleasantly, made himself agreeable to everyone, and in short, spent a very pleasant evening. Over dinner he drank one or two glasses of champagne, a wine which, as everyone knows, is not exactly calculated to dampen high spirits. The champagne put him in a reckless, adventurous mood: he decided not to go straight home, but to call on a lady of his acquaintance, Karolina Ivanovna, who was of German origin and with whom he was on the friendliest terms. Here I should mention that the Important Person was no longer a young man but a good husband and the respected head of a family. His two sons, one of whom already had a job in the Civil Service, and a sweet sixteen-year-old daughter with a snub nose that was nonetheless pretty, came every day to kiss his hand and say '*Bonjour, Papa*'. His wife, who still retained some of her freshness and had not even lost any of her good looks, allowed him to kiss her hand first, and then kissed his, turning it the other side up. But although the Important Person was thoroughly contented with the affection lavished on him by his family, he still did not think it wrong to have a lady friend in another part of the town. This lady friend was not in the least prettier or younger than his wife, but that is one of the mysteries of this world, and it is not for us to criticize. As I was saying, the Important Person went downstairs, climbed into his sledge and said to the driver: 'To Karolina Ivanovna's', while he wrapped himself snugly in his warm, very luxurious overcoat, revelling in that happy state of mind, so very dear to Russians, when one is thinking about absolutely nothing, but when, nonetheless, thoughts come crowding into one's head of their own accord, each more delightful than the last, and not even requiring one to make the mental effort of conjuring them up or chasing after them. He felt very contented as he recalled, without any undue exertion, all the gayest moments of the party, all the *bons mots* that had aroused loud guffaws in that little circle: many of them he even repeated quietly to himself and found just as funny as before, so that it was not at all surprising that he laughed very heartily. The boisterous wind, however, interfered with his enjoyment at times: blowing up from God knows where or why, it cut right into his face, hurling lumps of snow at it, making his collar billow out like a sail, or blowing it back over his head with such supernatural force that he had the devil's own job extricating himself. Suddenly the Important Person felt a violent tug at his collar. Turning round, he saw a smallish man in an old, worn-out uniform, and not without a feeling of horror recognized him as Akaky Akakievich. The clerk's face was as pale as the snow and was just like a corpse's.

But the Important Person's terror passed all bounds when the ghost's mouth became twisted, smelling horribly of the grave as it breathed on him and pronounced the following words: 'Ah, at last I've found you! Now I've, er, hm, collared you! It's *your* overcoat I'm after! You didn't care about mine, *and* you couldn't resist giving me a good ticking-off into the bargain! Now hand over *your* overcoat!' The poor Important Person nearly died. However much strength of character he displayed in the office (usually in the presence of his subordinates) – one only had to look at his virile face and bearing to say: '*There*'s a man for you!' – in this situation, like many of his kind who seem heroic at first sight, he was so frightened that he even began to fear (and not without reason) that he was in for a heart attack. He tore off his overcoat as fast as he could, without any help, and then shouted to his driver in a terrified voice: 'Home as fast as you can!'

The driver, recognizing the tone of voice his master used only in moments of crisis – a tone of voice usually accompanied by some much stronger encouragement – just to be on the safe side hunched himself up, flourished his whip and shot off like an arrow.

Not much more than six minutes later the Important Person was already at his front door. Coatless, terribly pale and frightened out of his wits, he had driven straight home instead of going to Karolina Ivanovna's. Somehow he managed to struggle up to his room and spent a very troubled night, so much so that next morning his daughter said to him over breakfast: 'You look very pale today, Papa.' But Papa did not reply, did not say a single word to anyone about what had happened, where he had been and where he had originally intended going. The encounter had made a deep impression on him. From that time onwards he would seldom say: 'How dare you! Do you realize who is standing before you?' to his subordinates. And if he did have occasion to say this, it was never without first hearing what the accused had to say. But what was more surprising than anything else the ghostly clerk disappeared completely. Obviously the general's overcoat was a perfect fit. At least, there were no more stories about overcoats being torn off people's backs. However, many officious and overcautious citizens would not be satisfied, insisting the ghost could still be seen in the remoter parts of the city, and in fact a certain police constable from the Kolomna[12] district saw with his own eyes a ghost leaving a house. However, being rather weakly built – once a quite normal-sized, fully mature piglet which came tearing out of a private house knocked him off his feet, to the huge amusement of some cab-drivers who were standing near by, each of whom was made to cough up half a copeck in snuff-money for his cheek – he simply did not have the nerve to make an arrest, but followed the ghost in the dark until it suddenly stopped, turned round, asked: 'What do *you* want?' and shook its fist at him – a fist the like of which you will never see in the land of the living. The constable replied: 'Nothing', and beat a hasty retreat. This ghost, however, was much taller than the first, had an absolutely enormous moustache and, apparently heading towards the Obukhov Bridge,[13] was swallowed up in the darkness of the night.

DIARY OF A MADMAN

October 3rd

Something very peculiar happened today. I got up rather late, and when Mavra brought my clean shoes in I asked her what the time was. When she told me it was long past ten I rushed to get dressed. To be honest with you, if I'd known the sour look I was going to get from the head of our department I wouldn't have gone to the office at all. For some time now he's been saying: 'Why are you always in such a muddle? Sometimes you rush around like a madman and make such a mess of your work, the devil himself couldn't sort it out. You start paragraphs with small letters and leave out the date and reference number altogether.' Damned old buzzard! Seeing me in the Director's office sharpening His Excellency's quills[1] must have made him jealous. To cut a long story short, I'd never have gone to the office in the first place if there hadn't been a good chance of seeing the cashier and making the old Jew cough up a small advance somehow or other. What a man! The Last Judgement will be upon us before you can get a month's pay out of *him* in advance. Even if you're down to your last copeck, you can go on asking until you're blue in the face, but that grey-haired old devil won't give in. I've heard people say his own cook slaps him on the face in his flat. The whole world knows about it. I don't see there's any advantage working in our department. No perks at all. It's a different story in the Provincial Administration or in the Civil or Treasury Offices. You'll see someone sitting there curled up in a corner scribbling away. He'll be wearing a filthy old frock-coat and just one look at his mug is enough to make you spit. But you should see the country house he rents! Just offer him a gilt china cup and all

he'll say is: 'That's what you give a *doctor*!' He'll only be
satisfied with a pair of racehorses, or a droshky, or a beaver
skin that cost three hundred roubles. To look at him you'd
think he was so meek and mild, and he talks with such refinement: 'Please be so good as to lend me that little knife to sharpen
my quills.' But just give him the chance and he'll strip any
petitioner until there's only the shirt left on his back. I must
admit, it's very civilized working in our department, everything's kept cleaner than you'll ever see in a provincial office.
And we have mahogany tables, and all the Principals use the
polite form of address. But really, if it weren't for the snob
value, I'd have given in my notice long ago.

I put on my old overcoat and took my umbrella, as it was
simply teeming down outside. There wasn't a soul about; except
for a few old peasant women sheltering under their skirts,
some Russian merchants under their umbrellas and one or two
messengers. As for better-class people, there weren't any, except
for one of our civil servants. I spotted him at the crossroads. As
soon as I saw him I said to myself: 'Aha, you're not going to the
office, my friend, you're after that girl dashing along over there –
and having a good look at her pretty little ankles into the bargain.' What beasts our civil servants are! Good God, they'd leave
any officer standing and get their claws into anything that goes
past in a bonnet. While I was engrossed with these thoughts, a
carriage drew up in front of a shop I happened to be passing.
I saw at once this was our Director's. He couldn't be wanting
anything in there, so he must have called for his daughter, I
thought. I flattened myself against the wall. A footman opened
the carriage door and out she fluttered, just like a little bird. The
way she looked first to the right, then to the left, her eyes and her
eyebrows flashing past . . . God in heaven, I thought, I'm lost, lost
forever! Strange *she* should venture out in all that rain! Now just
you try and tell me women aren't mad on clothes. She didn't
recognize me, and I tried to muffle myself up as best I could,
because my overcoat, besides being covered all over in stains,
had gone out of fashion ages ago. Nowadays they're all wearing
coats with long collars, but mine were short, one over the other.
And you couldn't really say the cloth had been waterproofed.

Her little dog wasn't quite quick enough to nip in after her and had to stay out in the street. I'd seen that dog before. She's called Medji. I hadn't been there more than a minute when I heard a faint little voice: 'Hullo, Medji!' Well, I never! Who was that talking? I looked around and saw two ladies walking along under an umbrella: one was old, but her companion was quite young. They'd already gone past when I heard that voice again: 'Shame on you, Medji!' What was going on, for heaven's sake? Then I saw Medji sniffing round a little dog following the two ladies. 'Aha,' I said to myself, 'It can't be true, I must be drunk.' But I hardly ever drink. 'No Fidèle, you're quite mistaken.' With my own eyes I actually saw Medji mouth these words: 'I've been, bow wow, very ill, bow wow.' Ah, you nasty little dog! I must confess I was staggered to hear it speak just like a human being. But afterwards, when I'd time to think about it, my amazement wore off. In fact, several similar cases have already been reported. It's said that in England a fish swam to the surface and said two words in such a strange language the professors have been racking their brains for three years now to discover what it was, so far without success. What's more, I read somewhere in the papers about two cows going into a shop to ask for a pound of tea. Honestly, I was much more startled when I heard Medji say: 'I *did* write to you, Fidèle. Polkan[2] couldn't have delivered my letter.' I'd stake my salary that that was what the dog said. Never in my life have I heard of a dog that could write. Only noblemen know how to write correctly. Of course, you'll always find some traders or shopkeepers, even serfs, who can scribble away: but they write like machines – no commas or full stops, and simply no idea of style.

I was really astonished at all this. To be frank, quite recently I've started hearing and seeing things I'd never heard or seen before. So I said to myself, 'I'd better follow this dog and find out who she is and what she's thinking about.' I unrolled my umbrella and followed the two ladies. We crossed Gorokhovaya Street, turned into Meshchanskaya Street, then Stolyanaya Street,[3] until we got to Kokushkin Bridge and stopped in front of a large house. 'I know this house,' I said to myself; 'it's

Zverkov's.'⁴ What a dump! Everybody seems to live there: crowds of cooks, foreigners, civil servants. They live just like dogs, all on top of each other. A friend of mine who plays the trumpet very well lives there. The ladies went up to the fifth floor. 'Fine,' I thought. 'I shan't go in now, but I'll make a note of the address and come back as soon as I have a moment to spare.'

October 4th

Today is Wednesday, and that's why I went to see the head of our department in his office. I made sure I got there early and sat down to sharpen all the quills.

Our Director must be a very clever man: his study is full of shelves crammed with books. I read some of their titles: such erudition, such scholarship! Quite above the head of any ordinary civil servant. All in French or German. And you should look into his face, and see the deep seriousness that gleams in his eyes! I have yet to hear him use *one* more word than is necessary. He might perhaps ask as you handed him some papers: 'What's the weather like?' And you would reply, 'Damp today, Your Excellency.' No, you can't compare him with your ordinary clerk. He's a true statesman. May I say, however, that he has a special fondness for me. If only his daughter . . . scum that I am! Never mind, better say nothing about that. I've been reading the *Little Bee*.⁵ A crazy lot, those French! What *do* they want? My God, I'd like to give them all a good flogging. There was a very good account of a ball written by a landowner from Kursk.⁶ They certainly know how to write, those landowners from Kursk! At that moment I noticed it was already past 12.30 and that our Director hadn't left his bedroom. But about 1.30 something happened that no pen could adequately describe. The door opened. I thought it was the Director and leapt up from my chair, clutching my papers: but it was her, herself in person! Holy Fathers, how she was dressed! Her dress was white, like a swan. What magnificence! And when she looked at me it was like the sun shining, I swear it! She nodded and said: 'Has Papa been here?' Oh what a voice! A canary, just like a canary! I felt like saying to her: 'Your Excellency, don't have me put to death, but if that is your wish, then let it be by your own noble hand.' But I was almost struck dumb, blast it, and all I could mumble was 'No, Miss.' She looked at me, then at the books, and dropped her handkerchief. I threw myself at it, slipped on the damned parquet floor and nearly broke my nose. I regained my balance however, and picked up the hand-kerchief. Heavens, what a handkerchief! Such a fine lawn, and smelling just like pure ambergris. You could tell from the smell it belonged to a general's daughter. She thanked me, and came so near to smiling that her sweet lips almost parted, and with that she left. I worked on for about another hour until a foot-man suddenly appeared with the message: 'You can go home now, Aksenty Ivanovich, the master's already left the house.' I can't stand that brood of flunkeys: they're always sprawled out in the hall and it's as much as you can do to get one little nod of acknowledgement from them. What's more, one of those pigs once offered me some snuff – without even getting up. Don't you know, ignorant peasant, that I am a civil servant and of noble birth? All the same, I picked up my hat, put my coat on *myself* – because those fine gentlemen wouldn't dream of helping you – and left the office. For a long time I lay on my bed at home. Then I copied out some very fine poetry:

> An hour without seeing you
> Is like a whole year gone by
> How wretched my life's become
> Without you I'll only fret and sigh.

Must be something by Pushkin.[7] In the evening I wrapped myself up in my overcoat and went to Her Excellency's house, and waited a long time outside the entrance just to see her get into her carriage once more. But no, she didn't come out.

November 6th

The head of the department was in a terrible mood. When I got to the office he called me in and took this line with me: 'Will you please tell me what your game is?' 'Why, nothing,' I answered. 'Are you sure? Think hard! You're past forty now, and it's time you had a bit more sense. Who do you think you are? Do you imagine I haven't heard about your tricks? I know you've been running after the Director's daughter! Take a good look at yourself. *What* are you? Just nothing, an absolute *nobody*. You haven't a copeck to bless yourself with. Just take a look in the mirror – fancy *you* having thoughts about the General's daughter!' To hell with it, his own face puts you in mind of those large bottles you see in chemists' windows, what with that tuft of hair he puts in curlers. And the way he holds his head up and smothers his hair in pomade! Thinks he can get away with anything! Now I can understand why he's got it in for me: seeing me get some preferential treatment in the office has made him jealous. I don't care a hoot about him! Just because he's a court counsellor he thinks he's Lord God Almighty! He lets his gold watch chain dangle outside his waist-coat and pays thirty roubles for a pair of shoes. He can go to hell! Does he think I'm the son of a commoner, or tailor, or a non-commissioned officer? I'm a gentleman! I could get promotion if I wanted! I'm only forty-two, that's an age nowadays when one's career is only just beginning. Just you wait, my friend, until I'm a colonel, or even something higher, God willing. I'll acquire more status than *you*. Where did you get the idea *you're* the only person whom we're supposed to look up to around here? Just give me a coat from Ruch's,[8] cut in the latest style; I'll knot my tie like you do: and then you won't be fit to clean my boots. It's only that I'm short of money.

November 8th

I went to the theatre today. The play was about the Russian fool, Filatka.[9] I couldn't stop laughing. They also put on some sort of vaudeville with some amusing little satirical poems about lawyers, and one collegiate registrar[10] in particular. So near the knuckle, I wonder they got past the censor. As for merchants, the author says straight out that they're swindling everyone and that their sons lead a dissolute life and have thoughts of becoming members of the aristocracy. There was a very witty couplet about the critics, saying they do nothing but pull everything to pieces, so the author asks for the audience's protection. A lot of very amusing plays are being written these days. I love going to the theatre. As long as I've a copeck in my pocket you can't stop me. But these civil servants of ours are such ignorant pigs, you'd never catch *those* peasants going, even if you gave them a ticket for nothing. One of the actresses sang very well. She reminded me of . . . ah! I'm a shocker! . . . Silence! The less said the better!

November 9th

At eight o'clock I set off for the office. The head of the department pretended he hadn't seen me come in. I played the same game, just as if we were complete strangers. Then I started checking and sorting out some documents. At four o'clock I left. I passed the Director's flat, but there didn't seem to be anybody in. After dinner I lay on my bed most of the evening.

November 11th

Today I sat in the Director's office and sharpened twenty-three quills for him – and for *her*. Ah, four quills for Her Excellency! He loves having a lot of pens around the place. Really, he must have a very fine brain! He doesn't say very much, but you can sense his mind is working the whole time. I'd like to know what he thinks of most, what he's hatching in that head of his. And those people with all their puns and court jokes – I wish I knew more about them and what goes on at that level of society.

Often I've thought of having a good talk with His Excellency, but somehow I'm always stuck for words, damn it: I begin by saying it's cold or warm outside, and that's as far as I get. I'd like to have a peep into the drawing-room but all I ever manage

to see is another door which is sometimes open, and leads off
to another room. Ah, what luxury! The china and mirrors! I'd
love to see that part of the house where Her Excellency . . . yes
that's what I'd dearly love to see, her boudoir, with all those
jars and little phials, and such flowers, you daren't even breathe
on them. To see her dress lying there, more like air than a dress.
And just one peep in her bedroom to see what wonders lie
there, sheer paradise, more blissful than heaven. One glance at
that little stool where she puts her tiny foot when she steps out
of bed. And then, over that tiny foot, she starts pulling on her
snowy white stocking. Ah, never mind, never mind, enough
said . . .

Today something suddenly dawned on me which made everything clear: I recalled the conversation I'd heard between the
two dogs on Nevsky Prospekt. I thought to myself 'Good, now
I'll find out what it's all about. Somehow I must get hold of the
letters that passed between those two filthy little dogs. There's
sure to be something there.' To be frank, once I very nearly
called Medji and said: 'Listen, Medji, we're alone now. If you
want I'll shut the door so no one can see. Tell me everything
you know about the young lady, who she is and what she's
like. I swear I won't tell a soul.'

But that crafty dog put her tail between her legs, seemed to
shrink to half her size, and went quietly out through the door,
as though she had heard nothing. I'd suspected for a long time
that dogs are cleverer than human beings. I was even convinced
she could speak if she wanted to, but didn't, merely out of
sheer cussedness. Dogs are extraordinarily shrewd, and notice
everything, every step you take. No, whatever happens, I shall
go to the Zverkovs tomorrow and cross-examine Fidèle, and
with any luck I'll get my hands on all the letters Medji wrote
to her.

November 12th

At two in the afternoon I set off with the firm intention of
seeing Fidèle and cross-examining her. I can't stand the smell
of cabbage; the shops along the Meshchanskaya just reek of it.

What with this, and the infernal stench coming from under the front doors of all the houses, I held my nose and ran for all I was worth.

If that's not bad enough, those beastly tradesmen let so much soot and smoke pour out of their workshops that it's quite impossible for any respectable gentleman to take a stroll these days.

When I reached the sixth floor and rang the bell, a quite pretty-looking girl with tiny freckles came to the door. I recognized her as the same girl I'd seen walking with the old lady. She blushed slightly and straight away I realized that the little dear needed a boyfriend. 'What do you want?' she said. 'I must have a talk with your dog,' I replied. The girl was quite stupid – I could see that at once. While I was standing there the dog came out barking at me. I tried to catch hold of her but the nasty little bitch nearly sank her teeth into my nose. However, I spotted her basket in the corner. That's what I was after! I went over to it, rummaged around under the straw and to my great delight pulled out a small bundle of papers. Seeing this, that filthy dog first bit me on the thigh and then, when she'd sniffed around and discovered I'd taken the papers, started whining and pawing me, but I said to her: 'No, my dear, goodbye!' and took to my heels. The girl must have thought I was mad, as she seemed scared out of her wits.

When I arrived home, I intended starting work right away sorting the papers out, because I can't see all that well by candlelight. But Mavra decided the floor needed washing. Those stupid Finns always take it into their heads to have a good clean up at the most inconvenient times. So I decided to go for a walk and have a good think about what had happened earlier. Now at last I would find out every little detail of what had been going on, what was in their minds, who was mainly behind it – and finally I would get to the bottom of everything: those letters would tell all. 'Dogs are a clever lot,' I told myself. 'They're well versed in diplomacy, and therefore everything will be written down, including a description of the Director and his private life. And there'll be something about *her*, but never mind that now . . . Silence!' I returned home towards the evening and spent most of the time lying on my bed.

November 13th

Well now, let's have a look: the letter is quite legible, though the handwriting looks a bit doggy. Let's see: 'Dear Fidèle, I still can't get used to your plebeian name. Couldn't they find a better one for you? Fidèle, like Rosa, is in very vulgar taste. However, all that's neither here nor there. I am very glad we decided to write to each other.'

The letter is impeccably written. The punctuation is correct and even the letter 'ye' is in the right place. Even the head of our department can't put a letter together so well, for all his telling us that he went to some university or other. Let's see what else there is: 'I think that sharing thoughts, feelings and experiences with another person is one of the greatest blessings in this life.' Hm! He must have found that in some translation from the German. The name escapes me for the moment.

'I am speaking from experience, though I've never ventured further than our front door. Don't you think I lead a very agreeable life? My mistress, whom Papa calls Sophie, is passionately fond of me.'

Ah! Never mind! Silence!

'Papa often likes to fondle and stroke me as well. I take cream with my tea and coffee. Ah, *ma chère*! I really must tell you, I don't get any pleasure out of those large half-gnawed bones our Polkan likes guzzling in the kitchen. I only like bones from game-birds, and then only if the marrow hasn't already been sucked out by someone else. A mixture of several different sauces can be very tasty, as long as you don't put any capers or greens in. But in my opinion there's nothing worse than feeding dogs on little pellets of dough. There's usually some gentleman sitting at the table who starts kneading bread with hands that not long before have been in contact with all sorts of filth. He'll call you over and stick a pellet between your teeth. It's rather bad manners to refuse, and you have to eat it though it's quite disgusting . . .'

What on earth does all that mean? Never read such rubbish! As if they didn't have anything better to write about! Let's look at another page and see if we can find something with a bit more sense in it.

'I should be delighted to tell you about everything that goes on in our house. I've already mentioned something about the head of the house, whom Sophie calls Papa. He's a very strange man.'

Ah, at last! Yes, I knew it all the time: their approach is very diplomatic. Let's see what they say about this Papa.

'. . . a very strange man. Says nothing most of the time. He speaks very rarely; but a week ago he kept on saying to himself: "Will I get it, will I get it?" Once he turned to me and asked, "What do you think, Medji? Will I get it, or won't I?" I couldn't understand a word he was saying. I sniffed his shoes and left the room. Then, *ma chère*, about a week later he came home beaming all over. The whole morning men in uniforms kept arriving to congratulate him on something or other. During dinner Papa was gayer than ever I'd seen him before, telling anecdotes, and afterwards lifting me up to his shoulders and saying: "Look, Medji, what's that?" It was some sort of ribbon. I sniffed at it, but it didn't have any sort of smell at all. Then I gave it a furtive lick, and it tasted rather salty.'

Hm! That dog, in my opinion, is going too far . . . She'll be lucky if she doesn't get a whipping! Ah, he's so ambitious! Must make a note of that.

'Goodbye, *ma chère*. I'm in a tearing hurry, etc. etc . . . I'll finish the letter tomorrow. Well, hullo, here I am again. Today my mistress Sophie . . .'

Aha! Let's see what she says about Sophie. Ah, you devil! Never mind, never mind . . . Let's get on with it.

'. . . my mistress Sophie was in such a tizzy. She was getting dressed for a ball, and I was delighted to have the chance of writing to you while she was gone. My Sophie is always thrilled to go to a ball, although getting dressed usually puts her in a bad temper. I really can't understand, *ma chère*, what pleasure there is in going to these balls. Sophie comes home about six in the morning, and I can always tell from the poor dear's pale, thin look that she's had nothing to eat. I must confess *that* would be no life for me. If I didn't have woodcock done in sauce or roast chicken wings I don't know what would become of me . . . Sauce goes very well with gruel. But you can't do anything with carrots or turnips, or artichokes . . .'

The style is amazingly jerky. You can see at once that it's not written by a human being. It starts off all right, and then lapses into dogginess ... Let's have a look at another letter. Seems rather long. Hm, there's no date either!

'Ah, my dear, how deeply I feel the approach of spring! My heart is beating as though it were waiting for something. There's a perpetual noise in my ears, and I often raise a paw and stand listening at the door for several minutes. In confidence, I must tell you I have a great many suitors. I often sit watching them out of the window. Ah, if you only knew how ugly some of them are! There's one very coarse mongrel, so stupid you can see it written all over his face, and he swaggers down the street thinking he's someone very important and that everyone else thinks the same. But he's wrong. I ignored him completely, just as if I'd never set eyes on him. And that terrifying Great Dane that keeps stopping by my window! If he stood on his hind legs (the coarse clodhopper's not even capable of that) he'd be a whole head taller than Sophie's Papa – and as you know, *he's* tall enough – and plump into the bargain. The great lump has the cheek of the devil. I growled at him, but a fat lot he cared. If only he frowned! But he stuck his tongue out, dangled his enormous ears and kept staring straight at the window – the peasant! But don't imagine, *ma chère*, that my heart is indifferent to all these suitors, ah, no ... If you'd seen one gallant called Trésor, who climbed over the fence from next door. Ah my dear, you should see his little muzzle!'

Ugh, to hell with it! What trash! Fancy filling a letter with such nonsense! I need *people*, not dogs! I want to see a human being; I ask for spiritual nourishment to feed and delight my soul, but all I end up with is that rubbish! Let's skip a page and see if there's something better.

'Sophie was sitting at a small table and sewing. I was looking out of the window as I love to see who's going by. All of a sudden a footman came into the room and said: "Teplov." "Ask him in," cried Sophie and threw her arms around me. "Ah, Medji, Medji, if you could only see him: a Guards Officer with brown hair, and his eyes – what eyes – black, and shining bright as fire!"

'Sophie ran up to her room. A minute later in came a young gentleman with black whiskers. He went up to the mirror, smoothed his hair and looked round the room. I snarled and settled down by the window. Soon Sophie appeared and gaily curtseyed as he clicked his heels. I kept looking out of the window just as if they weren't there, but I tried to catch what they were saying by cocking my head to one side. Ah, *ma chère*! What rubbish they talked! About a certain lady who danced the wrong step at a ball, and someone called Bobov who looked just like a stork in his jabot, and who nearly fell over. And there was someone called Lidina who thought she had blue eyes, whereas they were really green, and so on. How can one compare, I asked myself, this gentleman of the court with Trésor? Good heavens, they're whole worlds apart! First of all, the young gentleman's face is wide and very smooth and has whiskers growing all round it, just as if someone had bound it up with a black handkerchief. But Trésor's muzzle is very thin, and he has a white spot on his forehead. And you can't compare their figures. And Trésor's eyes, his bearing, aren't the same at all. What a difference! I really don't know what she can see in this Teplov. Why is she so crazy about him?'

It strikes me something's not quite right here. How can a young court chamberlain sweep her off her feet like that? Let's have a look:

'I think that if she can care for that court chamberlain then she can easily feel the same for the civil servant who has a desk in Papa's study. Ah, *ma chère*, if only you knew how ugly he is! Just like a tortoise in a sack.'

What is this civil servant like?

'He has a very peculiar name. All the time he sits sharpening quills. His hair looks just like hay. Papa always sends him on errands instead of one of the servants.'

I think that nasty little dog is referring to me. Who says my hair is like hay?

'Sophie can't stop laughing when she looks at him.'

You damned dog, you're lying! You've got a wicked tongue! As if I didn't know you're jealous! And who's responsible for this? Why, the head of the department! That man has vowed undying hatred for me and does me harm whenever he has the chance. Let's see though: there's one more letter. Perhaps the explanation's there:

'*Ma chère* Fidèle, please forgive me for being so long writing to you. I have been in raptures. The author who said love is a second life was absolutely right. Great changes have been taking place in our house. The gentleman of the court comes every day now. Sophie is madly in love with him. Papa is in very high spirits. I even heard from Grigory (one of our servants who sweeps the floor and seems to be talking to himself all the time) that the wedding's going to be very soon. Papa is set on marrying off Sophie either to a general, or a court chamberlain, or a colonel . . .'

Damnation! I can't read any more . . . It's always noblemen or generals. All the good things in this world go to gentlemen of the court or generals. People like me scrape up a few crumbs of happiness and just as you're about to reach out to grasp them, along comes a nobleman or a general to snatch them away. Hell! I'd like to be a general, not just to win her, and all the rest of it, but to see them crawling around after me, with all their puns and high and mighty jokes from the court. Then I could tell them all to go to hell. Damn it! It's enough to make you weep. I tore that stupid little dog's letter into little bits.

December 3rd

It's impossible! What twaddle! There just *can't* be a wedding. And what if he *is* a gentleman of the court? It's only a kind of distinction conferred on you, not something that you can see, or touch with your hands. A court chamberlain doesn't have a third eye in the middle of his forehead, and his nose isn't made of gold either. It's just like mine or anyone else's: he uses it to sniff or sneeze with, but not for eating or coughing. Several times I've tried to discover the reason for these differences. Why am I just a titular counsellor?[11] Perhaps I'm really a count or a general and am merely imagining I'm a titular counsellor? Perhaps I don't really know who I am at all? History has lots of examples of that sort of thing: there was some fairly ordinary man, not what you'd call a nobleman, but simply a tradesman or even a serf, and suddenly he discovered he was a great lord or a sovereign. So if a peasant can turn into someone like that, what would a nobleman become? Say, for example, I suddenly appeared in a general's uniform, with an epaulette on my left shoulder and a blue sash across my chest – what then? What tune would my beautiful young lady sing then? And what would Papa, our Director, say? Oh, he's so ambitious! But I noticed at once he's a mason,[12] no doubt about that, although he pretends to be this, that and the other; he only puts out two fingers to shake hands with. But surely, can't I be promoted to Governor General or Commissary or something or other this very minute? And I should like to know why I'm a titular councillor? Why precisely a *titular* counsellor?

December 5th

I spent the whole morning reading the papers. Strange things are happening in Spain. I read that the throne has been left vacant and that the nobility are having a great deal of trouble choosing an heir, with the result that there's a lot of civil commotion.[13] This strikes me as very strange. How can a throne be vacated? They're saying some 'donna'[14] must succeed to the throne. But she can't succeed to the throne: that's impossible. A king must inherit the throne. And they say there's no king anyway. But there *must* be a king. There can't be a government without one. There's a king all right, but he's hiding in some obscure place. He must be somewhere, but family reasons, or fears on the part of neighbouring powers – France and other countries, for example – force him to stay in hiding. Or there may be another explanation.

December 8th

I was about to go to the office but various reasons and considerations held me back. I couldn't get that Spanish business out of my head. How could a woman inherit the throne? They wouldn't allow it. Firstly, England wouldn't stand for it. And what's more, it would affect the whole of European policy: the Austrian Emperor, our Tsar ... I must confess, these events shook me up so much I couldn't put my mind to anything all day. Mavra pointed out that I was very absent-minded during supper. And, in fact, in a fit of distraction I threw two plates on to the floor, and they broke immediately. After dinner I walked along a street that led downhill. Discovered nothing very edifying. Afterwards I lay on my bed for a long time and pondered the Spanish question.

April 43rd, 2000

Today is a day of great triumph. There *is* a king of Spain. He has been found at last. That king is *me*. I only discovered this today. Frankly, it all came to me in a flash. I cannot understand how I could even think or imagine for one moment I was only a titular counsellor. I can't explain how such a ridiculous idea ever entered my head. Anyway, I'm rather pleased no one thought of having me put away yet. The path ahead is clear: everything is as bright as daylight.

I don't really understand why, but before this revelation everything was enveloped in a kind of mist. And the whole reason for this, as I see it, is that people are under the misapprehension that the human brain is situated in the head: nothing could be further from the truth. It is carried by the wind from the Caspian Sea.

The first thing I did was to tell Mavra who I was. When she heard that the King of Spain was standing before her, she wrung her hands and nearly died of fright. The stupid woman had obviously *never* set eyes on the King of Spain before. However, I managed to calm her and with a few kind words tried to convince her that the new sovereign was well-disposed towards her and that I wasn't at all annoyed because she sometimes made a mess of my shoes.

But what can you expect from the common herd? You just can't converse with them about the higher things in life. Mavra was frightened because she was sure all kings of Spain looked like Philip II.[15] But I explained that there was no resemblance between me and Philip and that I didn't have a single Capuchin friar under my sway ... Didn't go to the office today. To hell with it! No, my friends, you won't tempt me now. I've had enough of copying out your filthy documents!

86th Martober, between day and night

One of the administrative clerks called today, saying it was time I went to the office and that I hadn't been for three weeks. So I went – just for a joke. The head clerk thought I would bow to him and start apologizing, but I gave him a cool look, not too hostile, but not too friendly either. I sat down at my desk as though no one else existed. As I looked at all that clerical scum I thought: 'If only you knew who's sitting in the same office with you ... God, what a fuss you'd make! Even the head clerk himself would start bowing and scraping, just as he does when the Director's there.' They put some papers in front of me, from which I was supposed to make an abstract. But I didn't so much as lift a finger. A few minutes later everyone was rushing around like mad. They said the Director was coming. Many of the clerks jostled each other as they tried to be first to bow to him as he came in. But I didn't budge. Everyone buttoned up his jacket as the Director walked across the office, but I didn't make a move. Stand up when he comes in – *never*! So what if he's a departmental director. He's really a *cork*, not a director. And an ordinary cork at that – a common or garden cork, and nothing else, the kind used for stopping bottles. What tickled me more than anything else was when they shoved a paper in front of me to sign. Of course, they were thinking I would sign myself as: Clerk No. So-and-so, right at the very bottom of the page. Well, let them think again! In the most important place, just where the Director puts his signature, I wrote 'Ferdinand VIII'. The awed silence that descended on everyone was amazing; but I merely waved my hand and said: 'There's really no need for this show of loyalty,' and I walked out.

I went straight to the Director's flat. He wasn't at home. The footman wouldn't let me in at first, but what I said to him made his arms drop limply to his side. I made my way straight to *her* boudoir. She was sitting in front of the mirror and she jumped up and stepped backwards. I didn't tell her, however, that I was the King of Spain. All I said was that happiness such as she had never imagined awaited her, and that we would be together, in spite of hostile plots against us. Then I thought I'd said enough and left. But how crafty women can be! Only then did it dawn on me what they are really like. So far, no one has ever discovered whom women are in love with. I was the first to solve this mystery: they are in love with the devil. And I'm not joking. While physicians write a lot of nonsense, saying they are this and that, the truth is, women are in love with the devil, and no one else. Can you see that woman raising her lorgnette in the first tier of a theatre box? Do you think she's looking at that fat man with a medal? Far from it – she's looking at the devil standing behind his back. Now he's over there, hiding in his frock-coat and beckoning her with his finger! She'll marry him, that's for certain. And all those senior civil servants who curry favour everywhere they go, who aspire to be courtiers, insisting they are patriots, when all they want is money from rents![16] They'd sell their own mother, or father, or God for money, the crawlers, the Judases! And all this ambition is caused by a little bubble under the tongue which contains a tiny worm about the size of a pinhead, and it's all the work of some barber living in Gorokhovaya Street. I can't remember his name for the moment but one thing I'm sure of is that with the help of an old midwife he wants to spread Mahommedanism throughout the world. And I've already heard tell that most of the people in France are now practising the faith.

No date. The day didn't have one

I walked incognito down Nevsky Prospekt. His Imperial Majesty drove past. Every single person doffed his hat, and I followed suit. However, I didn't give any indication that I was the King of Spain. I considered it improper to reveal my true identity right there in the middle of the crowd, because, according to etiquette, I ought first to be presented at court. So far, the only thing that had stopped me was not having any royal clothes. If only I could get hold of a cloak. I would have gone to a tailor, but they're such asses. What's more they tend to neglect their work, preferring to take part in shady transactions, and most of them end up mending the roads. I decided to have a mantle made out of my new uniform, which I'd worn only twice. I decided to make it myself, so that those crooks shouldn't ruin it, and shut myself in my room so that nobody would see. I had to cut it all up with a pair of scissors, because the style's completely different.

I don't remember the date. There wasn't any month either. Damned if I know what it was

The cloak is ready now. Mavra screamed when I put it on. But I still can't make up my mind whether to present myself at court. So far no deputation's arrived from Spain and it would be contrary to etiquette to go on my own. It would detract from my dignity. Anyway I'm expecting them any minute now.

The first

I'm really astonished the deputation's so slow in coming. Whatever can have held them up? Could it be France? Yes, she's extremely hostile at the moment. I went to the post office to see if there was any news about the Spanish deputation. But the postmaster was extremely stupid and knew nothing about it. 'No,' he said, 'no Spanish deputation has arrived but if you care to send a letter, it will be despatched in the normal manner.'

To hell with it! Letters are trash. Only chemists write letters.

Madrid, 30th Februarius

So I'm in Spain now, and it was all so quick I hardly knew what was happening. This morning the Spanish deputation arrived and I got into a carriage with them. We drove very fast, and this struck me as most peculiar. In fact we went at such a cracking pace we were at the Spanish frontier within half an hour. But then, there are railways all over Europe now, and ships can move extremely fast. A strange country, Spain: in the first room I entered there were a lot of people with shaven heads. However, I guessed that these must either be grandees or soldiers, as they're in the habit of shaving their heads over there. But the way one of the government chancellors treated me was strange in the extreme. He took me by the arm and pushed me into a small room, saying: 'Sit there, and if you call yourself King Ferdinand once more, I'll thrash that nonsense out of you.' But as I knew that this was just some sort of test I refused, for which the chancellor struck me twice on the back, so painfully that I nearly cried out. But I controlled myself, as I knew that this was the normal procedure with Spanish knights before initiating someone into a very high rank and that even now the code of chivalry is still maintained over there. Left on my own I decided to get down to government business. I have discovered that China and Spain are really one and the same country, and it's only ignorance that leads people to think that they're two different nations. If you don't believe me, then try and write 'Spain' and you'll end up writing 'China'. Apart from all this, I'm very annoyed by a strange event that's due to take place at seven o'clock tomorrow: the earth is going to land on the moon.[17] An account of this has been written by the celebrated English chemist Wellington.

I confess I felt deeply troubled when I considered how unusually delicate and insubstantial the moon is. The moon, as everyone knows, is usually made in Hamburg, and they make a complete hash of it. I'm surprised that the English don't do something about it. The moon is manufactured by a lame cooper, and it's obvious the idiot has no idea what it should be made of. The materials he uses are tarred rope and linseed oil. That's why there's such a terrible stink all over the earth, which makes us stop our noses up. And it also explains why the moon is such a delicate sphere, and why people can't live there – only noses. For this reason we can't see our own noses any more, as they're all on the moon. When I reflected how heavy the earth is and that our noses might be ground into the surface when it landed, I was so worried I put my socks and shoes on and hurried into the state council room to instruct the police not to let the earth land on the moon. The grandees with their shaven heads – the council chamber was chock-full of them – were a very clever lot, and as soon as I told them: 'Gentlemen, let us save the moon because the earth intends landing there,' everyone fell over himself to carry out my royal wish. Many of them climbed up the walls to reach the moon. But just at this moment in came the mighty chancellor. Everyone fled when they saw him. Being the king, I stayed where I was. But to my astonishment the chancellor hit me with his stick and drove me back into my room. That shows you how strong tradition is in Spain!

January in the same year falling after February

Up to this time Spain had been somewhat of a mystery to me. Their native customs and court etiquette are really most peculiar. I don't understand, I really do *not* understand them. Today they shaved my head even though I shrieked as loud as I could that I didn't want to be a monk. And I have only a faint memory of what happened when they poured cold water over my head. Never before had I gone through such hell. I was in such a frenzy they had difficulty in holding me down. What these strange customs mean is beyond me. So foolish, idiotic! And the utter stupidity of their kings who have still not abolished this tradition really defeats me. After everything that's happened to me, I think I'm safe in hazarding a guess that I've fallen into the hands of the Inquisition, and the person I thought was a minister of state was really the Grand Inquisitor himself. But I still don't understand how *kings* can be subjected to the Inquisition. It could of course be France that's putting them up to it, and I mean Polignac[18] in particular. What a swine he is! He's sworn to have me done away with. The whole time he's persecuting me; but I know very well, my friend, that you're led by the English. The English are acute politicians and worm their way into everything. The whole world knows that when England takes snuff, France sneezes.

The 25th

Today the Grand Inquisitor came into the room, but as soon as I heard his footsteps I hid under the table. When he saw I wasn't there, he started calling out. First he shouted: 'Poprishchin!' – I didn't say a word. Then: 'Aksenty Ivanov! Titular Counsellor! Nobleman!' – still I didn't reply. 'Ferdinand the Eighth, King of Spain!' I was in half a mind to stick my head out, but thought better of it. 'No, my friend, you can't fool me! I know only too well you're going to pour cold water over my head.' He spotted me all the same and drove me out from under the table with his stick. The damned thing is terribly painful. But my next discovery that every cock has its Spain, tucked away under its feathers, made up for all these torments. The Grand Inquisitor left in a very bad mood however and threatened me with some sort of punishment. But I didn't care a rap about his helpless rage, as I knew full well he was functioning like a machine, a mere tool of the English.

Da 34 te Mth eary Fеbruary 349

No, I haven't the strength to endure it any longer! Good God, what are they doing to me? They're pouring cold water over my head! They don't heed me, see me or listen to me. What have I done to them? Why do they torture me so? What can they want from a miserable wretch like me? What can I offer them when I've nothing of my own? I can't stand this torture any more. My head is burning and everything is spinning round and round. Save me! Take me away! Give me a troika with horses swift as the whirlwind! Climb up, driver, and let the bells ring! Soar away, horses, and carry me from this world! Further, further, where nothing can be seen, nothing at all! Over there the sky whirls round. A little star shines in the distance; the forest rushes past with its dark trees and the moon shines above. A deep blue haze is spreading like a carpet; a guitar string twangs in the mist. On one side is the sea, on the other is Italy. And over there I can see Russian peasant huts. Is that my house looking dimly blue in the distance? And is that

my mother sitting at the window? Mother, save your poor son!
Shed a tear on his aching head! See how they're torturing him!
Press a wretched orphan to your breast! There's no place for
him in this world! They're persecuting him! Mother, have pity
on your poor little child . . .

And did you know that the Dhey of Algiers[19] has a lump
right under his nose?

THE CARRIAGE

* * *

The little town of B— brightened up considerably when the
*** cavalry regiment set up quarters there. Before then life had
been terribly dull. If you happened to be passing through and
took one look at those squat little adobe houses peering out
into the street with an incredibly sour expression – well, words
cannot describe the oppressive feeling that came over you! It
was as if you had lost at cards or blurted out something silly
and inappropriate: in short, really depressing. The plaster on
the houses has peeled off with the rain and walls that once were
white have turned piebald and blotchy. Most of the roofs are
thatched with reeds, as is usual in our southern towns. To
improve the general aspect of the place, the mayor had long
ago ordered the little gardens to be cut down. Rarely do you
meet anyone in the street – perhaps a cockerel might venture
across the road that becomes as soft as pillows when the least
drop of rain turns the inch-deep dust into mud. And then the
streets of the little town of B— are filled with those portly
beasts called 'Frenchies' by the mayor. Thrusting their proud
snouts into the air out of their 'baths', they emit such deafening
grunts that the traveller can only whip on his horses as hard as
he can. However, you would be hard put to find any travellers
at all in the town of B—; only very rarely some squire owning
eleven serfs and clad in his nankeen frock-coat clatters along
the road in a contraption that is a cross between a brichka and
a cart, peeping out from piles of flour sacks and lashing his bay
mare with her following foal. Even the market-place has a
rather forlorn look. The tailor's house has been built very
stupidly, with one corner to the street, so that it does not face

it squarely. Opposite, some brick edifice with two windows has
been under construction for the past fifteen years. Further on,
and standing by itself, is a stylish wooden fence, painted grey
to match the mud and erected by the mayor as a model for
other projects in his younger days, before he acquired the habit
of taking a nap immediately after dinner and drinking – as a
nightcap – some peculiar decoction distilled from dried goose-
berries. Elsewhere there were only plain wattle fences.

In the middle of the square are the tiniest stalls, where you
are sure to see a bundle of bread-rings, a market-woman in a
red kerchief, thirty-six pounds of soap, a few pounds of bitter
almonds, grapeshot for the huntsman, a roll of demicotton and
two shop boys playing pitch and toss[1] all day in front of them.
But the moment the cavalry regiment was stationed in the little
town of B— everything changed. The streets were filled with
life and colour – in fact, they were completely transformed.
Those squat little houses would often witness a sprightly, well-
turned-out officer passing by in his plumed hat, on his way to
chat about promotion, or the best tobacco with a friend – and
occasionally to play cards for what might justifiably be called
the 'regimental' droshky since, without ever leaving the regiment, it went the rounds of all the officers: one day the major
would be bowling along in it, the next it would turn up in the
lieutenant's stables and a week later – lo and behold! – the
major's batman would be greasing its axles again.

The wooden fence between the houses was always festooned
with soldiers' forage caps hanging in the sun; a grey overcoat
was invariably draped over a gate somewhere. In the side-streets
one would see soldiers with moustaches that bristled like boot
brushes. These moustaches were everywhere in view. If the
women of the town gathered at the market with their jugs, a
moustache was always to be glimpsed behind their shoulders.
By the town scaffold one could always see a mustachioed soldier
reprimanding some country bumpkin who would only grunt
and goggle by way of reply. The officers revitalized local society,
which until then had consisted only of the judge, who shared
lodgings with a deacon's widow, and the mayor, who, being a
very sensible man, was apt to spend all day sleeping from

lunch to dinner, from dinner to lunch. Social life expanded and became more interesting when the brigadier general was transferred to the town. Local squires whose existence no one would have suspected before took to visiting the town more frequently, calling on the officers – sometimes for a game of whist, of which they had a very hazy notion, so lumbered were their heads with crops, hares and instructions from their wives. I regret that I cannot remember what actually inspired the brigadier general to give a sumptuous dinner. The scale of the preparations for this grand event was vast: the clatter of chefs' knives could be heard almost as far as the town gates; the entire market was commandeered for this dinner, so that the judge and his deaconess had to subsist on buckwheat cakes and fish jelly. The small courtyard at the general's quarters was packed with droshkies and other carriages. The company was male, consisting of officers and sundry local landowners. Most eminent among the latter was one Pifagor Pifagorovich Chertokutsky, one of the foremost aristocrats in B— province, who made his voice heard above all others at the elections,[2] turning up in a very fancy carriage. Once he had served in a cavalry regiment and had been one of its most notable and prominent officers. At least, he was seen at numerous balls and gatherings wherever his regiment happened to be stationed: the young ladies of Tambov and Simbirsk provinces[3] can vouch for that. He might equally have acquired fame in other provinces had he not been obliged to resign his commission as a result of one of those incidents commonly called 'an unpleasant business'. Whether he had slapped someone's face in the old days, or whether someone had slapped his, I cannot say for certain. Whatever the facts, he had to resign. However, his authority was not diminished one bit. He gallivanted around in a military-style, high-waisted tail-coat, wore spurs on his boots and sported a moustache under his nose, for without one the local gentry might think that he had served in the infantry, which he sometimes contemptuously referred to as 'infantillery' and sometimes as 'infanfery'. He visited all the crowded fairs, where the very heart of Russia, consisting of mammas, daughters and fat squires, would flock to amuse themselves, in their brichkas, tarantasses and such preposterous carriages as you would never even see in your dreams. He had a pronounced talent for sniffing out a cavalry regiment's quarters, leaping with the utmost aplomb from his light carriage or droshky, and in no time at all he would make the officers' acquaintance. At the last election he had given a splendid dinner for the gentry, at which he announced that if only he were elected marshal he would not fail to 'set them up'. By and large, he lorded it like a real gentleman, as they say in the provinces, married a pretty girl with a dowry of two hundred serfs and several thousand in cash. These funds were immediately lavished on a team of six truly excellent horses, gilt locks for the doors, a tame monkey for the house and a French butler. The young lady's two hundred serfs, together with two hundred of his own, were mortgaged for some business transaction. In brief, he was an exemplary landowner, a real paragon. Apart from him, there were several other landowners at the general's dinner, but there is nothing much to say about them. The remaining guests were officers from the same regiment, and two staff officers: a colonel and a rather corpulent major. The general himself was rather stout and stocky, but, in the words of his officers, a good commander. He spoke in a rather thick, portentous bass.

The dinner was magnificent: the profusion of sturgeon, beluga sterlet, bustards, quails and partridges amply testified that the chef had gone without food and sleep for the past two days, and that four soldiers, knife in hand, had toiled all night to help him prepare fricassees[4] and gêlées.[5] The multitude of bottles – tall slender ones of Lafitte, short-necked ones of madeira, the fine summer's day, the wide-open windows, the plates of ice, the officers with their last waistcoat button undone, the crumpled shirt-fronts of the owners of exceedingly capacious tail-coats, the conversational crossfire drowned by the general's voice and lubricated with champagne – all made for perfect harmony.

After dinner the guests rose with an agreeable heaviness in their stomachs. When they had lit their long- and short-stemmed pipes, they stepped out on to the porch with cups of coffee in their hands. The general's, the colonel's and even the major's uniforms were completely unbuttoned, so that their pure silk, rather aristocratic braces were visible. But the other officers, duly observing regimental etiquette, kept their tunics fastened – except for the last three buttons.

'Now you can have a look at her,' the general was saying. 'Here, my dear fellow,' he muttered, turning to his adjutant – a rather smart young man of pleasant appearance – 'tell them to bring the bay mare. Then you can see for yourselves!'

At this the general took a pull on his pipe and released a plume of smoke. 'She's not properly groomed yet, there's no decent stabling in this wretched little town. But she's a very presentable . . . *puff* . . . *puff* . . . horse!'

'And has Your Excellency . . . *puff* . . . *puff* . . . had her long?' asked Chertokutsky.

'Well . . . *puff* . . . *puff* . . . *pu* . . . *ff* . . . well, not so long. It's only two years since I had her from stud.'

'And did Your Excellency take her broken in, or did you have her broken in here?'

'*Puff* . . . *puff* . . . *pu* . . . *pu* . . . *u* . . . *u* . . . *ff* . . . here' – and at this the general vanished completely in smoke.

Meanwhile a soldier sprang out from the stables, the clatter of hooves was heard and finally another soldier appeared, wearing white overalls and with enormous black moustaches, leading by the bridle a trembling, terrified mare which suddenly reared and almost lifted the soldier – moustaches and all – into the air.

'Now, now, Agrafena Ivanovna,' the soldier said, bringing her up to the porch steps.

Agrafena Ivanovna was the mare's name. As spirited and as wild as a southern beauty, she nervously stamped her hooves on the wooden steps and then suddenly stopped.

Putting down his pipe, the general began surveying her with evident satisfaction. The colonel came down from the steps and took Agrafena Ivanovna by the muzzle. The major patted Agrafena Ivanovna on the leg, while the others clicked their tongues in approval. Then Chertokutsky went down and followed the mare; the soldier holding the bridle and standing to attention stared the guests right in the eyes, as if he intended jumping right into them.

'Very fine, very fine!' exclaimed Chertokutsky. 'Excellent points. If I may ask Your Excellency, how does she go?'

'She has a good stride only – damn and blast! – that idiot of a vet gave her some sort of pills and for the past two days she's done nothing but sneeze.'

'She's a fine horse – very fine! And does Your Excellency have the right kind of carriage?'

'Carriage? But she's a saddle-horse.'

'I know. But what I really meant is – does Your Excellency have the right kind of carriage for your other horses?'

'Well, I don't have much in the way of carriages. I must confess that for some time I've been wanting an up-to-date calash. I've written to my brother in St Petersburg about it, but I've no idea if he's going to send me one or not.'

'In my opinion, Your Excellency . . .' observed the colonel, 'you can't beat a Viennese calash.'

'There you are right . . . *puff* . . . *puff* . . . *puff*.'

'I have an exceptional calash, of real Viennese make, Your Excellency!'

'Which one? The one you came in?'

'Oh no, that's purely for riding around in, for short trips. But as for the other, why, it's truly amazing – as light as a feather! And when you sit in it – if I may put it like this – it's as if your nurse were rocking you in the cradle.'

'You mean it's comfortable?'

'Very, very comfortable! The cushions, springs – all top-notch!'

'Well, that's nice!'

'And so roomy! Oh yes, I've never seen one like it, Your Excellency. When I was in the army I used to get ten bottles of rum and twenty pounds of tobacco into the boxes, not to mention six uniforms, underlinen and two pipes as long as tapeworms, if I may put it like that, Your Excellency. And you could stow a whole ox in the pockets!'

'That's good!'

'It cost four thousand, Your Excellency.'

'At that price it *should* be good. And did you buy it yourself?'

'No, Your Excellency. I acquired it by chance. It was bought by a friend of mine – a fine chap and childhood pal, a man with whom you would have got along perfectly. We used to share everything. I won it off him at cards. Now, would you do me the honour, Your Excellency, of coming to have dinner with me tomorrow? You could inspect the calash at the same time.'

'I really don't know what to say – it's a bit awkward, you know, coming on my own. Would you allow me to bring my fellow officers along?'

'The officers will be most welcome too! ... Gentlemen, I should consider it an honour to have the pleasure of entertaining you in my home!'

The colonel, major and the other officers thanked him with polite bows.

'In my opinion, Your Excellency, if one buys something it should be good and if it's no good there's no point in buying it. When you do me the honour of visiting me tomorrow I'll show you a few improvements I've introduced on my estate.'

The general glanced at him and blew more smoke out of his mouth. Chertokutsky was really delighted that he had invited the gentlemen officers. Mentally he was already ordering the pâtés and sauces as he cheerfully looked at them. For their part, the look in their eyes and their little gestures in the way of half-bows showed that they were twice as well disposed towards him as before.

Chertokutsky now became more free and easy and there was a languid note in his voice, as though it were simply weighed down with pleasure.

'There you will meet the lady of the house, Your Excellency.'

'That will be most pleasant,' replied the general, stroking his moustache.

After this Chertokutsky could not wait to return home and ensure that the preparations for receiving his dinner guests next day were made in good time. He was about to pick up his hat, but for some strange reason he stayed on a little longer.

Meanwhile card-tables had already been set up in the room. Soon the whole company was divided into foursomes for whist and sat down in different parts of the general's rooms. Candles were brought. Chertokutsky was a long time making up his mind whether or not to sit down to whist. But since the officers were pressing him, he considered that it might be terribly bad form to refuse and so he took a seat. As if by magic there suddenly appeared before him a glass of punch which he immediately downed, without thinking. After two rubbers there again appeared a glass of punch at Chertokutsky's elbow and he downed that too, again without thinking, declaring beforehand: 'It's really time I went home, gentlemen.' But again he sat down, to a second game. Meanwhile private conversations were struck up in various parts of the room. The whist players were rather quiet, but the others who were not playing sat to one side on sofas, engaged in conversation of their own. In one corner the staff captain who was reclining with a cushion thrust under one side, his pipe between his teeth, was regaling a group of fascinated listeners with a fairly spicy and flowing account of his amorous adventures. One extraordinarily fat squire with short hands rather like overgrown potatoes was listening with an unusually cloying expression as he made sporadic attempts to extract his snuff-box from his back pocket. In another corner a rather heated argument about squadron drill had broken out and Chertokutsky, who had about that time twice played a jack instead of a queen, suddenly interrupted the conversation that did not concern him at all, calling out from his corner: 'In which year? Which regiment?', oblivious of the fact that his questions were quite malapropos. Finally, a few minutes before supper, the whist came to an end, although the games continued verbally and everyone's head was bursting with whist. Chertokutsky clearly remembered that he had won a great deal, but he did not pick up his winnings. After getting up from the table he stood there for a long time, like a man who finds he has no handkerchief in his pocket. Meanwhile supper was served. It goes without saying there was no shortage of wine and that Chertokutsky felt almost compelled to refill his glass from time to time, as there were bottles to left and right of him.

An interminable conversation dragged on at table, but it was conducted rather oddly. One squire who had served in the 1812 campaign told of a battle that had certainly never taken place and then, for some mysterious reason, removed the stopper from a decanter and stuck it in the pudding. In brief, by the time the party started to break up it was already three in the morning and the coachmen had to carry several of the guests in their arms as if they were parcels from some shopping expedition. Despite his aristocratic pretensions, Chertokutsky bowed so low and with such a broad sweep of the head as he climbed into his carriage that he later found he had brought home with him two thistles in his moustache.

At home everyone was fast asleep. The coachman had difficulty finding a footman, who conducted his master across the drawing-room and handed him over to a chambermaid, whom Chertokutsky somehow managed to follow to the bedroom, and he lay down beside his pretty young wife, who was sleeping in the most enchanting posture in her snow-white nightdress. The jolt made by him falling on the bed woke her. Stretching, raising her eyelashes and blinking three times in quick succession, she opened her eyes with a half-angry smile, but when she realized that her husband had no intention of showing her any kind of endearment, turned over on her other side in pique. Resting her fresh cheek on her hand she fell asleep soon after him.

When the young mistress of the house awoke beside her snoring spouse it was at an hour that country folk would not consider early. Mindful that he had returned after three o'clock in the morning, she did not have the heart to wake him and so, donning her bedroom slippers that her husband had specially ordered from St Petersburg, her white nightdress draped around her like a flowing stream, she went to her dressing-room, washed herself in water as fresh as herself and went over to her dressing-table. After a couple of glances in the mirror she saw that she was looking really quite pretty that morning. This apparently insignificant circumstance led her to sit in front of her mirror exactly two hours longer than usual. Finally she dressed herself very charmingly and went out into the garden for some fresh air. As if by design, the weather was glorious, as only a summer's day in the south of Russia can be. The noonday sun beat down fiercely, but it was cool walking down the shady paths with their overarching foliage; the flowers were three times as fragrant in the warmth of the sun. The pretty young wife forgot that it was already twelve o'clock and that her husband was still asleep. The post-prandial snores of the two coachmen and the postilion, who were fast asleep in the stable behind the garden, already reached her ears, but she continued to sit in the shady avenue from which the totally deserted high road was clearly visible. Suddenly a cloud of dust in the distance caught her attention.

Straining her eyes, she soon made out several carriages, headed by an open two-seater trap, in which were sitting the general, his thick epaulettes glinting in the sun, with the colonel at his side. This was followed by a four-seater carriage with the major and the general's adjutant, with two other officers sitting opposite. This carriage was followed by the regimental droshky, familiar to all and which was then in the stout major's possession. The droshky was followed by a *bonvoyage* in which four officers were seated, with a fifth squeezed in. After the *bonvoyage* three officers on their fine dappled bays came into view.

'Surely they're not coming here?' wondered the mistress of the house. 'Oh, my God! They *are*! They've turned at the bridge!'

She shrieked, wrung her hands and dashed right across the flowerbeds and shrubbery to the bedroom, where her husband was sleeping like a log.

'Get up! Hurry now! Get up!!' she cried, tugging at his arm.

'Ehhhh?' Chertokutsky said, stretching, without opening his eyes.

'Get up, poppet! Do you hear? We've visitors!'

'Visitors? *What* visitors?' – and having said this he moaned plaintively, like a calf nuzzling its mother's udder. 'Mmm-mmm . . .' he mumbled, 'give me your little neck, sweetie, I want to kiss it.'

'Darling! For heaven's sake get up! At once! It's the general and the officers. Oh – you've a thistle in your moustache!'

'The general? So, he's on his way already? Why on earth didn't anyone wake me up? Now, about dinner . . . has everything been properly prepared?'

'What dinner?'

'But didn't I give instructions for dinner . . . ?'

'Give instructions? You came home at four o'clock in the morning and however hard I tried I couldn't get one word out of you . . . I didn't wake you, poppet . . . because I felt sorry for you . . . you needed your sleep.'

She spoke these last words in a particularly languid and pleading voice.

His eyes goggling, Chertokutsky lay on his bed for a minute as if struck by a thunderbolt. Finally he leapt out of bed with only his nightshirt on, forgetting that this was highly improper.

'God! I'm such an ass!' he exclaimed, slapping his forehead. 'Yes, I did invite them for dinner. So, what are we going to do? Are they far off?'

'No, they're not! They'll be here any minute.'

'Darling, you go and hide . . . Hey, who's there? Oh, it's you, you wretched girl! Now come here, you silly thing . . . what are you afraid of? Now, the officers will be here any minute, so you must tell them the master's not at home . . . tell them he won't be here at all . . . that he went away early this morning. Do you hear? And tell all the other servants. Now, hurry up!'

With these words he grabbed his dressing-gown and ran to hide in the carriage-shed, assuming he would be perfectly safe there. But as he stood in a corner he realized that even there someone might spot him.

'Now, this is better!' flashed through his mind and in no time at all he had pulled down the steps of the carriage standing right by him, jumped in and slammed the door after him. For greater security he covered himself with the leather apron and travelling rug and lay there absolutely still, huddled in his dressing-gown.

Meanwhile the carriages had driven up to the front steps. The general alighted and gave himself a little shake; the colonel followed, smoothing the plumes of his hat. Then out of the droshky jumped the stout major, his sabre under his arm. Then the slim subalterns sprang down from the *bonvoyage*, with the ensign who had been squeezed in with them. Lastly the officers who had been elegantly prancing about on horseback dismounted.

'The Master's not at home,' announced a footman as he came out on to the front steps.

'Not at home! I suppose he'll be back for dinner then.'

'Oh no, sir. Master's gone out for the day. He won't be back until around this time tomorrow.'

'Well I'll be damned!' said the general. 'What the hell's going on here!?'

'I must admit, it's all rather odd!' laughed the colonel.

'And how! What's he playing at?' continued the general, visibly put out. 'Hell and damnation! If he can't receive people why did he invite them in the first place?'

'I do agree, Your Excellency. I too cannot understand how anyone can behave so badly,' observed a young officer.

'*What!!?*' shouted the general, who was in the habit of using the interrogative particle whenever he addressed a junior officer.

'I was saying, Your Excellency . . . how could anyone behave like that?'

'Quite so . . . well, if something unexpected had happened he could at least have told us. Otherwise he shouldn't have invited us.'

'No, Your Excellency, there's nothing we can do about it . . . Let's go back,' said the colonel.

'Yes, of course, that's all we can do . . . but we might take a look at that carriage of his without him. I'm sure he wouldn't have gone away in it. Hey . . . you! Come here, old chap!'

'What can I do for Yer Excellency?'

'Are you the stable-boy?'

'That I am, Yer Excellency.'

'Well, show us the new calash your master bought recently.'

'If you'd please come into the carriage-shed, sir.'

The general went with his officers into the shed.

'Shall I move it out a bit, sir, it's rather dark in here.'

'Yes . . . enough . . . that's enough . . . that's fine!'

The general walked around the calash with his officers and carefully inspected the wheels and springs.

'Well, it's nothing special,' remarked the general. 'It's nothing out of the ordinary.'

'Yes, nothing much at all,' agreed the colonel. 'Can't say anything good about it.'

'It seems to me, Your Excellency, that it can't possibly be worth four thousand,' commented one of the young officers.

'*What!!?*'

'Your Excellency, I said that I don't think it's worth four thousand.'

'Four thousand – my eye! It's not even worth two thousand – sheer junk!'

'Well, perhaps there's something special about the inside. Please unbutton the apron, my dear chap.'

And right before the officers' eyes there was Chertokutsky, sitting in his dressing-gown and curled up in the most bizarre fashion.

'Aha! So here you are!' exclaimed the astonished general.

And with these words the general immediately slammed the door, pulled the apron back over Chertokutsky and rode off with his officers.

THE GOVERNMENT
INSPECTOR

CHARACTERS AND COSTUMES

Notes for the Actors

MAYOR A long-serving man, quite shrewd after his own fashion. Although a grafter, conducts himself with dignity. Rather serious and somewhat sententious. Speaks neither loudly nor softly, nor too much nor too little. Every word he says carries weight. Features are coarse and hard, typical of a man who has worked his way up from the lower ranks. Shifts from fear to joy, from servility to arrogance rather easily, like any coarse person. Normally goes around in a uniform with tabs and high boots with spurs. His hair is close-cropped and greying.

ANNA ANDREYEVNA His wife, a provincial coquette, on the verge of middle age, educated partly on novels and albums, partly by running a pantry and supervising the maids' room. Very inquisitive. Given the chance, displays vanity. Sometimes dominates husband, but only because the latter is at a loss for a reply. Her power over him is confined to trifles, however, and consists of mild reproaches and sneers. Changes her dress four times during the play.

KHLESTAKOV Young man of about twenty-three, thinnish, slightly built. Rather dim – 'not all there', as they say. The type known in government offices as feather-brained. Talks and acts without thinking first. Incapable of concentrating on anything for long. Speech is staccato; the words fly from his lips totally unexpectedly. The more sincerity and simplicity the actor performing this role displays, the more he will profit by it. Fashionably dressed.

OSIP His manservant. Like any other servant getting on in years. Talks seriously, with eyes downcast. A moralizer, he likes to recite to himself homilies intended for his master. His voice is almost flat, and when he speaks to his master it acquires a stern, sharp and even somewhat coarse tone. He is cleverer than his master and quicker to catch on, but he is rather taciturn and keeps his own counsel. Wears a shabby grey or blue frock-coat.

BOBCHINSKY *and* DOBCHINSKY   Both are short, dumpy and highly inquisitive. Almost indistinguishable. Both have little pot bellies. Both speak very rapidly, to the accompaniment of wild gesticulations. Dobchinsky is slightly taller and more serious, whereas Bobchinsky is more easy-going and livelier.

LYAPKIN-TYAPKIN   The judge. Has read five or six books, therefore something of a freethinker. Much given to conjecture and lends particular weight to every word. The actor must always maintain a portentous expression. Talks in a bass voice, drawling out each word; wheezes and huffs like an antique clock which hisses before striking the hour.

ZEMLYANIKA   Warden of Charities. Very plump, clumsy and sluggish man, but for all that a cunning rogue. Very servile and ready to please.

POSTMASTER   Simple-minded to the point of naïvety.

The other roles do not require special explanations. Their prototypes are almost always to be found before one's eyes. The actors must pay particular attention to the last scene. The last spoken word must produce a sudden electric shock on everyone, instantaneously. The entire group must change its position in the blink of an eye. The cries of astonishment must be uttered by the ladies all at the same time, as if from a single bosom. The whole effect may be lost if these remarks are ignored.

MEANINGS OF NAMES OF CHARACTERS

Skvoznik-Dmukhanovsky (mayor): A compound of *skvoznik* – 'a puff of wind' and the Ukrainian *dmukhati* – 'to blow'. *Skvoznik* also has the colloquial meaning of 'sly old fox', while *dmukhati* has associations with puffing oneself up with pride.

Khlopov (Inspector of Schools): From *khlop* or *kholop*, 'a serf', with subsidiary meanings of 'sycophant', 'groveller'. His first name and patronymic, Luka Lukich, suggest onions, of which he reeks.

Lyapkin-Tyapkin (judge): Derived from popular expression *lyap-tyap*, said of something done haphazardly, in a slapdash manner. The verb *tyapat'* means 'to pilfer, steal', while the colloquial *lyapat'* means 'to bungle, botch'.

Zemlyanika (Warden of Charities): Meaning 'wild strawberries'.

Shpekin (postmaster): Possibly from *shpik* – 'a police spy'; he likes to open and read private letters.

Khlestakov: From verb *khlestat'* – to lash, with secondary meaning of 'to speak idly', 'to prattle', 'to lie'. Nabokov has brilliantly described the wealth of associations of this name: 'Khlestakov's very name is a stroke of genius, for it conveys to the Russian reader an effect of lightness and rashness, a prattling tongue, the swish of a slim walking cane, the slapping sound of playing cards, the braggadocio of a nincompoop and the dashing ways of a lady-killer' (*Nikolai Gogol*, New Directions, New York, 1959).

Lyulyukov: From verb 'to rock in a cradle, to lull'.

Rastakovsky: Compunded from verb *takat'* – 'to be a "yes-man"'.

Korobkin: From *korobka* – 'a box'. (In *Dead Souls* we have the landowner Korobochka.)

POLICEMEN:

Ukhovyortov: From *ukho* – 'ear' – and *vertet'* – 'to twist'. Suggests rough treatment.

Svistunov: From *svistun* – 'a whistler.'

Pugovitsyn: From *pugovitsa* – 'a button'.

Derzhimorda: From *derzhat'* – 'to hold' – and *morda* – 'snout'. Implication that he treats his victims with great brutality. The word has passed into the language to mean a brutal policeman.

THE GOVERNMENT INSPECTOR

A Comedy in Five Acts

It's no good blaming the mirror if your mug's crooked
— Proverb

CHARACTERS

ANTON ANTONOVICH SKVOZNIK-DMUKHANOVSKY, *mayor*
ANNA ANDREYEVNA, *his wife*
MARYA ANTONOVNA, *his daughter*
LUKA LUKICH KHLOPOV, *Inspector of Schools*
KHLOPOV'S WIFE
AMMOS FYODOROVICH LYAPKIN-TYAPKIN, *judge*
ARTEMY FILIPPOVICH ZEMLYANIKA, *Warden of Charities*
IVAN KUZMICH SHPEKIN, *postmaster*
PYOTR IVANOVICH DOBCHINSKY
PYOTR IVANOVICH BOBCHINSKY } *local landowners*
IVAN ALEKSANDROVICH KHLESTAKOV, *government official
from St Petersburg*
OSIP, his servant
KHRISTIAN IVANOVICH HUEBNER, *district doctor*
FYODOR ANDREYEVICH LYULYUKOV
IVAN LAZAREVICH RASTAKOVSKY } *retired officials,
respected citizens*
STEPAN IVANOVICH KOROBKIN
KOROBKIN'S WIFE
STEPAN ILICH UKHOVYORTOV, *chief of police*

SVISTUNOV
PUGOVITSYN   } *police constables*
DERZHIMORDA
ABDULIN, *shopkeeper*
FEVRONYA PETROVNA POSHLYOPKINA, *locksmith's wife*
A SERGEANT'S WIDOW
MISHKA, *mayor's servant*
A WAITER
Guests, merchants, townsfolk, petitioners

ACT I

[*A room in the mayor's house.*]

Scene I

[MAYOR, WARDEN OF CHARITIES, INSPECTOR OF SCHOOLS, JUDGE, CHIEF OF POLICE, DISTRICT PHYSICIAN, *two* CONSTABLES.]

MAYOR   I've called you here, gentlemen, to tell you some news that you're not going to like. A government inspector[1] is coming to pay us a visit.

JUDGE, WARDEN OF CHARITIES [*together*] What? An inspector?

MAYOR   Yes, a government inspector from St Petersburg – incognito. And with secret instructions, what's more.

JUDGE   Well! What do you say to that!

WARDEN OF CHARITIES   As if we didn't have enough on our plates!

INSPECTOR OF SCHOOLS   Good God! And with secret instructions!

MAYOR   I had a kind of premonition about this. All last night I dreamt about a couple of extraordinary rats – they were black and absolutely enormous. They came in, took a few sniffs and off they went. Now, let me read you this letter from Andrey Ivanovich Chmykhov – you know him, Artemy Filippovich. This is what he writes: 'My dear old friend, cousin and benefactor (mutters under his breath as he rapidly scans the letter) . . . to warn you . . .' Hm . . . here it is . . . 'I hasten to warn you, among other things, that a government official has arrived with instructions to inspect the entire province – and our district[2] in particular. [*Raises one finger meaningfully*]. 'This has come to me from the most reliable sources, although I understand he's posing as an ordinary person. And since I know very well that like everyone else you've been guilty of the odd little peccadillo, because you're a smart fellow and not stupid enough to let anything slip through your fingers . . .' Hm . . . 'as we're all friends here I advise you to take the necessary precautions, as he could turn up at any time, if he's not there already, staying somewhere incognito . . . Yesterday I . . .' Hm . . . the rest is all about family matters – '. . . my cousin Anna Kirilovna is here with her husband. Ivan Kirilovich has put on a lot of weight and he's still playing the fiddle . . .' and so on. Well, that's how things are!

JUDGE   Oh yes, an extraordinary state of affairs, most extraordinary! There's more in this than meets the eye, I can tell you!

INSPECTOR OF SCHOOLS   But why, Anton Antonovich? What does it mean? Why should an inspector want to visit us?

MAYOR   I reckon it's fate, that's what [*sighs*]. So far, thank God, they've always gone snooping around other towns. Now it's our turn.

JUDGE   Do you know what I think, Anton Antonovich? There must be some subtle political reason behind all this. I'll tell you what it means: Russia . . . yes, Russia . . . wants to go to war and the Ministry's sent an official to root out any traitors.

MAYOR   That's a bit far-fetched! Call yourself an intelligent man! I ask you – traitors in our neck of the woods! Do you think we're on the frontier here? Why, you could gallop away for three years without even reaching a foreign country!

JUDGE   That may well be, but I'm telling you . . . er . . . you don't understand. Those government officials in St Petersburg have got eyes like hawks! Oh yes! No matter how far away we may be, *nothing* gets past that lot.

MAYOR   Whether it does or doesn't you've been given fair warning, gentlemen. For my part I've given a few instructions and I'd advise you to follow suit. Particularly you, Artemy Filippovich. There's no doubt whatsoever that the government inspector will first want to inspect the charitable institutions in your charge. Make sure everything looks neat and tidy and that the patients' nightcaps are clean, so that they don't look like chimney-sweeps, the way they do when they're at home.

WARDEN OF CHARITIES   Don't you worry yourself about that. We can get them clean nightcaps, that's no problem.

MAYOR   Good. And then you must write something over the patients' beds in Latin, or some other learned language – that's your department, Dr Huebner: what illness, when the patient fell ill, the date, day of week ... And see they stop smoking that foul tobacco. Whenever you enter the wards you sneeze your head off. And you'd better thin the patients out a bit, otherwise he might think the hospital's badly run, or that the doctor's incompetent.

WARDEN OF CHARITIES   Oh no! Dr Huebner and I have our own methods as regards treatment: let Nature take its course. We have no time for expensive medicines. After all, man's not very complicated: if he dies, he dies, if he recovers, he recovers. Besides, Dr Huebner can't make himself understood to the patients, as he can't speak a word of Russian.[3]

[Dr Huebner utters a sound midway between an 'i' and an 'e'.]

MAYOR   And as for you, Ammos Fyodorovich, I'd advise you to take that courthouse of yours in hand. Your watchmen have been raising geese in the vestibule where petitioners usually wait and the goslings get under everyone's feet. Of course, I've nothing against poultry-keeping, it's an admirable pastime for anyone. And why shouldn't the watchmen take it up? But a courthouse is no place for that ... I meant to point this out before, but somehow it kept slipping my mind.

JUDGE   I'll see they're all driven into the kitchen right away. Now, why don't you pop over for dinner tonight?

MAYOR   And another thing. There's all kind of rubbish hanging up to dry in your own chambers. That simply won't do. As for that hunting whip right over the cabinet with all the court files! I know you're keen on hunting, but for the time being you'd better have it taken down. You can hang it up again when the inspector's gone. And there's that district assessor of yours . . . no doubt he's a man of learning, but he stinks just as if he'd stepped out of a distillery. We can't have that either. I've been wanting to mention this to you for some time now, but I was too busy with other matters. You know, there's remedies for that kind of thing – if it really is his natural odour, as he says. Advise him to eat onions, or garlic or something. Or perhaps Dr Huebner might be able to prescribe something.

[*Dr Huebner emits the same sound.*]

JUDGE   No – he just can't get rid of it. He says that when he was a baby his nurse dropped him and there's been a whiff of vodka about him ever since.

MAYOR   Well, I just thought I'd point it out to you. Now, as for my private arrangements and what Chmykhov calls peccadilloes in his letter, I don't know what to say. I don't need to tell you that there isn't a man alive who hasn't some little indiscretion on his conscience. That's how the good Lord created us – and those Voltairean[4] freethinkers can say what they like!

JUDGE   But what do you understand by 'little indiscretions', Anton Antonovich? I mean, there are sins and there are sins. I can tell you quite openly that I take bribes, but what do they amount to? Borzoi puppies! Now, that's something quite different!

MAYOR   Whether they're puppies or whatever they're still bribes.

JUDGE   I can't go along with you, Anton Antonovich. What if someone accepts a five-hundred rouble fur coat, or a shawl for his wife, for example?

MAYOR   Well, supposing all you take by way of bribes is borzoi puppies. But then, you don't believe in God and you don't go to church. At least I'm a firm believer. I'm in church every Sunday. But you . . . I know you only too well – once you start talking about the creation of the world it's enough to make your hair stand on end!

JUDGE   Well, at least I worked it out all by myself, with my own brains.

MAYOR   Too much grey matter can be worse than none. However, I just thought I'd mention the courthouse. If truth be told, no one's likely to go poking his nose in there – it appears to be one of those privileged institutions under divine protection. But you, Luka Lukich, as Inspector of Schools, really must take those teachers of yours in hand. Of course, I do realize they're scholars, educated at different colleges. But their behaviour is extremely odd. Well, that's only natural with learned men. For example, one of them – that fellow with the fat face . . . I can't remember his name . . . who's incapable of standing behind his desk without pulling the most hideous faces⁵ . . . like this [*pulls a face*] . . . and then he starts stroking his beard under his necktie. It wouldn't matter if he only pulled a face at one of his pupils. Oh yes, it might even be necessary – I'm no judge of that. But imagine if he did that in front of our visitor! Why, that could be disastrous! A government inspector could take it as a personal insult and all hell might break loose.

INSPECTOR OF SCHOOLS   So what am I to do with him? I've mentioned it to him several times. Only the other day, when the Director came into the classroom, he made the most hideous face I've ever seen! He didn't mean any harm,⁶ but I was really hauled over the coals for allowing our young people's heads to be filled with radical ideas.

MAYOR   And it's the same with the history teacher, I must tell you. He's a learned fellow, his head's crammed with facts, but he gets so excited explaining things that he completely forgets himself. I listened to him once – everything was fine as long as he was talking about the Assyrians and Babylonians. But the moment he came to Alexander of Macedon I can't begin to tell you what came over him. Heavens! I thought the place was on fire! He leapt from behind his desk, grabbed a chair and banged it on the floor as hard as he could. Well, he obviously meant to convey that Alexander of Macedon was a great hero. But that's no reason to go smashing chairs up . . . the Government will have to bear the cost.

INSPECTOR OF SCHOOLS   Yes, he's very enthusiastic! I've pointed it out to him several times and all he says is: 'Say what you like, but I'm ready to lay down my life in the cause of learning!'

MAYOR   Yes, it's fate's inscrutable law that clever men are either drunkards or pull faces horrible enough to shock the saints.

INSPECTOR OF SCHOOLS   God help anyone who goes in for teaching![7] You're scared of putting a foot wrong, everyone interferes, everyone wants to prove he's as smart as the next man.

MAYOR   Well, that wouldn't really worry us, but there's that damned incognito business. Suddenly he might look in and say: 'Ah! Here you are, my dear friends! Tell me, who's the judge here?' 'Lyapkin-Tyapkin,' I say. 'Fetch Lyapkin-Tyapkin! And who's Warden of Charities?' 'Zemlyanika,' I reply. 'Send Zemlyanika too!' Now, that's the rotten thing about it.

Scene II

[*The same, with* POSTMASTER.]

POSTMASTER   Please tell me, gentlemen, what's this about a government inspector coming here?

MAYOR   Haven't you heard?

POSTMASTER   I heard something from Pyotr Ivanovich Bobchinsky – he was at the post office just now.

MAYOR   Well, you tell me what you think about it.

POSTMASTER   What I think? I think we're going to war with the Turks!

JUDGE   That's right. My thoughts entirely!

MAYOR   You're both barking up the wrong tree.

POSTMASTER   No – there's going to be war with the Turks – it's the French up to their dirty tricks again.

MAYOR   What war with the Turks? *We're* the ones who are going to suffer, not the Turks. That's a fact. I've a letter to prove it.

POSTMASTER   Then there's not going to be any war with the Turks!

MAYOR   Well, what are your thoughts on the subject, Ivan Kuzmich?

POSTMASTER   Me? No – what do *you* think, Anton Antonovich?

MAYOR   What do I think? I'm not scared . . . well, just a bit. It's the shopkeepers and townsfolk who cause me concern. They've been complaining that I squeeze them hard, but as God is my witness, if I do sometimes accept a little trifle from them I do it without any ill feeling. I have a suspicion [*takes* POSTMASTER *by the arm and leads him to one side*] – yes, I suspect someone may have informed on me. If you stop to consider, why should they send an inspector to us? Now listen, Ivan Kuzmich. For everyone's benefit, do you think you could manage to open every letter that goes through the post office – just a teeny bit – and read it, to see if someone's informing or if it's simply everyday correspondence.[8] If it's harmless you can seal it again. In fact, you could even deliver it 'opened in error'!

POSTMASTER   Yes, I know! You don't need to tell me. No, I don't do it as a precaution but more out of curiosity. I'm dying to know what's going on in the world! And let me tell you, letters provide fascinating reading. Some are a sheer joy to read, the way things are described in them . . . and they're so edifying! Better than the *Moscow Gazette*[9] any day!

MAYOR   Now tell me, have you come across anything about an official from St Petersburg?

POSTMASTER   No, nothing at all about a St Petersburg official. But there's plenty about officials from Kostroma and Saratov.[10] It's a pity, though, that you don't read these letters. Such marvellous things in them. Only the other day a lieutenant wrote to a friend and he described a ball in the most sprightly manner – excellent it was! 'My life is wending its way through Elysian fields, my dear friend . . . so many girls, bands playing, flags unfurling . . .' And written with such feeling! I simply had to keep that one for myself. Would you like me to read the rest?

MAYOR   No, I've no time for that now. But do me a favour, Ivan Kuzmich – should you come across a complaint or denunciation, don't have any qualms – just keep it back.

POSTMASTER   Of course, with the greatest pleasure.

JUDGE   You two had better watch out or you'll find yourselves in hot water!

POSTMASTER   Oh, don't say that!

MAYOR   Don't worry – it's not as if we were going to let the public know. After all, these are private matters.

JUDGE   There's trouble brewing, I know it! Well, what I really came for, Anton Antonovich, was to give you a little present – a nice puppy. She's the sister of that hound I was telling you about. I suppose you've heard that Cheptovich and Varkhovinsky are suing each other, so now I'm in clover! I can go hunting on both their estates now!

MAYOR   Good God! I couldn't care less about your hares right now – I can't get that damned incognito out of my mind. Any minute I expect the door to fly open and – lo and behold!

Scene III

[*The same. In rush* BOBCHINSKY *and* DOBCHINSKY, *both out of breath.*]

BOBCHINSKY   A most extraordinary occurrence!

DOBCHINSKY   Such unexpected news!

ALL   What is it?

DOBCHINSKY   Something quite unforeseen. We'd just gone to the inn . . .

BOBCHINSKY   [*interrupting*] We'd just gone to the inn, Pyotr Ivanovich and I . . .

DOBCHINSKY   [*interrupting*] Please, Pyotr Ivanovich! Let me tell them the story.

BOBCHINSKY   No, let me . . . you're no good at telling stories, you don't have the knack . . .

DOBCHINSKY   But you'll get muddled up and leave half of it out.

BOBCHINSKY   Oh no I won't, I swear it! Now, don't interrupt and let me tell them. Gentlemen . . . please tell Pyotr Ivanovich to stop butting in.

MAYOR   For God's sake get on with it! My heart's in my mouth. Please sit down, gentlemen. Here's a chair for you, Pyotr Ivanovich.

[*They all sit around the two Pyotr Ivanoviches.*]

So, tell us what it's all about.

BOBCHINSKY   All right then, I'll tell you everything, in the right order. Well, as soon as I'd had the pleasure of leaving you – just after you'd been so upset about that letter – I ran off immediately – please don't interrupt, Pyotr Ivanovich, I remember everything! As I was saying, please take note, I dashed over to Korobkin's. As Korobkin wasn't at home I went off to Rastakovsky's and as he was out I dropped in on Ivan Kuzmich to tell him your news. And just as I was leaving I bumped into Pyotr Ivanovich.

DOBCHINSKY   [*interrupting*] Near the stall where they sell pies.

BOBCHINSKY   Near the stall where they sell pies. So, I meet Pyotr Ivanovich and I say: 'Have you heard the news Anton Antonovich received in his letter from a reliable source?' But Pyotr Ivanovich had already heard about it from your housekeeper, Avdotya, who'd just been sent to Pyotr Ivanovich Pochechuyev's[11] for something or other . . .

DOBCHINSKY   For a French brandy keg.

BOBCHINSKY   [*pushing Dobchinsky's hands away*] Yes, for a French brandy keg. So, off we go to Pochechuyev's – please don't interrupt! – and on the way Pyotr Ivanovich suddenly says: 'Let's stop at the inn. I haven't eaten a thing since this morning and my stomach's rumbling like mad.' Yes, Pyotr Ivanovich's stomach, that is. 'They've just had a delivery of fresh salmon at the inn so we can go and have a bite to eat,' he says. And the moment we entered we saw a young man . . .

DOBCHINSKY   [*interrupting*] Quite well turned out he was . . . and in mufti.

BOBCHINSKY   Well turned out and in mufti. He started walking around the room with such a thoughtful expression . . . and there was something about his features, his refined manners – and lots on top! [*Flutters his hand in front of his forehead.*] At once I had a hunch and I tell Pyotr Ivanovich: 'There's more in this than meets the eye.' And Pyotr Ivanovich snaps his finger for the landlord to come over . . . you know, old Vlas – his wife had a baby three weeks ago, such a bright little boy. One day he'll keep an inn, just like his dad. So, Pyotr Ivanovich whispers to Vlas: 'Who's that young gentleman?' and Vlas replies: 'That . . . that young . . .' Hey! Stop interrupting, Pyotr Ivanovich! Please stop it! You're hopeless at telling stories. You lisp and one of your teeth whistles! 'That young gent,' Vlas tells me, 'is an official from St Petersburg. His name's Ivan Aleksandrovich Khlestakov, he's on his way to Saratov province. There's something fishy about the way he's been behaving. Been here a fortnight and never sets foot outside the place, has everything charged to his account and won't pay a copeck for anything.' The moment he told me this it dawned on me. 'Aha!' I say to Pyotr Ivanovich.

DOBCHINSKY   No, Pyotr Ivanovich, it was I who said 'Aha!'

BOBCHINSKY   All right, you said it and then I said it. We both said 'Aha!' And I ask: 'Why is he staying cooped up here when he's supposed to be heading for Saratov?' Oh yes, no doubt about it. He's the inspector, that's who he is!

MAYOR   Who? What inspector?

BOBCHINSKY   The inspector you received news of . . . the *Government* Inspector!

MAYOR   [*terrified*] Good God! What are you saying? It can't be him!

DOBCHINSKY   Oh yes it is! He doesn't pay for a thing, doesn't show his face anywhere. Who else could he be? And his order for horses[12] is made out for Saratov.

BOBCHINSKY   Oh yes, it must be him. He's got eyes in the back of his head, doesn't miss a thing. When he saw we were eating salmon – because of Pyotr Ivanovich's stomach . . . Well! He even peered right into our plates. I was scared out of my wits, I can tell you!

MAYOR   Lord have mercy on us sinners! What room is he in?

DOBCHINSKY   Number five, under the stairs.

BOBCHINSKY   The same room where those officers started a brawl last year.

MAYOR   And has he been here long?

DOBCHINSKY   Well, it must be already two weeks. He arrived on St Basil the Egyptian's Day.[13]

MAYOR   Two weeks! [*Aside*] Holy mackerel! Saints and martyrs deliver us! During the past two weeks the sergeant's widow's been flogged, the prisoners haven't had their rations and the streets are like a pigsty – filth everywhere! Oh the disgrace of it! The humiliation! [*Clutches head.*]

WARDEN OF CHARITIES   So, what do you think, Anton Antonovich? Shall we make an official visit to the inn – in full ceremonial dress?

JUDGE   Well, the head of the town should go first, then the clergy, then the shopkeepers. That's what it says in *The Acts of John the Mason* . . . [14]

MAYOR   No, let me handle it. I've been in some tight corners and I've always muddled through. What's more, I even got thanked in the end! So perhaps God will help us out of this one. [*Turning to Bobchinsky*] You say he's a young man?

BOBCHINSKY   Yes, no more than twenty-three or four.

MAYOR   All the better. It's much easier to feel out a young man, we could have had a lot of bother if they'd sent some old fogey, but a youngster's like an open book. Now, gentlemen, go and get your departments in order and I'll stroll over to the inn on my own, or with Pyotr Dobchinsky – casually, as it were – to make sure the visitors are being treated well. Hey, Svistunov!

SVISTUNOV   Yes, sir?

MAYOR   Hurry up and fetch the chief of police. No, hold on . . . I need you here. Just tell someone else to bring him here as soon as possible – and come back right away. [SVISTUNOV *dashes off.*]

WARDEN OF CHARITIES   We'd better be going, Ammos Fyodorovich, I think something nasty's about to happen.

JUDGE   What are you scared of? Just put clean nightcaps on the patients and no one will be any the wiser.

WARDEN OF CHARITIES   Nightcaps are the least of my worries. The patients are supposed to have oatmeal porridge, but there's such a stench of cabbage[15] wafting down the corridors you have to hold your nose!

JUDGE   Well, I've nothing to worry about on that score. In fact, who on earth would want to inspect a courthouse? And if anyone did look in to examine the files he'd rue the day. Fifteen years I've sat on the bench and one glance at a case report drives me to despair. Solomon himself couldn't sort out what's true or false in them.

[*Exeunt* JUDGE, WARDEN OF CHARITIES, INSPECTOR OF SCHOOLS *and* POSTMASTER. *They collide in the door-way with the returning* SVISTUNOV.]

Scene IV

[MAYOR, BOBCHINSKY, DOBCHINSKY *and* SVISTUNOV.]

MAYOR   Is the droshky ready?

SVISTUNOV   It's ready, sir.

MAYOR   Go into the street . . . no . . . wait! Go and fetch . . . but where are all the others? You're the only one? Surely I ordered Prokhorov to be here too? Where's Prokhorov?

SVISTUNOV   Prokhorov's at the police station, but he's not fit for duty.

MAYOR   Why's that?

SVISTUNOV   Well, this morning he was carried back dead drunk. We soused him with two tubs of water, but he still hasn't sobered up.

MAYOR   [*clutching his head*] Oh my God, oh my God! Now, go outside and . . . no . . . wait . . . first run up to my room and fetch my sword and new hat. Got it? Good. Let's go, Pyotr Ivanovich.

BOBCHINSKY   And me too, let me come, Anton Antonovich.

MAYOR   No, Pyotr Ivanovich, it's out of the question, it's too awkward. Besides, we couldn't all fit into the droshky.

BOBCHINSKY   I don't mind, I'll manage . . . yes, I'll hop along behind – look, like this! All I want is to peep through a crack in the door to see those elegant manners again.

MAYOR   [*taking off his sword, to Svistunov*] Now, hurry and round up the other constables and tell each one to take a . . . Hell! My sword's scratched all over. That damned shop-keeper Abdulin knows very well the mayor's sword's in poor condition and still he doesn't send me a new one. Oh, they're a crafty lot! I bet those bastards are already cooking up petitions against me on the sly. Now, tell each constable to

take a street in his hand and start ... Damnation! I mean,
take a broom in his hand and sweep the street that leads to
the inn – and make sure it's swept spick and span ... D'ye
hear?! You watch out now, I know your type. You get
friendly with everyone and then slip the silver spoons down
your jackboots ... You watch it! You can't pull the wool
over my eyes. What did you do to that draper Chernayev,
eh? He gave you two yards of cloth for a new uniform and
you swiped the whole roll! You watch out! You're taking
bribes above your rank! Get going!

Scene V

[*The same, with* CHIEF OF POLICE.]

MAYOR   Ah, Stepan Ilich! Where on earth have you been?
What the hell's going on here?

CHIEF OF POLICE   I was here ... right by the gates.

MAYOR   Now look here, Stepan Ilich! That official from
St Petersburg has arrived. What arrangements have you
made?

CHIEF OF POLICE   Just as you instructed. I've sent Constable
Pugovitsyn and the others to clean up the pavements.

MAYOR   Where's Derzhimorda?

CHIEF OF POLICE   Derzhimorda's gone on the fire engine.[16]

MAYOR   And Prokhorov's drunk?

CHIEF OF POLICE   Yes, sir.

MAYOR   How could you let such a thing happen?

CHIEF OF POLICE   God knows. There was a brawl outside
town yesterday and he went to restore order – and he came
back plastered.

MAYOR   Now you listen, this is what you must do. Constable
Pugovitsyn is very tall, so station him on the bridge to create
a good impression. And tell them to pull down that old fence
by the shoemaker's and stick up some poles to make it look
like a building site. The more we pull down the busier the
mayor will appear. Oh God! I clean forgot about that refuse
they've dumped by the fence! About forty cartloads of it. What

a rotten town this is! As soon as you put up some monument or a simple fence they pile all sorts of rubbish against it. The devil knows where they get it from! [*Sighs.*] And if that inspector should happen to ask the constables if they're contented, make sure they reply: 'Perfectly happy, Your Excellency!' But if anyone says he's unhappy I'll give him something to be unhappy about later. Oh, oh! I've sinned, I've sinned a lot. [*Picks up hatbox instead of his hat.*] God help me out of this mess quickly and I'll light the most enormous candle you've ever seen.[17] I'll make each swine of a shopkeeper stump up for a hundred pounds of wax. Oh my God! Let's go . . . Pyotr Ivanovich. [*Puts on the box instead of his hat.*]

CHIEF OF POLICE   But Anton Antonovich! That's a box, not a hat!

MAYOR   [*throwing it down*] So it is, damn it! If the inspector asks why the hospital chapel – you know, the one for which funds were allocated five years ago – hasn't been built yet, don't forget to say that we did start it, but it burned down. I even sent in a report to that effect, otherwise someone might have been fool enough to say it was never even begun. And tell Derzhimorda not to be so free with his fists. He thinks keeping good order means distributing shiners all round, to innocent and guilty alike. Let's go, Pyotr Ivanovich. [*Goes out and returns.*] And don't let the soldiers go out into the street half-naked. That garrison riff-raff like to wear their uniforms with nothing on down below.

[*Exeunt all.*]

Scene VI

[ANNA ANDREYEVNA *and* MARYA ANTONOVNA *run on stage.*]

ANNA ANDREYEVNA   Where are they, for heaven's sake? Oh, goodness me! [*Opens door.*] My husband! Anton! Antosha! [*Speaking quickly*] It's all your fault, always you! The way you fuss about and waste time. 'I need a pin, I need a scarf.' [*Runs to window and cries out.*] Anton! Where are you

going? What's that? He's arrived? The inspector? Does he
have a moustache? What kind of moustache?

MAYOR   I'll tell you later. Later, dear.

ANNA ANDREYEVNA   Later? Whatever next – later! I don't
want your 'later' . . . I only want to know if he's a colonel.
Eh? [*Scornfully*] Now he's gone. You'll pay for this. And
what with you and your 'Mama! Mama! Won't be a moment
. . . I just want to fasten my scarf.' You and your moment!
Because of you we've found nothing out – you little flirt! She
hears the postmaster's here and starts preening herself in
front of the mirror, first from this side and then the other.
You think he's interested, but he pulls faces at you the
moment your back is turned!

MARYA ANTONOVNA   So, what shall we do, Mama? We'll
know everything in a couple of hours anyway.

ANNA ANDREYEVNA   A couple of hours! Thank you very
much! Most obliged for your answer. Why not a couple of
months – we'd know even more by then. [*Leans out of
window.*] Hey, Avdotya! What did you hear? Eh? Has anybody arrived? You didn't hear? Stupid girl! They shooed you
away? Well, what of it – you still could have asked him. You
couldn't? I'm not surprised. All you can think of is men.
What's that? They drove off too quickly? But you should
have run after the droshky. Now, hurry up! Do you hear?
Run and find out where they've gone. And be sure to find
out who he is, what he looks like. Do you hear? Peep through
the keyhole and find everything out – if his eyes are black.
And mind you come back right away – do you hear? Now
hurry, hurry! [*Keeps shouting as the curtain falls in front of
the two of them standing at the window.*]

ACT II

[*A small room at the inn. A bed, table, empty bottle, shoes, clothes-brush and so on.*]

Scene I

OSIP [*lying on his master's bed*] To hell with it! I'm starving and my stomach's rumbling like a regimental band going full blast! At this rate we'll never get home, that's for sure. My dear master's blown all his money on the road and now he's stuck here with his tail between his legs and doesn't do a damn thing. We'd plenty of cash for the journey – more than enough. But no: he has to show off in every town. [*Mimics him.*] 'I say, Osip,' he tells me, 'fish around and find me the best room and order a first-rate dinner – no inferior cooking for me, nothing but the best will do.' It wouldn't be so bad if he really was a somebody, but he's just a lousy little clerk. If he meets a stranger on the road it's out with the cards. Now look where you've landed us! Ugh, I'm sick to death of this life. Oh yes, you can have an easy time of it in the country. True, not much going on, but there's less to worry about. Get yourself a woman and lie in bed all day and stuff yourself with pies. But let's face it, there's no place like St Petersburg. All you need is some cash and then you can lead a nice rafeened life – theatters, performing dogs – anything you want! And they speak all so polite and genteel – as good as noblemen. Just you trot along to Shchukin Market[18] and the stallholders'll call you sir. Take the ferry and you'll find yourself rubbing shoulders with government officials. If it's company you want then go into any shop and some old campaigner'll spin you a yarn about camp-life and tell you what the stars hold, so everything's as clear as daylight. Or an officer's missus'll drop in – and sometimes a lady's maid – wow! [*Bursts out laughing and shakes his head.*] Oh, all so frightfully rafeened, I'm sure! You'll never hear a rude word and everyone calls you sir. And if you're tired of hoofing it, just take a cab and sit back like the master. And if you don't want to pay – no problem. Every house has a back door as well as a front so you can do a bunk – and the devil himself couldn't catch you!

But there's one snag: some days you can stuff yourself silly – and then you starve to death, like now. And it's his fault! What can I do with him? His old man sends him money, enough to keep him going. And what happens? Off he goes, out on the town, driving around in cabs. And poor old me has to go and collect theatre tickets every night. And before the week's out he'll send me to the flea market to flog his new tail-coat. Sometimes he'll flog everything until all he has left is some scruffy old jacket or overcoat. Honest, it's true! He'll fork out 150 roubles for a new dress-coat – finest English cloth – and then go and flog it for twenty. And his trousers'll go for a song.[19] Any why? All because he won't do an honest day's work. You won't catch *him* going to the office: he'll be strolling down the boullivards and playing cards. Oh, if his old man got wind of it! His being a civil servant wouldn't matter a damn – it'll be up with the tails and he'll get such a tanning he won't be able to sit down for days. You've got a job, so why don't you get on with it! And now the landlord's saying there's no more food until we've paid for what we had. And what if we don't pay? [*Sighs.*] God! What wouldn't I give for a bowl of cabbage soup! I'm that starving I could eat a horse . . . Oh, someone's knocking . . . must be him. [*Hurriedly jumps off the bed.*]

Scene II

[OSIP *and* KHLESTAKOV.]

KHLESTAKOV   Here, take these [*Hands* OSIP *his cap and cane.*] So, loafing around on my bed again?

OSIP   Why should I loaf around on your bed? Haven't I seen a bed before?

KHLESTAKOV   You're lying, you've been loafing around on it. Just look – it's all rumpled.

OSIP   But why should I need a bed? Do you think I don't know what a bed is? I've got legs, I can stand on them. What do I want with your bed?

KHLESTAKOV   [*pacing the room*] See if there's any tobacco left in my pouch.

OSIP   How could there be any tobacco? You smoked the last scrap four days ago.

KHLESTAKOV   [*walking up and down and pursing his lips into various shapes. Then he says in a loud, determined voice*] Now you listen to me, Osip!

OSIP   What is it, sir?

KHLESTAKOV   [*in a loud but not so determined voice*] You go down.

OSIP   Down where?

KHLESTAKOV   [*in a decidedly undetermined, almost pleading voice*] Down to the dining-room. Tell them I want some lunch.

OSIP   Oh no! I'm not going down there!

KHLESTAKOV   How dare you disobey me – you oaf!

OSIP   It wouldn't do no good even if I did go. The landlord says he won't give us no more to eat.

KHLESTAKOV   How dare he refuse! What a cheek!

OSIP   And he says he's going to complain to the mayor. He says: 'You've been here two weeks and haven't paid a thing. You're a pair of crooks and your master's a swindler. We've seen conmen and spongers like you before!'

KHLESTAKOV   And you enjoy telling me all this, you pig!

OSIP   'At this rate,' says he, 'anyone can come along, make himself at home, run up a bill and we'd never get rid of him. I'm telling you straight, I'm off to get you two clapped in gaol.'

KHLESTAKOV   That's enough, you moron! Now, go and tell him to send up some lunch. What a swine!

OSIP   I'd better get the landlord up here, so you can have it out.

KHLESTAKOV   What do *I* want with the landlord? Tell him yourself.

OSIP   But sir . . .

KHLESTAKOV   Go, damn it! Tell him to come here!

[*Exit* OSIP.]

Scene III

[KHLESTAKOV *alone*.]

I'm absolutely famished! I thought I could walk my appetite off, but no – it damned well won't go away! Yes, if I hadn't had that fling in Penza I'd have enough to get home. That infantry captain really rooked me. The hands that bastard dealt himself! We only sat down for a quarter of an hour and he cleaned me out. Still, I'd dearly love to have another crack at him, but fat chance of that! This town's a real dump. The grocers won't give you a thing on tick, the mean buggers! [*First whistles an air from* Robert,[20] *then the 'The Red Sarafan',*[21] *then nothing in particular.*] Why don't they come?

Scene IV

[KHLESTAKOV, OSIP *and* WAITER.]

WAITER   The landlord sent me to ask what you'll be wanting, sir.

KHLESTAKOV   Why, hullo old chum! How are you today? Well, I hope?

WAITER   Very well, sir.

KHLESTAKOV   How's things at the inn? Business good?

WAITER   Oh yes, thank God.

KHLESTAKOV   Plenty of guests?

WAITER   Yes, there's enough.

KHLESTAKOV   Now listen to me, old chum. They haven't brought me my lunch yet, so tell them to get a move on. You see, I've important business to attend to later.

WAITER   The landlord said he won't be serving you no more. Matter of fact, he's meaning to complain to the mayor today.

KHLESTAKOV   Complain? What about? Put yourself in my shoes, old chum. What am I supposed to do? A man has to eat. If I go on like this I'll waste away ... I'm absolutely starving – and I'm not joking.

WAITER   Yes, sir. The landlord said: 'I won't give him nothing more till he's paid for what he's had.' That's exactly what he said.

KHLESTAKOV   Reason with him, persuade him.

WAITER   But what should I tell him?

KHLESTAKOV   Try and make him understand that I've got to eat. You don't have to worry about money ... that peasant thinks if he can go a day without food then others can do the same. That's rich, that is!

WAITER   All right, I'll tell him.

Scene V

[KHLESTAKOV *alone*.]

Well, things look pretty rough: what if he doesn't give me food? I've never been so hungry in my life! Perhaps I could flog a few clothes – my trousers perhaps? No, I'd rather starve to death than show up at home without my St Petersburg suit. A pity Joachim[22] wouldn't rent me that carriage in St Petersburg – it would have been marvellous, dammit, driving home in a carriage, bowling along in grand style right up to some neighbouring landlord's porch, lamps blazing and Osip sitting behind me in his livery. I can just imagine all the commotion: 'Who is it? Whose carriage is this?' they would ask. And then the footman [*stiffens up as he imperson-*

ates a footman] announces: 'Ivan Aleksandrovich Khlestakov of St Petersburg! Will you receive him?' Those country bumpkins haven't the foggiest what 'receiving' means. If some cloddish landowner goes visiting he'll barge straight into the drawing-room like a clumsy bear! But I'll waltz over to the pretty daughter and say, 'Charmed, I'm sure, mamselle . . .' [*Rubs his hands and scrapes his foot.*] Pfoo! [*Spits.*] I'm sick with hunger!

Scene VI

[KHLESTAKOV, OSIP *and* WAITER.]

KHLESTAKOV Well?

OSIP They're bringing lunch.

KHLESTAKOV [*Claps his hands and does a little jig on his chair.*] Hurrah! It's coming!

WAITER [*with plates and a napkin*] The landlord says it's for the last time.

KHLESTAKOV Landlord! Damn your landlord! What have you got there?

WAITER Soup and a joint.

KHLESTAKOV What? Only two courses?

WAITER That's all, sir.

KHLESTAKOV It's an outrage! I won't stand for it! You go and ask him what the hell he's playing at. It's nowhere near enough.

WAITER The landlord says it's too much.

KHLESTAKOV And is there no gravy?

WAITER We don't have none, sir.

KHLESTAKOV Why not? I saw them preparing gallons of the stuff when I went past the kitchen. And only this morning there were two dumpy little characters gorging themselves on salmon in the dining-room – and plenty more besides.

WAITER Well, perhaps there is and perhaps there ain't.

KHLESTAKOV What do you mean *ain't*?

WAITER There just ain't.

KHLESTAKOV No smoked salmon, fried fish, cutlets?

WAITER   All that's for our proper customers, sir.

KHLESTAKOV   You're a damned idiot!

WAITER   Yes, sir.

KHLESTAKOV   A filthy little pig ... how is it they're given food and not me? Aren't I a hotel guest, just like them?

WAITER   But they're not the same as you.

KHLESTAKOV   What are they then?

WAITER   They're the regular sort. They pays their bills.

KHLESTAKOV   I'm not going to argue, you imbecile. [*Ladles himself some soup and eats.*] Call this soup? You just poured dishwater into a bowl, that's what. It's got no taste and it stinks. I don't want this soup, bring me something else.

WAITER   I'll take it back, sir. The landlord says if you don't want it you don't have to eat it.

KHLESTAKOV   [*shielding the soup with his hands*] No, no! Leave it where it is, you idiot! And I would advise you not to try it on with me. [*Eats.*] My God! What disgusting soup! [*Carries on eating.*] I don't suppose mortal man ever tasted such slops! There's feathers floating around in it instead of fat. [*Cuts the chicken in the soup.*] Ugh! Where on earth did you get that old hen! Now, give me the joint ... there's a drop of soup left, Osip ... you can have it. [*Carves the joint.*] What's this supposed to be? It's no joint, that's for sure!

WAITER   What is it then?

KHLESTAKOV   The devil only knows, but it's not roast meat. They must have gone and roasted the kitchen cleaver instead of the beef! [*Eats.*] What muck they're feeding me on, the rogues! One mouthful's enough to give you jaw-ache. [*Picks his teeth.*] Villains! It's just like tree bark, I can't pick it out! My teeth will turn black from this stuff. Crooks! [*Wipes his mouth with napkin.*] Anything else?

WAITER   That's all, sir.

KHLESTAKOV   The rotten bastards! The swine! Not even a fish course, or dessert! Layabouts! All they know is how to fleece travellers.

[WAITER *clears away and goes out with* OSIP.]

Scene VII

KHLESTAKOV   Honestly! I feel as if I've eaten nothing at all,
only whetted my appetite. If only I had a little cash I'd send
out for some rolls.

OSIP   [*Enters.*] The mayor's downstairs – he's making
inquiries about you.

KHLESTAKOV   [*terrified*] Oh God – the Mayor! It's all up with
me! That swine of a landlord's managed to complain already.
What if he really does put me behind bars? Well, if they treat
me like a gentleman perhaps I'll . . . Oh, no, no! I'm damned
if I'll go! There's officers hanging around the inn and just to
show off. I swapped a few winks with that shopkeeper's pretty
daughter. No, I won't go! How dare he! And who does he take
me for – some shopkeeper or common workman? [*Plucks up
courage and stands erect.*] Yes, I'll tell him straight to his face:
'How dare you . . . how *dare* you . . . ? [*The door knob turns.*
KHLESTAKOV *grows pale and cringes.*]

Scene VIII

[KHLESTAKOV, MAYOR, DOBCHINSKY. *On entering the*
MAYOR *stops dead in his tracks.* KHLESTAKOV *and*
MAYOR *stare at each other for a few minutes, terrified
and eyes popping.*]

MAYOR   [*recovering slightly and standing to attention*] May I
offer you my humble greetings, sir!

KHLESTAKOV   [*Bows.*] The honour's mine.

MAYOR   Please forgive the intrusion.

KHLESTAKOV   Please don't worry.

MAYOR   It is my duty, as mayor of this town, to ensure that
all visitors and people of quality suffer no inconvenience.

KHLESTAKOV   [*stammering a little at first, but speaking loudly
by the end of his speech*] What could I do? It's not my fault.
I'll pay up, honest I will. They'll send money from home.
[BOBCHINSKY *peeps around door.*] It's the landlord who's

more to blame. Serves meat as tough as old boots – and as for the soup! The devil only knows what he tipped in it. I had to chuck it out of the window . . . He's been starving me for days now . . . And the tea's quite peculiar – it reeks of fish! And why should I? . . . I mean to say . . . I ask you!

MAYOR [*frightened*] Forgive me, but it's not my fault, really – it's not. There's always top-quality meat at the market, supplied by sober and honest butchers from Kholmogory.[23] I've no idea where he could have got that meat from. But if things are not to your liking, may I suggest you accompany me to other accommodation?

KHLESTAKOV Oh no! I won't go! I know what you mean by other accommodation! You mean the gaol! What right have you, how can you have the nerve . . . I hold a government post in St Petersburg [*becomes heated*] I . . . I . . . I . . .

MAYOR [*aside*] Good Lord! He's in a terrible temper! He knows everything! Those confounded shopkeepers must have blabbed.

KHLESTAKOV [*growing bolder*] You can fetch the entire constabulary – I won't budge! I'll go straight to the Minister! [*Thumps his fist on the table.*] Who do you think you are? Tell me!

MAYOR [*standing to attention and shaking all over*] Have mercy, don't ruin me! I've a wife and little ones . . . Don't ruin me . . .

KHLESTAKOV I won't go! Really! What's it to do with me – just because you have a wife and children I have to go to prison! Very nice! [BOBCHINSKY *peers around the door and hides in fright.*]
      Thank you very much, but I'm not going!

MAYOR [*trembling*] It was my inexperience, sheer inexperience, honestly. All through inexperience. And my wretched salary. Please judge for yourself, sir. An official's pay isn't even enough for tea and sugar. And if I did take a few bribes – well, they were simply trifles – something for the table, a piece of cloth for a suit. And as for that story about the sergeant's widow – the one who keeps a stall at the market and whom I'm supposed to have had flogged – I swear it's all malicious gossip, pure slander cooked up by those who wish me harm, the kind of people who wouldn't hesitate to do away with me.

KHLESTAKOV   So what! What the hell's that got to do with me? On the other hand – why are you telling me all this, about enemies and that sergeant's widow? A sergeant's widow is one thing, but don't you dare flog *me*! What a nerve! I ask you! Yes, I'll pay my bill, I'll pay up, but I don't have any money right now. That's why I'm stuck here – because I'm broke.

MAYOR   [*aside*] He's a sly customer. So, that's his game! What a smokescreen he's laid! Sort that out if you can! There's no knowing what line to take with him. But I'll have a shot at it and see what happens. What will be will be! [*Aloud*] If you're actually short of funds, I can be of service immediately. It's my duty to assist travellers.

KHLESTAKOV   Right! Then give me a loan and I'll be able to settle up with the landlord right away. About two hundred should do it, or even less, perhaps.

MAYOR   [*offering notes*] There's exactly two hundred roubles. You don't need to count them.

KHLESTAKOV   Much obliged. I'll repay you the moment I'm home . . . I always pay on the dot. I can see you're a gentleman. Now I don't envisage any problems.

MAYOR   [*aside*] Well, thank God for that! He took the money, so all will be plain sailing from now on, I hope. And I slipped him an extra two hundred.

KHLESTAKOV   Hey, Osip!
    [*Enter* OSIP.]
    Tell that waiter to come back! [*To* MAYOR *and* DOBCHINSKY] But why are you standing, gentlemen? Please be seated. [*To* DOBCHINSKY] Here, take a seat.

MAYOR   It's all right, we prefer to stand.

KHLESTAKOV   Really! Please do sit down! Now I can see what sincere and genuine people you are! I must confess, I'd thought you'd come here to . . . to . . . [*To* DOBCHINSKY] Why don't you sit down! [MAYOR *and* DOBCHINSKY *sit down.* BOBCHINSKY *peeps in at the door and listens.*]

MAYOR   [aside] I must be bolder. He wants to remain incognito. All right, we can play the same game too: we'll pretend we haven't the faintest idea who he is. [Aloud] While Pyotr Ivanovich Dobchinsky – one of our local landowners – and I were going about our business, we called at the inn to see that the guests were being well looked after. That's because I'm not the kind of mayor who doesn't give a hoot about such things. Oh no! As a true Christian, from pure love of my fellow men, I go beyond the call of duty and I like to see that everyone is given a warm welcome. And now fate has rewarded me with the pleasure of making such an agreeable acquaintance.

KHLESTAKOV   It's my pleasure too. If it hadn't been for you I'd have been stuck here for ages. I had no idea how I was going to pay the bill.

MAYOR   [aside] A likely story! Didn't know how he'd pay his bill! [Aloud] May I venture to inquire where your destination lies?

KHLESTAKOV   I'm going to my estate in Saratov.

MAYOR   [aside, with a sarcastic expression] Saratov indeed! And he doesn't even blush! Oho, you have to be on your toes with this fellow! [Aloud] Travelling is a most delightful undertaking, sir! On the one hand changing horses can be a great inconvenience, but on the other it diverts the mind. I dare say you're travelling chiefly for pleasure?

KHLESTAKOV   Oh no, my father sent for me. The old boy's cross because I haven't made much headway in St Petersburg. He thinks the moment you arrive at the office they'll pin a St Vladimir[24] on you. I'd like to make *him* join the office rat race!

MAYOR   [aside] Just listen how he piles it on! He's even dragged in his old father. [Aloud] And will you be staying here long, sir?

KHLESTAKOV   I really don't know. My father's an obstinate old fogey and as thick as two planks. But I'll tell him straight to his face: as you wish, but I cannot live anywhere except St Petersburg. And why should I waste my life among peasants? Today's needs are different: my soul thirsts for the higher things in life.

MAYOR [*aside*] What a web he spins! One lie after the other – and he never wavers for one moment! He's nothing to look at either – so pint-sized I could squash him with my thumbnail. You just wait! I'll make you spill the beans somehow! [*Aloud*] That's absolutely true: what can you do out here in the sticks? Take this place, for instance. You slave away, you don't sleep at night, you do your best for your country, you don't spare yourself – and what do you get for it? [*Glances around the room.*] Seems a bit damp in here, don't you think?

KHLESTAKOV It's a lousy room. And as for the bedbugs! I've never seen the like of them – they bite like dogs!

MAYOR That's disgraceful! A distinguished visitor like you and look what he has to put up with. Bedbugs that should never have been created in the first place! And the room's a little on the dark side, isn't it?

KHLESTAKOV Yes, it's pitch-black in here! The landlord's taken to refusing me candles. Now and then I feel the urge to do something – a little reading. Or if I feel like it, some writing. But I can't, as it's so dark!

MAYOR Might I venture to suggest . . . but no! I'm not worthy of such an honour.

KHLESTAKOV What is it?

MAYOR No, really. I'm unworthy.

KHLESTAKOV What are you talking about?

MAYOR If it's not too presumptuous . . . well, there's an excellent room at home, so cheerful, so quiet . . . But no – the honour would be too great! Please don't be offended, I merely offered it in all sincerity, from the purest motives.

KHLESTAKOV On the contrary! I'd be delighted! I'll be far better off in a private home than in this dosshouse.

MAYOR It will make me so happy! My wife will be overjoyed. Yes, that's the way I am. Ever since I was a child I've always tried to be hospitable – especially if the guest is a cultured gentleman like yourself. Please don't think I'm saying this to flatter you. No: that's not one of my vices. I speak from the bottom of my heart!

KHLESTAKOV Much obliged, I'm sure. And I'm like you – I've

no time for two-faced people. I find your frankness and cordiality most gratifying. I do confess that I ask for nothing more out of life than devotion and respect, respect and devotion.

Scene IX

[*The same. Enter* WAITER, *followed by* OSIP. BOBCHINSKY *peeps round the door.*]

WAITER   You called, sir?

KHLESTAKOV   Yes – give me the bill.

WAITER   But I've given you the bill every single day . . .

KHLESTAKOV   I can't keep track of your stupid bills. Tell me: how much does it come to?

WAITER   You had a full dinner the first day, sir – and on the second some salmon. After that everything was on credit.

KHLESTAKOV   Idiot! He's itemizing every single thing! Just tell me – how much altogether?

MAYOR   Now please don't concern yourself with it . . . he can wait. [*To* WAITER] Get out! You'll be sent the money.

KHLESTAKOV   That's fine with me. [*Puts the money away.*]

[*Exit* WAITER. BOBCHINSKY *peeps around door.*]

Scene X

MAYOR   Would you care to inspect some of the local institutions – the charity hospital, for example?

KHLESTAKOV   Why? What's there to see?

MAYOR   Well, you could see how we run things . . . the way we organize everything.

KHLESTAKOV   By all means. At your service!

[BOBCHINSKY *pokes his head through the doorway.*]

MAYOR   And if you so wish, we can proceed to the district school and you may observe how we instruct our students.

KHLESTAKOV   Why of course – by all means!

MAYOR   And afterwards you might care to see the prison, to see how criminals are looked after here.

KHLESTAKOV   Why the prison? I'd really prefer to inspect the charitable institutions.

MAYOR   As you please. Will you take your carriage or come with me in the droshky?

KHLESTAKOV   Oh, I'd better come with you.

MAYOR   [to DOBCHINSKY] There won't be any room for you, Pyotr Ivanovich.

DOBCHINSKY   It's all right, I'll manage.

MAYOR   [aside, to DOBCHINSKY] Now listen: run as fast as your legs will carry you with two notes – one for Zemlyanika at the charity hospital and the other for my wife. [To KHLESTAKOV] If you will allow me, I'll just dash off a few lines to my wife, so that she can prepare to receive our distinguished guest.

KHLESTAKOV   Why bother? Anyway, here's some ink, but I don't know about paper ... Could you use the bill instead?

MAYOR   Oh yes ... [Writes and talks to himself] And now we'll see how things go after a good lunch and a nice fat bottle of Madeira! We have a local Madeira – doesn't look strong but it would knock an elephant off its feet. As long as I can find out what his game is and what I have to fear from him ... [After finishing the notes he hands them to DOBCHINSKY, who walks to the door. At that moment it falls off its hinges and the eavesdropping BOBCHINSKY comes flying on to the stage with it.]

   [Loud exclamations. BOBCHINSKY picks himself up.]

KHLESTAKOV   Are you all right? I hope you haven't injured yourself.

BOBCHINSKY   No, it's nothing! Nothing at all to worry about, sir – just a slight bruise on the tip of my nose, that's all. I'll run over to Dr Huebner's – one of his special plasters will heal it up in no time.

MAYOR   [Wagging his finger reproachfully at BOBCHINSKY. To KHLESTAKOV] It's really nothing, sir. Now, if you'd come with me I'll tell your man to bring your luggage over. [To OSIP] Be a good chap and bring everything over to the mayor's house – anyone will show you the way ... No – after you, sir! [Lets Khlestakov go first, but then turns round *and gives Bobchinsky a taste of his tongue.*] That's just typical! Couldn't you find anywhere else to fall flat on your face? Spreadeagling yourself like the devil knows what! [*Exit, followed by* BOBCHINSKY.]

[*Curtain.*]

ACT III

[*The same room as in ACT I.*]

Scene I

[ANNA ANDREYEVNA, MARYA ANTONOVNA *are standing at the window in the same positions.*]

ANNA ANDREYEVNA So, we've been waiting a whole hour, thanks to you and your stupid preening. You were dressed very nicely, but no – you had to carry on fussing with your toilette! Really, I should have ignored you, it's so annoying. To make matters worse, there's not a soul about. The whole town seems dead!

MARYA ANTONOVNA Really, Mama, in a couple of minutes we'll know everything. Avdotya's bound to be back soon. [*Looks out of window and shouts.*] Ah, Mama, Mama! Someone's coming – look, at the end of the street!

ANNA ANDREYEVNA Where? You're just imagining things again. Oh yes, someone is coming. Who is it? Very short, in a frock-coat. Who can it be? Eh? This is quite maddening. Who on earth could it be?

MARYA ANTONOVNA It's Dobchinsky, Mama.

ANNA ANDREYEVNA Dobchinsky! I ask you! Always imagining things! It's definitely not Dobchinsky. [*Waves her handkerchief.*] Hey you! Come here! Quickly!

MARYA ANTONOVNA But it *is* Dobchinsky, Mama!

ANNA ANDREYEVNA There you go again – always arguing with me. I tell you it's not Dobchinsky.

MARYA ANTONOVNA   There! What did I tell you, Mama! Do you see?

ANNA ANDREYEVNA   Oh yes, now I can see. So, why are you arguing? [*Shouts from window.*] Hurry up. Don't dawdle! Well, where are you? What? You can shout from there, it doesn't matter. What's that? He's very stern? What? And what about my husband? [*Steps back from window in annoyance.*] The man's a fool – he won't tell us a thing until he's indoors.

Scene II

[*The same, with* DOBCHINSKY.]

ANNA ANDREYEVNA   Well, aren't you ashamed of yourself? I was counting on you, as I thought you were a decent man, but you had to go flying after the rest of them. Now I'm left without a scrap of news. Aren't you ashamed? I was godmother to your Vanechka and Lizanka and this is how you treat me!

DOBCHINSKY   As God is my witness, I ran so fast to pay my respects that I'm completely out of breath. Good day, Marya Antonovna!

MARYA ANTONOVNA   Good day, Pyotr Ivanovich!

ANNA ANDREYEVNA   Well, tell me all about it. What's happening?

DOBCHINSKY   Here's a note from Anton Antonovich.

ANNA ANDREYEVNA   But what kind of man is he? A general?

DOBCHINSKY   No, not a general, but he's as good as one. So cultured, so dignified.

ANNA ANDREYEVNA   So he must be the one they wrote about to my husband?

DOBCHINSKY   Oh yes! Pyotr Ivanovich and I were the first to spot him.

ANNA ANDREYEVNA   Please tell us about it.

DOBCHINSKY   Thank God everything's going well. At first he was a little hard on Anton Antonovich, became very angry and refused to go with him and said he wasn't going to prison

on his account. But later, when he realized it wasn't Anton
Antonovich's fault and the two of them got talking, he soon
changed his tune and thank God things went smoothly. Now
they've gone off to inspect the charity hospital. But at the
beginning Anton Antonovich wondered if someone had
secretly informed on him. I was a bit worried myself.

ANNA ANDREYEVNA But what do *you* have to be afraid of?
You don't work for the government.

DOBCHINSKY No, but when a bigwig like him speaks it really
makes you scared.

ANNA ANDREYEVNA But why? What nonsense! Now, tell us
what he's like. Is he young or old?

DOBCHINSKY He's young – quite young. About twenty-three.
But he talks like an old man. 'If you please,' he says, 'I shall
go here and I shall go there . . .' [*Waves arms.*] And all so
upper class! 'I,' says he, 'am fond of reading and writing, but
I can't as the room's so dark.'

ANNA ANDREYEVNA But what's he like? Dark or fair?

DOBCHINSKY I'd say light-brown – and his eyes dart about
like two ferrets: it really makes you nervous.

ANNA ANDREYEVNA Well, let's see what my husband has to
tell me. [*Reads.*] 'I hasten to inform you, my love, that I was
in a sorry state, but now, trusting in God's mercy . . . for two
pickled cucumbers and half a portion of caviare one rouble
twenty-five copecks . . . [*Stops.*] I can't make head or tail of
anything! What have cucumbers and caviare to do with it!'

DOBCHINSKY Anton Antonovich was in a great hurry when
he wrote that. It's some old bill, I think.

ANNA ANDREYEVNA Oh yes, I can see. [*Carries on reading.*]
'. . . trusting in God's mercy all will turn out well in the end.
Now hurry and prepare a room for our distinguished guest
– the one with the yellow wallpaper. Don't worry about
dinner as we'll be eating at the charity hospital with Artemy
Filippovich. But mind you order plenty of wine. Tell Abdulin
to send the very best or I'll go and turn his cellar inside out.
I kiss your hand, my darling, Your Loving Anton Skvoznik-
Dmukhanovsky.' Oh dear! We must hurry! Mishka! Are you
there?

DOBCHINSKY   [*Runs to door and shouts.*] Mishka! Mishka!
   [*Enter* MISHKA.]

ANNA ANDREYEVNA   Now listen, Mishka ... run over to
   Abdulin's ... no, wait ... I'll give you a note. [*Sits at table
   and speaks as she writes.*] Give this note to Isidor and tell
   him to hurry over to Abdulin's for the wine. And then go at
   once and get the spare room ready for our guest. Put in a bed
   and a washstand and everything ...

DOBCHINSKY   I think I'll shoot off now and see how the
   inspection's going, Anna Andreyevna.

ANNA ANDREYEVNA   Yes, you'd better go. I won't keep you.

Scene III

[ANNA ANDREYEVNA *and* MARYA ANTONOVNA.]

ANNA ANDREYEVNA   Now, Mashenka, we have to decide
   what to wear. He's a Petersburg man-about-town, so I hope
   he won't laugh at us. Your pale-blue dress with the little
   flounces would be most becoming.

MARYA ANTONOVNA   Oh no, Mama! Not the pale-blue one!
   I don't like it one bit! Miss Tyapkin-Lyapkin wears pale blue,
   so does Zemlyanika's daughter. No, I'll wear the frock with
   the floral pattern.

ANNA ANDREYEVNA   Floral pattern indeed! You only say that
   to spite me. The pale blue will be far more suitable, because
   I want to wear yellow. I simply adore that yellow dress.

MARYA ANTONOVNA   But Mama, not yellow! It doesn't suit
   you at all.

ANNA ANDREYEVNA   And why not?

MARYA ANTONOVNA   It really doesn't! To wear yellow you
   must have dark eyes.

ANNA ANDREYEVNA   Get away with you! So you're saying
   my eyes aren't dark? They're as dark as can be! What nonsense you talk! Of course they're dark – I always tell my
   fortune by the Queen of Clubs.[25]

MARYA ANTONOVNA   Ah, Mama! You're more like the Queen
   of Hearts!

ANNA ANDREYEVNA   What utter nonsense! I was never the
Queen of Hearts. [*Exit hurriedly with* MARYA ANTONOVNA
and still talks off stage.] Honestly, the ideas you get! Queen
of Hearts indeed! I've never heard such a thing.

[*A door opens as they go out and* MISHKA *sweeps out the
rubbish. From another door* OSIP *enters with a suitcase
on his head.*]

Scene IV

OSIP   Where shall I put it?

MISHKA   This way, grandpa . . . in here.

OSIP   Hang on . . . let me get my breath back. God, it's a dog's
life! Everything's heavy on an empty belly!

MISHKA   Tell me, grandpa, is the general coming soon?

OSIP   What general?

MISHKA   Well, your master. Who else?

OSIP   My master? So you think he's a general?

MISHKA   Well, isn't he one?

OSIP   Yes, he's a general, but bottom side up.

MISHKA   Is that more or less than a real general?

OSIP   More.

MISHKA   You don't say! So that's why there's all this commotion around here.

OSIP   Now listen, lad. I can see you're a smart young fellow,
so how about fixing me up with some grub?

MISHKA   There's nothing ready for you yet, grandpa. You
wouldn't be wanting plain grub and when your master sits
down to dinner you'll get the same as him.

OSIP   But what do you have in the way of plain grub?

MISHKA   There's cabbage soup, porridge and meat pies.

OSIP   Very good! I'll have cabbage soup, porridge and meat
pies! I'll eat anything, I'm not choosy. Now give me a hand
with the suitcase. Is that another way out of here?

MISHKA   That's right.

[*They carry the suitcase into a side room.*]

Scene V

[CONSTABLES *open both halves of the double doors. Enter* KHLESTAKOV, *followed by* MAYOR, WARDEN OF CHARITIES, INSPECTOR OF SCHOOLS, DOBCHINSKY *and* BOBCHINSKY *with a plaster on his nose. The* MAYOR *points out a piece of paper on the ground to the* CONSTABLES *who rush to pick it up, colliding in their haste.*]

KHLESTAKOV   Well, the institutions are really first class! I like the way you show visitors round. In other towns they didn't show me a thing.

MAYOR   In other towns, if I may say so, mayors and other officials are more concerned with feathering their own nests. But here – and I can say this in all honesty – our only concern is to merit the approval of the authorities by vigilance and attention to law and order.

KHLESTAKOV   That lunch was delicious. I really ate too much! Do you lunch like that every day?

MAYOR   No, it was specially prepared for our most welcome guest.

KHLESTAKOV   I'm mad about good food. But what else is life for except to pluck the blossoms of pleasure . . . What was the fish we had?

WARDEN OF CHARITIES   [*running up*] Salt cod, sir – labberdaan.[26]

KHLESTAKOV   And very tasty too! Where was it we had lunch? At the charity hospital?

WARDEN OF CHARITIES   Yes indeed, sir, at the charity hospital.

KHLESTAKOV   Oh yes, I remember seeing the empty beds. Have all the patients recovered, then? There didn't seem to be many there.

WARDEN OF CHARITIES   There's about ten of them at the moment – no more. The others have recovered. All that is due to the excellent organization and administration we have here. You may not believe this, but since I took charge the patients have been recovering like flies. The moment a patient sets foot in the hospital he's cured. And it's not so much the medicine we use as honest and efficient management.

MAYOR   If I may say so, a mayor's duties are enough to make one's head go round. There's so much to attend to – sanitation, repairs, general improvements – all this would put a strain on the ablest of men. But thank God everything is running smoothly. Of course, other mayors are only concerned with looking after their own interests, but even when I lie down to sleep one thought possesses me: 'Almighty God!' I say to myself, 'teach me to please my superiors so that they take note of my diligence and are satisfied with me.' Of course, it rests with them whether they think fit to reward me or not. But at least I'll have a clear conscience. When good order prevails in the town, when the streets are swept, the prisoners well treated and when there's hardly any drunkenness – what more could I want? I'm not seeking honours – oh no! I know they tempt a certain kind of person, but compared with virtue all is vanity.

WARDEN OF CHARITIES   [aside] Just listen how thick he lays it on, the grafter! I wish I had his gift of the gab!

KHLESTAKOV   That's so true. I must admit that I occasionally like to dabble in philosophy myself; sometimes I turn out a piece of prose or toss off a few light verses.

BOBCHINSKY   [to DOBCHINSKY] Perfectly true, isn't it, Pyotr Ivanovich? So nicely put – it's obvious he's a scholar.

KHLESTAKOV   Now please tell me what you have to offer here in the way of amusements – I mean societies where one can meet for a little game of cards, for example?

MAYOR   [aside] Oho my fine fellow! I can see what you're driving at! [Aloud] Oh no! God forbid! We would not tolerate such societies in this town. I myself have never picked up a card in my life. I don't even know how to play. I simply cannot look at them without getting angry. The sight of a King of Diamonds or any other card fills me with revulsion. Once – merely to amuse the children – I built a house of cards and all night long I had nightmares about the blasted things! Heavens! How can people waste precious time on them?

JUDGE   [*aside*] And the lying bastard took a hundred roubles off me only last night.

MAYOR   I prefer to devote my time to the service of my country.

KHLESTAKOV   Well, I can't agree with you there. It all depends on how you look at it. If you stick when you should raise your stake . . .[27] then . . . No! I find the occasional game most enjoyable.

Scene VI

[*The same, and* ANNA ANDREYEVNA *and* MARYA ANTONOVNA.]

MAYOR   Allow me to introduce my wife and daughter, Your Excellency.

KHLESTAKOV   [*bowing*] I am delighted, Madam, to have the pleasure, so to speak, of your company.

ANNA ANDREYEVNA   It is even more of a pleasure for us to entertain such a distinguished guest.

KHLESTAKOV   [*posturing*] If you'll permit me to say so, Madam, the pleasure is all mine.

ANNA ANDREYEVNA   How can you say that? You only mean to flatter us! Please do take a seat.

KHLESTAKOV   Merely standing near you is happiness itself. But if you really insist, then I shall sit down. How delightful to be seated at your side!

ANNA ANDREYEVNA   My goodness! I dare not presume to think that your compliments are intended for me. After life in St Petersburg travelling around the provinces must be most disagreeable.

KHLESTAKOV   Yes, most disagreeable! Accustomed as I am – *comprenez-vous* – to mixing in high society and then suddenly to find oneself on the road – all those filthy inns, that benighted ignorance . . . well . . . I do confess that if it weren't for the good fortune [*looking at* ANNA ANDREYEVNA *and posturing in front of her*] that has so amply compensated me for . . .

ANNA ANDREYEVNA   Yes, you really must find it most disagreeable.

KHLESTAKOV   Indeed I do, Madam. But now I find everything
most agreeable.

ANNA ANDREYEVNA   Oh sir! You are only flattering me. I am
not worthy of such flattery.

KHLESTAKOV   And why not? You *are* worthy of it.

ANNA ANDREYEVNA   I live in the depths of the country.

KHLESTAKOV   Yes ... but the country too has its little knolls
and rivulets ... Of course, you can't compare it to
St Petersburg. Ah, St Petersburg! That's the life! You may
think all I do is copy documents. Far from it! I'm on the
friendliest of terms with the head of the department. He'll
slap me on the shoulder and say: 'Come and have dinner, old
man!' Normally I drop in at the office for a minute or so,
just to say: 'Do this! Do that!' and in a flash that little rat of
a copy clerk will be scratching away like mad ... scr ... scr
... scr ... They even wanted to promote me to collegiate
assessor,[28] but I thought: 'What's the point?' And the porter
often flies after me with a brush: 'Allow me, sir, to polish your
boots,' he says. [*To* MAYOR] But why are you all standing,
gentlemen? Please be seated.

MAYOR	Men of my rank can stand.
WARDEN OF CHARITIES [*together*]	We'd rather stand.
JUDGE	Don't worry about us, sir!

KHLESTAKOV   I'm not concerned with rank ... now do sit
down.

[MAYOR *and everyone sit down.*]

No, I'm not one for ceremony. On the contrary, I always do
my best to steal around unnoticed. But it's impossible to
avoid attention, quite impossible! The moment I step outside
people will say: 'There's Ivan Aleksandrovich!' Once I was
even taken for the Commander-in-Chief himself. The soldiers
leapt out of the guardroom and presented arms. Afterwards
an officer – a great friend of mine – told me: 'Well, old man,
we really did think you were the Commander-in-Chief!'

ANNA ANDREYEVNA   Well fancy that!

KHLESTAKOV I'm known everywhere. I'm acquainted with all the pretty actresses and I've written little vaudevilles for them. I mix chiefly with the literary set – Pushkin and I are great pals. Many's the time I've asked him: 'How's it going, Pushkin old chap?' And he'll reply: 'So-so, old boy. Fair to middling.' What a card that Pushkin is!

ANNA ANDREYEVNA So you write too? It must be so gratifying to be an author. I suppose you write for the magazines?

KHLESTAKOV Yes, I do some work for the magazines. But then, there's no end to what I've written – *The Marriage of Figaro*,[29] *Robert le Diable*, *Norma*[30] – why, I can't even remember their titles. It all came about by chance. I didn't really want to write, but those theatre directors kept pleading with me: 'You simply must write something for us, old man.' So I thought about it. 'Well, why not? I'll have a go.' And that very same evening, you know, I dashed the whole lot off and stunned everyone. You know, I'm blessed with amazing mental agility. Everything under the name of Baron Brambeus,[31] 'The Frigate *Hope*',[32] the *Moscow Telegraph*.[33] I wrote all of that!

ANNA ANDREYEVNA Well I never! So in fact *you* are Baron Brambeus!

KHLESTAKOV Oh yes! I correct everyone's articles. Smirdin[34] pays me forty thousand roubles a year for it.

ANNA ANDREYEVNA I suppose *Yury Miloslavsky*[35] is yours too?

KHLESTAKOV Yes, that's mine.

ANNA ANDREYEVNA I guessed it at once.

MARYA ANTONOVNA But Mama, it says it's by Mr Zagoskin on the front cover.

ANNA ANDREYEVNA There you go again! I knew you'd find something to argue about!

KHLESTAKOV But she's right. That one's by Zagoskin, but there's another *Yury Miloslavsky* – that one I wrote.

ANNA ANDREYEVNA Of course. I thought I must have read yours – it's so beautifully written.

KHLESTAKOV I must admit that I live for literature. I keep the best house in St Petersburg. It's known as Khlestakov

House. [*Addressing everyone*] Gentlemen, if you're ever in St Petersburg do look me up. I also give balls.

ANNA ANDREYEVNA   I can just imagine how magnificent and elegant they must be!

KHLESTAKOV   Words cannot describe them. On the table I'll have one melon that cost seven hundred roubles. The soup is brought in special tureens on a steamer from Paris. And the aroma when you lift the lid – well, nothing can compare with it! I'm at a ball every day of the week. Or I throw my own little whist parties, with the Foreign Minister, the French, English, German ambassadors and myself. And we play until we're ready to drop – quite incredible. And then I'll dash up to my fourth-floor apartment and I just tell the cook: 'Hey, Mavrushka, take my coat!' Now what am I talking about. Of course, I mean *first*-floor apartment! The staircase alone is worth . . . well . . . And you should take a look into the entrance-hall before I'm up – it's most interesting! Counts and princes jostling each other and buzzing like so many bees – all you hear is bzz.bzz.bzz. Sometimes a cabinet minister drops by.

[*The* MAYOR *and the others tremble as they rise to their feet.*]

My letters are even addressed 'Your Excellency'. Once I ran a whole department. Yes, a strange thing happened. The Director suddenly vanished – no one knew where. Naturally there were all sorts of arguments and people asked: 'What are we going to do now? Who will take his place?' Many of the top brass were keen on the job, but they just couldn't cope: at first sight it all seemed so easy, but it turned out infernally difficult. They were all at sea, so they sent for me. Right away courier after courier came galloping down the streets. Can you imagine – thirty-five thousand couriers! 'What's the problem?' I ask. 'Ivan Aleksandrovich! You must come and take charge of the department!' Well, I ask you! I was quite taken aback. At the time I was in my dressing-gown and I really felt like refusing, but then I realized that the Tsar might get to hear about it – and there was my service record to consider. 'Very well, gentlemen, if you insist I'll take over, but I'm warning you that I won't stand for any nonsense. Oh no! You have to be on your toes when I'm around!' And in fact whenever I passed through the department you'd have thought there'd been an earthquake – everyone was quivering and shaking like a leaf.

[*The* MAYOR *and others tremble in terror.* KHLESTAKOV *gets even more carried away.*]

Oh no, I'm not to be trifled with! So, I read them the riot act. Even the Cabinet's scared stiff of me. And why shouldn't they be? That's the kind of person I am. No one gets the better of me!! I tell all and sundry 'I know who I am all right!'

I'm everywhere, just everywhere. I drop in at the Palace every day. Tomorrow I'm being promoted to field marshal. [*Slips slightly and nearly falls down, but is respectfully supported by the officials.*]

MAYOR [*approaching and trembling all over in an effort to articulate his words*] Yo . . . Yo . . . Yo . . . Exc . . .

KHLESTAKOV [*in rapid staccato*] What is it?

MAYOR Yo . . . Yo . . . Excell . . .

KHLESTAKOV Can't understand a thing, it's all gibberish.

MAYOR Wouldn't Yo . . . Yo . . . Exc . . . care to rest for a while? The room's ready, with everything you may require.

KHLESTAKOV Rest? What nonsense! Ah well, perhaps I will. That was an excellent lunch, gentlemen! . . . Very nice, really nice! [*Declaiming: Labberdaan! Labberdaan! goes into a side room, followed by* MAYOR.]

Scene VII

[*The same, without* KHLESTAKOV *and* MAYOR.]

BOBCHINSKY [*to Bobchinsky*] Now there's a man for you, Pyotr Ivanovich! That's what I call a man! I've never been in the presence of such an important personage. I very nearly died of fright! What do you think his rank is?

DOBCHINSKY I should think he's almost a general.

BOBCHINSKY Well, if you ask me, a general's not fit to tie his

bootlaces. He must be at least the *generalissimo*. You heard
how he made mincemeat of the Cabinet. Let's run and tell
Ammos Fyodorovich and Korobkin. Goodbye, Anna
Andreyevna!

DOBCHINSKY   Good day to you, ma'am!

[*Exeunt.*]

WARDEN OF CHARITIES *to* INSPECTOR OF SCHOOLS I'm
simply terrified, but I can't tell you why. We're not even in
uniform! I only hope that after he's sobered up he doesn't
whip off a report to St Petersburg. [*Goes out, deep in thought,
together with* INSPECTOR OF SCHOOLS, *saying: Good day to
you, ma'am!*]

Scene VIII

[ANNA ANDREYEVNA *and* MARYA ANTONOVNA.]

ANNA ANDREYEVNA   What a charming gentleman!

MARYA ANTONOVNA   Oh yes – a real darling!

ANNA ANDREYEVNA   And so refined. You can tell at once he's
from the Capital . . . such polish! Oh, it's wonderful! I have
a passion for young men like him, I'm simply bowled over.
And I could see he liked me – he couldn't take his eyes off
me.

MARYA ANTONOVNA   But Mama, it was me he was looking
at!

ANNA ANDREYEVNA   Get away with you! Will you never stop
arguing!

MARYA ANTONOVNA   But Mama, he was! Really!

ANNA ANDREYEVNA   There you go again. Heavens! – you and
your arguing. Why on earth should he want to look at you?

MARYA ANTONOVNA   Really, Mama, he was looking at me
the whole time. And when he talked about literature he
looked right at me – and again when he told us how he
played whist with the ambassadors.

ANNA ANDREYVNA   Well, perhaps he did give you the odd
glance, but only out of politeness. 'Ah well,' he must have
thought, 'I might as well give her a look.'

Scene IX

MAYOR   [entering on tiptoe] Sh . . . shhh!

ANNA ANDREYEVNA   What is it?

MAYOR   I'm sorry. I gave him so much to drink. What if only
half he told me is true? [Becomes thoughtful.] And why
shouldn't it be true? When a man's had too much to drink it
all slips out. Of course, he did embroider things a bit, but
you never hear anything that doesn't have a few fibs in it.
Says he plays cards with ministers and calls at the Palace.
Well, the more I think about it . . . hell! . . . my head's going
round! I feel as if I were perched on top of a steeple or as if
I had a noose round my neck.

ANNA ANDREYEVNA   He didn't make me feel in the least
intimidated. In my opinion he's a man of culture and good
breeding. I don't give a rap about his rank.

MAYOR   Ugh! – there's women for you, you and your frippery
and flounces! Without rhyme or reason they'll blurt out
any old rubbish and escape with a thrashing. But I'll get my
marching orders! And carrying on like that, my dear, with a
young man, as if he were some run-of-the-mill Pyotr Ivanovich Dobchinsky or other . . .

ANNA ANDREYEVNA   I wouldn't worry about it if I were you.
We women know a thing or two! [Looks at daughter.]

MAYOR   [to himself] Oh, what's the use of talking! I'm in a
real quandary. I still can't get over the fright he gave me.
[Opens door and calls out.] Mishka! Call those constables
Svistunov and Derzhimorda – they're just outside by the gate.
[After a brief pause.] The whole world's gone topsy-turvy.
You expect him to look the part, but no! He's just a skinny
little pipsqueak. How could anyone tell who he is? If he were
an army officer you'd know immediately, but in that tail-coat
he's like a fly with clipped wings. Back at the inn he kept up
an act for some time. With all his lies and claptrap I thought
I'd never make him open up. But in the end he gave himself
away, spilled more than he needed to. He's obviously a mere
greenhorn.

Scene X

[*The same, with* OSIP. *All beckon and rush to him.*]

ANNA ANDREYEVNA   Come here, my dear man!

MAYOR   Shhh! . . . what's the matter? Is he asleep?

OSIP   No, just stretching a bit.

ANNA ANDREYEVNA   Now, tell me your name.

OSIP   Osip, ma'am.

MAYOR   [*to wife and daughter*] That's enough from you two!
[*To* OSIP] Tell me, old chum, did they feed you well?

OSIP   They did and all, sir, really well, thanking you kindly.

ANNA ANDREYEVNA   Now tell me – I imagine a good many
counts and princes call on your master, eh?

OSIP   [*aside*] What do I say? Well, they fed me very well just
now, so it can only get better later on. [*Aloud*] Yes, counts
and all calls on him.

MARYA ANTONOVNA   Osip, dear, your master's so good-
looking!

ANNA ANDREYEVNA   Tell me, Osip, is your master . . . ?

MAYOR   That's enough! All you do is interfere with that stupid
chatter. Now, old chum, tell me . . .

ANNA ANDREYEVNA   What's your master's rank?

OSIP   Er . . . the usual kind.

MAYOR   Oh God! You with your silly questions again! When
I want to discuss serious matters I can't get a word in edge-
ways. Is he hard on people? Does he blow them up?

OSIP   Yes, he likes everything to be just right, everything's got
to be done real proper.

MARYA ANTONOVNA   I really like your face, I must say! You
seem to be a decent fellow . . . Now, what does . . . ?

ANNA ANDREYEVNA   Tell me, Osip, when your master's in
St Petersburg, does he go around in uniform or . . . ?

MAYOR   Shut up, you chatterboxes! It's a really serious matter
and a man's life is at stake! [*To* OSIP] Now listen, old chum,
I've taken a real liking to you. When you're on the road I'm
sure an extra glass of tea's always welcome, especially now,
in this chilly weather. So here's a couple of roubles for you.

OSIP [*taking the money*] Thank you most kindly, sir. God grant you good health for helping a poor man.

MAYOR You don't have to mention it – it's a pleasure. Now, tell me, old chap . . .

ANNA ANDREYEVNA Osip! Please tell us what kind of eyes your master likes most.

MARYA ANTONOVNA Darling Osip! What a sweet little nose your master has!

MAYOR Shut up you two and let me get a word in! [*To* OSIP] Tell me, my friend, what kind of thing interests your master most? I mean, what does he enjoy when he's travelling?

OSIP It all depends on the circumstances. More than anything he likes warm hospitality and good food.

MAYOR Good food!

OSIP Oh yes! Good food! Now, take me – I'm only a serf but he always sees I'm well treated, honest he does! After stopping somewhere he'll always ask: 'Did they feed you well?' If I reply: 'Very badly, Your Excellency', he'll say: 'Well, Osip, he must be a lousy host. Just remind me when we get back to St Petersburg!' 'Well,' I usually think to myself [*waves his hand dismissively*] 'it's not for me to make a fuss.'

MAYOR That's good! Now you're talking sense. Well, I've given you money for tea, so here's something for a bun.

OSIP It's most kind of you, sir. [*Puts the money away.*] I'll drink Your Honour's health with it.

ANNA ANDREYEVNA And if you come to my room, Osip, I'll give you something too.

MARYA ANTONOVNA Osip, dear, give your master a kiss for me!

        [KHLESTAKOV'S *light coughing is heard from the next room.*]

MAYOR Shhh! [*Stands on tiptoe. The rest of the scene is whispered.*] God help you if you make a sound! Now, off with you both. I've just about had enough of your prattling.

ANNA ANDREYEVNA Come along, Mashenka, there's something I've noticed about our guest that we can only discuss in private.

MAYOR Oh my God! The way they go on and on . . . it's

enough to make you plug your ears! [*Turns to* OSIP.] Now, old chum . . .

Scene XI

[*The same.* DERZHIMORDA, SVISTUNOV.]

MAYOR   Shhh! You clumsy clodhoppers barging in here with your boots on! I thought a ton of bricks had fallen off a cart! What the devil are you doing here?

DERZHIMORDA   I've been acting on instructions, sir . . .

MAYOR   Shhh! [*Claps his hand over* DERZHIMORDA'*s mouth.*] Just listen to him – cawing like an old crow! [*Mimics him.*] 'Acting on instructions' he says! You bumbling great blunderer! [*To* OSIP] Now you run along and see your master has all he needs. Everything in this house is at your disposal.

[*Exit* OSIP.]

As for you two – you can go and stand at the front door. And don't you dare budge from there! Don't let any of that lot in, especially those shopkeepers. If you so much as let even one in I'll . . . The minute you spot anyone with a petition, or even someone who looks as if he might be considering one, grab him by the scruff of the neck and kick him out, good and hard. Like this! [*Illustrates a kick.*] Understand? Shh! Shhhh! [*Tiptoes out after the constables.*]

ACT IV

[*The same room in the mayor's house.* JUDGE, WARDEN
OF CHARITIES, POSTMASTER, INSPECTOR OF SCHOOLS,
BOBCHINSKY, DOBCHINSKY *enter gingerly, almost on
tiptoe, all in full-dress uniform. The whole scene is conducted in hushed voices.*]

Scene I

JUDGE   [*making everyone stand in a semicircle*] For heaven's
sake, gentlemen, hurry up and stand nice and orderly please.
Remember: this man goes to the Palace and tells the Cabinet
off! Now, get into formation, like trained soldiers. And you,
Pyotr Ivanovich, go over there . . . and you, Pyotr Ivanovich
Dobchinsky, stand here.
   [*Both Pyotr Ivanoviches run to their places on tiptoe.*]
WARDEN OF CHARITIES   It's all very well, Ammos Fyodoro-
vich, but we need to take some sort of action.
JUDGE   And precisely what?
WARDEN OF CHARITIES   Well, you know what . . . I mean to
say . . .
JUDGE   Slip him something?
WARDEN OF CHARITIES   Yes, let's slip him something.
JUDGE   It's too risky, damn it! He might raise the roof – after
all, he's a statesman . . . well . . . perhaps we could pass it off
as a donation from the local gentry towards some monument?
POSTMASTER   Or we could say: 'Look. Some money's come
in the post and we don't know who it belongs to.'

WARDEN OF CHARITIES   Mind he doesn't post *you* somewhere a long way off! Now, listen to me. This just isn't how
things are done in a well-ordered community. What's the
good of a whole squadron of us descending on him? We
should pay our respects one by one – *tête-à-tête* so to speak,
behind closed doors, so no one sees or hears. That's how
things are done in a well-ordered society. You'd better go in
first, Ammos Fyodorovich.

JUDGE   No, you'd better go first. After all, it was in *your* hospital that our distinguished visitor took luncheon with us.

WARDEN OF CHARITIES   No, I think Luka Lukich should go
in first, in the capacity of one who enlightens and instructs
our young people.

INSPECTOR OF SCHOOLS   No, I can't, gentlemen, I really
can't. It's the way I was brought up. If an official who is only
one rank higher happens to speak to me I go to pieces and
my tongue sticks to my throat. No, gentlemen, you really
must excuse me! I just can't!

JUDGE   Well, Ammos Fyodorovich, that leaves you. With that
elegant turn of phrase of yours it's just as if Cicero himself
were tripping off your tongue.

INSPECTOR OF SCHOOLS   Get on with you! I ask you –
Cicero! Whatever next! Just because I get carried away at
times by my packs of hounds.

ALL   [*badgering him*] But it's not only dogs – you can talk
about the Tower of Babel – about anything! No, Ammos
Fyodorovich, don't let us down, be a father to us. Please,
Ammos Fyodorovich!

JUDGE   Oh, leave me alone, gentlemen!

  [*Just then footsteps and coughs come from* KHLES-
  TAKOV's *room. All rush panic-stricken to the door, scram-
  bling and colliding. Stifled exclamations.*]

BOBCHINSKY'S VOICE   Ouch! You're treading on my foot,
Pyotr Ivanovich!

WARDEN OF CHARITIES' VOICE   Step aside, gentlemen,
you're squashing me to death!

  [*More 'ouches'. Finally all squeeze out and the stage is
  empty.*]

Scene II

[*Enter* KHLESTAKOV, *alone, bleary-eyed.*]

KHLESTAKOV   Well, I reckon that was a really good snooze. But where on earth did they get those mattresses and eiderdowns from? I'm simply dripping with sweat. Seems they plied me with something very potent at lunch yesterday, my head's pounding like mad. Now it looks like I can have a really good time here. Nothing can compare with fine hospitality, particularly when it's given from a genuine will to please and not from ulterior motives. Well, the mayor's daughter is not a bad-looking piece ... even the mother might do very well ... Oh yes, all said and done I've taken quite a fancy to the life here.

Scene III

[KHLESTAKOV *and* JUDGE.]

JUDGE   [*entering then stopping to talk to himself*] Oh Lord, see me through this safely. My knees are giving way. [*Aloud, standing to attention, hand on sword*] I have the honour of introducing myself, Collegiate Assessor Lyapkin-Tyapkin, Judge of the District Court.

KHLESTAKOV   Please do sit down. So, you're the judge here, eh?

JUDGE   I was elected in 1816 for a three-year term by the gentry. I have held the office ever since.

KHLESTAKOV   Do you do well from being a judge, eh?

JUDGE   After my third term I was awarded the Order of St Vladimir, Fourth Class, with commendation. [*Aside*] God! This money is burning a hole in my fist!

KHLESTAKOV   I'm fond of the Vladimir. Much more impressive than the St Anne Third Class.[36]

JUDGE   [*thrusting his clenched fist slightly forwards. Aside*] Oh God! I just don't know where I am! I feel as if I'm on hot coals!

KHLESTAKOV   What's that in your hand?

JUDGE   [*becoming flustered and dropping some banknotes on to the floor*] Nothing, sir.

KHLESTAKOV   What do you mean – nothing? Haven't you dropped some money?

JUDGE   [*trembling all over*] Oh no, sir. [*Aside*] Oh God, I'm as good as in prison. I can hear the police cart coming to take me away.

KHLESTAKOV   [*picking it up*] Yes, that's money.

JUDGE   [*aside*] Well, it's all over now. I'm finished.

KHLESTAKOV   I tell you what. Why don't you lend me it?

JUDGE   [*hurriedly*] Certainly, sir ... of course ... with the greatest pleasure. [*Aside*] Courage! Save me, Holy Mother of God!

KHLESTAKOV   I left myself a bit short on the road, what with one thing and another ... But I'll pay you back as soon as I'm home.

JUDGE   Not to think of it! How can you even suggest such a thing? I consider it an honour! I always endeavour – to the best of my meagre abilities – to serve my superiors diligently and devotedly ... to merit ... [*Rises from chair and stands to attention, hands at sides.*] I dare not trouble you with my presence a moment longer. Does Your Excellency have any instructions?

KHLESTAKOV   Instructions?

JUDGE   Well, I mean to say, you might wish to give instructions to the district court.

KHLESTAKOV   What for? I don't need the district court just now!

JUDGE   [*bowing and leaving. Aside*] Well, all is saved!

KHLESTAKOV   [*As he goes out.*] A nice chap, that judge!

Scene IV

[*POSTMASTER enters in uniform, stiffly, sword in hand.*]

POSTMASTER   I have the honour to present myself, Court Counsellor[37] Shpekin, postmaster.

KHLESTAKOV   Delighted, I'm sure! I simply love congenial
company. Now please take a seat. I suppose you've always
lived here?

POSTMASTER   That's right, sir.

KHLESTAKOV   I've taken a real fancy to this little town. Of
course, it's not a big town, but what of it? After all, it's not
St Petersburg. Isn't that so, eh?

POSTMASTER   Perfectly true, sir.

KHLESTAKOV   Only in the Capital can one find *bon ton* – none
of your country bumpkins there! What do *you* think?

POSTMASTER   Perfectly true, sir. [*Aside*] He's not a bit stuck
up. Asks my opinion about everything.

KHLESTAKOV   But one can live very well in a small town,
don't you agree?

POSTMASTER   Oh yes, sir.

KHLESTAKOV   After all, what does one really need? Only to
be respected and genuinely liked. Isn't that so?

POSTMASTER   Oh yes, sir!

KHLESTAKOV   I'm glad you share my opinion, I do confess.
You know, some people find me rather odd, but that's how
I am. [*Peers right into* POSTMASTER*'s eyes. To himself*]
Perhaps I can touch this postmaster for a loan! [*Aloud*] It's
really most peculiar how it happened, but I spent all my
money on the road. You couldn't possibly lend me three
hundred roubles, could you?

POSTMASTER   Of course I could! It will make me supremely
happy. Here, sir, please accept it. I'm only too pleased to be
of service.

KHLESTAKOV   Thank you, I'm most grateful to you. I loathe
having to deny myself anything when I'm travelling. Why
should I, in my case? Isn't that so?

POSTMASTER   Oh, quite so, sir. [*Gets up, stands to attention
and grasps sword.*] I dare not impose my presence on you
any longer. Perhaps Your Excellency has some comments
regarding the postal system?

KHLESTAKOV   No, none at all.

[POSTMASTER *bows and leaves.*]

[*Lighting a cigar*] The postmaster strikes me as a

thoroughly decent chap too. At least he wants to please. I like his type.

Scene V

[*Enter* KHLESTAKOV *and* INSPECTOR OF SCHOOLS, *who is virtually propelled through the doorway. Offstage a muffled voice is heard:* 'What the hell are you scared of?']

INSPECTOR OF SCHOOLS [*standing stiffly, trembling and holding his sword*] I have the honour to present myself, Titular Counsellor[38] Khlopov, Inspector of Schools.

KHLESTAKOV Delighted, I'm sure. Now, do sit down. Would you care for a cigar? [*Offers him one.*]

INSPECTOR OF SCHOOLS [*hesitantly, to himself*] This is tricky! I never expected this! Shall I take it or not?

KHLESTAKOV Do take it. It's not a bad little cigar. Of course, not the quality you get in St Petersburg. There, old chap, I pay twenty-five roubles a hundred. One puff's enough to make you smack your lips! Here, light up. [*Hands him a candle.*]

[INSPECTOR OF SCHOOLS *trembles all over as he tries to light up.*]

KHLESTAKOV That's the wrong end!

INSPECTOR OF SCHOOLS [*Drops the cigar from fright, spits, gestures in despair and says to himself*] To hell with it! My damned shyness is my ruination!

KHLESTAKOV I can see you're not a connoisseur when it comes to cigars, but I must confess they're a weakness of mine. Cigars and women – I can't resist them. And what about you? Which do you prefer – blondes or brunettes?

[INSPECTOR OF SCHOOLS *is at a complete loss what to say.*]

Tell me frankly – blondes or brunettes?

INSPECTOR OF SCHOOLS I dare not contemplate such matters.

KHLESTAKOV Come on, don't try and wriggle out of it. I'd really like to know which you prefer.

INSPECTOR OF SCHOOLS   If I may hazard an opinion ...
[*Aside*] No, what am I saying!

KHLESTAKOV   Aha! You don't want to tell me? I fancy some
little brunette has led you a dance! That's right, isn't it?

[INSPECTOR OF SCHOOLS *is silent.*]

Aha! You're blushing! You see, you see! Come on, why
don't you tell me?

INSPECTOR OF SCHOOLS   I'm too sshhy, Your Hon ... Exc
... High ...   [*Aside*] My blasted tongue's done for me
again!

KHLESTAKOV   Too shy? Yes, something in my eyes does
inspire fear. At least, I know for sure that no woman can
resist them. Isn't that so?

INSPECTOR OF SCHOOLS   Perfectly true, sir.

KHLESTAKOV   Now listen. The strangest thing happened to
me – I ran completely out of cash on the road ... You
couldn't lend me three hundred roubles, could you?

INSPECTOR OF SCHOOLS   [*frantically rummaging in his
pocket, to himself*] A fine thing if I don't have them. Phew!
Here they are ...   [*Takes the money out and trembles as he
hands over the notes.*]

KHLESTAKOV   I'm much obliged!

INSPECTOR OF SCHOOLS   [*stiffening and grasping his sword*]
I dare not trouble you further with my presence.

KHLESTAKOV   Goodbye then.

INSPECTOR OF SCHOOLS   [*aside, practically flying out of the
room*] Well, thank God for that! Perhaps he won't inspect
the schools now.

Scene VI

[KHLESTAKOV *and* WARDEN OF CHARITIES, *who stands
to attention, hand on sword.*]

WARDEN OF CHARITIES   I have the honour of presenting
myself, Court Counsellor Zemlyanika, Warden of Charities.

KHLESTAKOV   How do you do? Please sit down.

WARDEN OF CHARITIES   I had the honour of accompanying

you and receiving you personally at the charitable institutions under my supervision.

KHLESTAKOV   Oh yes, I do remember! That was a splendid lunch you served.

WARDEN OF CHARITIES   I am only too pleased to be of service to my country.

KHLESTAKOV   I must confess fine cuisine is one of my weaknesses. Now, please tell me: weren't you a bit shorter yesterday?

WARDEN OF CHARITIES   That's quite possible. [*Brief silence.*] I can honestly say that I don't spare myself in zealously performing my duties with the utmost diligence. [*Moves his chair closer and whispers.*] You couldn't say the same about the postmaster – he doesn't do a blessed thing! Lets everything go to pot. Parcels are always being delayed . . . please feel free to investigate yourself. And there's the judge – he was here just before me. All he does is hunt hares. He kennels his dogs in the courthouse – and as for his morals – and I am duty-bound to point this out for the sake of my country, despite his being a friend and relative – they're absolutely shocking. There's a local landowner by the name of Dobchinsky – you've already met him, Your Excellency. Well, the moment this Dobchinsky leaves the house the judge is there, snuggled up with his wife. It's the truth and I'd take an oath on it. You just have to look at the children – not one of them looks like Dobchinsky – all of them, even the little girl, are the spitting image of the judge.

KHLESTAKOV   Well, fancy that! I'd never have thought it!

WARDEN OF CHARITIES   And as for the Inspector of Schools – I cannot understand how the authorities could have appointed him in the first place. He's worse than a Jacobin[39] and he crams the pupils' heads with such subversive ideas that words fail me. Would Your Excellency like me to put it all down in writing?

KHLESTAKOV   Yes, please do write it down, I'd like that very much. I really enjoy having some light reading when I'm bored. Now, what's your name? – I keep forgetting.

WARDEN OF CHARITIES   Zemlyanika.

KHLESTAKOV   Oh yes! Tell me – do you have any children?

WARDEN OF CHARITIES   I do, sir. Five of them – two are already grown up.

KHLESTAKOV   Grown up! You don't say! And what do they . . . er . . . what's their . . . ?

WARDEN OF CHARITIES   Is Your Excellency being so kind as to inquire about their names?

KHLESTAKOV   Yes. What are they called?

WARDEN OF CHARITIES   Nikolay, Ivan, Elizaveta, Marya and Petunia.

KHLESTAKOV   Oh, very nice!

WARDEN OF CHARITIES   I dare not intrude a moment longer and occupy time that is dedicated to sacred duties. [*Bows as if to leave.*]

KHLESTAKOV   [*seeing him out*] Don't mention it! I find what you've told me very amusing . . . some other time . . . I enjoy that kind of thing. [*Turns round and shouts after him, after opening the door*] Hey! I keep forgetting your first names.

WARDEN OF CHARITIES   Artemy Filippovich.

KHLESTAKOV   Could you do me a favour, Artemy Filippovich? It's really most odd what happened. Well, I managed to run through all my money on the road. You don't have four hundred to lend me, do you?

WARDEN OF CHARITIES   Of course I have.

KHLESTAKOV   Well, what luck! I'm most obliged to you.

Scene VII

[KHLESTAKOV, BOBCHINSKY *and* DOBCHINSKY.]

BOBCHINSKY   I have the honour of introducing myself, Pyotr Ivanovich Bobchinsky, resident of this town.

DOBCHINSKY   Landowner Pyotr Ivanovich Dobchinsky.

KHLESTAKOV   Oh yes, I've seen you before. Weren't you the one who took a tumble? How's your nose?

BOBCHINSKY   It's fine, thank God. Please don't worry about it. It's completely healed up now.

KHLESTAKOV   Healed up? That's good! I'm glad ... [*Suddenly, and abruptly*] Got any money on you?

BOBCHINSKY   Money? What money?

KHLESTAKOV   [*loudly and quickly*] A thousand roubles you could lend me?

BOBCHINSKY   I really don't have anything like that much on me, I swear it. Do you, Pyotr Ivanovich?

DOBCHINSKY   No, not on me. The fact is, please be informed, all my money's on deposit at the Office of Social Welfare.[40]

KHLESTAKOV   Well, if you can't manage a thousand, a hundred will do.

BOBCHINSKY   [*rummaging in his pockets*] Do you have a hundred on you, Pyotr Ivanovich? All I have is forty, in notes.

DOBCHINSKY   [*looking into his wallet*] All I have is twenty-five roubles.

BOBCHINSKY   Do look a little harder, Pyotr Ivanovich! I know there's a hole in the right-hand side of your pocket. It's possible some money's fallen through into the lining.

DOBCHINSKY   No, I assure you there's nothing there!

KHLESTAKOV   Never mind. No harm in asking. Well, lend me the sixty-five. [*Takes the money.*]

DOBCHINSKY   May I presume to ask for Your Excellency's advice on a very delicate matter?

KHLESTAKOV   Fire away.

DOBCHINSKY   A most delicate matter, Your Excellency. You see, my eldest son was born out of wedlock.

KHLESTAKOV   You don't say!

DOBCHINSKY   Well, he was – in a manner of speaking. He was born just as if I had been married. Subsequently, as was right and proper, I of course assumed the lawful bonds of matrimony, Your Excellency. So you see, if you would be good enough, I want him to be made my legitimate son and to take my name – that is, Dobchinsky.

KHLESTAKOV   All right, let him be called Dobchinsky. I don't see any problem in that.

DOBCHINSKY   I wouldn't have troubled you, but I feel sorry for the boy – he's so gifted and should go far: he can recite all kinds of poems by heart and if he happens to get hold of a penknife he'll carve you a miniature horse and cart as skilfully as a magician, Your Excellency. Pyotr Ivanovich will vouch for it.

BOBCHINSKY   Yes, the boy's very talented.

KHLESTAKOV   All right, I'll do what I can . . . I'll put in a word with . . . I hope something can be done . . . yes . . . [*Turning to* BOBCHINSKY] Is there anything you have to tell me?

BOBCHINSKY   Oh yes, I have a very humble request.

KHLESTAKOV   Well, what is it?

BOBCHINSKY   I humbly beg you, when you are back in St Petersburg, you say 'Your Highness' or 'Your Excellency' and then tell all the dignitaries, the senators[41] and admirals and the rest, that in such and such a town lives a man by the name of Pyotr Ivanovich Bobchinsky. Just tell them 'Pyotr Ivanovich Bobchinsky lives there'.

KHLESTAKOV   Very well.

BOBCHINSKY   And if you should happen to meet the Tsar, then just tell him: 'Your Imperial Majesty, Pyotr Ivanovich Bobchinsky is living in such and such town.'

DOBCHINSKY ⎫ Do forgive us for imposing our presence on
BOBCHINSKY ⎭ you.

KHLESTAKOV   Not at all! It's been a pleasure. [*Shows them out.*]

Scene VIII

[KHLESTAKOV *alone.*]

This place is crawling with officials. But I have the feeling they've taken me for a man from the ministry. Well, I suppose I did lay it on a bit thick yesterday! What a bunch of halfwits! Yes, I should write and tell Tryapichkin in St Petersburg. He can give them a nice little mauling in one of those newspaper articles he dashes off! Here, Osip! Bring me paper and ink!

[OSIP *peers round the door and says* 'Right away'.]

If that Tryapichkin gets his teeth into anyone – why, he wouldn't spare his own father for the sake of a joke and he's partial to money as well. But those civil servants are a decent lot really. At least, they did me a favour with those loans. I must tot it all up: three hundred from the judge, three hundred from the postmaster – six hundred, seven, eight – ugh! What a greasy banknote! . . . nine hundred. Oho! Over a thousand. Yes, my dear infantry captain! Just you cross my path again. We'll see who comes out on top!

Scene IX

[KHLESTAKOV *and* OSIP, *with ink and paper*.]

KHLESTAKOV Now you can see, you imbecile, how I'm fêted and welcomed everywhere. [*Starts writing*.]

OSIP And how! But there's one thing, Ivan Aleksandrovich.

KHLESTAKOV [*writing*] What's that?

OSIP We must get out of here. God knows it's time we left.

KHLESTAKOV Nonsense! Why should we?

OSIP Well, I think we should. While the going's good! We've had a gay old time for two days and enough's enough. No point in hanging around with that lot any longer. To hell with them! Who knows – someone else might turn up! We could gallop away now and they wouldn't see us for dust.

KHLESTAKOV [*writing*] No, I want to stay a bit longer – tomorrow, perhaps.

OSIP Why tomorrow? For God's sake, let's go now, Ivan Aleksandrovich! I know they're treating you like a lord, but we'd better make tracks while the going's good. They've taken you for someone else, that's what! Besides, your father'll hit the roof if we're not home soon. We'd be given the best horses and drive off in grand style!

KHLESTAKOV Oh, all right then. But first post this letter – and you can order the horses at the same time. Mind they're good ones! Tell the coachmen I'll tip them a rouble each to drive me as fast as an Imperial courier and sing songs to me! [*Carries on writing*.] I can just picture Tryapichkin now – he'll die laughing!

OSIP I'll send one of the servants over with it. And I'd better get a move on with the packing, so's not to waste any time.

KHLESTAKOV   [*writing*] Good. Just bring me a candle.

OSIP   [*Exits and speaking offstage*] Hey, old pal! Take this letter for us to the post office and tell the postmaster there's no charge. And tell them my master wants the best troika they have – the type Imperial messengers use. And you can say the master won't pay nothing for that neither, seeing as we're on government business. And look lively, or the master'll get angry. Hold on, the letter's not ready yet.

KHLESTAKOV   [*continues writing*] I'd like to know where he's living these days, in Post Office or Gorokhovaya Street? He's the same as me – decamps when the rent's due! Well, I'll take a chance on Post Office Street. [*Folds it and addresses it.* OSIP *brings a candle.* KHLESTAKOV *seals the letter. Meanwhile* DERZHIMORDA's *voice can be heard.*] 'Where d'ye think you're going, old beardie? I've orders to let no one in.'

[KHLESTAKOV *gives* OSIP *the letter.*]

There, take it.

SHOPKEEPERS' VOICES   Let us in, sir! You can't keep us out – we're here on business!

DERZHIMORDA'S VOICE   Clear off! Beat it! He ain't seeing no one – he's asleep.

[*The noise grows louder.*]

KHLESTAKOV   What's going on, Osip? Go and see what it's all about.

OSIP   [*Goes up to window.*] Some shopkeepers want to come in, but the constable won't let 'em. They're waving papers about. Looks as if it's you they want to see.

KHLESTAKOV   [*going up to window*] Well, what can I do for you fine fellows?

SHOPKEEPER'S VOICE   We've come to appeal to Your Worship. Please let us present our petitions, sir.

KHLESTAKOV   Let them in. Let them in, Osip! Tell them they can come in.

[*Exit* OSIP.]

[*Takes the petitions through the window, unrolls one of them and reads:*]

To His Most Noble Supreme Excellency Lord High Financier, from shopkeeper Abdulin.

What the hell's that supposed to be!? There's no such title!

Scene X

[KHLESTAKOV *and* SHOPKEEPERS *with a basketful of wine and loaves of sugar.*]

KHLESTAKOV   What can I do for you, my friends?

SHOPKEEPERS   We humbly beg a favour from Your Worship.

KHLESTAKOV   What do you want?

SHOPKEEPERS   Save us from ruin, Your Worship! We haven't deserved the harsh treatment we're getting.

KHLESTAKOV   And who is responsible?

A SHOPKEEPER   It's the mayor, sir. There's never been a mayor like him, sir. The way he's ground us down – well, you wouldn't believe it. He's ruining us by billeting all those soldiers on us and we're at the end of our tether. He'll grab us by the beard and tell us we're heathens! Honest to God! And it's not as if we didn't show him respect – we always do our duty: if it's a small length of cloth to make his wife and daughter dresses – we don't jib at that. But it's not enough. He'll come into the shop and take anything he can lay his hands on. If he spots a roll of cloth he'll say: 'Hey, old chap, that's very nice material. Send it over to my place.' Well, of course you have to send it – and that roll could have a hundred feet in it!

KHLESTAKOV   You don't say! He's an out-and-out crook!

SHOPKEEPER   Not half! No one can remember a mayor like him. You have to hide everything away in your shop when you see him coming. And I don't only mean fancy food – he'll take any old rubbish. For example, prunes that have been mouldering seven years in a barrel – even my shop boy wouldn't touch them with a barge pole. But he'll go and grab a whole handful. When his name-day comes round – St Anthony's Day, that is – you'd think you'd given him all the presents a man could want. But no, it's not enough for him. And then he'll tell us he has another name-day –

St Onufry's! So we have to take him presents on St Onufry's Day too!

KHLESTAKOV   The man's nothing less than a highway robber.

SHOPKEEPERS   You can say that again! And just you cross him and he'll billet an entire regiment on you. Or he'll have you locked up in your own house. 'I won't have you flogged,' he says, 'and I won't torture you, as it's against the law. But I'll have you eating salted herring[42] by the time I've finished with you!'

KHLESTAKOV   Oh – what a swine! He could go straight to Siberia for that.

SHOPKEEPERS   Wherever Your Worship decides to send him is all right with us. The further away the better. Now, please accept our little tokens of hospitality, Your Worship – a few loaves of sugar and some wine.[43]

KHLESTAKOV   No, you can forget it. I never accept bribes of any kind. But if you were to offer me a loan of three hundred roubles that would be quite a different matter. I could accept a loan.

SHOPKEEPERS   By all means, Your Worship. [*They take out money.*] But why a measly three hundred? Take five, only please help us!

KHLESTAKOV   All right. I'll take it. I've no objection to loans.

SHOPKEEPERS   [*bringing him the money on a silver salver*] And please accept the salver as well.

KHLESTAKOV   Oh! I don't object to that either.

SHOPKEEPERS   [*bowing*] And please take some sugar too, sir.

KHLESTAKOV   Oh no, I never take bribes!

OSIP   Go on, take it, Your Excellency! Take it! It'll come in handy on the road. Now, give me the sugar and the basket. Give me the lot – it'll be handy. What's that? You've some rope? Give us that too, we might have to use it on the road – if parts of the carriage fall off we can tie them back on again.

SHOPKEEPERS   Please help us with our petition, Your Honour! If you don't, there's no knowing what might happen! . . . we might as well go and hang ourselves . . .

KHLESTAKOV   Of course, of course! I'll do everything I can.

[*Exeunt* SHOPKEEPERS. *A woman's voice is heard: 'No, don't you dare turn me away, I'll complain to him in person, that I will. Ouch! Stop pushing – you're hurting me!'*]

Who's there? [*Goes over to window.*] What's the matter, my good woman?

VOICES OF TWO WOMEN   Have mercy on us, kind sir! Please hear us out!

KHLESTAKOV   [*Goes to window.*] Let them in!

Scene XI

[KHLESTAKOV, LOCKSMITH'S WIFE *and* SERGEANT'S WIDOW.]

LOCKSMITH'S WIFE   [*bowing down to ground*] Have mercy on us!

SERGEANT'S WIDOW   Have mercy on us!

KHLESTAKOV   Who are you, good women?

SERGEANT'S WIDOW   I'm Ivanovna, Sergeant Ivanov's widow.

LOCKSMITH'S WIFE   Fevronya Petrova Poshlyopkina. My husband's the the town locksmith and . . .

KHLESTAKOV   Hold on a minute. One at a time! Now, what do you want?

LOCKSMITH'S WIFE   Please have pity on us, sir. It's the mayor I want to complain about. May the good Lord send down every plague and affliction on his head! May that crook and his children, uncles and aunts never prosper!

KHLESTAKOV   Heavens! What for?

LOCKSMITH'S WIFE   Well, he had my husband sent off into the army when it wasn't his turn. Oh, the swine! What's more, it's against the law – seeing as he's a married man!

KHLESTAKOV   How *dare* he do that?!

LOCKSMITH'S WIFE   Well he did and all, the rotten crook! God damn him in this world and the next! May he and his aunt – if he's got one – suffer every filthy trick, may he die like a dog, may he choke till kingdom come, the bastard! By rights he ought to have sent the tailor's son into the army instead, but the boy's a drunkard and his parents bought the mayor off with a fancy present. Then he went after Mrs Panteleyevna's son and she sent three lengths of cloth to his wife and he comes to me and says: 'What do you need your husband for? He's no use to you.' And I says: 'It's for me to say if he's any use or not, you rotten devil!' 'He's a thief,' he says. 'Maybe he hasn't stolen anything yet, but it makes no difference – he's bound to steal before long. And even if he doesn't he'll be conscripted next year anyway!' 'So,' I says, 'how will I manage without my husband ... I'm a helpless woman and you're a dirty rotten bastard! May none of your kinsfolk ever see the light of day again. And if you have a mother-in-law may she ...'

KHLESTAKOV   All right, all right. [*Sees the old woman out.*] Well, what about you?

LOCKSMITH'S WIFE   [*As she leaves.*] Don't forget, kind sir! Please be merciful!

SERGEANT'S WIDOW   It's about the mayor, Your Honour.

KHLESTAKOV   Well? Tell me what you've come for. Make it short.

SERGEANT'S WIDOW   He had me flogged, Your Honour! Honest he did!

KHLESTAKOV   How was that?

SERGEANT'S WIDOW   It was all a mistake, kind sir! Some womenfolk had a bit of a scrap in the market-place and the police showed up too late. So they had to arrest someone and so they grabs me and gives me such a thrashing I couldn't sit down for two days.

KHLESTAKOV   Well, what can *I* do about it?

SERGEANT'S WIDOW   There's nothing that can be done now, of course. But you could fine him for his mistake – I don't want to turn my back on a little windfall and I could use the money right now.

KHLESTAKOV   Very well. Now, run along. I'll see to it.
      [*Hands holding petitions are thrust through the window.*]
      Oh no! Not more of them! [*Goes to window.*] Go away! I don't want to see them, I really don't! I'm sick to death of them. Don't let anyone else in, Osip!

OSIP   [*shouts out of window*] Now clear off! Scram! We don't have time for you lot.

[*The door opens and a figure in a coarse woollen coat appears, unshaven, with swollen lip and bandaged cheek. Behind him are a few others upstage.*]

Clear off! Where d'ye think you're going?

[*Shoves the first intruder in the belly and squeezes out with him into the hall, slamming the door.*]

Scene XII

[KHLESTAKOV *and* MARYA ANTONOVNA.]

MARYA ANTONOVNA   Oh!

KHLESTAKOV   Did something frighten you, mamselle?

MARYA ANTONOVNA   No, nothing at all.

KHLESTAKOV   [*posturing*] Let me assure you, mamselle, that I'm really flattered that you think I'm the kind of man who ... May I inquire as to where you were going?

MARYA ANTONOVNA   I wasn't going anywhere in particular.

KHLESTAKOV   But why, may I ask, weren't you going anywhere in particular?

MARYA ANTONOVNA   I thought Mama might be here.

KHLESTAKOV   Yes, but I'd really like to know why you should be going nowhere in particular.

MARYA ANTONOVNA   I'm afraid I've bothered you when you're so occupied with important business.

KHLESTAKOV   Your eyes are better than any business. How could you possibly bother me? On the contrary, you can only bring me pleasure.

MARYA ANTONOVNA   That's the way they talk in St Petersburg!

KHLESTAKOV   But only to a ravishing creature like you! May I aspire to the happiness of offering you a chair? But no – it's a throne you deserve!

MARYA ANTONOVNA   Honestly, I don't know ... I really should be going now. [*Sits down.*]

KHLESTAKOV   What a beautiful scarf you're wearing!

MARYA ANTONOVNA   You city-dwellers can only make fun of
a simple country girl!

KHLESTAKOV   How I would like to be your scarf, mamselle,
so that I might embrace your lily-white neck!

MARYA ANTONOVNA   I don't understand what you mean . . .
it's just an ordinary scarf . . . what extraordinary weather
we're having today!

KHLESTAKOV   Your lips, mamselle, are more beguiling than
any weather.

MARYA ANTONOVNA   Oh, the things you say! Now, I'd like
you to write some verses in my album, as a keepsake. I'm
sure you know a lot of them.

KHLESTAKOV   For you, mamselle, I'd do anything. Just tell
me which kind of poetry you would like.

MARYA ANTONOVNA   Oh, any kind . . . well, something pretty
and new.

KHLESTAKOV   Ah yes! That's easy . . . I know so many poems.

MARYA ANTONOVNA   But do tell me which ones you are going
to write down for me.

KHLESTAKOV   But why should I do that? I know them well
enough without any need for that.

MARYA ANTONOVNA   I simply adore poetry.

KHLESTAKOV   Well, I know so many different kinds. So how
about this: 'O man, who in thy grief vainly complainest
against the Lord . . .'[44] And I know others like that, only I
can't remember them just now. Anyway, that doesn't matter.
I'd much rather declare the love I feel for you, when one
glance from your eyes . . .
[Moves chair closer.]

MARYA ANTONOVNA   Love! I don't understand what you
mean by love – I know nothing about love . . . [Moves chair
away.]

KHLESTAKOV   [moving chair closer] Why do you move your
chair away? It's much cosier sitting close to one another.

MARYA ANTONOVNA   [moving away] But why close to one
another? Further away is perfectly all right.

KHLESTAKOV   [moving closer] But why far apart when we can
be close together?

MARYA ANTONOVNA   But what's the point of all this?

KHLESTAKOV   [*moving closer*] You're only imagining that we're close together, but in reality we're far apart. How happy it would make me, mamselle, if I could enfold you in my arms.

MARYA ANTONOVNA   [*Looks out of window.*] Something just flew by. A magpie, wasn't it?

KHLESTAKOV   [*Kisses her shoulder and looks out of window.*] Yes, a magpie.

MARYA ANTONOVNA   [*Stands up in a huff.*] Well now, you've gone too far! What impudence!

KHLESTAKOV   [*holding her back*] Do forgive me, mamselle. It was only for love of you . . . only true love . . .

MARYA ANTONOVNA   You must take me for some country girl . . . [*Attempts to leave.*]

KHLESTAKOV   [*still holding her back*] Yes, it was love, true love. But it was not meant seriously, Marya Antonovna! Don't be angry! I'll even go down on my knees to beg forgiveness. [*Sinks to his knees.*] Do forgive me! See, I'm on my knees.

Scene XIII

ANNA ANDREYEVNA   [*Sees* KHLESTAKOV *on his knees.*] Good heavens! Such goings-on!

KHLESTAKOV   Damn it!

ANNA ANDREYEVNA   [*to daughter*] What's the meaning of this, young lady? What sort of behaviour is this?

MARYA ANTONOVNA   But Mama, dear . . .

ANNA ANDREYEVNA   Leave the room at once – do you hear? Get out! And don't you dare show your face in here again.
    [*Exit* MARYA ANTONOVNA *in tears.*]
    Do forgive me, I was absolutely shocked . . .

KHLESTAKOV   [*aside*] She's quite a tasty dish too – not at all bad looking. [*Falls on his knees.*] Madam, you can see that I'm consumed with love!

ANNA ANDREYEVNA   What are you kneeling for? Oh, do get up, please, the floor's so dusty in here!

KHLESTAKOV   No, I must kneel, I really must! I need to know my fate – will it be life or death?

ANNA ANDREYEVNA   Forgive me, but I don't quite follow the drift of what you're saying. If I'm not mistaken, you're proposing to my daughter?

KHLESTAKOV   Oh no, it's *you* I'm in love with! My life hangs by a thread. If you reject my undying love I shall be unworthy of earthly existence. With heart ablaze I ask for your hand.

ANNA ANDREYEVNA   Please let me point out that – in a manner of speaking – I'm a married woman.

KHLESTAKOV   No matter! True love knows no barriers. As the poet said:[45] ' 'Tis laws that condemn . . .' – but together we shall fly to the shade of a distant stream . . .[46] Your hand – I implore you! Your hand!

Scene XIV

[*The same and* MARYA ANTONOVNA, *who suddenly rushes in.*]

MARYA ANTONOVNA   Mama! Papa says he'd like you to . . . [*Sees Khlestakov on his knees and shrieks.*] Heavens! Such goings-on!

ANNA ANDREYEVNA   Why . . . well . . . what's the matter with you – scatterbrain! Rushing in here like a scalded cat! What are you so surprised about? Whatever's got into your head? Really, you're behaving like a little child of three! No one would think you're eighteen years old. When will you learn some sense and start behaving like a well-brought-up young lady? When will you learn how to conduct yourself?

MARYA ANTONOVNA   [*through her tears*] Really, Mama, I didn't know . . .

ANNA ANDREYEVNA   There's a kind of whirlwind blowing around in your head! Why take those Lyapkin-Tyapkin girls as an example? Why imitate them? There are better examples for you to follow – your own mother! There's an example for you!

KHLESTAKOV   [*grasping the daughter's hand*] Anna Andrey-

evna! I beg you – don't stand in the way of our happiness!
Give your blessing to our undying love.

ANNA ANDREYEVNA   Oh, so it's *her* you're . . . ?

KHLESTAKOV   Decide now: is it life or death?

ANNA ANDREYEVNA   There – do you see, you stupid girl! For
a worthless creature like you His Excellency has been so good
as to go down on his knees. And you have to come bursting
in here like a lunatic. Now, it would serve you right if I were
to refuse my consent – you're unworthy of such happiness.

MARYA ANTONOVNA   I won't do it again, Mama. Honestly I
won't!

Scene XV

[*The same and* MAYOR, *in a hurry.*]

MAYOR   Your Excellency! Don't ruin me! Please don't ruin
me!

KHLESTAKOV   What's the matter with you?

MAYOR   It's those shopkeepers – they've been complaining to
Your Excellency. Word of honour, I assure you that not half
of what they say is true. They're the ones who cheat and
short-change their customers. And the sergeant's widow who
told you I had her flogged – she's lying! She flogged herself,
I swear it!

KHLESTAKOV   To hell with the sergeant's widow, I've other
things to think about.

MAYOR   Don't believe them, don't believe them. They're such
liars – even a little child would never trust them. The whole
town knows they're damned liars. And as for swindling, I
venture to inform you that they're the biggest crooks the
world has ever seen.

ANNA ANDREYEVNA   Are you aware of the great honour Ivan
Aleksandrovich is bestowing on us? He's asked for our
daughter's hand in marriage.

MAYOR   What? A likely story. You're out of your mind! Please
don't be angry, Your Excellency, she's a little touched. Her
late mother was just the same.

KHLESTAKOV   But it's true. I'm asking for your daughter's hand.

MAYOR   I can't believe it, Your Excellency.

ANNA ANDREYEVNA   Not even when you're being told to your face?

KHLESTAKOV   I'm in real earnest. I could go out of my mind, I'm so in love!

MAYOR   I can scarcely believe it, Your Excellency. I'm unworthy of such an honour.

KHLESTAKOV   It's true – and if you refuse to give Marya Antonovna's hand in marriage there's no knowing what I might do to myself!

MAYOR   I just can't believe it ... No ... well, I see Your Excellency likes to have his little joke!

ANNA ANDREYEVNA   What a dunderhead you are! Even when everything's been explained to you, you still don't believe it!

MAYOR   I can't believe it.

KHLESTAKOV   Give her to me, give her! I'm a desperate man and I'd stop at nothing. When I've put a bullet through my brains they'll bring you to trial for it.

MAYOR   Oh God! Heavens! No! Please don't be angry with me! I'm not to blame, neither in thought nor deed. I'll do whatever Your Excellency thinks fit. Oh, my head's going round! God knows what's happening to me – I've made a complete fool of myself.

ANNA ANDREYEVNA   All right ... give them your blessing.

[KHLESTAKOV *comes forward with* MARYA ANTO-NOVNA.]

MAYOR   May God bless you. I'm not to blame, I swear it!

[KHLESTAKOV *kisses* MARYA ANTONOVNA. *The* MAYOR *stares at them.*]

What the devil! So it's true! [*Wipes eyes.*] They're kissing. Saints alive! They're kissing, just like an engaged couple. Well, what do you say to that! [*Shouts and jumps for joy.*] Hey, Anton! Bravo! Bravo! Well done, Mr Mayor! I never expected things to turn out like this!

Scene XVI

OSIP   The horses are ready.

KHLESTAKOV   Er . . . fine . . . won't be a minute.

MAYOR   What's that, Your Excellency? You're leaving?

KHLESTAKOV   Yes, I'm leaving.

MAYOR   But when . . . I mean to say . . . well. Your Excellency did mention something about a wedding, didn't you?

KHLESTAKOV   I won't be away long – one day. To see my uncle, a rich old boy. I'll be back tomorrow, of course!

MAYOR   We would not presume to detain you and look forward to your safe return.

KHLESTAKOV   Of course, of course . . . back in no time. Farewell, my love, farewell . . . no – words fail me. Farewell, my darling! [*Kisses her hand.*]

MAYOR   Is there anything you might need for the road? I remember Your Excellency mentioning you were . . . that you were rather short of funds.

KHLESTAKOV   Oh no, why talk of such things now? [*Short pause for thought.*] Well, perhaps I . . . if you really don't mind . . .

MAYOR   How much would you like?

KHLESTAKOV   You lent me two hundred before – I mean to say, it was four hundred, but I wouldn't want to take advantage of your mistake. Perhaps the same again, to make it a round eight hundred?

MAYOR   At once, Your Excellency! [*Takes the money from his wallet.*] And it's all in new banknotes!

KHLESTAKOV   Ah yes! [*Examines the notes.*] That's great – as they say, new money brings new happiness!

MAYOR   That's right, Your Excellency!

KHLESTAKOV   Farewell! Cheerio, Anton Antonovich. Much obliged for your hospitality. I can honestly say that I've never had such a warm reception. Farewell, Anna Andreyevna! Farewell, Marya Antonovna, my darling!

[EXEUNT.]

[*Offstage:*]

KHLESTAKOV'S VOICE   Farewell, Marya Antonovna, my angel!

MAYOR'S VOICE   What's this? Surely you're not travelling in that broken-down post-chaise?

KHLESTAKOV   Why yes, I'm used to it. Smooth rides give me a headache.

COACHMAN'S VOICE   Whoa there! Whoa!

MAYOR'S VOICE   At least let me spread something over the seat – a rug, perhaps? Shall I get you one?

KHLESTAKOV'S VOICE   No, what for? It's not necessary. On the other hand a rug would be nice . . .

MAYOR'S VOICE   Hey, Avdotya! Run to the storeroom and fetch the best rug – the Persian one with the blue border. And make it snappy!

COACHMAN'S VOICE   Whoa!

MAYOR'S VOICE   When may we expect Your Excellency?

KHLESTAKOV'S VOICE   Tomorrow – or the day after.

OSIP'S VOICE   Ah, is that our rug? Give it here and spread it like this. And some hay this side.

COACHMAN'S VOICE   Whoa!

OSIP'S VOICE   On this side. There! A bit more! That's fine. He'll be very comfortable. [*Pats rug.*] Would Your Excellency care to be seated?

KHLESTAKOV'S VOICE   Farewell, Anna Andreyevna.

MAYOR'S VOICE   Farewell, Your Excellency.

WOMEN'S VOICES   Farewell, Ivan Aleksandrovich!

KHLESTAKOV'S VOICE   Farewell, Mama!

COACHMAN'S VOICE   Giddyup, my beauties. Giddyup!

[*Coach bells ring. Curtain.*]

ACT V

Scene I

[MAYOR, ANNA ANDREYEVNA, MARYA ANTONOVNA]

MAYOR Well, what do you say to that, Anna Andreyevna? Eh? Have you given it some thought? What a prize catch, damn it! You must admit it's beyond your wildest dreams ... one day a small-time mayor's wife and then suddenly to ... By God, dammit! You're a mother-in-law to that dashing young devil!

ANNA ANDREYEVNA Not at all. I've known for a long time now. You're so surprised because you're so common. You've never mixed with refined people, of quality.

MAYOR What! I'm a person of quality, my dear! Come to think of it, Anna Andreyevna, we're birds of a different feather now, you and I! Now we're flying high, dammit! Just you wait, I'll make it hot for all those lousy two-timing complainers and informers. Who's there?

[*Enter* CONSTABLE.]

Oh, it's you, Ivan Karpovich! Now go and fetch all those rotten shopkeepers. I'll teach those sneaking bastards. Complain about me, eh? Ugh, you stinking Jews! You just wait, my little darlings! So far I've only had you by the whiskers, but now I'll pull your beards out! I want the names of all those who've been griping about me – especially those filthy scribblers who concocted petitions for them.[47] And make sure everyone in this town knows how God has honoured their mayor – I'm not marrying my daughter off to some little jerk, but to a man the likes of whom the world has never seen, a man who can do anything. Anything! Tell everyone about it, shout it from the rooftops, ring the church bells, damn it! Now's the time to celebrate!

[*Exit* CONSTABLE.]

So there you are, Anna Andreyevna! And where are we going to live – here or in St Petersburg?

ANNA ANDREYEVNA   Why, in St Petersburg of course. How could we stay in this place any longer?

MAYOR   If you say St Petersburg, then St Petersburg it shall be. But I wouldn't mind staying here either. I reckon I could say goodbye to being a mayor.

ANNA ANDREYEVNA   Of course you could. After all – what's a mayor?

MAYOR   So, what do you think, Anna Andreyevna? I could fix myself up with a top job now, seeing as the Inspector hobnobs with ministers and calls regularly at the Palace. He could pull strings. Given time, I might even be a general. What do you think, Anna Andreyevna? Could I become a general?

ANNA ANDREYEVNA   I should say so! Of course you could!

MAYOR   It would be marvellous to be a general, dammit, what with a sash draped across your shoulder. Now, what sash shall it be, Anna Andreyevna. Red or blue?[48]

ANNA ANDREYEVNA   Well, blue. It's more impressive.

MAYOR   Listen to her! So that's what you've set your heart on! Red isn't bad either. Well now, why am I so keen to become a general? Because when you're travelling somewhere, special messengers and adjutants will gallop ahead of you, shouting: 'Horses for the general!' You'd get priority[49] at posting-stages – all those titular counsellors, captains, mayors are crying out for horses and you won't give a damn! Off you'd go to dine with the Governor and some poor old mayor will be sitting there fuming, waiting his turn. That's the nicest part about it. Ha! ha! ha! Bet your life it is!

[*Bursts into laughter.*]

ANNA ANDREYEVNA   You've only ever liked coarse things, but please remember that from now on our lives will be completely different. You won't have any more friends like that dog-crazy judge to go hunting with, or that Zemlyanika.

None of that riff-raff any more! Oh no! You'll be mixing with highly refined and cultivated people, such as counts and aristocrats. But I have to say there's one thing that worries me – your behaviour . . . and sometimes you let slip the kind of words you'd never hear in polite society.

MAYOR   What of it? Words can't harm you.

ANNA ANDREYEVNA   That was all very well for some common or garden provincial mayor, but life in the Capital will be completely different.

MAYOR   Yes . . . I've heard there's two kinds of fish there – eels and smelts – they make your mouth water at the very first bite.

ANNA ANDREYVENA   Fish! I suppose that's all you can think of! But I do want to have the very best house in the Capital. There'll be such an exquisite odour when you enter my boudoir that it will make you close your eyes! [*Closes eyes and sniffs.*] Oh, how wonderful!

Scene II

[*Enter* SHOPKEEPERS.]

MAYOR   What ho, my darlings!

SHOPKEEPERS   We wish you good health, Your Honour.

MAYOR   Well, how's tricks, my pets? Eh? How's business? So, you tea-swilling hucksters thought you'd go and complain about me, didn't you? You master crooks, twisters, fiddlers, double-dealing scum went and complained! And where did it get you? Thought you'd put me behind bars, eh? Do you know what? I chuck a host of devils and a filthy witch in your faces!

ANNA ANDREYEVNA   Goodness gracious! What language, Antosha!

MAYOR   [*irritated*] To hell with my language! Do you know that the government official you ran to complain to is going to marry my daughter? What do you say to that, eh? I'll fix you lot! Oooooooh! Cheating simple townsfolk, signing government contracts so you can swindle it to the tune of a hundred thousand roubles by supplying rotten cloth, you swine! And then 'generously' donating twenty yards to charity and expecting a medal for it. If they ever found out they'd give you . . . Look at that one over there, swaggering about with his fat belly. 'I'm a shopkeeper,' he says, 'you mustn't lay a finger on me! I'm as good as the nobility.' Fine nobleman, you with the ugly mug! A true nobleman studies science and even if he's whipped at school it doesn't matter as long as he learns what's useful. But you lot! You're born swindlers and your boss beats you if you can't cheat. Before you've even memorized the Lord's Prayer you're short-changing people and as soon as your paunch fills out and your pockets are stuffed you start acting all high and mighty. Ugh, what wonders of creation! Just because you swill sixteen samovars of tea a day you think you can behave like lords! I spit on your heads and your swanky ways!

SHOPKEEPERS [*bowing*] It's all our fault, Anton Antonovich . . .

MAYOR Wanted to complain, did you? And who helped you with that fiddle with the bridge, charging twenty thousand for timber when there wasn't even a hundred roubles' worth? It was *me*, you with the goat's beard! Slipped your mind, eh? If I'd blabbed on you I could have had the lot of you packed off to Siberia. What do you say to that, eh?

SHOPKEEPERS We're guilty, Anton Antonovich, the devil led us astray, Your Honour. We swear never to do it again. We'll do anything to please you, only don't be so angry with us!

MAYOR Don't be angry! Now you can grovel at my feet all right. And why? I'll tell you. Because I've come out on top. But if things had gone your way you scum would have trampled me into the mud and dumped logs over me into the bargain.

SHOPKEEPERS [*bowing down to ground*] Don't ruin us, Anton Antonovich!

MAYOR Now it's 'Don't ruin us'! And what did you say before? I've a good mind to take you all . . . [*Gesticulates.*] May God forgive you . . . Well, that's enough. I'm not the sort to bear grudges. But from now on you'd better watch your step. I'm not marrying my daughter to just anybody, so you'd better make sure I'm properly congratulated – do you follow? I won't be fobbed off with lousy bits of herring or loaves of sugar this time. Now, on your way.

[*Exeunt* SHOPKEEPERS.]

Scene III

[*The same, with* JUDGE, WARDEN OF CHARITIES, *then* RASTAKOVSKY.]

JUDGE [*still in doorway*] Are these rumours to be believed, Anton Antonovich? Has some extraordinary good fortune come your way?

WARDEN OF CHARITIES   I have the honour to congratulate you on your extraordinary good fortune. I was absolutely overjoyed when I heard about it. [*Kisses Anna Andreyevna's hand.*] Anna Andreyevna! [*Kisses Marya Antonovna's hand.*] Marya Antonovna!

RASTAKOVSKY Allow me to congratulate you, Anton Antonovich. God grant you and the young couple long life. May He bless you with numerous offspring – grandchildren and great-grandchildren! Anna Andreyevna! [*Goes and kisses her hand.*] Marya Antonovna! [*Goes and kisses her hand.*]

Scene IV

[*The same,* KOROBKIN *and his wife,* LYULYUKOV.]

KOROBKIN   I have the honour to congratulate you, Anton Antonovich! Anna Andreyevna! [*Goes and kisses her hand.*]

KOROBKIN'S WIFE   My heartfelt congratulations on your new-found happiness.

LYULYUKOV   I have the honour of congratulating you, Anna Andreyevna! [*Kisses her hand and then turns to onlookers and clicks his tongue with an air of bravado.*] Marya Antonovna! I'm honoured to congratulate you! [*Kisses her hand and turns to onlookers with same air of bravado.*]

Scene V

[*A crowd in dress- and tail-coats first go and kiss* ANNA ANDREYEVNA's *hand, saying 'Anna Andreyevna!' Then to* MARYA ANTONOVNA, *saying 'Marya Antonovna!'* BOBCHINSKY *and* DOBCHINSKY *push their way to the front.*]

BOBCHINSKY   I have the honour of congratulating you!

DOBCHINSKY   Anton Antonovich! I have the honour of congratulating you!

BOBCHINSKY   On this auspicious occasion!

DOBCHINSKY   Anna Andreyevna!

BOBCHINSKY   Anna Andreyevna!
    [*As they go to kiss her hand they collide and bang their heads together.*]

DOBCHINSKY   Marya Antonovna! [*Goes and kisses her hand.*] I have the honour of congratulating you. You will be terribly happy and parade in a cloth-of-gold dress and dine on many exquisite soups. You'll have a superb time!

BOBCHINSKY   [*interrupting*] Marya Antonovna! I have the honour to congratulate you! God grant you wealth, piles of gold and a bouncy baby boy ... so tiny ... [*Demonstrates with his hand.*] ... so tiny you could sit him on the palm of your hand. Oh yes! And the little fellow will cry, Wah! Wah!

Scene VI

[*Several more guests come up to kiss the ladies' hands, among them the* INSPECTOR OF SCHOOLS *and his wife.*]

LUKA LUKICH   I have the honour ...

LUKA LUKICH'S WIFE   [*running ahead of him*] I congratulate you, Anna Andreyevna!
    [*They kiss.*]
Honestly, I was *so* delighted when I was told that Anna Andreyevna's daughter is engaged. 'Ah, goodness me!' I thought. I was *so* thrilled I just had to tell my husband:

'Listen, Lukanchik dear, such happiness has overtaken Anna Andreyevna!' And I thought: 'Thank heavens for that!' and I went on: 'I'm so excited I simply can't wait to tell Anna Andreyevna in person . . .' 'Ah goodness me!' I thought, 'Anna Andreyevna was always hoping to find a good match for her daughter and now her wish has been granted.' I was so over-joyed, my dear, I was lost for words. I sobbed my heart out, I did. And Luka Lukich asked: 'Why are you sobbing like that, Nastenka dear?' And I replied: 'Luka dear, I don't know myself – the tears are just streaming down my face.'

MAYOR   Please be seated, ladies and gentlemen! Hey, Mishka! Bring some more chairs!

[*The guests sit down.*]

Scene VII

[*The same*, CHIEF OF POLICE *and* CONSTABLES.]

CHIEF OF POLICE   Allow me to congratulate you, Your Honour, and wish you long life and prosperity.

MAYOR   Thank you, thank you. Please sit down, gentlemen!

JUDGE   Now tell us, Anton Antonovich, how it all happened, the exact course of events . . .

MAYOR   The course of events was really quite extraordinary. His Excellency was pleased to propose in person.

ANNA ANDREYEVNA   And in an exceedingly polite and most refined manner. He expressed himself beautifully: 'Anna Andreyevna,' he said, 'I do this out of the respect I have for your fine virtues . . .' And such a handsome, well-bred gentleman, of the noblest principles! 'Believe me, Anna Andreyevna,' he says, 'life without you isn't worth living. I'm doing this out of respect for your rare qualities.'

MARYA ANTONOVNA   But Mama, he said that to *me*!

ANNA ANDREYEVNA   Silence! What do you know? Now, mind your own business! 'I, Anna Andreyevna,' he said, 'am amazed . . .' And the compliments just poured out in a stream! I was about to reply: 'We do not dare dream of such an honour', when he suddenly fell on his knees and said – in the noblest manner – 'Anna Andreyevna, don't make me the unhappiest of men! Please reciprocate my feelings or I shall put an end to my life.'

MARYA ANTONOVNA   Honestly, Mama! He said that to *me*!

ANNA ANDREYEVNA   Why yes, of course it was you. I don't deny it.

MAYOR   And he gave us quite a scare. He kept saying: 'I'll shoot myself, I'll shoot myself!'

CHORUS OF GUESTS   You don't say!

JUDGE   Well, I'll be blowed!

WARDEN OF CHARITIES   The hand of destiny was at work . . .

INSPECTOR OF SCHOOLS   Destiny my foot! These are the just deserts of devoted service. [*Aside*] Some pigs have all the luck!

JUDGE   If you like, Anton Antonovich, I'll sell you that puppy we were bargaining about.

MAYOR   I've no time for puppies now.

JUDGE   Well, if not that one, perhaps we could strike a deal over another.

KOROBKIN'S WIFE   Ah, Anton Antonovich. You cannot imagine how thrilled I am!

KOROBKIN   May I ask where our distinguished visitor is? I think I heard he had to leave town for some reason.

MAYOR   Yes, he's gone, just for the day, on exceedingly important business.

ANNA ANDREYEVNA   To see his uncle to ask for his blessing . . .

MAYOR   Yes, to ask his blessing. But tomorrow he'll be back.
   [*Sneezes.*]
   [*One deafening roar of 'Bless You!'*]
Thank you very much. Yes, he'll be back tomorrow. [*Sneezes.*]
   [*Above the general clamour voices can be heard:*]

BOBCHINSKY   A hundred years and a sack of gold coins!

DOBCHINSKY   May you live to forty times four!

WARDEN OF CHARITIES   You can go to hell!

KOROBKIN'S WIFE   Damn and blast you!

MAYOR   Thank you very much. And the same to all of you.

ANNA ANDREYEVNA   Of course, we plan to live in St Petersburg. The air here is, I must say, so very *provincial*. Yes, most disagreeable. As for my husband, he's going to be made a general.

MAYOR   Yes, ladies and gentlemen, I must confess that I'd love to be a general, dammit!

LUKA LUKICH   May God grant your wishes come true!

RASTAKOVSKY   With God all things are possible.

JUDGE   Great ships need deep waters.

WARDEN OF CHARITIES   Honour where it is due.

JUDGE   [aside] What a laughing-stock he'll make if he's made a general – like putting a saddle on a cow! No, my friend, you've still a long way to go for that! There's those with far cleaner copy-books than you and they're not generals.

WARDEN OF CHARITIES   [aside] I ask you – he's set his sights already on being a general. Who can say, he might even make it. God only knows he's puffed up enough. [Turns to MAYOR.] You won't forget your old pals, Anton Antonovich?

JUDGE   And if we have any trouble here, if we need your help in an emergency, I trust you will take us under your wing.

KOROBKIN   Next year I shall be taking my son to St Petersburg to enter him in the civil service. Can I rely on you to give him a helping hand and be like a father to the poor little orphan?

MAYOR   Yes, I shall do everything in my power . . .

ANNA ANDREYEVNA   Oh, you're always too free with your promises, Antosha! Firstly you won't have time to think about such things. Secondly, why should you burden yourself with promises like that?

MAYOR   Why not, my dearest! Sometimes these things are possible.

ANNA ANDREYEVNA   Perhaps they are, but you can't start giving your protection to all the small fry that happen to come along.

KOROBKIN'S WIFE   Did you hear what she called us?

FEMALE GUEST   Oh, she's always been like that. I know her only too well. You can always tell a pig from its grunt.

Scene VIII

[*The same.* POSTMASTER *comes rushing in with an opened letter in his hand.*]

POSTMASTER   The most amazing thing's happened, ladies and gentlemen! The official we took to be a government inspector isn't an inspector at all!

ALL   What do you mean – not an inspector?

POSTMASTER   He's not an inspector – I found it out from this letter.

MAYOR   What are you talking about? *What* letter?

POSTMASTER   A letter he wrote himself. They brought it to me at the post office. When I saw the address was Post Office Street[50] I was thunderstruck. 'Oh yes,' I thought, 'he must have found irregularities in the postal department and he's reporting me to the authorities.' So I went and opened it.

MAYOR   How could you do such a thing?

POSTMASTER   I can't rightly say – I was driven on by some supernatural force. I was about to send it off special delivery, but curiosity the like of which I'd never felt before got the better of me. 'I can't open it, I can't,' I thought, but then something kept tugging at me, drawing me on. In one ear I heard a voice telling me: 'Hey, don't open it, or you're a dead duck.' And in the other some demon kept whispering: 'Go on – open it! Go on!' The moment I broke the seal I had a burning sensation in every vein. But when I opened it I simply froze – honest to God I did! My hands shook and my head started going round.

MAYOR   How dare you open the private letter of such a powerful personage!

POSTMASTER   Well, that's just it! He's not powerful at all and he's not even a personage!

MAYOR   Then tell me who you think he is?

POSTMASTER   He's a complete nobody, just a little squirt.

MAYOR   [*heatedly*] What do you mean – a *nobody*? How dare you! I'll have you arrested for that!

POSTMASTER   Who? *You!?*

MAYOR   Yes, me!

POSTMASTER   Just you try!

MAYOR   Are you aware that he is to marry my daughter, that I am going to be a dignitary myself and that I could pack you off to Siberia at the drop of a hat?

POSTMASTER   Hold on! What's all this about Siberia? It's a far cry to Siberia! Now, I think I'd better read it out to you, gentlemen. Shall I read it, ladies and gentlemen?

ALL   Yes, read it!

POSTMASTER   [reads] 'I hasten to inform you, my dear Trya-pichkin, of the wondrous things that have befallen me. On the way here I was completely cleaned out by an infantry officer and mine host the innkeeper was all set to put me behind bars when suddenly, thanks to my St Petersburg looks and my clothes, the whole town took me for some governor general. Here I am, staying with the mayor now, having a gay old time and flirting like mad with his wife and daughter – only I haven't decided which one to go for first. Probably the mother, as she looks as if she'd oblige at the flick of a finger. Remember the times when you and I were on the breadline and had to scrounge and sponge for our meals? Remember that pastry cook who chucked me out for charging pies to the King of England?[51] Now the boot's on the other foot: they lend me as much as I want. You'd die laughing – they're all such dreadful freaks. Now, those little sketches you write for the magazines – why not stick them in? Take the mayor, for example. He's as stupid as a mule.'

MAYOR   That's a load of rubbish! It can't possibly say anything of the sort!

POSTMASTER   [showing the MAYOR the letter] Well, read for yourself.

MAYOR   '. . . as stupid as a mule'. It's not possible! You made that bit up yourself!

POSTMASTER   And how could I have done that?

WARDEN OF CHARITIES   Read it all out!

JUDGE   Read on!

POSTMASTER   [continuing] '. . . the mayor's as stupid as a mule . . .'

MAYOR   What the hell! Must you repeat it – it's bad enough
as it is.

POSTMASTER   Hm . . . hmm . . . '. . . as stupid as a mule. The
postmaster's a fine specimen too . . .' [*Stopping*] There's
something rude about me too.

MAYOR   Go on, read it!

POSTMASTER   What for?

MAYOR   To hell with it! It was your idea to read it!

WARDEN OF CHARITIES   Give it to me, I'll read it. [*Puts on
his spectacles and reads.*] 'The postmaster is the spitting
image of Mikheyev, our office porter – and he probably
drinks like a fish too, the old devil!'

POSTMASTER   [*to onlookers*] He's a filthy brat who deserves
a good thrashing – that's what I say!

WARDEN OF CHARITIES   [*continuing*] '. . . the Warden of
Charit-it-it-ie . . .' [*Stammers.*]

KOROBKIN   Why did you stop?

WARDEN OF CHARITIES   The writing's not clear. Anyway, the
man's obviously a rotter.

KOROBKIN   Give it to me! I think my eyesight's better than
yours.

[*Tries to grab letter.*]

WARDEN OF CHARITIES   [*holding on to letter*] No, we can
skip that bit, it's easier to read lower down.

KOROBKIN   No, let me do it. I know how to.

WARDEN OF CHARITIES   No, I'll do the reading. It's legible
lower down.

POSTMASTER   No! Read the lot! We haven't skipped anything
so far!

ALL   Give Korobkin the letter, Ammos Filippovich, give him
the letter.

[*To* KOROBKIN] *You* read it!

WARDEN OF CHARITIES   Wait a minute . . . [*Hands over
letter.*] We're here . . . [*Covers part of it with finger.*] Start
from here . . .

[*All crowd around.*]

POSTMASTER   Now read, read! I don't want any nonsense!
Read the lot!

KOROBKIN   [*reading*] 'The Warden of Charities is a perfect pig in a skull-cap.'[52]

WARDEN OF CHARITIES   That's not even funny! A perfect pig in a skull-cap, I ask you! Whoever heard of a pig in a skull-cap?

KOROBKIN   [*continuing*] 'The Inspector of Schools reeks to high heaven of onions.'

LUKA LUKICH   I've never eaten an onion in my life! As God is my witness!

JUDGE   [*aside*] Thank God there's nothing about me.

KOROBKIN   [*reading*] '. . . and the judge . . .'

JUDGE   What the hell! There *is* something! Really, gentlemen, what on earth's the point of reading all that rubbish?

LUKA LUKICH   It's not rubbish.

POSTMASTER   No! Carry on!

WARDEN OF CHARITIES   Read every word!

KOROBKIN   [*continuing*] 'Judge Lyapkin-Tyapkin is the last word in *mauvais ton*.' [*Stops.*] Hm . . . must be French.

JUDGE   The devil knows what it is! It's not so bad if all it means is crook, but it could be something far worse!

KOROBKIN   [*continuing*] 'For all that, they're a good-hearted bunch, very hospitable. Well, goodbye, Tryapichkin old man, I've made my mind up to follow your example and take up literature. It's such a bore living the way I do. In the long run a man hungers for spiritual nourishment. I realize one's concern should be with the higher things in life. Write to me in Saratov province. [*Turns letter over and reads.*] To: Ivan Vasilyevich Tryapichkin, Esq., 97 Post Office Street, St Petersburg, Third Floor, First on Right.'

A LADY   We hardly expected such a slap in the face!

MAYOR   Well, he's finished me off, done for me! I'm a broken man, played out. All I can see are pigs' snouts everywhere instead of faces. Bring that fellow back! Bring him back! [*Waves his arms.*]

POSTMASTER   Fat chance of that! If things weren't bad enough, I told the stationmaster to give him the fastest horses available. What's more, I gave orders for horses in advance – *and* a priority warrant! The devil himself must have prompted me!

KOROBKIN'S WIFE   What an unparalleled mess!

JUDGE   And the worst of it is, gentlemen – he borrowed three hundred roubles from me.

WARDEN OF CHARITIES   And from me.

POSTMASTER   And from me!

BOBCHINSKY   And sixty-five from Pyotr Ivanovich and myself. Oh yes sir!

JUDGE   [*throwing up his arms in bewilderment*] How did it happen, gentlemen? How could we have blundered like that?

MAYOR   [*Strikes forehead.*] How could I? How *could* I have been such an idiot? I've gone soft in the head, I'm like an old sheep. Thirty years I've been in service and not once has a shopkeeper or contractor ever put one over on me. I've outsmarted swindler after swindler, nailed scoundrels, rogues capable of robbing the whole world! I've bamboozled three governors! Oh yes! And what are governors after all – not worth wasting your breath on!

ANNA ANDREYEVNA   But it can't be true, Antosha! He's engaged to our Masha . . .

MAYOR   [*excited*] Engaged! Engaged, my arse! You can stuff the engagement, that's what! I've got engagement before the eyes . . . Just take a look at me! Let the whole world, all Christendom, see how your mayor's been duped. Fool! Imbecile! Blockhead! [*Shakes fist at himself.*] You thick-nosed idiot – taking that little squirt, that bloody pipsqueak for a powerful personage! I can just picture him now, bowling along to the sound of jingling bells, letting the whole world know about it! And as if it's not bad enough being a laughing-stock already, along will come some hack, some miserable pen-pusher and stick us all in a comedy. That's what really hurts! He won't give a rap for rank or reputation as long as the audience grins from ear to ear and claps its hands. [*Stamps furiously on floor.*] What are you laughing at? You're laughing at yourselves, that's what!⁵³ Ooh – you lot! I'd like to get my hands on all you blasted scribblers. Oooh! You lousy hacks, damned liberals,⁵⁴ devil's spawn! I'd like to tie you all up together, grind you to powder and send you down to hell, right into the devil's maw! [*Strikes out with his fist, pounds his heel on stage floor. After a brief pause*] I can't get over it. Yes, they say those whom the gods want to punish they first drive insane.[55] Was there anything *like* a government inspector about that whippersnapper? Absolutely damn all. Not by a long chalk! Everyone suddenly starts yapping: the Inspector! The Inspector! Now, who started this rumour about a government inspector? Answer me! Somebody tell me!

WARDEN OF CHARITIES [*spreading his arms wide*] I can't explain how it all came about, for the life of me. I feel as if a thick fog has blinded us. It's the work of the devil!

JUDGE I'll tell you who started it. It was those two fine specimens over there. [*Points to* DOBCHINSKY *and* BOB-CHINSKY.]

BOBCHINSKY It wasn't me, honestly. It never entered my head . . .

DOBCHINSKY I didn't say a thing! Nothing at all!

WARDEN OF CHARITIES Of course it was you!

INSPECTOR OF SCHOOLS It stands to reason. You rushed from the inn like lunatics, shouting: 'He's arrived, he's arrived, and he doesn't pay for anything . . .' A fine inspector *you* found!

MAYOR It couldn't have been anyone else. Town gossips, damned liars!

INSPECTOR OF SCHOOLS You and your government inspectors and your fairy-tales can go to hell!

MAYOR Only good at gallivanting around town stirring up trouble, you damned windbags! All you can do is spread rumours, you jabbering magpies!

JUDGE Damned bunglers!

INSPECTOR OF SCHOOLS Morons!

JUDGE Pot-bellied shrimps!

[*Everyone crowds round them.*]

BOBCHINSKY I swear it wasn't me – it was Pyotr Ivanovich.

DOBCHINSKY Oh no, Pyotr Ivanovich. *You* were the first to . . .

BOBCHINSKY Oh no, I wasn't. *You* started it.

Last Scene

[*Enter gendarme.*][56]

GENDARME   The official who has just arrived from St Petersburg by Imperial command requires your presence at the inn immediately.

[*These words strike everyone like a thunderbolt. All the ladies cry out at once in astonishment. The whole group suddenly changes position and stands as if turned to stone.*]

Mute Scene[57]

The MAYOR *stands in the middle like a pillar, arms outstretched and head thrown back. On his right are his wife and daughter, straining to reach him. Behind him the* POSTMASTER, *transformed into a question mark, stands facing the audience. Behind him is the* INSPECTOR OF SCHOOLS *in a state of innocent bewilderment. Behind him, right at the edge of the stage, are three ladies leaning against each other, directing the most sarcastic looks at the mayor's family. To the left of the* MAYOR *stands the* WARDEN OF CHARITIES, *his head slightly cocked to one side, as if he were listening for something. Behind him is the* JUDGE, *arms spread wide, squatting almost to the floor and puckering his lips as if about to whistle or mutter: 'Now we're really in the cart!' Behind him is* KOROBKIN, *winking towards the audience and directing contemptuous looks at the* MAYOR. *Behind him, right at the very edge of the stage, stand* BOBCHINSKY *and* DOBCHINSKY, *arms outstretched towards each other, mouths gaping, eyes popping. The other guests are simply transformed into pillars. The petrified group maintains this position for about a minute and a half.*

[*Curtain.*]

Publishing History and Notes

IVAN FYODOROVICH SHPONKA AND
HIS AUNT

Completed at the end of 1831, this story was first published in 1832, in the second book of the collection of stories set in the Ukraine, *Evenings on a Farm Near Dikanka*, which first established Gogol's reputation. The apparently unfinished state of the story is deliberate: here is emphasized the utter emptiness and meaninglessness of the 'hero's' life. The story could end anywhere and in his preface Gogol amusingly tells us that the 'incompleteness' can be explained by the fact that the end of the manuscript had been lost, having been used by an old woman for making pie papers. Contemporaries viewed this 'unfinished' state as a deliberate artistic device, possibly deriving from Laurence Sterne (1713–68).

The story anticipates many motifs and characterizations in Gogol's later work, particularly *Dead Souls*: in Storchenko we have an embryonic Petukh/Sobakyevich. The description of the infantry regiments is further developed in 'The Carriage'.

The hero's surname carries a special meaning. According to Gogol's *Lexicon of Ukrainian Words*, 'shponka' is another word for 'cuff-link'. One of Shponka's favourite occupations is cleaning his uniform buttons and by this surname Gogol is underlining his essential triviality.

1. *Gadyach*: Town in Poltava province (Ukraine) on the Psyol River.
2. *tax-farmer*: Here, someone who has received, for payment of a predetermined sum, a monopoly on certain goods. From 1827 the most widely held monopoly in Russia was on wine and vodka.
3. *Vytrebenky*: Caprices, whims, as defined by Gogol in his notebook *Odds and Ends*.
4. *Deyeprichastiye*: This surname means 'gerund'.

5. *scit*: (Latin) 'he knows (it)'.

6. *strong spirits made from frozen liquor*: Alcoholic drinks that have lost part of their water content by freezing, thereby gaining in strength.

7. *Mogilyov*: Town in eastern Belorussia, on the River Dnieper, formerly with a high Jewish population.

8. *address book*: A kind of calendar or directory, giving the names and duties of civil servants in all government departments.

9. *staying in some Russian inn*: The action is actually taking place in the Ukraine, not Russia proper.

10. *Trokhimov vodka*: Originally vodka was very crudely distilled and it was flavoured with herbs, honey or lemon zest to hide the unpleasant smell and flavour. After improvements in distillation, flavoured vodkas became a speciality in their own right. Centaury is a bitter-tasting herb, used for upset stomachs.

11. *Korobeynikov's Journey to the Holy Land*: An account of a journey made to Jerusalem and Egypt in 1583. This book was not published until 1783 and was reprinted many times.

12. *kvass*: A home-brewed drink usually made from rye bread and malt.

13. *He took off his hat – and there was a wife sitting in it*: Shponka's chaotic dream is apparently based on the declaration of love by the German Trumpf to Tsar Vakula's daughter Podshchipa in I. A. Krylov's mock tragedy *Trumpf* (1797), a violently satirical play directed against the regime of Paul I and not published until 1871.

HOW IVAN IVANOVICH QUARRELLED WITH IVAN NIKIFOROVICH

This story was first published in 1834, in the almanac *Housewarming*, issued by the publisher A. F. Smirdin on the occasion of moving to new premises. It is the last story in the *Mirgorod* series and was almost certainly completed before the other three stories in the *Mirgorod* collection (1835).

When the censors excised several long passages in the first version, Gogol wrote a preface, affirming that all the events in the story belonged to the past and that now everything had turned out for the best. This sarcasm did not go unnoticed and at the last moment the preface itself was prohibited by the censors. As the forthcoming collection had already been typeset and any resetting would have been extremely costly, Gogol was forced to add, very quickly, two pages to the preceding story ('Viy') to make up the gap.

The most direct antecedent for this story, in its comic treatment of provincial mores and judicial system, can be seen in 'The Two Ivans or Passion for Litigation' (1825) by Gogol's fellow-Ukrainian, V. T. Narezhny (1780–1825). Narezhny's story of a prolonged lawsuit between two neighbours – Ivan Zubar and Ivan Khmara – with their neighbour Khriton Zanoza, is less satirical than Gogol's story, being sentimental and didactic. Also, Gogol had been familiar with prolonged litigation (as in the story) in his own family, and in a letter of 30 April 1829 he wrote to his mother: 'Give my respects to grandfather. Please ask him how his lawsuit's going. Will it ever end?'

After hearing Gogol read the story to him Pushkin remarked: 'Very original and very funny.'

1.   *Gapka*: Popular form of Agafiya.
2.   *Poltava*: Large town in Ukraine where Peter I defeated Charles XII of Sweden in 1709.
3.   *Khorol*: District town in Poltava province (Ukraine).
4.   *Koliberda*: Small town on the Dnieper, in Kremenchug district of Poltava province.
5.   *Pupopuz*: 'Pup' = 'navel', 'puz' = 'belly'.
6.   *rather like the letter 'V'*: Last letter of Church Slavonic and pre-1918 alphabet.
7.   *Sorochintsy*: Small town in Ukraine, Gogol's birthplace.
8.   *All together . . . a striking picture*: This scene strongly anticipates the famous Mute Scene at the close of *The Government Inspector*.
9.   *printed by Lyubya, Garya and Popov*: Reference to the publishers of Madame de Genlis's *La Duchesse de la Vallière* (Moscow, 1804–5). This same novel is read by Chichikov in *Dead Souls* (ch. 10).
10. *Mirror of Justice*: A pyramid-shaped glass case with the Statutes of Peter the Great; a symbol of justice.
11. *Dovgochkhun*: 'Long sneeze'.
12. *Santurinsky or Nikopolsky liqueur*: Popular wines named after place of production: Santorin – Greek island; Nikopol – town on River Dniester.
13. *following statement*: Besides being a parody of the legal officialese of the day, this passage is intentionally meaningless in parts, being concocted by a half-witted clerk with a smattering of legal knowledge.

NEVSKY PROSPEKT

Written between 1833 and 1834 'Nevsky Prospekt' was first published in the Petersburg cycle of stories, *Arabesques*, in 1835. Ever fearful of the censors, Gogol asked Pushkin to look through the story. Pushkin replied: 'I read it with great pleasure. It seems all can be passed. But it's a pity to leave out the flogging. It strikes me as essential for the full effect of the evening mazurka' (letter of 15 October to 9 November 1834). Gogol was extremely worried that the censors would take offence at the scene where the drunken Germans punish Pirogov: the lieutenant would not have been flogged had he appeared in full uniform, which would have commanded respect, so in the original draft Pirogov appears in civilian dress.

Called Gogol's 'fullest' work by Pushkin, 'Nevsky Prospekt' shows the influence of E. T. A. Hoffmann (then very popular in Russia): there are striking parallels between the artist Piskarev and Anselmus in Hoffmann's *Der Goldene Topf* (*The Golden Pot*). V. Vinogradov has pointed out a striking resemblance to Thomas de Quincey's *Confessions of an English Opium Eater* (1821; widely read in Russia at the time): Piskarev turns to opium.

In a letter to his mother of 30 April 1829, shortly after his arrival in St Petersburg for the first time, Gogol gives an interesting description of his first impressions of the city: 'People stroll about a lot. In winter, all those with nothing to do promenade from 12 to 2 (at this time those working in offices are busy) along Nevsky Prospekt.' In the detailed descriptions of St Petersburg artists' lives in the story Gogol's own time as a student at the Academy of Arts (1830–33) finds reflection. Writing to his mother (3 June 1830) he states: '. . . through my acquaintance with artists – even very distinguished ones – I'm able to take advantage of facilities inaccessible to many. Not to mention their talent, I can't enthuse too greatly over their character and whole attitude. What people! . . . such humility with the greatest talent!'

1. *Nevsky Prospekt*: About two and a half miles long, St Petersburg's main thoroughfare runs from the Admiralty to the Alexander Nevsky Monastery. As in Gogol's day, it is still the hub of the city's shopping and entertainment, lined with a colourful medley of shop fronts, restaurants and art galleries. It was laid out in the early eighteenth century as the start of the main road to Novgorod.

2. *Morskaya, Gorokhovaya, Liteynaya, Meshchanskaya and other*

streets: Streets in central St Petersburg. Gogol lived from 1833 to 1836 in (Malaya) Morskaya Street.

3. *Vyborg*: On the north side of the Neva River.

4. *Peski*: 'Sands' – a district of St Petersburg.

5. *Ganymede*: Handsome Trojan youth, seized by the gods and a favourite of Zeus. Here a shop boy. He was cup-bearer to the gods – hence the point of the humour.

6. *Yekaterinsky Canal*: Now called Griboyedov Canal, it was one into which sewage flowed. Gogol is being sarcastic when he speaks of its 'cleanliness'.

7. *strong language that they would never hear even in the theatre*: Reference to the low-life vaudevilles that appeared on the Russian stage in the 1830s, with civil service clerks and tradesmen as their heroes (see note 18).

8. *Foreign Collegium*: Peter the Great established a system of twelve colleges, all being government departments. The Foreign Collegium was the Ministry of Foreign Affairs.

9. *Admiralty spire*: The gilded spire of the old Admiralty, headquarters of the Russian navy from 1711. This spire is a St Petersburg landmark and is easily visible from Nevsky Prospekt.

10. *Hungry titular, court and others counsellors*: See general note on Table of Ranks (p. xxxv).

11. *Perugino's Bianca*: Reference to the Madonna in Perugino's *The Adoration of the Magi* in the chapel of Santa Maria dei Bianchi in Città della Pieve.

12. *and sent her carriage for you*: An anecdote possibly borrowed from *A Russian Gil Blas* (1814), a novel by Gogol's fellow-Ukrainian V. T. Narezhny (1780–1825).

13. *Kammerjunkers*: A Kammerjunker was 'Gentleman of the bedchamber', a courtier's rank introduced by Paul 1 in 1797. Pushkin was ignominiously appointed Kammerjunker at an age well past the usual one for this appointment.

14. *Okhta*: Old cemetery.

15. *Bulgarin*: F. V. Bulgarin (1789–1859), writer and journalist, co-editor of the journal *Northern Bee* with N. I. Grech. Police informer, plagiarist, cut-throat journalist, he was known as the 'reptilian journalist', vilely attacking Pushkin, Gogol and most leading writers. He enjoyed great commercial success with *Northern Bee* (see note 26) and his worthless, didactic, picaresque novels such as *Ivan Vyzhigin* (1829). His fear of commercial rivalry led him to engage Pushkin and others in vicious squabbles. Pushkin's devastating satirical articles, such as 'A Few

Words about Mr Bulgarin's Little Finger' effectively destroyed Bulgarin as man and author.

16. *Grech*: N. I. Grech (1787–1867). Not quite so unscrupulous as Bulgarin, Grech left interesting memoirs, a book on Russian grammar and an often reprinted *History of Russian Literature* (1822), as well as several very mediocre novels.

   The novels of Bulgarin and Grech were aimed at the un-demanding middle-class reader loyal to the government. The comic juxtaposition of Pushkin with these hack journalists and writers cannot have escaped Gogol's readers. In particular, Gogol is being sarcastic about the officers' meagre literary education by their linking the name of Pushkin with those of Bulgarin and Grech.

17. A. A. Orlov: Author (1791–1840) of numerous mediocre novels, partly a continuation of Bulgarin's own novel *Ivan Vyzhigin*. His works became the laughing-stock of literary critics and (for commercial reasons) were vilely attacked by Bulgarin. In his brilliant article 'The Triumph of Friendship, or A. A. Orlov vindicated' Pushkin compares Bulgarin and Orlov as 'two geniuses'.

18. *one of those Filatkas*: A popular vaudeville from the life of the common people by P. I. Grigoryev, author of *Filatka and her Children* (1834), and *Filatka and Miroshka* (1831) by P. G. Grigoryev, which enjoyed enormous success. Critics from the aristocracy reproached the author of the latter for breaching 'the norms of good taste'.

19. *Dmitry Donskoy*: Published 1806, patriotic five-act verse tragedy by A. A. Ozerov (1769–1816), performed in 1807.

20. *Woe from Wit*: Published 1833–4, famous comedy by A. S. Griboyedov (1795–1829). One of the great classics of the Russian stage.

21. *the anecdote about a cannon . . . a unicorn another*: Prince P. A. Vyazemsky (1792–1878) retells this in his *Old Notebook*: ' "I could never really understand the difference between a cannon and a unicorn", Catherine the Great once told a general . . . "There's a world of difference," he replied, "and I'll tell Your Majesty right away. Please understand that a cannon is one thing and a unicorn is another." "Ah, now I know," replied the Empress.' A unicorn was a cannon with unicorns engraved on it. Its range was about three miles.

22. *rappee*: A coarse type of snuff made from inferior tobacco leaves, originally produced by rasping a piece of tobacco.

23. *Swabian*: Swabia is a region of south-west Germany, noted for the industry of its inhabitants.

24. *He considered Siberia and a flogging the very least punishment Schiller deserved*: These lines were excised by the censors in the original version.

25. *should the punishment designated by it be inadequate*: These lines were also excised by the censors.

26. *Northern Bee*: The first large-scale privately owned journal in Russia, published first by Bulgarin (see note 15) and then by both Bulgarin and Grech. The circulation reached ten thousand – an enormous number for the times. It was controlled by the government and was the only journal allowed to publish political articles. Gogol gives a highly critical account of the *Northern Bee* in his article 'On the Movement of Journalistic Literature in 1834 and 1835'. The journal became synonymous with triviality and bad taste.

27. *Control Commission*: Ministry of Statistics and Accounts.

28. *arch of the Staff Headquarters*: Part of the General Staff building on Palace Square, designed by the Italian architect K. I. Rossi and commenced in 1823.

29. *church that is being built*: The Lutheran church of St Peter and Paul, begun in 1833 by A. P. Bryullov.

30. *Lafayette*: Marie Joseph, Marquis de Lafayette (1757–1834), French general and statesman who took part in the American War of Independence. Commanded National Guard in the Revolutions of 1789–92 and 1830.

THE NOSE

'The Nose', written between 1833 and 1835, was first published in 1836, in Pushkin's *The Contemporary* (no. 3), after being rejected by the *Moscow Observer* as 'dirty' and 'trivial'. On publication Pushkin provided the following editorial note: 'N. V. Gogol has long withheld publication of this story; but we have found in it so much that is unexpected, fantastic, amusing, original, that we have prevailed upon him to allow us to share with the public the pleasure that his manuscript has afforded us.'

The historian and publicist M. P. Pogodin, who had been pressing Gogol for a story for the *Moscow Observer*, was the editor who actually turned down the story. In a letter of 31 January 1835 to Pogodin Gogol had written: 'Tell our gentlemen that I'm burning with desire . . . I swear that I cannot send this story any earlier than for the third issue. I've so much trouble at the moment it doesn't bear thinking about.' (The 'trouble' concerned Gogol's ill-fated university teaching career.) In March 1835 he wrote to the literary historian and critic S. P. Shevyrov (1806–64): 'I hope to have my story for the *Moscow Observer* finished any day now', and finally, on 18 March, he sent the story to the journal. However, when it was rejected, Gogol wrote to Pogodin asking him to return 'The Nose' as soon as possible. Pogodin evidently delayed and in January the following year Gogol wrote: 'Do me a favour, send me my "Nose". I need it desperately. I want to rework it a little and include it in a small collection that I'm preparing for the press': Gogol's real intent was to have it published in *The Contemporary*.

Noses, snuff-taking and snuff-boxes appear constantly in Gogol's writing. Besides his own obsession with his nose, contemporary anecdotes and jokes about noses had a great attraction for him: the literature of the time abounded in nosological material. V. V. Vinogradov, in his *The Subject and Composition of* 'The Nose': *Poetics of Russian Literature* (Moscow, 1976), has compiled a very lengthy list of contemporary stories and plays concerned with noses, such as N. I. Khmelnitsky's *My Little Ball* and A. I. Pisarev's *The Magic Nose*. Gogol was also possibly influenced by Laurence Sterne, whose *Tristram Shandy* was published in Russian translation between 1804 and 1807. Parts of 'The Nose' distinctly recall Slawkenbergius's tale, with its mock-serious dissertation on noses. The digressive self-parodying style, the nebulous 'asides', where the author confesses that he himself is mystified as to what is going on, are all strongly reminiscent of Sterne.

Gogol had great trouble with the censorship over this story – e.g., see note 6, p. 315. In the original manuscript all details concerning the policeman, loaves of sugar, bribe-taking and the nose's entry into a cathedral were excised. In this first draft the disappearance of Kovalyov's nose is described as a dream, but in the first published edition (for *The Contemporary*) this is eliminated. For the third edition of his collected works (1842), Gogol again revised the ending, shortening the epilogue and introducing new episodes such as Kovalyov's conversation with his servant Ivan, the visit to the pastry-shop and the meeting with the staff officer's wife, Mrs Podtochin, and her daughter.

1. *Collegiate Assessor*: Eighth rank in the civil service hierarchy. According to a statute of 1802, titular counsellors (one rank lower) could be promoted to collegiate assessors only on completion of a university course or by passing an examination. However, it was easier to attain this rank in the Caucasus, far from the bureaucratic nerve centre in St Petersburg. In his *Journey*

to Arzrum Pushkin writes: 'Young titular counsellors come here to get an assessor's rank.' See also Table of Ranks, p. xxxv.

2. *variety appointed in the Caucasus*: See note 1.

3. *never called himself collegiate assessor, but 'Major'*: The civil service ranks had their equivalent in the army and navy.

4. *Nevsky Prospekt*: See 'Nevsky Prospekt', note 1, page 310.

5. *state counsellor*: Holder of the fifth of the fourteen ranks in the civil service hierarchy. A collegiate assessor was three grades lower.

6. *Kazan Cathedral*: Such was the severity (and idiocy) of the censorship in Gogol's day that in the original version the Cathedral was ordered to be replaced by a shopping arcade (Gostiny Dvor), on the grounds that for a nose to enter a cathedral and pray there was blasphemous. At the time Gogol wrote to his friend Pogodin: 'If your stupid censors start quarrelling that a nose could not visit the Kazan Cathedral then I might let it go to a Catholic church instead. However, I cannot believe that they've taken leave of their senses to such an extent as this.' Influenced in style by St Peter's, Rome, the Cathedral was built 1801–11 by A. N. Voronikhin. It now houses the Museum of the History of Religion and Atheism.

7. *Voskresensky Bridge*: Formerly a floating bridge across the Neva.

8. *Anichkov Bridge*: Stone bridge across the Fontanka, near the Anichkov Palace. Built in 1715. Four statues of rearing horses, designed by Baron Klodt von Jurgensburg, were added in 1841.

9. *lieutenant-colonel*: The equivalent rank in the civil service was court counsellor.

10. *Northern Bee*: See 'Nevsky Prospekt', note 26, p. 313.

11. *rappee*: See 'Nevsky Prospekt', note 22, p. 312.

12. *Berezinsky*: A cheap type of snuff (probably named after River Berezina).

13. *wanted to make you look foolish*: Lit. leave you with a nose. Russian has many idioms referring to the nose, most of which have the meaning of fooling someone. In this case a clever pun!

14. *dancing chairs in Konyushenny Street*: An entry in Pushkin's *Diary* (17 December 1833) mentions a story about furniture jumping about in one of the houses attached to the Royal Stables in what was then Konyushenny (now Stable) Street. In 1832 a certain lady by the name of Turchaninovna was exiled from St Petersburg for deceiving people into thinking that she could will objects to move.

15. *Tavrichesky Park*: Once the private garden of Catherine the

Great's lover Potyomkin, for whom she had the gardens laid out and the neighbouring Tavrichesky Palace built 1783–9.

16. *Khozrev-Mirza*: (1813–75) A Persian prince who had come to Russia with official apologies for the murder of the playwright A. S. Griboyedov in Tehran in 1828. (Griboyedov had gone to Tehran to negotiate with the Shah regarding the Peace of Turkmenchai.)

17. *Gostiny Dvor*: The same shopping arcade substituted by the censorship for Kazan Cathedral in the original version. It was redesigned and built in the eighteenth century by Rastrelli and Vallin de la Mothe after the original wooden structure was destroyed by fire in 1736. About three-quarters of a mile long, it opens off Nevsky Prospekt.

THE OVERCOAT

With the original title of 'The Civil Servant who Stole Overcoats', 'The Overcoat' (the most famous story in Russian literature) was written between 1839 and 1841 and first published in the third volume of the collected works, 1842. According to the memoirist Pavel Annenkov, Gogol first conceived the idea for the story (before he went abroad in 1836) based on an anecdote he had heard at a tea party about an indigent government clerk who, after undergoing enormous sacrifices to buy himself a new rifle, loses it on his very first duck-shooting expedition, when it is knocked out of the boat by some thick reeds. After vainly trying to retrieve it he returned home and became seriously ill and only fully recovered after his sympathetic civil service colleagues clubbed together and bought him a new rifle. Annenkov records: 'Everyone laughed at the story, based on a true event, except Gogol, who listened thoughtfully with lowered head. This anecdote provided the initial idea for his wonderful story "The Overcoat" . . .' (P. V. Annenkov, *Literaturnye Vospominaniya*, Moscow, 1960). Gogol very often took his themes from external facts and anecdotes provided by others – the prime examples are *Dead Souls* and *The Government Inspector*, based on anecdotal material given him by Pushkin.

In the 1830s and 1840s there was a proliferation of humanitarian stories with the oppressed and downtrodden (especially government clerks) as their subjects. The scholar A. Tseytlin lists no fewer than 150 stories on this theme. Among these may be mentioned: E. Grebenka's 'Luka Prokhorovich' (1838), F. Bulgarin's 'Fomich Openkin' and N. Pavlov's 'The Demon' – admired by Pushkin and Gogol – with a petty clerk as its protagonist. Dostoyevsky continued this tradition (although with far deeper psychological analysis) in his *Poor Folk* (1846): it has been stated that this first work of Dostoyevsky's 'came out from under "The Overcoat"'.

There is also some personal basis to the story from Gogol's own experiences when he first came to St Petersburg and wrote to his mother on 2 April 1830 that, unable to order warm clothes, he resigned himself to the fact and got through the whole freezing winter in a summer coat.

In the first drafts the 'hero' had no Christian name, becoming subsequently Akaky ('mild, inoffensive'), conveying the character of a downtrodden clerk; and the original surname Tishkevich was later changed to Bashmachkevich and finally Bashmachkin.

Gogol had great problems with the censors when preparing the story for publication and was forced to excise various passages, chiefly those disrespectful towards high government officials. The original passages were later restored in Soviet editions, following the original manuscript.

1. *rank in the civil service*: See also Table of Ranks (p. xxxv). A titular counsellor belonged to the ninth rank (out of fourteen).

2. *bashmak*: Shoe.

3. *calendar*: The Russian Orthodox Church calendar, containing a large number of saints' days and their names.

4. *state counsellor*: See 'The Nose', note 5, p. 315.

5. *only then did he realize he was not in the middle of a sentence but in the middle of the street*: In a letter of 30 April 1829 Gogol wrote to his mother about St Petersburg civil servants: '. . . Everything is stifled, everything has sunk deep in the aimless, futile labours in which they fruitlessly lead their lives. It's quite amusing to meet them in an avenue or on the pavement – they are so deep in thought that if you draw level with any of them you can hear them cursing or talking to themselves . . .'

6. *Falconet's statue*: In this famous statue in St Petersburg the rearing horse is on its hind legs, with its tail as a third support. The work of the French sculptor E. M. Falconet (1716–91), it was dedicated in 1782, and bears the inscription: To Peter I from Catherine II – 1782.

7. *marked by a cross in the calendar*: In the calendar of the Orthodox Church, major festivals were printed in red and the less important saints' days marked with a cross.

8. *He took the overcoat out of the large kerchief he had wrapped it in*: In the eighteenth and nineteenth centuries handkerchiefs were extremely large, the size of a pillow-case.

9.   *cheap cabmen*: Gogol here uses the word *Vanka* (diminutive of
     Ivan), the popular term for a cabman with an old, slow horse
     and ramshackle cab.
10. *sealed off*: The police normally sealed off the house or flat of
     someone dying without family or heirs.
11. *Kalinkin Bridge*: Last bridge across the Fontanka before it meets
     the Neva. The Fontanka was a major waterway four miles long,
     once forming the border of St Petersburg and plied by boats and
     barges.
12. *Kolomna*: District of St Petersburg on right bank of the Fontanka.
     Formerly on outskirts of the city.
13. *Obukhov Bridge*: Formerly a stone drawbridge over the Fontanka.

DIARY OF A MADMAN

'Diary of a Madman' was first published in the collection *Arabesques*
(1835), with the subtitle 'Fragments from the Notes of a Madman'.
Although it was written in the autumn of 1834, Gogol conceived the
basic idea for it in 1832. In his *Literaturniye Vospominaniya* (Moscow, 1960) the memoirist P. V. Annenkov records that on his first
visit to Gogol an elderly gentleman was sitting among the company
'telling of the habits of the insane, of the strict, almost logical sequence
in the development of their stupid ideas. Gogol moved his chair closer
to him and listened attentively to his narrative. Most of the material
collected for the stories told to Gogol by the gentleman was used by
Gogol in his "Diary of a Madman".' In 1852, the year of Gogol's
death, Dr A. T. Tarasenkov, who treated him during his final illness,
had a conversation with him about 'Diary of a Madman', as follows:
'When I told him that I constantly observe psychopaths and even
possess authentic notes, I wanted to discover from him if he read
similar accounts before he wrote this work. He replied: "I did, but
afterwards." "So how is it all so close to reality?" I asked. "That's
easy, I just had to imagine it"' (A. T. Tarasenkov, *The Last Days of
the Life of N. V. Gogol*, Moscow, 1902).
    At the time of writing this story Gogol was deeply interested in the
subject of madness: his censored play, *The Order of Vladimir, Third
Class* (1832–8), deals with this subject. ('Diary of a Madman' is
usually linked to this unfinished comedy, in which a careerist goes
mad from not receiving the Order of Vladimir and finally comes to
believe that he *is* the order.) Also, the question of insanity was highly
topical. The journal the *Northern Bee* was filled with stories of asylum
inmates – in one article it was stated that a certain St Petersburg

asylum was filled with patients who were previously civil servants – in itself a scathing indictment, perhaps, of the ruthless bureaucratic machine! In addition, wild reports were current of a young girl purportedly with two noses; of a young Frenchman who affirmed that he had accidentally swallowed a captain of hussars when the latter fell into his wineglass – and so on.

In a letter to Pushkin of December 1834 Gogol records sarcastically that he had encountered severe problems with the censorship over the story: ' "Diary of a Madman" met with a rather unpleasant little snag from the censor yesterday. But thank God things are a little better today. At least, all I have to do is throw out the *best parts*.' The 'best parts' were: the entry of 3 October that only noblemen can write correctly; the conversation about orders and comparison of a Kammerjunker with the dog Trésor in the entry of 13 November; and the remark in Martober 86 about patriots who will sell their own families for money and honours. These excisions were later restored from original drafts.

At the time the War of the Spanish Succession was very topical and received detailed coverage in the reactionary *Northern Bee*. Possibly Poprishchin identified himself with Schiller's Don Carlos, who is handed by Philip II to the Inquisition.

There are possibly links with Hoffmann's *Kapellmeister Kreisler*, which has an artist as a central figure; there are also echoes of Hoffmann's *Kater Murr*; and of *Nachricht von den neusten Schicksalen des Hundes Berganza* in the correspondence of the dogs. In addition Cervantes' *Coloquio de los Perros* (Novelas Ejemplares) may also have been an influence.

1. *sharpening His Excellency's quills*: Sharpening pens in government departments was the responsibility of most minor clerks, who could sometimes further their careers by sharpening pens according to the taste of their superiors.

2. *Polkan*: Common Russian name for a dog – as opposed to the more 'aristocratic'-sounding French *Fidèle*.

3. *Gorokhovaya Street ... Stolyanaya Street*: Gogol lived in this part of St Petersburg for a time.

4. *Zverkov's*: In 1830 Gogol had lodgings in this tall building near the Kokushkin Bridge. It no longer exists.

5. *the Little Bee*: The arch reactionary St Petersburg journal *Northern Bee*. See also 'Nevsky Prospekt', note 26, p. 313.

6. *Kursk*: Large, ancient town about three hundred miles south of Moscow.

7. *Must be something by Pushkin*: Actually from a poem by the

minor poet and dramatist N. P. Nikolev (1758–1851). Some of his verse was included in popular songbooks. His solemn poem celebrating Prince Bagration is mentioned in *War and Peace*.

8.   *Ruch's*: A fashionable St Petersburg tailor of the time.

9.   *The play was about the Russian fool, Filatka*: Reference to the popular folk vaudeville *Filatka and her Children* by P. I. Grigoryev (performed at the Aleksandrinsky Theatre in November 1831), and *Filatka and Miroshka*, by P. G. Grigoryev, staged that same year. The latter retained its popularity until the 1850s.

10. *collegiate registrar*: Lowest rank (number fourteen) in the civil service Table of Ranks. See also Table of Ranks, p. xxxv.

11. *titular counsellor*: Ninth rank in civil service hierarchy. See also Table of Ranks, p. xxxv.

12. *he's a mason*: Freemasonry was widespread in eighteenth-century Russia, and viewed with great suspicion and hostility by the Tsarist authorities. Among other things, masons were suspected of being associated with the Decembrist Revolt of 1825.

13. *civil commotion*: By civil commotion Gogol is referring to the dispute over the succession to Ferdinand VII of Spain, who died in 1833.

14. *'donna'*: Ferdinand's under-age daughter Isabella, raised to the throne in 1833. The succession was disputed by Don Carlos, her uncle.

15. *Philip II*: (1527–98), King of Spain, whose reign was devoted to increasing the power of Spain and the Catholic Church.

16. *insisting they are patriots, when all they want is money from rents!*: The rents were income paid, by imperial decree, monthly, for services to the state. After 1837 land was awarded instead. On 3 June 1830 Gogol wrote to his mother: 'Previously the man who had given loyal service over several years was awarded whole estates, a thousand serfs ... but now they give this no longer, as you yourself know.' When the story first appeared, the lines from 'And all those senior civil servants' to '. . . the Judases!' were cut by the censors.

17. *the earth is going to land on the moon*: Poprishchin's insane thoughts possibly reflect the worldwide sensation caused by the English astronomer John Herschel's apparent discovery. In 1834, in New York, an anonymous brochure appeared which stated that Herschel, with the aid of a powerful telescope, had discovered an atmosphere, flora, fauna, and thinking beings on the moon. This brochure, which aroused furious argument among

European scholars, was published in a Russian translation in 1836.

18. *Polignac*: Jules Armand, Prince de Polignac (1780–1847), French statesman, prime minister (1829–30). His reactionary government precipitated the 1830 Revolution. He was chiefly responsible for the French occupation of Algeria during the 1830s.

19. *Dhey of Algiers*: Reference to deposition of Hussein Pasha by the French in 1830. The title was disused after the French occupation.

THE CARRIAGE

First published in volume 1 of Pushkin's *The Contemporary* (1836), 'The Carriage' was written the previous year and originally destined for inclusion in an almanac that Pushkin intended publishing but which never materialized. (In October 1835 Pushkin had written to P. A. Pletnyov (poet and journalist, and close friend): 'Thanks, many thanks to Gogol for his "Carriage" – the almanac will travel far in it. But if you want my opinion, "The Carriage" should not be published for nothing. A price must be agreed. Gogol needs the money.'

Like many of Gogol's stories 'The Carriage' is loosely based on an anecdote, in this case an amusing story concerning a close St Petersburg friend, Count M. Yu. Vielgorsky, renowned for his extreme absentmindedness. As V. A. Sollogub (Vielgorsky's brother-in-law) writes in his *Memoirs*: '. . . his absent-mindedness was legendary. Once, having invited the whole diplomatic corps then living in St Petersburg to a great banquet at his house, he completely forgot about it and went off to dine at his club.' There is a connection, albeit fairly tenuous, between Vielgorsky and the forgetful Chertokutsky in the story.

The censors were severe concerning Gogol's portrayal of the free and easy mores of the 'gentlemen officers', considering them 'improper', and Gogol was compelled to make a number of cuts, restored in later editions.

In a letter to Alexey Suvorin, publisher of *New Times*, in May 1889, Chekhov commented: '. . . how spontaneous, how powerful Gogol is – and what an artist! His "Carriage" alone is worth 200,000 roubles. Nothing but pure delight.' And Tolstoy considered it Gogol's best work – 'the peak of perfection'. Since a number of carriages are mentioned in this story they are listed in this opening paragraph. The carriage referred to in the title of this story is a *kolyaska*, similar to a calash or barouche (derived from the original Polish *kolaska*) – a light, low-wheeled carriage with a removable folding hood.

brichka: Light carriage, sometimes covered.

tarantas: Springless four-wheeled carriage.

droshky: Low four-wheeled open carriage.

bonvoyage: Four-seater carriage (from French for 'good journey').

1.   *pitch and toss*: The ancient game of *svayka*, where players throw a large thick nail or spike with a large head into a ring lying on the ground.

2.   *elections*: Of marshals of the gentry and other provincial functionaries.

3.   *Tambov and Simbirsk province*: Provinces south-east of Moscow. The Volga flows through Simbirsk province.

4.   *fricassees*: Meats fried or stewed, served with a thick white sauce.

5.   *gêlées*: Savoury jellies with meat, fish or eggs.

THE GOVERNMENT INSPECTOR

The Government Inspector was written towards the end of 1835, apparently in the astonishingly short period of two months. The first performance took place at the Aleksandrovsky Theatre in St Petersburg on 19 April 1836; and in Moscow on 25 May in the same year, when the role of the mayor was brilliantly played by the famous actor M. S. Shchepkin. However, Gogol was bitterly disappointed with both performances because of the 'vaudeville' methods of most of the actors. (There is an interesting parallel here with the first performance of Chekhov's *The Seagull* sixty years later.) First published in the *Collected Works* of 1836, it underwent numerous corrections and alterations until the definitive edition of 1842. In 1838 Gogol, in a letter to M. P. Pogodin, had expressed a wish to reissue the play 'corrected and perfected', but he made these corrections only towards the early part of 1841. The most fundamental change was the reworking of the first scenes of Act IV. In 'A Fragment of a Letter written by Gogol the author shortly after the first performance of *The Inspector General* to a Man of Letters', Gogol gives the reason for this: 'At the time of the performance I noticed that the beginning of Act IV was cold. It seems as if the flow of the play, hitherto smooth, has stopped or runs lazily.' To preserve the continuity of action and to accelerate its movement, Gogol started Act IV with the town officials' conference as to how to bribe Khlestakov instead of with Khlestakov's monologue. In a later edition (1851) some minor stylistic changes were made.

As with *Dead Souls*, Gogol asked Pushkin to 'give him a plot': 'Do me a favour, give me a plot, it doesn't matter whether it is amusing or not, so long as it is a purely Russian anecdote. Meanwhile I am itching to write a comedy ... Do please give me a plot. I'll produce a five-act comedy in one burst and I swear it will be devilishly funny! ... For God's sake! My mind and my stomach are famished' (letter of 7 October 1835). Although in his later 'Author's Confession' (1847) Gogol claims that Pushkin did in fact give him the plot, according to the memoirist Pavel Annenkov Gogol possibly appropriated the theme from Pushkin, who is reported to have said: 'One has to be very wary with this Ukrainian; he robs me before I have time to shout for help.' Moreover, no reply by Pushkin to Gogol's letter of October 1835 exists. It is possible that Pushkin himself intended to write a play on the subject, and wrote a brief sketch. At the time there were numerous stories circulating of travellers to the provinces passing themselves off as ministry inspectors and fleecing the locals. Pushkin himself, when visiting Orenburg province in 1833 to collect material for his *History of Pugachov*, was taken for an important official, as was the journalist Pavel Svinin, who when in Bessarabia posed as an important official. In *The Provincial Actors* (1835) A. F. Veltman had touched on the subject; but closest to Gogol's plot is his fellow-Ukrainian Grigory Fyorodovich Kvitka's (pseudonym Osnovyanenko) *The Visitor from the Capital, or Uproar in a Provincial Town* (written 1827, pub. 1840), which Gogol, however, does not mention as a source. However, the last word may be said to rest with the critic Belinsky, who stated that 'Gogol had no model, no precursors either in Russian or foreign literatures'.

Since civil ranks are referred to very frequently, a full list with explanatory notes is given separately, on p. xxxv, Table of Ranks.

ACT I

Scene I

1. *government inspector*: The post was introduced by Peter the Great to seek out and then report back on corruption and inefficiency in the provinces. Because of the vast distances, the inspectors took so long to reach their destination that the locals had ample warning and were thus well prepared beforehand to cover things up. Dostoyevsky records in his *Notes from the House of the Dead* (1860): 'A government inspector is coming from St Petersburg ... Everyone's clearly scared, running around and wanting to show everything in the best light.'

2. *the entire province – and our district*: In 1708, under Peter the Great, Russia was divided into eight large administrative provinces, each with its own governor, and subsequently divided into smaller districts.

3. *he can't speak a word of Russian*: In Gogol's time most doctors were German.

4. *Voltairean*: Synonymous with sceptics, freethinkers.

5. *without pulling the most hideous faces*: It has been suggested that Professor N. N. Sandunov of Moscow University was the prototype for this character. As any open criticism of the law and government was prohibited, disapproval could be expressed by grimaces or gestures.

6. *He didn't mean any harm*: This has a factual basis, as in the time of Nicholas I many academic freethinkers were dismissed for the propagation of so-called subversive ideas – including teachers from Gogol's own school at Nezhin.

7. *God help anyone who goes in for teaching*: Very possibly autobiographical reference to Gogol's own keen interest in education and his ill-fated lectureship in history at St Petersburg University. Gogol wrote several articles concerned with education, such as 'On the Teaching of Universal History' (1833). For a time (1831) he taught at the Patriotic Institute, a boarding-school for daughters of high-ranking army officers.

Scene II

8. *do you think you could . . . everyday correspondence*: The interception of private letters by agents of the Third Department was commonplace. Pushkin bitterly complains of his letters to his wife being subjected to this treatment.

9. *Moscow Gazette*: Liberal and subsequently conservative journal published by Moscow University, 1756–1917.

10. *Kostroma and Saratov*: Large trading centres on the Volga.

Scene III

11. *Pochechuyev*: Derived from colloquial word for 'piles'.

12. *order for horses*: An official travel document, bearing the stamp of the Imperial Eagle, entitling holder to request coach, driver and horses according to rank.

13. *St Basil the Egyptian's Day*: Possibly feast-day of St Basil, martyred at Alexandria in AD 202 under Septimus Severus.

14. *The Acts of John the Mason*: Reference to *Self-Knowledge: A Treatise* (London, 1745), a book by the English nonconformist preacher John Mason, translated into Russian in 1783 by I. P. Turgenev, a prominent mason. Gogol concluded that it was a guidebook to masonic ritual, whereas it was actually a book of

sermons. (The author's name could be read in Russian as John *the* Mason.)

15. *such a stench of cabbage*: Gogol similarly expresses his dislike of the vegetable in 'Diary of a Madman', where the shops along Meshchanskaya Street reek of cabbage.

Scene V

16. *gone on the fire engine*: In Gogol's time the police also acted as firemen.

17. *and I'll light the most enormous candle you've ever seen*: Church candles were truly enormous. Here the mayor is talking of placing a candle in church before an image of his patron saint, Antony, as thanksgiving for safe deliverance.

ACT II

Scene I

18. *Shchukin Market*: An open-air market destroyed by fire in 1862. Its site is now occupied by a large department store.

19. *go for a song*: In a letter to his mother (1 September 1830) Gogol complains that he has to sell off things to raise money: the cost of living in St Petersburg was very high.

Scene III

20. *Robert*: *Robert le Diable*, opera by Giacomo Meyerbeer, first performed in Paris in 1831 and three years later in St Petersburg. It was very popular throughout Europe. In his article 'Petersburg Notes for 1836', Gogol mentions the highly enthusiastic reception of this opera, with its 'wild music'.

21. *'The Red Sarafan'* Song written by N. G. Tsyganov, with music by A. E. Varlamov.

Scene V

22. *Joachim*: Johann Albert Joachim (1762–1834), famous St Petersburg coach-builder.

Scene VIII

23. *Kholmogory*: Town fifty miles south-east of Archangel; the area was famous for high-quality beef.

24. *a St Vladimir*: Order of St Vladimir, founded in 1782, with four classes, awarded for long service or merit.

ACT III

Scene III

25. *the Queen of Clubs*: In patience the King of Hearts was supposed to foretell a man's marriage, the Queen of Clubs that of a woman.

Scene V

26. *labberdaan*: (Eng. haberdine), from Dutch word meaning large type of cod used for salting, fished by Basques near Bayonne. It derives from Labourdain, ancient name for area around Bayonne (in Latin: Lapurdum).

27. *you should raise your stake*: In games such as faro or bank, a punter would declare he was sticking by saying *basta* (enough) and bend over a corner, then a second and third of his winning card to show he was doubling his stake.

Scene VI

28. *collegiate assessor*: Eighth grade in civil service, equivalent to army rank of major. See Table of Ranks, p. xxxv.

29. *The Marriage of Figaro*: Famous comedy by Beaumarchais, first performed in Paris in 1784, staged in Russia (in French) the following year. It was very popular in Russia in the 1830s.

30. *Norma*: Opera by Vincenzo Bellini, first performed in Milan in 1831. Highly popular, it was performed in St Petersburg by a German opera company in 1835.

31. *Brambeus*: *Nom de plume* of Osip Senkovsky (1800–58), editor of Russia's most widely read journal, *Library for Reading*. With an incredibly cavalier attitude to editing, he 'corrected' manuscripts by giving them new endings, rewrote passages, 'collated' stories from different authors in a quite random and haphazard fashion, and plagiarized endlessly. A brilliant orientalist, his Far Eastern travels are reflected in his *The Fantastic Journeys of Baron Brambeus*. Gogol ridicules him in his article for Pushkin's *Contemporary*, 'On the Movement of Journalistic Literature in 1834 and 1835', calling *Library for Reading* a 'fortress of vulgarity': it was very popular among provincial readers and lower-ranking civil servants, with a very high circulation.

32. 'The Frigate *Hope*': Not by Brambeus: a story by A. Bestuzhev-Marlinsky (1797–1837), author of romantic tales of adventure, highly popular at the time.

33. *Moscow Telegraph*: Highly respected journal, published in Mos-

cow by Nikolay Polevoy from 1825 until 1834, when it was closed down for publishing an unfavourable review of N. V. Kukolnik's ultra-patriotic play, *The Hand of the Almighty Saved the Fatherland*. Bracketing the publisher of the *Moscow Telegraph* with that of *Library for Reading* must have struck serious readers as ridiculous.

34. *Smirdin*: A. F. Smirdin (1795–1857), leading St Petersburg publisher of the 1830s, founder of *Library for Reading*. His famous bookshop on Nevsky Prospekt was frequented by the leading writers of the day, including Pushkin. The first publisher in Russia to pay his authors proper remuneration, his overgenerosity brought about his bankruptcy. The critic Belinsky called the 1830s the 'Smirdin period in Russian literature'.

35. *Yury Miloslavsky*: *Yury Miloslavsky, or the Russians in 1812* (1829): Historical novel (heavily indebted to Sir Walter Scott), by M. N. Zagoskin (1789–1852). This novel, which went through four editions in three years, was praised (exaggeratedly) by Pushkin.

ACT IV

Scene III

36. *St Anne Third Class*: Order of St Anne, established in 1735 by Karl Friedrich Ulrich, Duke of Holstein-Gottorp, in memory of his wife, daughter of Peter the Great. The St Anne Third Class was three degrees lower than the St Vladimir Fourth Class and it was most commonly awarded to civil servants.

Scene IV

37. *Court Counsellor*: Seventh grade in civil service, equivalent to lieutenant-colonel. (See Table of Ranks p. xxxv.)

Scene V

38. *Titular Counsellor*: Ninth grade in civil service. In *The Overcoat* Akaky Akakievich holds this low rank.

Scene VI

39. *Jacobin*: Club of French revolutionaries formed in 1789. The name came to be associated with extreme radicals and free-thinkers in Russia.

Scene VII

40. *Office of Social Welfare*: Set up by Catherine the Great and authorized to perform the function of banks. In Gogol's time there were no private banks, which did not come into being until the 1860s.

41. *senators*: The Senate was established in 1711 by Peter the Great and supervised the judicial and financial activities of the state. By the time of Nicholas I it had lost much of its authority.

Scene X

42. *salted herring*: Prisoners were commonly tortured by being fed on salty food, without water.

43. *a few loaves of sugar and some wine*: Sweet foods such as honey and sugar were heavily taxed and were a great luxury. They were often given as bribes.

Scene XII

44. *'O man, who in thy grief . . . against the Lord'*: Opening lines of *Ode, adapted from Job* (1751) by Mikhail Lomonosov. Every Russian schoolboy would have been able to recite this poem by heart.

Scene XIII

45. *As the poet said*: The line is from the poem in the story 'The Island of Bornholm' (1794) by N. M. Karamzin, the leading figure in Russian sentimentalism, which Gogol is mocking here. The first stanza reads:

> 'Tis laws that condemn
> The object of my love;
> But who, oh my heart,
> Can offer resistance to thee?

46. *we shall fly to the shade . . . of a distant stream*: Here Gogol is mocking Rousseauistic worship of the simple bucolic life, as advocated by sentimentalism. The idea of streams affording shade is gently satirical!

ACT V

Scene I

47. *filthy scribblers who concocted petitions for them*: Illiterate merchants and others paid clerks to write letters of complaint for them.

48. *Red or blue*: The Order of St Andrey was blue, that of St Aleksandr Nevsky red. Both were very senior, but the St Andrey was the higher.

49. *You'd get priority*: Couriers were given priority at posting-stations.

Scene VIII

50. *Post Office Street*: The postmaster is alarmed because Post Office Street was where the central administration of the postal service was situated.

51. *charging pies to the King of England?*: That is, without paying. Similar phrases were 'charge it to the Sheremetyevs' (an extremely wealthy family), or to the 'Chinese Emperor'.

52. *perfect pig in a skull-cap*: Cf description of Poprishchin in *Diary of a Madman* – 'a perfect tortoise in a sack'.

53. *Engaged! ... laughing at yourselves, that's what!*: Gogol considerably expanded this speech from the earlier, 1836 version. Here the mayor is made a mouthpiece for the same kind of abuse directed against the play on its first performance (1836). The famous words 'What are you laughing at ... ?' are usually directed at the audience, as in Stanislavsky's great production of 1921.

54. *liberals*: This word was added in later editions: those who expressed criticism of the government were branded as liberals, and many reactionaries called the play the work of a dangerous liberal. Here Gogol is again attacking his critics.

55. *they first drive insane*: From the Latin translation of a line by Euripides: 'Quos Deus vult perdere, prius dementat.'

Last Scene

56. *gendarme*: The Corps of Gendarmes was established by Nicholas I in 1827, under the command of the head of the notorious Third Department, a secret police force.

57. *Mute Scene*: Gogol was very concerned that this scene should be correctly performed and after it was interpreted extremely badly

in the original production he issued detailed instructions. Similar 'mute' or 'dumb' scenes occur in *Dead Souls*: Manilov's reaction to Chichikov's proposal to buy dead serfs; and in 'How Ivan Ivanovich Quarrelled with Ivan Nikiforovich'.

THE STORY OF PENGUIN CLASSICS

Before 1946 ... 'Classics' are mainly the domain of academics and students; readable editions for everyone else are almost unheard of. This all changes when a little-known classicist, E. V. Rieu, presents Penguin founder Allen Lane with the translation of Homer's *Odyssey* that he has been working on in his spare time.

1946 Penguin Classics debuts with *The Odyssey*, which promptly sells three million copies. Suddenly, classics are no longer for the privileged few.

1950s Rieu, now series editor, turns to professional writers for the best modern, readable translations, including Dorothy L. Sayers's *Inferno* and Robert Graves's unexpurgated *Twelve Caesars*.

1960s The Classics are given the distinctive black covers that have remained a constant throughout the life of the series. Rieu retires in 1964, hailing the Penguin Classics list as 'the greatest educative force of the twentieth century.'

1970s A new generation of translators swells the Penguin Classics ranks, introducing readers of English to classics of world literature from more than twenty languages. The list grows to encompass more history, philosophy, science, religion and politics.

1980s The Penguin American Library launches with titles such as *Uncle Tom's Cabin*, and joins forces with Penguin Classics to provide the most comprehensive library of world literature available from any paperback publisher.

1990s The launch of Penguin Audiobooks brings the classics to a listening audience for the first time, and in 1999 the worldwide launch of the Penguin Classics website extends their reach to the global online community.

The 21st Century Penguin Classics are completely redesigned for the first time in nearly twenty years. This world-famous series now consists of more than 1300 titles, making the widest range of the best books ever written available to millions – and constantly redefining what makes a 'classic'.

The Odyssey continues ...

The best books ever written

PENGUIN CLASSICS

SINCE 1946

Find out more at www.penguinclassics.com